ALL THAT IS WITHIN US

LORI ROBERTS

Crecelius

Crecelius Haus Publishing

ISBN 978-1-7370597-5-2 Hardback
ISBN 978-1-7370597-6-9 Paperback
ISBN 978-1-7370597-7-6 ebook

Cover Design: Canva
Cover Layout: Lori Roberts
Interior Design- Suzanne Minae

Crecelius Haus Publishing, LLC
31 Sir William Drive
Bedford, IN 47421
Printed in the United States of America
First Edition

Acknowledgments

I want to take this opportunity to thank everyone who helped make The Lowcountry Ghost Trilogy possible.

First, to my sister and brother-in-law, Lisa and Dennis Collins, thank you for the countless trips around Wadmalaw Island, Johns Island, and Charleston. A special thanks to Dennis for painting the covers of both *Cries in the Night: A Lowcountry Ghost Story* and *Where the Sweetgrass Grows*.

I also extend my gratitude to Dr. Suzanne Abel, the inspiration for the character Dr. Brooke Armstrong in the trilogy. Thank you for allowing me multiple visits to your forensics classroom at the College of Charleston and for giving me the incredible opportunity to join you at your second workplace, the Charleston Coroner's Office. I appreciate you letting me immerse myself in the study of bones and bodies. You have become a dear friend along the way.

I want to express my deepest gratitude to my husband, Doug, who has been my unwavering supporter throughout my writing journey. There have been many nights when you have gone without a hot meal while I focused on writing, editing, and attending various literary events. I am excited to share the moment when we walk down the red carpet together at the premiere of "Where the Sweetgrass Grows."

I also want to thank Karen Mahoney for encouraging me to complete book three so that you can enjoy reading it! You have traveled long distances to attend my book signings and have shared my books with everyone you meet. You are not just a cousin; you are a dear friend.

I want to express my heartfelt gratitude to S.G. Minae for her assistance in formatting the manuscript into a finished book. I look forward to future collaborative endeavors.

I also want to extend my deepest thanks to my greatest supporter and encourager, my mother, Janet Johnson, who believed in me from the very beginning. I love you more than words can express.

Additionally, I am grateful to my editor, Grace Augustine, for her meticulous attention to detail and the care she has devoted to this project and others we have worked on together.

Finally, a sincere thank you to you, the readers. I truly appreciate the book clubs that have read my books and invited me to speak at your meetings. Your interest, insights, questions, and comments mean a great deal to me. To the folks I've met at events who have picked up a book and returned to buy another, thank you.

I would love to hear from you.

Kind regards and happy reading!

Lori Roberts

PROLOGUE

NINE YEARS EARLIER~

Carly Tabor placed her phone on the kitchen table, feeling a wave of heaviness washing over her. Weak-kneed, she sank into a chair. The sound of horses' hooves clattering down King Street broke the silence—another tour group was sightseeing historic homes, and hers was among them.. *Dead.* Carly whispered the word aloud, eager to celebrate the end of a nightmare. He received what he deserved. Karma, destiny, fate—whatever the reason, it had finally caught up with James Van Ness.

Carly recalled her escape from the fishing cabin. She heard the gunshot behind her and felt the sharp sting of pain before everything went dark.

She closed her eyes, attempting to erase the memory. A sense of satisfaction washed over her as she imagined the fear in James Van Ness's eyes. She pictured the girls' faces flashing before him with each thrust of the killer's knife.

"What lies behind us and
what lies before us
are tiny matters compared to
what lies within us."

~Ralph Waldo Emerson

"All of our lives we are searching,
when all of our lives
we need only to look within."

~author unknown

Chapter One

May 2025

Carly pulled into the gated parking area beside her King Street home after dropping off her children, Freddy, ten, and Viviene, six, at their school. She tossed her keys on the hall table, hurried upstairs, and changed clothes before her best friend, Delaney, arrived. Delaney Warrick and Carly became friends when Carly arrived in Charleston ten years earlier. The two women shared the gift of communicating with the deceased. A knock on the lower piazza door brought Carly to the first floor. Homes in the historic district of Charleston customarily featured two doors on the lower level, a formal entrance opening to the street, and another door off the lower piazza allowing family and friends to enter.

"Hey, girl." Carly hugged Delaney. "Come on in. I'm a mess trying to pack for ten days. We'll have the time of our lives."

"I've never ventured to Europe, only Mexico on a cruise twenty-five years ago with Mark when he received a company award," Delaney said, placing a coffee pod in the Keurig. She waited a moment as her cup filled with her favorite caramel latte. "Carly Tabor never packs until the last minute; why the rush?"

"I'm antsy about *this* trip for some reason. I haven't been out of the country for several years." She popped a vitamin in her mouth and downed the rest of her water.

"It's quite an opportunity for us, sweetie. Not only a chance to have a girls' trip, but also exploring England, Scotland, and Wales!" Delaney's eyes lit up with excitement.

"The conference site is a Tudor-era Abbey," Carly noted.

"We could do worse! Will your folks stay with the kids?"

"Mom and Dad want Freddy and Vivi to stay a couple of weeks with them in Kansas. Since their summer break begins on Saturday, it works out. Their cousins plan to stay a day or two as well."

Carly dumped the rest of her cup of coffee into the sink and sat at the counter with Delaney.

"I'm sure they're thrilled to spend a few weeks with the kids on the farm." Delaney changed the subject. "How's the presentation coming along?"

"I've started several times. I'm struggling to explain my earliest encounters with ghosts." Carly picked at her French manicured nails. "I remember people appearing, but I never connected with any of them until Freddy Richards."

"I'm a nervous wreck thinking about speaking in public. My nurse practitioner prescribed something for panic attacks," Delaney said. "Come to think of it, ghosts have always surrounded me. It's the living that scares me."

"I wish Austin could tag along with us since he isn't on rotation at the hospital. He spends more time with us since he and Dr. Elston share a practice."

"I'm sure he doesn't miss being a new doctor on staff. He established his reputation at the hospital," Delaney said.

Dr. Austin Tabor finished his residency as a pediatric neurosurgeon on staff at Roper Medical Center after Carly's abduction. He realized his family needed him at home during the night. After the COVID-19 pandemic, they contemplated returning to Kansas to be closer to their families. Austin wanted to protect her, but he failed.

"I enjoy having Austin at home almost every night. He kept his credentials at the hospital to assist or operate when needed. I think he misses being a surgeon."

"Having him at home cuts into *my* time," Delaney said and winked at Carly.

"Oh, no worries. We'll have *our* time together, Austin insists."

Delaney checked her phone. "If we hurry, we can get down to Poogan's Porch before the primo tables fill up."

"I'll drive. Did you park behind me?" Carly asked.

"Yes, so let me drive. Boyd asked me to stop by the Historical Society to gather information on the McLeod Plantation. I'll swing by on my way back."

Delaney parked her car near Poogan's Porch, a popular spot for locals and visitors. The restaurant, a two-story building resembling the homes along Queen Street, featured haint blue ceilings on both the lower and upper piazzas, which complements the soft yellow wood siding. The outdoor seating area was dotted with black faux wrought-iron tables and chairs, while the interior offered a more upscale dining experience. Carly and Delaney sat at a table on the lower piazza, enjoying watching the people around them.

During brunch, the restaurant seemed less crowded than usual. Delaney asked Carly what she would like to have, and Carly responded that a mimosa with bacon and waffles sounded good. Delaney suggested something healthier with fruit mixed in, and Carly mentioned needing something more potent than coffee, as Austin had awakened her from another dream. Charla, their server, took their order, recognizing Delaney from a ghost tour she'd attended.

"Delaney and I became friends after one of her ghost tours years ago. She's the best in Charleston," Carly said as she winked at a blushing Delaney.

After placing their orders, Carly continued to share her recurring dream.

"My dream is about a mother and her children. She is holding a little girl in her arms, and both are crying."

Delaney suggested the dream may be related to a traumatic event Carly had experienced, but Carly was reluctant to revisit that dark place. Delaney patted Carly's hand, reassuring her that talking about it could help.

Carly started to comment, but an incoming call from her cell phone stopped her. The number belonged to Dr. Brooke Armstrong.

She mouthed to Delaney, "I'll just be a minute."

Delaney nodded and resumed her habit of people-watching.

"Hey, Brooke. How's it going?"

Dr. Brooke Armstrong was now the Deputy Coroner for the Charleston Coroner's office since the retirement of long-time Coroner Rona Warren. The previous deputy coroner won the election and moved into Rona's position.

"Hi, Carly. Is this a bad time?" Brooke asked, hearing the street and patrons in the background.

"Delaney and I are having breakfast at Poogan's Porch this morning. Can I call back on my way to the station in about an hour?"

"Sure, that's fine. I'm on my way to the office now."

"Okay, I'll call in a bit." Carly put her phone inside her purse.

"I haven't seen Brooke in a while. How's she doing?"

"She's expecting her first child in August."

"How exciting, not to mention a major life adjustment," Delaney smiled.

"It's exciting for sure. I can't imagine having my first baby at 42," Carly said, then added, "I'll finish the last bite of my waffle, and we can be on our way."

"I doubt my mission for Boyd will take too long. I have a hair appointment at two."

"Good luck finding all the information," Carly said, reaching into her purse for cash. "I'll get the waitress's attention for the check."

Carly waved goodbye, closed the door and hurried upstairs to change.

She chose a Lilly Pulitzer dress, a vibrant print in pink, teal, and yellow. She also picked out a pink stone necklace and matching earrings that she had purchased while she and Austin stayed in Key West the previous summer. To complete the outfit, she slipped on dark pink sandals.

Once in her vehicle, Carly put in her earbuds and phoned Brooke. She pulled onto King Street and traveled out of town, waiting for Brooke to answer her phone.

"Sorry, Carly. I finished talking with an officer in Georgia who needed the identification of a drop-site victim off the highway in Walterboro. The reason I called earlier is about a favor."

Carly had asked Brooke for plenty of favors over the years. "What kind of favor?"

"Larry Deveroux called me last night right before I left work. He's working in Savannah now as the coroner and wanted your opinion on a case."

Carly tensed. Larry Deveroux worked as the Deputy Coroner in 2014 when Carly found human remains in her cellar. He respected Carly's paranormal ability and kept her case in his files.

"Are you still there?" Brooke asked.

Carly exhaled. "Yes, I'm here. What's going on with Larry?"

Someone interrupted Brooke. Carly waited a few seconds as she overheard a muffled conversation between Brooke and another person.

"It's busy here today. What's your schedule like later?" Brooke asked.

"I'm headed to work now. I'm meeting with the new co-anchor who is replacing Chad."

"I loved watching Chad Flannery with you on Channel 5. The news isn't going to be the same without him. You worked so well together," said Brooke.

Carly sighed. "I'll miss working with him. I'm happy for Chad and Josie, though. They plan to buy a motor home and travel."

Chad Flannery took Carly under his wing when she arrived at Channel 5. The two exhibited strong chemistry from the first newscast they co-anchored. After her brush with death, she gained Chad's most profound admiration. Carly felt the utmost respect for Chad, and the thought of him leaving her with Jeffrey Sullivan caused her to roll her eyes.

"Why don't you stop by my place on the way home? I want to show you my ultrasound pictures. The little nugget is growing," Brooke said.

"Sure, I'll head over around eleven-thirty. Will that work?"

"Yes, it's perfect. I'm going to finish up here and have lunch. We'll talk later."

Carly slid her phone inside her purse as she pulled into Channel 5's fenced lot. She grabbed her credentials lanyard and hurried inside the studio.

The station's general manager, Bauer Donahue, sat in his office drinking the last of a Dr. Pepper. Bauer's dark blue eyes and tan skin made him look younger than his actual age, especially since his dark hair came from a bottle. Recently divorced from his second wife, his focus shifted back to the station and its high ratings. His tolerance of Carly's absences from paranormal engagements and conferences waned after Carly's extended absence following her abduction and hospitalization. She tried to limit her time off, and he reluctantly agreed when she asked to be away for the upcoming paranormal conference.

"Hi, Carly, come on in. I'm expecting Jeff any moment," Bauer said. He offered Carly a drink, which she declined.

Bauer, sixty, has held the General Manager's position for twenty-five years. He wasn't planning on retiring anytime soon. Carly got along with Bauer and knew how to get her way when she wanted to pitch a new story idea, somehow making him think he had come up with it himself.

"So, will Jeffrey Sullivan start at the end of the month?" Carly asked, putting her things on the chair beside her.

"He left his current position at WXFT in Boston three weeks ago. He's already found a condo to rent by the harbor. He says he loves being near the water."

"Oh, he's a hahba guy from Bahstan," Carly mocked in her best Boston accent.

"Not too bad with the accent," a voice said behind Carly.

She turned to face her new co-host, who just happened to be standing in the doorway. With a tanned face and athletic build, Jeff looked more like someone from Kiawah than someone from Boston. Rising from her chair, she extended her hand.

"Hi, I'm Carly Tabor, and I didn't mean any disrespect." Her face flushed.

"Jeffrey Sullivan, but please, call me Jeff, no offense taken."

Bauer pushed back his chair and said, "Jeff, Carly co-anchors the six o'clock news. She joined the team in 2014 and worked her way up from investigative reporter to news anchor." He walked over to a small refrigerator and grabbed another Dr. Pepper.

"I hope I receive lots of grace in the beginning. I know next to nothing about the Lowcountry. In no time, I'll say "y'all and 'bless your pea-pickin' heart' at the right time, I promise," Jeff said, getting a playful dig at Carly.

"I'm not a southern girl, I'm a Jayhawker," Carly explained.

Bauer ended the exchange. "After we discuss a few things, we will have time to get better acquainted."

Jeff winked at Carly. He seemed nothing like Chad. Maybe fuller of himself than Chad ever thought about being, Carly thought.

"Jeff, you've got an impressive list of awards from the Boston area. We're glad to have you as part of our team. You're entering a position where the previous anchor received the highest ratings of all the competing anchors in Charleston. Carly added to our station's rising numbers and Emmy awards," Bauer added.

"I hope everyone goes easy on this Yankee. I want to put my best foot forward with the viewers."

"There's nothing to worry about. Everyone welcomed me with open arms when I started here." Carly reassured the new hire.

"Well, then, I'll let Carly play tour guide. I have a meeting downtown." Bauer shook Jeff's hand. "Welcome aboard."

Carly hid her disappointment in being the one to play tour guide.

"Okay, I'll lead the ten-cent tour." Carly grabbed her purse, keys, and lanyard from the chair.

"Channel 5 is smaller than what I'm coming from, but I like the vibe already," Jeff said, closing Bauer's door behind them.

Carly took Jeff to the break room last, walking in on the new intern orientation. "Oh, excuse me. I didn't mean to interrupt."

"You're not interrupting, come on in," Millie Cobb, head of human resources, said.

Carly introduced Jeff to Millie. She, in turn, introduced the interns to Jeff and Carly.

Carly noted that Jeff's left hand did not have a ring. He made eye contact with everyone and made small talk.

I bet he's related to the Kennedy clan... with his perfect teeth, flawless looks, and schmoozing personality.

Millie added, "Carly, let me introduce Addie Guillim. Jeff, this is Griffin Potts, our new summer intern."

"Hello, Griffin. Hello, Addie. Welcome to Channel 5," Jeff said, adding,

"Griffin, it looks like we're going to learn the ropes together."

Carly noticed the break room clock. "I'm sorry I can't stay and introduce the noon team, but I have an appointment at eleven thirty."

"Oh, no worries," Jeff said. "I'm flying home to Lexington this afternoon to close the sale on my house tomorrow. The new owners are anxious to move in."

Carly's eyebrows raised, "Lexington, as in 'the shot heard round the world' Lexington?"

"Sure do. I loved working where the American Revolution began, not to mention all the colonial history nearby."

Can this guy do anything wrong? "I majored in history and journalism in college. I've always been a history geek."

"I'm a history geek as well. I'm looking forward to learning more about Charleston. I hear the Lowcountry cuisine is amazing," he made a chef's kiss with his fingers.

"That's true. I think I put on ten pounds in the first month of living here. Have a safe trip back to Boston," she said as she headed for the parking lot.

"Thanks. I'll be back next week to move into my new condo. Take care." Jeff's eyes locked on Carly walking down the hall to the back exit. He admired the scenery.

Once inside her SUV, Carly clicked her seatbelt buckle and pulled through the gate. She merged into traffic on Savannah Highway. The drive to James Island gave her time to mull over the new hire. *He seems nice enough, but a little too perfect.* She wondered what lured him to the South. A messy divorce or a mid-life crisis? *Me thinks there's more to Jeff Sullivan's story.*

Carly pulled onto Whippoorwill Court on James Island, a street that was part of an older, established neighborhood. She admired the well-manicured lawns landscaped with palm trees and blooming bushes.

She drove a short distance before the number on the side of Brooke's mailbox and house came into view. The home, a stylish two-story house in a coastal beige tone, featured an expansive wrap-around front porch. Boston ferns hanging on the porch swayed with the gentle breeze. Haint blue covered the ceiling, floor, and accents on the porch steps and columns. Overstuffed teal, beige, and navy-blue pillows lay scattered on the dark wicker furniture, making the space inviting for guests.

Cary grabbed her cell phone and purse, exited her vehicle, and locked the door. She waved to Brooke, who was standing on the porch, her hair styled in an updo with a clip. She wore white yoga pants and an oversized University of Charleston T-shirt, her baby bump fully stretching the material.

"Long time no see." Brooke hugged Carly.

"It's been too long. How are you doing?" Carly followed Brooke inside.

"Oh, you know, I have good days and bad days. Everyone says it's a good sign if you have morning sickness." Brooke rubbed her stomach.

"I suffered from morning sickness during all of my pregnancies. You're glowing," Carly noted.

"Thanks. It's all the water I drink. Would you like something?"

"Um, I think water for me, thanks." Carly surveyed Brooke's spacious living room. She admired the coastal decor and plantation shutters at each window.

Brooke came back carrying two glasses, handing one to Carly.

"So, catch me up on your two gorgeous kiddos. What is Freddy and Vivi up to?"

Carly took out her wallet and shared pictures of her children. "Both attend Charleston Day School and love it. Freddy is like Austin, athletic and outgoing. Vivi is more serious and reserved. She is interested in the visual arts. She loves to draw and is quite good, if I say so myself," Carly said.

"You and Austin have a beautiful little family."

"Thanks. Some days, I don't think I'll ever have it together." Carly took a drink and set the glass on the tile coaster. "So, what is Larry Deveroux up to these days?"

"He moved down to Savannah after the pandemic. Yesterday, he reached out to me and said he got called out to Bethesda Academy, where the house parents found bones... a lot of them."

"I don't think I'm familiar with Bethesda. What is it?" Carly took a sip of water, her interest piqued.

"Oh, you're going to love this." Brooke's eyes lit up, and she continued. "Bethesda began as an orphanage in the early 1740s. If you know your colonial history, you'll recognize George Whitefield."

Carly's eyebrows rose. "I do remember studying about him. He evangelized throughout Europe and founded the Methodist church. Oh, wait, I'm thinking of John Wesley, my mistake."

"I did a Google search. It states that Whitefield came to Georgia and established the orphanage as a place of 'strong Gospel influence and discipline.' Having raised the money by his preaching, Whitefield insisted on sole control of Bethesda." Brooke read from a small slip of paper she removed from a notepad.

"You mentioned that someone found bones. I suppose that connects to a haunting?" Carly sighed.

"I'm sorry," Brooke apologized. "Maybe I should have asked Delaney instead. After all that you've been through, it isn't something you want to jump into again."

"No. It's okay. I've conquered my demons," Carly reassured Brooke. "Fill me in on what Deveroux told you."

For the next ten minutes, Brooke recounted the situation as Larry had told her.

"So, the owners discovered a burial site behind one of the original dwellings, and they claim strange noises are coming from inside the house," Carly restated.

"Yeah, that is the long and short of it. Larry said he thought the graves belonged to a slave cemetery, but the Chatham County forensic anthropologist dated them older than he first thought."

"How old are you thinking?" Carly asked, sure of the answer.

"That is why I called you. You connect with children's spirits." Brooke adjusted her legs in the chair. "We're thinking maybe during the mid to late 1700s."

"Oh, the graves contain children." Carly turned away, her eyes closed for a moment.

"Well, eight children and four adults. It appears the skeletal remains are in a common grave and have been covered over at some point with one of the original outbuildings."

Brooke repositioned herself in the chair. "If you have time, the house parents are amenable to your walking around the place to investigate who is causing the disturbances." Brooke added, "Bethesda is a religious boys' school. I don't think they want to draw attention to the paranormal."

"Delaney and I are flying out for a conference in the UK next week. I suppose I can squeeze in a trip to Savannah before we leave," Carly offered. "I understand about the school not wanting to advertise ghosts on campus. I've gotten used to skeptics and scoffers over the years."

"Thanks. Larry will get a kick out of seeing you again." Brooke handed Carly a Post-it note with his phone number and the address of Bethesda Academy in Savannah."

Carly called Delaney on the way home. "Hey, got a minute?"

"Sure, what's going on?"

"If you have some free time this week, I'm going to Savannah and need my partner in crime."

"I'm supposed to go to McLeod Plantation the day after tomorrow on an investigation with Boyd. Other than that, I'm free."

Carly thought for a moment, bringing up her Google calendar on her phone. "How is Tuesday, the twenty-first?"

"Sounds good to me. I'm looking forward to going to Savannah for the day," Delaney replied.

Austin and Carly waited until Freddy and Vivi fell asleep before discussing Carly's latest case. Sitting on Austin's lap, she took several sips from a glass of wine. The wine started to relax her. She nuzzled his neck, her lips grazed beneath his ear. She loved the way his stubble grazed her forehead.

"Why don't we do this more often?" Austin asked, kissing the top of Carly's head.

"I don't know. I've missed it, and I've missed us."

Austin repositioned his arm. "Did you have a good day?"

She turned to face Austin. "I went out to visit Brooke Armstrong this afternoon."

He reached for his glass of wine. "Brooke Armstrong? What's new with her?"

Carly told him about the pregnancy and her house on James Island, then got to the point. "Brooke got a call from Larry Deveroux, the former coroner from Charleston."

"Oh, sure. I remember Deveroux coming to the house to investigate our finding Freddy's skeleton in the cellar," Austin said.

"Right. Well, Larry moved on to a new job as the assistant coroner in Savannah. Last week, he received a call from the house parents at

Bethesda Academy. They had discovered a burial site behind one of the dormitories."

She waited for Austin's reaction.

"I'm assuming he wants you to get involved because he thinks the bones are children," Austin uttered matter-of-factly.

"Yes, several children, it seems. He thought I might be able to connect with them and find out what's behind the hauntings. The owners accidentally found the graves. They aren't part of a known cemetery." Carly waited for Austin to dampen the conversation.

"Now that Freddy and Vivi are older, I want to keep them away from the spirit world." Austin raised an eyebrow, giving one of his authoritative looks.

She shifted her position on the couch. "I understand. I try to keep them isolated from my sensitive abilities. It isn't something I want them involved in." Carly knew Austin wanted to avoid discussing the paranormal in front of the children, and she never spoke of her abilities in their presence.

"Good, I'm glad we're still in agreement."

Carly bristled, "Of course, but if I can help the spirits at Bethesda find rest, I will."

Austin's phone pinged. He looked at it, then returned it to his pocket. "I always said you're the champion of lost children," he said as he pulled Carly close.

CHAPTER TWO

May 21st, 2025

The drive from Charleston to Bethesda Academy, via Interstate 95 to Highway 17, took almost three hours. Carly and Delaney spent the time discussing their upcoming conference in the UK. A text alert on Bluetooth distracted Carly when she merged onto Ferguson Avenue, the location of the Bethesda Academy. Bauer Donahue's secretary, Mally Perkins, texted, *We're planning cocktails and finger food on June 8th at Hall's Chop House for Jeffery Sullivan, Channel 5's new anchor. Hope you and Austin can attend.*

Carly sighed. "Looks like the new guy at work is getting a welcome party."

"I take it you haven't gotten over Chad retiring." Delaney saw Carly's eye roll.

"Well, truth be told, I'm comfortable with Chad. He gets me, and he knows about my past." Carly turned at the entrance of Bethesda Academy.

"I get it. You're afraid the new guy might think your cheese slid off your cracker."

Carly gave Delaney the side-eye and smiled, "Yeah, something like that."

"Y'all are going to give Chad a proper send-off, aren't you?"

"Yes, I already have it planned. It's the 15th at Henry's."

"Sounds swanky. I'm sure Chad will be surprised. It is a surprise, I assume?"

Carly knew better than to try anything with Chad. He always seemed to know things before anyone else did. "No, I'm consulting Josie for her opinion on this," Carly said.

She compared Josie to Mother Teresa because she believed anyone who put up with Chad Flannery for forty years deserved sainthood.

Carly's GPS alerted her to turn left. She pulled her vehicle over to the side of the driveway and took in the beauty before her. A massive, brick archway framed the Spanish-moss-laden oak-lined drive. Inscribed within the brick were the words BETHESDA, and below it, in smaller letters, FOUNDED 1740.

"Brooke told me Bethesda became an orphanage in 1740." Carly put the SUV in gear and continued down the driveway. The administrative offices sat on the right with a statue of a man and two children holding his hands. Carly assumed they represented the children who lived here at one time, as well as one of the administrators.

"There are two Civil War soldiers standing in the field to the left," Delaney said matter-of-factly.

"I wonder if a battle happened on the grounds or if Bethesda became a makeshift hospital?"

"I asked Google," Delaney began. "It says a battle nearby at Fort McAllister happened in 1864, and the Union Army used part of the grounds for a field hospital."

Carly scanned both sides of the road and continued at a snail's pace. The drive split into two directions. To the right, she noticed a two-story school building, a multipurpose building atop a bluff overlooking the Moon River.

To the left, the road formed a semicircle. A brick chapel sat amid expansive pine and oak trees. The herringbone brick sidewalk leading up to the front door was original to the building. The wrought iron latch on the door and the iron side lanterns on the church also appeared original. Above the door, a palladium window with a single candle in the center caught Carly's eye.

Beyond the chapel, flanking the road, several centuries-old oak trees with Spanish moss lifted in a river breeze welcoming them. At the center of the semi-circle drive, an ancient live oak with wooden benches flanked the tree.

As Carly closed her door, a couple in their late thirties came out from behind the first dormitory.

"You must be Ms. Carly. Thank you for coming," the man said. "I'm Darrick Summerfield, and this is my wife, Jamesetta."

The African American couple wore matching light blue polo shirts with the Bethesda Day School emblem on them. Jamesetta wore her hair braided beneath a stylish straw hat. Both approached with outstretched hands.

"So nice to meet you." Carly took their outstretched hands. "This is my dear friend, Delaney Warrick. I asked her to join me."

After they exchanged pleasantries, the couple led Carly and Delaney to the side of the building.

"I'm not sure what you know about our situation," Darrick began. "Are you familiar with Bethesda's history?"

"Only what my friend, Dr. Armstrong, shared. I'm afraid I'm unfamiliar with its history," Carly replied.

Darrick and Jamesetta give Carly and Delaney a brief history of Bethesda's early years as an orphanage. They mentioned the dormitories had been used as a Union hospital during the Civil War.

Carly glanced at Delaney, recognizing the reference. They explained that in the 1990s, the orphanage transformed into a boarding and day school, replacing the term "orphanage" with it.

"So, how did you find the bones?" Carly asked, intrigued by the history of the place.

"Let's walk to the back, and we'll show you where we found the cemetery," Jamesetta said.

As Carly and Delaney followed Jamesetta and Darrick, the moans and cries for relief from Civil War soldiers were audible only to them. Carly glanced over at Delaney, who nodded to an unseen enslaved person carrying a sweetgrass basket full of amputated limbs from the rear of the dormitory.

Darrick stopped next to where a police tape barricaded an area approximately 10 feet by 10 feet. The area gave the appearance of a crime scene dig, now covered.

Darrick lifted the barricade for Carly and Delaney. "We telephoned a contractor to come out a few weeks ago because we thought the septic system had leaked. An area showed up where the grass started to hold water," he explained.

Delaney and Carly walked under the police tape, each taking a different part of the area. Carly's eyes scanned an area of graves prepared in haste. Both encountered images of the deceased.

"I count twelve gravesites: eight children and four adults," Carly said.

Delaney squatted on the ground and touched the fresh gravesite.

"These graves didn't belong to the enslaved people who built Bethesda or the soldiers who died here. They are buried elsewhere on the grounds." She surveyed the yard, seeing a small cemetery fifty yards away, surrounded by a low stone wall.

Darrick and Jamesetta looked at one another, their eyes wide.

"How do you do it? I mean, how can you see and hear spirits?" Jamesetta asked and walked under the tape.

Carly shrugged her shoulders. "It's something I've experienced since childhood. I can't explain it."

"Carly and I experience different things at times. It's what makes our investigating together important," Delaney said, moving to another spot.

"Are the sounds coming from inside the dormitory from children, or are you hearing something else?" Carly asked.

Darrick hesitated, then said, "Well, we've both experienced things since we took the job here as house parents."

"We've heard children whispering and a woman crying. I've also heard what I think are hobnail shoes walking the hallways at night," Jamesetta said. "Some of the boys also have said they hear things when they are in their rooms after we've gone to sleep."

Carly started to duck under the police tape but stopped.

Delaney caught the expression on Carly's face. "Do you see something else?"

"One of the adult bones is a woman holding a newborn, and a young girl is beside her."

Jamesetta's eyes darted to her husband. "I believe only one set of bones found belongs to a baby, to my knowledge. You're correct on number twelve. The anthropologist who came with the coroner called earlier in the week."

"Oh, what did he say?" Carly asked, wiping off her Capri pants.

"He said they assembled the bones collected in the grave. Eight are children of various ages, ranging from an infant to eight years old. The adults are three females: two are teens, and the other is in her twenties. An adult male is in his thirties," Jamesetta said.

The couple led Carly and Delaney across the yard to the summer kitchen. Both women walked through the brick building. The spacious fireplace still held the spider and iron post that extended to hold heavy pots over the fire. A cast-iron cook stove stood in its original place before the Civil War. Shelves held pieces of crocks and pottery found on the grounds, as well as more recent reproductions of what a summer kitchen would have contained. A worn wooden dough board sat atop a cupboard built into the wall. A butcher block with at least two centuries of use sat near a dry sink and counter. Neither Delaney nor Carly connected with any ghosts. They emerged a few moments later.

"Would you like to go inside the dormitories? All the students are in class today. Tomorrow is their last day, then their families will come to Honor Day and take them back to their homes," Darrick said.

"I assumed Bethesda is a day school, not a boarding school," Delaney said.

"We recently opened the dorms again for boarding. Once the renovations ended, the noises became more frequent." Darrick opened the door, allowing Carly, Delaney, and Jamesetta to walk inside.

Multiple updates had been done to the interior, including improvements to the plumbing, electricity, and modern facilities. Darrick and Jamesetta took turns giving a brief history of the 1740s dormitories. They learned that the orphans came from England and the surrounding communities.

The foursome walked through the rooms downstairs and climbed the expansive staircase to the second floor. At the top of the landing, an original Palladian window opened to the massive live oak in front of the building.

Children's images appeared in the gravesite. Delaney walked to the window and recognized each child's familiar features. The children's eyes sank as if they had been afflicted with an illness.

She pulled Carly back, "Take a look at the children outside."

Carly moved to get a better view. "Yes, I see them."

Several children stood beside their graves. She counted seven, and each stared back with hollow eyes.

The Summerfields finished the second-floor tour. On the way downstairs, Jamesetta asked Carly and Delaney if they would like to visit the room where Bethesda Academy kept the orphan records.

"The library holds books from the early days of Bethesda. The orphanage managers kept impeccable records of all the children, and any staff employed here," Darrick stated.

Carly checked the time. She allowed enough time to stop for lunch if they left for Charleston now.

"I wish we could explore the records while we're here. Can we try again another time?" Carly asked.

"You're welcome to come back and go through whatever records are here," said Darrick.

Jamesetta walked the women to the door.

"We'd appreciate any suggestions on how to stop the noises."

"If you agree, I'll bring in the company with whom I investigate after the students are gone for the summer. It will allow us to spend more time identifying the children and adults," Delaney offered.

"Yes, thank you. Just listening to you both today is fascinating," Jamesetta said.

"Delaney and I are attending a conference in the UK next week. What about next month? We'll be available the second week in June if that works."

"Yes, we can do that. Thank you for coming today, and we look forward to an in-depth investigation on the grounds," Darrick added.

Carly and Delaney left their business cards with the couple and walked to Carly's SUV. She started the engine, then snapped her seatbelt in place. "All the children appear to suffer from illness at the time of death. I'm not sure about the woman and children with her," Carly said.

Delaney pulled her seatbelt strap into place. "I'll bet Tucker and Boyd will jump at the chance to investigate Bethesda."

"Let's try to find information on orphanages in London when we have time away from the conference," Carly said as she drove away from Bethesda.

∾

May 25, 2025

Carly and Austin waved goodbye as Curt and Paula Evans, Carly's parents, and Frederick and Vivi, drove out of sight.

"The house will be quiet without the kids," Carly said, slipping her arm around Austin's waist.

"I'll be lonely not having you or the kids here each day," Austin replied. "I know they'll enjoy spending time with your folks."

Carly knew Frederick and Vivi were safe. "I don't want to cook tonight. Let's take advantage of our time alone."

Austin agreed. They drove to Folly Beach for an evening of relaxation at Rita's, their favorite spot. Austin and Carly seldom enjoyed time alone, given their busy schedules and the presence of small children. After dinner, they walked along the coast, the warm surf on their bare toes. The breeze carried sea spray across their arms and faces, prompting Carly to slide her sunglasses in place from where they were still perched on her head.

The crowded beach surprised Carly. Most days, it cleared up in the early evening as families went to change and eat dinner. Carly and Austin felt like young lovers as they walked hand in hand down to the pier. The previous month, they celebrated their fourteenth wedding anniversary with dinner at Hall's Chop House. Boyd and Delaney offered to stay with Freddy and Vivi. At the same time, the Tabors enjoyed an evening alone. Since Carly's abduction, the couple vowed never to take their marriage for granted.

∾

Monday, May 27th

Austin walked into the kitchen for a bottle of water. Not seeing Carly downstairs, he went upstairs to change out of his doctor's coat and scrubs. Carly sat cross-legged on the floor in front of her open suitcase, earbuds in and singing along to the music. Seeing Austin enter the room, she took out one earbud. "It's impossible to keep it under fifty pounds. I took that pile out." Carly motioned to a stack of discarded outfits.

"You pack better than anyone. Just roll and go," Austin said as he rubbed the top of her head.

Carly grabbed his hand. "Thanks for the advice."

Austin sat on the floor beside Carly. "I haven't pressed you for any details since the trip to Bethesda. Is something bothering you?"

Carly pulled her knees up to her chest. "I'm not sure how I can help the Summerfields. Several spirits haven't crossed over. Some are from the Civil War era and others from the colonial period."

Austin waited for a moment before answering. "I'm uncertain how it works with you, but I believe you have a gift for solving wrongs done to children."

"That's just it. It isn't only children who appear to me. There's also a woman." Carly pulled herself up on the side of the bed. "I keep seeing the same woman, and I don't understand why."

"Didn't you say it'll take a while to get results from the carbon dating? Why not wait for Deveroux to contact you with the results before you're too involved?"

Austin started to walk out of the room. "The sooner you solve this haunting, the sooner we can get our lives back to normal," he said.

Carly slammed the suitcase closed. Austin's words settled in her craw. "You're right, as usual. Either way, I'm looking forward to the conference."

Austin shrugged his shoulders and shook his head. He thought it was easier to walk away than engage and possibly end up in a misunderstanding.

Carly walked into the open landing and then upstairs to her office. The warm afternoon sun heated the room, so she turned on the two window air conditioners. The spacious third floor housed an efficiency apartment with a small kitchen and dining area, a bedroom, a bathroom, a living room, and an office.

Austin's sister, Ainsleigh Tabor, arrived in the summer of 2018 to live in the upstairs apartment. She moved out a year later when she decided Charleston's humidity 'sucked the life out of her', as she put it. A month before the COVID-19 pandemic hit the United States, she met a realtor from Asheville, North Carolina, and the two moved in together. They married in 2023, leaving Carly the finished space to make her own.

Carly walked over to her desk and turned on her computer. She opened the slide deck for her presentation and paused, looking at the ghostly image of Freddy Richards, which her father captured in the nursery. Next to it, she saw photographs of the centuries-old, stacked rum barrels along the back wall of the cellar, where they discovered Freddy Richards' skeletal remains.

Carly thought about the original owners of her home, Andrew and Celeste Pettigrew, whom Ben Hastings murdered in cold blood. Their spirits and the orphan Freddy Richards haunted the Tabor home until Carly and Delaney solved the mystery. After they located the remains, television reporters clamored to interview her and Austin, making their story headline news throughout the South.

Skeptics doubted Carly's sensitivity and questioned how she used her abilities to resolve the haunting and the murders in her home. Some prank callers phoned her office at Channel 5, and occasional whispers followed her at social events. Carly grew accustomed to the lingering stares when she and Delaney went out for lunch.

Carly thought she had buried her sensitive ability with Freddy's remains and with the birth of her child, Frederick, later that year. She enjoyed a short reprieve from paranormal activity until the summer of 2016.

She advanced to the next slide and the image of Fairlight, the two-hundred-year-old Trescott-Whaley plantation home on Johns Island, South Carolina. Seeing it brought a smile to her face. She and the home's owner, Iyla Faye Whaley, became friends in the summer of 2018 when Carly solved the forty-year string of cold cases on Johns Island involving Iyla Faye's daughter.

After Amy Whaley's memorial service, Iyla Faye decided to leave her ancestral Trescott plantation home. "Waiting for Amy to come home is the only reason I stayed after Jameson passed away, you know," Iyla Faye told Carly.

In 2022, Iyla Faye sold Fairlight to her nephew from Murrell's Inlet. She now resides in a senior living community on James Island. Carly visits Iyla Faye monthly.

Carly tensed when she advanced the slide to the fish camp near Cherry Point on Wadmalaw Island. The cabin and pit where she discovered the girls brought tears to her eyes. She saw James Van Ness's face. *You'll never hurt anyone again.*

Carly's throat tightened when the slide with Joella McGee appeared next. Beautiful Jo-Jo, as Frederick called her. A tear escaped and she quickly wiped it away.

A collage with photos of Amy Whaley, Abbey Lawson, Cassie Moore, and Cadence Davis followed Joella's. Carly remembered the peace and closure enveloping her when their spirits left the room at the Charleston Coroner's office. The parents were finally able to have their daughter's remains laid to rest. Abbey Lawson continues to be the exception. Both her mother and grandmother passed away before knowing what happened to Abbey.

Carly and Austin bought a plot next to Freddy Richards at Magnolia Cemetery in Charleston for Abbey Lawson. The ordeal ended, or so she thought, with the death of James Van Ness. The spirits of children no longer haunted her. Life returned to normal until the vivid dreams of people, places, and, more recently, the mysterious woman and children. She used a slow breathing technique to release anxiety from her body, as her therapist, Dr. Jane Durban, suggested.

Carly printed the notes she needed for her presentation and turned off the computer and window units. Her shadow appeared on the wall as she descended the stairs to the second-floor landing, as the sun shone through the window. She noticed another shadow appear, and her breath caught in her throat. Delaney and Carly reached the landing at the same time.

"You scared the daylights out of me," Carly said, punching Delaney in the shoulder. "I didn't hear you come in."

"Sorry. Austin told me I'd find you up here." Delaney followed Carly downstairs to the kitchen. "Are you finished packing?"

"Yes, it took me a while to decide what to take. I've done all I can do for my presentation. Now I'm thinking about sightseeing," Carly said.

The ping of Carly's phone interrupted the conversation. Larry Deveroux's name appeared on the screen.

"Hello, Carly. I wondered if you had a chance to drive down to Bethesda?"

"Hi, Larry. Delaney Warrick and I visited the grounds and dormitory last week. We saw several spirits lingering at the property."

"I believe the bones date back at least two hundred years," he said. "Did you see the children?"

"We connected with enslaved people, soldiers, and children. A woman with her small children appeared to me. The infant skeletal remains might be her child as well."

"The results of the carbon dating will take several weeks. It makes my job easier, confirming the bones are from antiquity."

"I'm not a textile expert, but the clothing style they wore dates before the 1800s," Carly surmised.

"Time will tell. I'll contact you as soon as the report on the carbon dating comes back," Larry said.

"Thanks, Larry. It's good to hear from you. Goodbye." Carly shoved her phone into her open purse.

"Did Larry know how long it takes to get the results from the carbon dating?" Delaney asked.

"He said several weeks."

"Let's investigate again before Deveroux receives the results," Delaney suggested.

The grandfather clock downstairs chimed at nine o'clock. Delaney reached for her purse and keys on the counter. "I think I'll head home. We have an early wake-up call in the morning."

"I have my phone alarm and the bedside clock set for four-thirty. What time is Boyd picking you up in the morning?"

"I told him to be at my house by three. I printed out my boarding pass and tickets before I came here. I'm good to go," Delaney confirmed.

"I'll see you at the terminal then. Drive safe, and try to get a good night's sleep," Carly said as the two women hugged.

"I might need a shot of Captain Morgan before I hit the sheets," Delaney said as she closed the door.

Carly laughed. The image of Delaney hitting the bottle before bed reminded her of the time the two went to Baton Rouge for a paranormal convention. Delaney and Carly mingled with other guests during a meet and greet at the hotel bar. Delaney drank one too many rum and Coke concoctions that evening, and she entertained Carly performing the Whip and Nae Nae for a solid hour.

Austin waited for Carly to get into bed before they called her parents. They caught Freddy and Viviene just in time to FaceTime with them to say goodnight.

After saying goodnight, Carly turned up the volume on her phone. "I don't want to sleep through my alarm in the morning."

She turned off the bedside lamp and curled up behind Austin. His slow and steady breathing soon soothed her into matching his cadence. She dreamed about the woman and children aboard a ship going out to sea, the wind cold on their faces as they stood on deck. The woman pulled a wool blanket tight around her growing belly and turned her back to the town behind her.

Chapter Three

Tuesday, May 28th

Carly and Austin shared one last embrace before they reached the terminal entrance. "I'll text you when we reach Coombe Abbey. The hotel information is on the bar in the kitchen along with Mom and Dad's cell numbers."

Austin nodded. "I already have their cell numbers in my phone. Don't worry, everyone and everything will be fine. Enjoy yourself. I love you."

Carly exhaled. "I love you, and I'll see you in nine days." She kissed him again and walked through the security area to her terminal.

She saw Delaney already there with an open folder on her lap, looking over her notes and sipping a drink through a red straw.

"Hey, girl. You're drinking early," Carly teased.

"I got here an hour ago. I didn't want to be late. A drink doesn't sound half bad, but this is a mocha latte," Delaney said.

"Our flight doesn't leave until eight, not to mention the long layover in Philadelphia," Carly added. "I think I'll order one of those."

Passengers heading to Philadelphia and beyond started to fill the terminal. Carly and Delaney's flight arrived the following morning at London Heathrow in the UK.

Delaney removed a small gift bag from her carry-on. "Here's something to get our *Carlaney 2025 Adventure* off in style," she said.

"What's this? Did you have that printed on a t-shirt for me?"

"You'll have to dig in there to find out."

The bag contained a faux fur sleep mask and a travel-sized bottle of lavender mist.

"I love it, and lavender is supposed to help with relaxation. Thank you."

"I ordered them for both of us to use during the flight and at the hotel." Delaney smiled. "I like your idea of putting it on a t-shirt. I can't believe I didn't think of it."

The voice over the PA system announced that early boarding was about to begin for first-class. As a perk for speaking at the conference, Carly and Delaney received upgrades to first-class. The duo grabbed their carry-ons and walked through the jet bridge. The line inched toward the inside of the plane. They found their seats in the third row. Carly let Delaney have the window seat. An elderly gentleman waited for Carly to get to her seat and then sat across from her.

Delaney and Carly greeted him, and he returned the hello while snapping his seatbelt. She texted Austin before the crew delivered the usual directions in case of cabin pressure loss, turbulence, or worse. The captain addressed the passengers, and Carly felt Delaney's left hand grab hers.

Moments later, the Jet Blue airplane taxied down the runway and lifted off, with Delaney squeezing her eyes tight, holding Carly's hand in a death grip.

As the plane ascended to its maximum altitude, Carly noticed Delaney gazing down at the city shrinking below them, transforming the landscape into a patchwork quilt.

"Well, that wasn't so bad," Delaney said as she released Carly's hand and unbuckled her seatbelt.

Carly noticed the imprint of Delaney's nails in her hand. She reached into her purse for a tour book of Wales and reclined her seat.

The layover in Philadelphia gave Carly and Delaney time to eat lunch and people-watch. The packed terminal for the British Airways flight to London Heathrow offered a diverse range of travelers: parents with children, young adults in pajama pants and hoodies, business travelers, and small tour groups.

A young gentleman with a lanyard displaying the name of his group walked over to sit beside Carly.

"Do you mind if I take this seat?" he asked. "I'm Jordan Fentress. I'm with Spirit Seekers USA. You're Carly Tabor, aren't you?"

Carly recognized Jordan from the information she and Delaney received in their conference packets.

"Yes, I am. It's good to meet you."

Delaney and Jordan introduced themselves and shook hands.

"The conference is full, as of last count. Several countries and over 120 people are planning to attend. I'm glad you're joining us. We've wanted you as a speaker for several years."

Carly's cheeks flushed at the compliment. "Thank you. I'm excited to have the opportunity to attend."

"Delaney, I look forward to your presentation as well. You both will add so much to the conference."

While conversing, a couple noticed Jordan and joined the trio. Delaney recognized the man immediately. Byron Harris, the host of a paranormal television program, Historical Haunts, renowned for its specials on haunted locations. And by his side was Alexandria Diaz, a sharp-dressed Hispanic woman. She entered the supernatural scene in

2018, claiming she remained in a coma for several days following a car crash and traveled back in time. Delaney found the woman interesting, and Byron forged a friendship with her over the last two years, bringing her to his television program and conferences. Carly estimated her to be in her early forties.

Jordan introduced the pair to Carly and Delaney, and the foursome spent the next hour talking about the conference and the historic Coombe Abbey, now a convention site and hotel.

The flight to Heathrow lasted over eight hours, allowing Carly and Delaney to don their sleep masks. Surprisingly, both women managed to sleep for a few hours during the overnight flight. At five-fifty a.m. the following morning, the plane touched down at their destination.

After claiming their baggage from the carousel, a woman with a Spirit Seekers UK Paranormal Conference sign stood near the baggage claim area where others gathered. Jordan explained she was their tour group coordinator and co-founder of the event, Katherine Hawkins-Cooke. Katherine and her husband, Graham, own a cottage in the town of Warwickshire, located near Coombe Abbey. The home has remained in Graham's family since the twelfth century. She and Jordan forged a partnership in creating the Spirit Seekers Paracon Conference in 2018, and, since its inception, the conference has changed locations annually. Katherine formally introduced herself and distributed packets with each person's name, including conference information, a lanyard, maps, tour information, and hotel accommodation details.

Carly had received an itinerary and hotel information before the conference, but little else. Katherine explained that the other flights would arrive soon, and Jordan would take their group of twenty-five in a shuttle to the location. They could settle in and sight-see on the grounds until five p.m., when the conference opened.

Two shuttles waited outside the airport to transport the attendees to the London Euston train station. From there, the train traveled an hour to Coventry Station.

Green pastures and fenced farmland dotted the Warwickshire countryside. The train crossed picturesque fields where sheep grazed inside ancient stone walls, and thatched-roof barns graced the pastoral setting. Looking out the opposite window on the train, Carly and Delaney noticed the gardens around quaint cottages. The location spoke to Carly's love of history. Her phone battery needed a charge, but she continued to take pictures as the train pulled into Coventry Station.

"I remember seeing scenes like this on *Downton Abbey*," Carly shared.

"Wait until you see Coombe Abbey," Byron said, overhearing Carly's comment. "It's magnificent."

The tour group departed from the train station and waited for taxis to arrive. Carly and Delaney shared a cab with two middle-aged men. Dr. Alston Curry from Glasgow, Scotland, and Pierce Rynders from London introduced themselves and recounted their paranormal experiences during the twenty-minute ride.

Dr. Curry, a professor in parapsychology at the University of Glasgow, spent the last twenty-five years researching paranormal phenomena across the UK. His white hair, trimmed goatee, and mustache reminded Carly of Sean Connory, another Scotsman. Pierce noted he leads a local ghost-investigating group, Beyond the Veil Ghost Investigation Service. He looked to be about thirty, donning a baseball cap and a silver stud in his right ear. The conversation centered on the conference and what the next three days had in store for the attendees.

As the taxi entered the driveway to Coombe Abbey, Carly and Delaney focused on the spectacular view outside the window. The building resembled a sixteenth-century manor house, complete with a moat and drawbridge. Guests arrived at the hotel via the circular drive, where porters, dressed in red and black attire, waited to assist the visitors with their luggage.

~

Weeks before the trip, Carly researched the conference location and learned about the history of Coombe Abbey. It was built in the twelfth century. Richard de Camville presented the Abbey to Cistercian monks, but the monks lost it in 1539 when King Henry VIII dissolved all monasteries. The Abbey had changed ownership many times, with one notable owner being James VI, the Scottish King of England. He sent his daughter, Princess Elizabeth, to live at the Abbey.

The Abbey underwent a series of improvements, including the moat, gardens, and east and west wings, which enlarged the estate. Today, the Abbey and surrounding buildings are a 4-star hotel. It is considered one of the most haunted places in England.

"It's no wonder Spirit Seekers UK chose the site for its conference. The history of the Abbey dates to the twelfth century," Carly said.

The taxi drove across the stone bridge which spanned a moat filled with lily pads and swans. Carly pointed out the metal drawbridge below the Abbey. Three more taxis pulled inside the circular, flat stone drive. Thistle, buttercups, wild primrose, and white clover covered the surrounding fields. The nursery, gardens, and landscape, designed by Capability Brown, graced the park, trails, and paths over five hundred acres.

Carly and Delaney put their lanyards around their necks and lugged their carry-on bags inside. A porter brought a gold-plated rolling cart to load their luggage from the taxi. Byron and Pierce followed behind the women. Inside the hotel, the decor transported guests back to the Medieval era.

"This is beyond anything I imagined," Delaney commented.

Carly agreed as her eyes panned the massive wooden beams and arched doorways in the registration area. Byron and Pierce went to the hotel reception desk to check in for the conference. A young, twenty-something brunette woman named Layla left her computer screen to welcome the guests. Carly and Delaney waited for their turn to check in.

"I overheard Byron say that the speakers received the best rooms. I guess that is why the registration costs more," Carly said.

"I haven't been anywhere for so long. I want to go big or go home!" Delaney remarked, bringing chuckles from the registration attendant.

Layla finished Byron's registration and asked, "Who's next?" Delaney motioned Carly to the desk.

Another young girl walks up to the counter to handle Delaney's registration. "Ms. Tabor, we have your room, The Princess Elizabeth. It is one of our most popular Grand Feature rooms." Layla handed Carly the plastic key card.

Disappointed, Carly expected her to hand over an exquisitely carved skeleton key instead of the modern one. "Thank you. I feel as though I've stepped back in time. If my room is half as beautiful as I've seen, I'll be in heaven."

Her luggage was placed on a transport cart. A steward said, "When you're ready, I will follow you to your room."

"Thank you. I'm waiting for my friend to finish her registration. I'll join you in a minute."

The attendant handed Delaney the key to her room. "Your room, The Gibson, overlooks the moat. Your room is down the hall from your friend's."

"I can't wait to see it," Delaney said.

Another steward came with Delaney's luggage and followed Carly and her steward to an elevator.

"Your room is on the next floor. You can ride the elevator or use the stairs if you wish."

Carly asked Delaney. "You want to walk instead?"

"Sure, I need to stretch my legs."

Carly told the stewards she and Delaney would meet them at the landing. They turned and found the massive stairway leading to the next level. As they strolled down the hallways that were lined with stone busts and tapestries hanging from the walls, the atmosphere transported them to the twelfth century.

"I read in the brochure that Queen Elizabeth I visited here, as it belonged to her father, King Henry VIII. I get chills thinking about the history that is surrounding us." Delaney smiled.

Carly went inside her room, admiring the impressive four-poster bed and fabric-covered walls in deep red and gold. She pulled back the rich damask draperies and viewed the long, tree-lined driveway. The moat below the window caught her eye. She turned back to the steward, giving him £ 5.00. She thanked him as he placed her luggage onto a wooden baggage rack.

"If there is anything else you need, madam, please let me know," he said.

She thanked him again and closed the door, latching the deadbolt. She noticed the stairway leading to a private bath in the turret. Giddy, she climbed the stairs to explore her room further.

After admiring the amenities in her room, she texted Austin: *We're here! Love, C.*

While she put her things inside the ornate armoire, her phone pinged.

Have a great time. Leave the spooks there. Love, A. Carly chuckled softly. *I can't promise anything.*

Carly's and Delaney's rooms featured four-poster beds upon a raised platform with rich fabric curtains to match the period-style spread. Above, the ornate plaster details on the ceiling reminded Carly of something she saw in a television program about Highclere Castle. The bathrooms showcased roll-top tubs and stone floors.

After a few moments, Delaney texted Carly a picture of her suite, and Carly returned the favor. The welcome meet and greet, set to start in two hours, gave them time to freshen up and change for the evening.

~

Spirit Seekers Paracon UK welcomed one hundred twenty guests from around the UK, Canada, the United States, Wales, and Scotland. Two guests traveled from Austria and one from Australia. The conference began today, Wednesday, May 29th at five p.m. and ended on Saturday, June 1st.

Carly noticed the speakers seated near the front of the hall at two oval tables. Katherine gave a slight wave to her and Delaney as they entered the room. The attendees dressed in various clothing styles, some wearing T-shirts bearing their paranormal group names, while others wore formal attire, and several opted for casual wear. Carly opted for a navy top paired with white capri slacks, while Delaney selected a khaki pair of slacks and a multi-colored floral top. Both felt at ease with their choices, appreciating the various styles on display. They took seats beside Alexandria Diaz and Byron Harris. Katherine and Graham sat in the front row by the podium next to Jordan Fentress. After a clank of her fork alongside her glass, the room stilled, and she welcomed the attendees to Coombe Abbey.

Carly flipped through the conference booklet. She found her picture and bio in the section listing the speakers and guests of honor. She cringed—she didn't remember sending her most recent headshot. They used one of her photos from Channel 5's website.

Delaney approved of the professional photograph taken of her months earlier.

Katherine thanked the staff of Coombe Abbey and the founders of Spirit Seekers USA for hosting the event with the UK branch.

"I trust your stay at the Abbey or in one of the adjoining buildings will meet every expectation. We have a packed schedule for the next four days with tours, panels, and keynote addresses by our distinguished guests of honor," she said, waving her hand toward Carly and Delaney's table.

Delaney leaned over and whispered, "I love listening to the different accents. I feel like a clod hopper compared to the other speakers."

Carly whispered, "I feel the same way."

The opening statements included an overview of the conference, a list of ghost investigations offered to guests, and a description of the various spirits said to haunt the Abbey and grounds.

Carly craned her neck to see around Byron. A man entered the room and walked to the stage. Katherine paused, acknowledging the gentleman, who appeared embarrassed. He gave a slight nod to the audience and took his seat.

"Well, that's a skosh awkward," Delaney said in low tones.

Carly smiled. *Poor guy.* The man took his seat beside Graham Cooke and Jordan Fentress.

Katherine moved away from the podium to speak in soft tones. The men shared a laugh, and Katherine continued. "Our final guest, Drake Taylor, finally joins us due to an unforeseen delay."

The crowd applauded, and several guests flipped through the program booklet to find his picture and bio.

"He sure is a looker," Carly said behind her napkin, nudging Delaney in her side.

Delaney's brows furrowed. "I wonder what his story is?"

Drake thanked Katherine, giving a quick wave to the guests. He scanned the faces looking back at him, noticing Carly. He acknowledged her with a slight nod. She smiled and glanced at the back section of attendees in her program. *His picture is complimentary, but he's much better looking in person.*

Katherine stepped aside as Jordan Fentress walked up to the podium. "Welcome, everyone, to Spirit Seekers Paracon 2025. I'll begin the evening by introducing our distinguished guests."

After Carly and Delaney's introductions, Carly resumed reading Drake's bio. *Drake is the Lead Investigator for Spectral Investigations and the manager of The London Foundling Home Museum.* Carly felt a chill settle over her and saw small faces peering from a second-story window. In an instant, the vision left her.

She didn't realize how much of the opening speech she'd missed. Jordan took his seat as people entered the dining hall to eat dinner.

"Earth to Carly," Delaney said as she moved away from the table. "I'm starving, and you're in la-la land."

Carly snapped to attention at the sound of Delaney's voice. "I think I have jet lag. The struggle is real. Sorry, lead the way."

CHAPTER FOUR

The attendees and guests dined together in one of the dining halls, The Court House, a former eighteenth-century tennis clubhouse, sat the conference attendees and speakers together. Carly admired the ornate decorations and table coverings as she followed the server to her seat. Carly sat with a group of six attendees. She scanned the room and saw Delaney seated beside Drake Taylor. She smiled and turned back to her table.

"Ms. Tabor! What a treat to sit with you," Dr. Alston Curry remarked, scooting his chair closer to the table.

"Thank you, Dr. Curry," Carly said, squinting to see his name on the lanyard. "Please, call me Carly."

"I hope you'll catch my presentation on psychic phenomena tomorrow," he said.

"I find the study of ESP and Psychokinesis fascinating," Carly replied. "I look forward to it."

A young woman across the table commented, "I came to the conference from Australia just to hear your presentation," she said to Carly.

"Oh, my. What an honor! Thank you," Carly replied.

"I'm Sheree Carver. I grew up in Brisbane but now live in Perth. I'm part of Ghosts Down Under, a paranormal investigation group."

Sheree's coal-black hair was in a loose bun with pink sparkly thread interwoven. On one arm was a red rose tattoo. On her wrist, a chain of purple and red flowers, and on the other forearm, a Celtic cross. Her nails were painted black, and she wore a dark purple short-sleeved maxi dress with black velvet pumps.

"I'm pleased to meet you, Sheree, and thank you for coming to the conference."

An Arabic couple in their mid-forties, Hakim and Ravon Said, from Vancouver, said they attended the conference each year, making the trip part of their vacation to Europe.

Myles Frasier of Edinburgh, Scotland, producer of a paranormal television show called Ghosts of the Isles, sat across from the couple. He shared his own experiences with those seated around him. The Saids asked Myles Frasier for his autograph on their program, and he obliged.

"Delaney, my friend, and I are traveling to Wales and Scotland before we return to Charleston," Carly remarked.

"My show airs on Wednesday afternoons on the stations in Edinburgh. I hope you'll enjoy it," Myles said as he handed the program back to the Saids just as the food was being served.

Carly enjoyed the leek and potato velouté, the starter for the evening meal. The main course, a Southwest lamb leg, paired with a dessert of Bramley apple and mixed spice crumble, received rave reviews from everyone at the table, except the Saids. They chose a vegetarian menu and alternate choices for the weekend.

After the meal, everyone gathered in the Great Hall, where the spirit tour began. Carly found Delaney talking with Eleanor Murphy, a paranormal enthusiast from Dublin. Carly introduced herself and joined them on the tour.

For the next hour, guests walked the Abbey alone to the most active locations on the property. Due to darkness and a sudden shower, everyone opted for the indoor locations. Carly and Delaney perused the list of spirits said to haunt Coombe Abbey.

"Let's go upstairs and walk the corridor near our rooms. Since we're in the old part of the Abbey, I expect to hear or see someone tonight," Carly said as they took the stairs instead of the elevator.

"Did you notice that none of the other conference speakers seemed interested in the tour?" Delaney asked.

"Maybe this isn't their first rodeo. I guess they have other plans," Carly replied. "Besides, we seem to attract spirits, wanted or not."

The ghosts of Abbot Geoffrey, Matilda, the stable girl, and a Victorian bike rider top the list of the most active spirits at Coombe. While strolling along the corridors, the women neither heard nor saw anything paranormal. Carly absorbed the building's history, taking in all the sights and furnishings of the Medieval era.

At nine-thirty, both felt the effects of a long day. Carly suggested, "Why don't you come to my room, and we'll order something from room service."

Delaney declined, "I think the soaking tub is calling my name. Jet lag is the real deal."

"It sounds heavenly. Enjoy! Tomorrow is another day," Carly bid Delaney goodnight.

~

After some time in the massive tub, Carly grabbed her notes for tomorrow's presentation and climbed the two wooden steps into bed.

The furnishings and curtains around the massive four-poster bed gave the room a medieval feeling. She turned up the volume on the television to muffle the sound of her voice as she read her notes out loud. Her life played like a movie before her eyes as she rehearsed her speech.

Carly's earliest memories of spirits appearing dated back to the summer she spent at her grandmother and grandfather's farm in rural Kansas. On a trip to the local cemetery with Granny Eddleman to place flowers on family graves, she encountered a spirit.

A girl near Carly's age stood beside a dead cedar tree, her own grave next to it. At first, Carly thought the child had slipped away from her parents. She said hello to the girl, but she didn't reply.

Granny turned to ask Carly who she was talking to, and Carly told her about the little girl beside the cedar tree. Granny nodded and took Carly's hand, leading her away. She didn't tell Carly that she didn't see anyone or that Carly made up the little girl as an imaginary friend, as her brother and sister did. Her grandfather passed away from lung cancer before her tenth birthday. She dreamed of Pop Eddleman holding her hand and walking together into the barn to feed the cows. He appeared as a young man and sang a silly song to her. When she told her mother, she seemed to be confused. "Daddy always sang that song to me," Paula said.

Carly leaned against the soft pillows propped behind her as she remembered her mother discouraging her imaginary friends and inventive imagination growing up. Granny Eddleman always listened with interest when Carly told her of such things when she stayed with her and Pop Eddleman.

As Carly grew into adulthood, she didn't talk about the people she had seen as a child. Neither her sister nor brother spoke of similar experiences growing up and brushed off Carly's "imaginary friends". Paula Evans, her mother, avoided the topic altogether.

When Carly reached her teenage years, the paranormal encounters ceased, and the family avoided discussing the topic in the future. She continued to spend time with Granny. The two shared a closeness not felt by her other grandchildren.

The summer the Tabors purchased their home on King Street brought their idyllic life to an abrupt halt. Months of Poltergeist activity led to Carly experiencing full-body apparitions, violent attacks, and voice communication with an assemblage of the original owners haunting their homes. Not until the image of Freddy Richards, the young child murdered in their home in 1796, appeared in a family photograph taken by Curt Evans, did her abilities surface with her family. During a visit in 2013, Carly posed with her mother in a spare bedroom she hoped would be the future nursery. Upon seeing the photograph, the Evanses realized that Austin and Carly had been sharing their home with spectral beings.

In the summer of 2016, Paula came to stay with Carly after James Van Ness kidnapped and shot her. Paula listened as Carly explained her capture and how the deceased girls helped her escape, and officers discovered their remains buried in a pit at the Van Ness fishing camp.

She retold the experiences of Celeste and Andrew Pettigrew's murder playing out before her eyes, and the angry killer, Ben Hastings, trying to do her harm. She broke down in gut-wrenching sobs as she described searching until she found Freddy Richards's remains behind the wall in the cellar. Paula stayed silent as Carly shared her earliest memories of seeing filmy visions of long-dead family members and strangers.

Afterward, she exhaled the last of the repressed anxiety over the years.

Paula kneaded the material of her T-shirt as she spoke. "All my life, I knew of such things. When you started seeing people the rest of us couldn't, I knew, but I didn't want to believe it."

Carly's breath caught in her throat as she waited for her mother to continue.

"Sweetheart, what you've experienced with ghosts came to you through my mother and her grandmother before her," Paula said.

Carly shuffled her notes. The memory brought a smile to her face. Knowing she inherited the blessing from Granny Eddleman helped Carly accept her psychic ability instead of running from it. A sound from outside her room caught her by surprise. The discussion grew louder, and Carly moved closer to the door to look through the peephole. Dr. Alston Curry voiced his displeasure with the small room provided for his panel discussion. The event liaison appeared taken aback and tried to diffuse the situation, remaining calm. Carly couldn't imagine why Dr. Curry objected, but she left her post by the door and resumed rehearsing her notes for tomorrow.

The draperies around Carly's bed fluttered, drawing her away from her podcast. The flutter of the bed curtain brought Carly to an upright position, eyes darting around the room. Something caught her eye in front of the door. The light from beneath the door shone on a small slip of paper lying on the floor.

Curious, Carly put on her slippers and crossed the room to retrieve the paper. A note on the hotel stationery read, "I need to speak to you if you're awake. I'll be waiting in the chairs beside the confession box, next to the knight in shining armor."

The thought crossed her mind that the note came from Delaney as a joke. She texted her and waited for a reply. She hurriedly put on the clothes she'd taken off earlier. Carly reached for her key and shoved it, the note, and her phone inside the pocket of her slacks. She hurried down the corridor to Delaney's door and knocked twice.

She didn't hear any sound from inside. Delaney must've fallen asleep as soon as she returned to her room.

She studied the handwriting on the note. It wasn't Delaney's.

If Delaney didn't leave the note, then who did?

Throwing caution to the wind, she headed downstairs to the lobby. The walls inside the hotel corridors displayed Baroque tapestries and paintings from Coombe Abbey's early days. Down another flight of stairs, through a massive wooden archway, she noticed the cloisters, where the monks meditated and prayed.

Carly saw two Tudor-era ladies walking up the stairs toward her. They seemed startled when Carly acknowledged them. "Ladies," she said, lowering her eyes.

"Your friend is waiting for you," one lady said so low that only Carly could hear.

Friend? Carly didn't know the identity of the sender of the note. "Thank you," she replied, and continued her descent of the stairs past the spectral guests. When she turned to see which direction they went, they vanished.

Carly's eyes scanned across the expanse of the area. To her right, restored confession boxes lined the wall beside an elevated, carved wooden pulpit. A massive stone fireplace claimed most of the seating area on her left, along with various oil paintings and medieval armored knights. Above her, massive beams covered the ceiling, flags displaying multiple coats of arms from the families who once made Coombe Abbey their home.

Carly noticed a couple sipping wine inside an alcove, looking out at the circular stone drive, sharing an intimate moment with a kiss.

Closer to the pulpit, a gentleman sitting alone scrolled on his phone.

As she approached, she could see the top of his dark hair from behind. He sat cross-legged, jiggling his foot, engrossed in a text message.

Carly approached the man. When he saw her, he put away his phone, smiled, and rose from his chair.

"Thank you for meeting me, Ms. Tabor," Drake Taylor said, extending a warm hand.

CHAPTER FIVE

"I love a good mystery," Carly replied, intrigued by the secretive meeting.

"Please, sit," Drake said, motioning to the empty chair.

The hotel staff stood behind the massive counter, discussing an issue with a Wi-Fi glitch, oblivious to the guests who milled about. Even at this late hour, the seating areas were starting to fill.

"Mr. Taylor, I'll admit I didn't expect you as the note's sender."

Drake moved his chair closer to hers. "Please, call me Drake. I apologize for my forwardness, but when I saw your picture in the conference booklet, I knew I must speak to you privately."

"Oh? This sounds intriguing. I'm Carly, by the way."

"Truth be told, I almost didn't attend the conference, but when I saw you this evening, I experienced an overwhelming sense of urgency to speak with you."

Carly registered the seriousness in Drake's tone. "Urgency? I'm not following you."

Drake leaned closer to Carly, lowering his voice, as another couple occupied the high-back chairs to their right.

"It's the strangest thing. While working in the museum two nights ago, I saw an apparition of a beautiful woman standing in front of the door where the Foundling Hospital keeps the records."

"I don't understand the connection to me, though. Did the apparition speak to you?"

"No, not directly, but I heard the name Bethesda."

Carly's mouth opened to take in a gulp of air. "Bethesda?"

Drake felt his arms prickle with gooseflesh. "You've heard of Bethesda before?"

Carly told Drake of her recent trip to Bethesda Academy after the owners discovered bones on the site. She added, "They've noticed an increase in paranormal activity since the discovery of the small cemetery."

"I found the information for the conference on my bureau with the page turned to your bio. Strange, wouldn't you say?"

Carly digested the information, saying, "The spirits reach out in ways we never expect. Delaney, my friend, and I are traveling from the conference to Wales and Scotland. We have some wiggle room before checking in at our hotel. Would you mind if we stopped by the Foundling Home Museum?"

"No, not at all. I'd be delighted to show you the records and the museum." Drake smiled and added, "I want to hear more about your experiences if you don't mind sharing."

"Yes, of course, and your experiences too." Carly found Drake easy to talk with, not thinking about the time.

The hotel lobby lights dimmed as it approached midnight.

"It looks like they're closing up shop," Carly remarked. "I suppose I should go upstairs since we have an early start tomorrow." She thanked Drake for the information, extending her hand in return.

"Thank you for meeting me. It's been a pleasure, Carly," Drake said. He felt an unexplained energy pass between them.

Carly stood, "You're welcome. Good night, Drake."

The connection of the Foundling Museum to Bethesda piqued her curiosity and sixth sense. Could the bones discovered at Bethesda be the orphans from England? Who were the adults buried with them? The Summerfields said the orphans came from England during the early days of Bethesda. She couldn't wait to get upstairs and jot down what Drake shared. She would explain everything to Delaney.

Drake waited a moment before walking to the elevator. He felt the two were former acquaintances from his past. He couldn't place her, though.

Carly awoke after a blissful night of rest. The four-poster bed was delightful. She had kept the curtains drawn to experience the full medieval effect. As soon as she brushed her teeth, a loud rap on the door jolted her from the royal treatment.

"Carly, it's me!" an excited voice said from the hallway.

Pulling on one of the hotel-provided robes, she peered through the peephole. Delaney, clad in yoga pants and a University of North Carolina sweatshirt, tapped louder on the door.

Carly opened the door and pulled her friend inside. "You're going to wake the dead with all that racket."

Delancy walked past Carly and turned on her heels with her eyebrows raised. "Well, are you going to leave me hanging? Talk about it, girlfriend."

"I tried to get you to go with me last night, but you didn't answer the door," Carly said in a huff.

"Oh, well, I sprayed the lavender on my sheets and donned my sleeping mask. It was all over in a matter of seconds."

Carly remembered the gift she had given her at the airport, inside her carry-on. "Well, I received this note under my door last night," Carly said, handing the note to Delaney.

Delaney read the note and gave it back to Carly. "Who in the world does this?"

"Drake Taylor." Carly paused, then added, "I wrote down everything he said after returning to my room."

The idea that Carly took such a careless risk ruffled Delaney's feathers. "You realize this could have been some sex trafficker kidnapper who wanted to sell you..."

Carly held up her hands and stopped her in mid-sentence.

"I didn't even think about it. Besides, I would have missed the two ladies on the stairway if I hadn't gone."

Delaney swallowed her protest. "Ladies? You mean you saw former residents at the Abbey?"

"I did, and one of them spoke to me. The ghost told me, 'Your friend is waiting for you.' How about that?"

Delaney took a moment to process the information. "So, you saw two intelligent spirits that knew Drake Taylor wanted to speak to you. Go on, I'm listening."

Carly told Delaney about the woman Drake saw two nights ago. When she finished, Delaney finally spoke.

"Okay, that was worth a walk downstairs into the unknown! Now we *have* to go to the Foundling Museum."

Carly nodded. "I agree, and I know you wouldn't mind another chance to be with the handsome Drake Taylor."

"I've already scoped out his bio. He's single." Delaney winked and closed the door behind her.

Carly met Delaney at the Garden Room Conservatory at six-thirty for breakfast. Delaney chose a table near one of the floor-to-ceiling windows overlooking one of the many gardens.

The breakfast options were endless, and both women chose the buffet. When they reached their table, Jordan Fentress and Alexandria Diaz approached them.

"Good morning," Carly and Delaney greeted in unison.

Alexandria balanced her plate of bacon, eggs, and fruit in one hand while holding a glass of tomato juice in the other.

"Do you mind if we join you this morning?"

Carly smiled and offered the chair beside her. "No, we'd love for you to sit with us."

Delaney gathered their notes and handbags and placed them on the remaining chair beside her. "Isn't the buffet amazing?" she asked.

After the foursome devoured their breakfast, they discussed the panel discussions planned for the day. The honored guests would each speak forty-five minutes during the conference. Half of the speakers would give their presentations on the first day, and the other half would present on the second day. The rest of the time, attendees would go on day trips to nearby historical sites and evening ghost hunts.

Alexandria frequently spoke at conferences, primarily in the southwestern United States and Canada. "This will be my first time speaking at this conference. I didn't sleep well last night. Jitters, I guess."

"I'm nervous, too, if that makes you feel any better," Delaney admitted.

Jordan reassured them. "It's all good. People aren't here to judge, they're here to learn."

"Thank you, that's what I keep telling myself," Carly said, nervous about her presentation.

The first panel began at eight a.m. Carly and Delaney had enough time to return to their rooms and freshen up before their presentations. Carly's presentation would be in the Walnut Room. The conference room featured floor-to-ceiling walnut paneling. The fifteen-foot ceilings gave the room an expansive feeling, while keeping the guests close to the speaker. Two expansive windows flanking an antique gold mirror overlooked the western terrace and formal gardens.

Carly admired the royal blue carpet, featuring gold, red, and white geometric designs accented with royal blue lines. A marble hearth and mantle surrounded the fireplace. Carvings of medieval scenes and vines covered the front and sides.

The spirit of a young boy standing sentinel at the fireplace with a bucket full of ashes nodded as Carly made her way to the walnut podium. She returned his greeting with a nod of her own. The Saids, already seated at one of two expansive banquet tables, made note of Carly's behavior.

"Do you see a spirit, Carly?" Hakim asked with excitement in his voice.

Carly smiled at the young boy. "Why, yes, I do. He's waiting to empty his bucket of ashes as soon as his Mistress dismisses him."

The Saids watched with interest, but neither saw the boy. "We want to experience something while we're here. This is as close as we've come," Ravon commented as if it were a consolation prize.

The room filled, and Carly placed her note cards on the podium. She never used notes or cheat sheets at conferences, but the number of spirits vying for Carly's attention was notable, acknowledging her courage in sharing her thoughts. The notes were there if she needed them.

Delaney, Jordan, Drake Taylor, and Alston Curry were seated to her left. The other thirty seats were filled with attendees. In the front row, Sheree Carver, the enthusiastic fan from Australia, sat beaming with a wide grin. Carly gave a slight wave, which caught the attention of those sitting beside her.

"My maternal grandmother shared the same abilities," Carly began, "and passed the gift on to me. My family tried to pass off my abilities as 'imaginary friends' and a 'wild imagination.'"

Delaney winked at Carly, acknowledging her courage in sharing her story.

Carly continued with the slides she'd prepared at home and sent to

Katherine to upload. The room stilled as she talked about the house on King Street and the photo of her family in the nursery with Freddy Richards's ghostly image. She spoke for the next twenty minutes about the Pettigrews and Ben Hastings and the hauntings she endured for weeks before finding Freddy Richards's remains.

She continued with the slide displaying the faces of Amy Whaley, Cassie Moore, Abbey Lawson, and Cadence Davis. She explained how Cadence appeared to her, and eventually, all the girls helped her find their remains.

Carly advanced the slide to Joella McGee and explained how she became Van Ness's final victim. The last slide she shared showed the pit with yellow police tape surrounding it.

Several women in the room wiped tears as Carly retold her own near-death experience, and how James Van Ness received the final verdict of death.

After concluding her presentation, Carly opened the floor to questions. "Carly, how do you interact with spirits, and do you see and hear them all the time?" Sheree asked.

"Thank you for your questions, Sheree. It's like being in the room with a clock that chimes and ticks every day, all day long. After a while, I don't notice. If the spirit tries to get my attention for help, I experience dreams and other manifestations."

Drake Taylor listened to Carly's presentation, mesmerized by her abilities. Alston Curry made notes during the presentation and didn't make eye contact.

After fielding various questions and taking pictures with several attendees, including Sheree and the Saids, Alston Curry waited for a moment out of earshot of the others.

He handed Carly a business card and said, "When you're ready, I can help you."

"Thank you," Carly said, accepting the card. "Help me to do what?"

Alston paused, "When you're ready, please contact me." He shook Carly's hand and left the room.

Carly tried to make sense of the exchange. She put the business card into her leather binder and joined Delaney.

"Aside from leaving a puddle of sweat behind the podium, I survived."

"Your presentation left me in awe of what you do, even though I witnessed most of it."

"Pardon me for intruding," Drake interjected. "I hope you'll forgive my staring at you throughout your presentation. I'm astounded by what you've encountered."

Carly thanked Drake for his kind comment. "I'm looking forward to your presentation tomorrow."

Jordan waited for Carly, Delaney, and Drake to exit the room. He moved the slide projector screen and closed the door behind him. He thought he had heard a child laughing and went back inside to check. The room was empty.

CHAPTER SIX

Carly and Delaney made a quick trip to the restroom before catching Alexandria Diaz's presentation in The Kelley, a meeting room down from Delaney's suite. The room that overlooked the moat was called the library. The mahogany-paneled walls extended to the massive, beamed ceilings. Centuries-old books bound in leather, and some covered in heavy material, perched on shelves that lined the walls. The windows gave the room abundant natural light, bathing it in the morning sun.

They took their seats near the front of the room. Delaney took a sip from the hotel's bottled water and whispered to Carly, "What did creepy Dr. Curry say to you?"

Carly unwrapped a peppermint and put it in her mouth before answering. "He gave me his business card and said that when I'm ready, he can help me."

Delaney raised an eyebrow, wanting to know more. "What in the world does he mean? Help you do what?"

Carly shrugged. She repeated the conversation back to Delaney. "I guess I'll know when I know, you know?" Carly laughed.

"It takes all kinds. Chalk it up to one in every crowd." Delaney stifled a chuckle as Alexandria started her presentation.

Carly tried to concentrate on Alexandria, imagining how odd it was to travel to one place while the body remained in another. Listening to her explain life in 1840s New York grabbed her attention. The details she gave about caring for immigrants who arrived during the potato famine piqued her interest even more. *She might have made the whole thing up, but who am I to discount what someone else claims to have experienced?*

When the program opened to questions, Delaney wanted to know the names of the people she encountered during her time travel. She shared validations from her time away from her physical body, which caused the guests to gasp in surprise.

"I wish I could go back and meet my ancestors," Carly whispered.

"Alexandria didn't get to choose. She awoke in 1847 without knowing a soul. Talk about culture shock," Delaney replied.

Carly raised her hand. "How did you return to the present?"

Alexandra paused, thanking Carly for asking the question, then answered. "That is the strangest part of the story. I remained in a coma for six weeks. One morning, my heart rate began to slow and eventually came to a stop. The crash cart team entered my room and began measures to shock my heart. In 1840, at the very same moment, I stepped in front of a team of horses rushing down the street. I assume the crushing weight of the horses killed me the instant the doctors brought me back to life with the defibrillator."

Carly and the rest of the audience gasped and nodded at the explanation. Alexandria sipped her water as the crowd commented about her strange experience. She turned the crowd's attention to a newspaper page on the projector screen. She read, *"The New York Daily Herald - March 11, 1847: Mary Catherine Stice, 25, was killed yesterday when a draft team of Mr. Ellery ran over her. She has no family, and the undertaker took her to the pauper cemetery near the tenement house.*

She nursed many Irish children who arrived in the city last December."

Alexandria advanced the screen to the next slide, showing the plot where a small stone read, *M. Stice*.

After answering a few more questions, Alexandria concluded her presentation to a round of applause.

Carly and Delaney waited until the crowd moved out of the room before thanking Alexandria for an exciting program. Byron Harris joined them at the podium.

"She's lived through an amazing experience. Science and the medical doctors couldn't explain it, but they have continued to discuss her case at medical conventions now and again."

"I found your experience amazing. I loved Matheson's book on time travel. The movie, *Somewhere in Time,* was based on his book," Carly added.

Their discussion ended as Katherine stepped into the room. "Pardon me, but we'll gather in the Cloisters for lunch. There will be a trip into Warwickshire later, if you're interested."

"Wanna go sightseeing tonight?" Carly asked Delaney.

"Sure, I'd love to experience the locals."

Carly flipped the pages of the program booklet she'd placed in her bag. Spirit Seekers listed the places to visit in Warwickshire that sounded interesting. Most of them touted a spirit or two lingering in the establishment. The afternoon trip on Friday included Shakespeare's home in Stratford-Upon-Avon, a must-see for both women.

The light lunch consisted of sandwiches, fruit, cheese, crackers, and delicious desserts. Carly and Delaney chose a table with Drake Taylor, Katherine Hawkins-Cooke, and Graham.

During the buffet lunch, Jordan Fentress provided an update on paranormal events scheduled for 2026 in the United States with Spirit Seekers USA. He announced that the 2026 conference location would be in Massachusetts. He outlined various places that the convention attendees could visit during the four-day conference.

"I'm in! The plan is to visit Lizzie Borden's house and take a trip to where the Witch Trials began in Danvers," Carly said.

Delaney suggested asking Boyd Hawley to join them. Carly agreed. He wouldn't pass up the chance.

Katherine walked to the podium to remind anyone interested that the tour of haunted locations in Warwickshire would begin in twenty minutes.

The women went to their rooms to change into more comfortable clothing and met the tour group at noon. Forty-eight people crowded into the shuttle buses provided. Carly and Delaney shared a row of seats with Drake Taylor and Myles Frasier. On the way into town, Carly and Delaney wrote the addresses for the Foundling Museum.

"If you have time to spare, I'd be delighted to invite you both to my paranormal program as my guests. I don't get to interview many Americans on my show. It would be a treat," Myles invited.

Carly and Delaney were speechless. The planned excursions included the conference and sightseeing in and around London and Wales.

The days following the conference would include touring several locations featured in the *Outlander* television show. Carly and Delaney spoke in hushed tones about an additional excursion.

"Yes, thank you. I think we can squeeze in a visit to your studio." Carly's excitement for visiting the Foundling Museum paled in comparison to a television appearance. On the other hand, Delaney found both Drake and Myles easy on the eyes and anxiously awaited another chance to hang out with them.

❧

Katherine distributed a schedule of shuttle departures for tours of the various locations. Carly knew seeing everything was next to impossible. The shuttles will take the group to St. Mary's Guildhall, Ford's Hospital, and Coventry Cathedral.

Sheree, from Australia, and Eleanor Murphy, from Ireland, joined Carly and Delaney on their walk to St. Mary's Guildhall. Built during the 1340s, the Guildhall boasted beautiful stained-glass windows, sculptures, and tapestries. Its rich history dated back to the Medieval times of King Henry VI.

Carly noticed a young apprentice standing outside the entrance. Sheree commented that she felt her face burning on the side facing the young boy as the women approached the doorway.

"I see a young boy, and his face suffered burns from a fire," Carly shared.

"It feels like someone slapped my face. It's stinging!" Sheree brought her hand up to rub her cheek.

Delaney walked to the entrance. She bent down as if to speak to a young child. "His master backed into him, knocking him off balance. He fell onto the fire, burning his face and hands."

"Poor mite," Eleanor said. "I don't see him, but I feel his sadness."

Delaney stood, wiping off the knees of her slacks. "He suffered for several days. He doesn't know he's dead."

The boy appeared to be about Vivi's age, and Carly felt a tug at her heartstrings. "I can't bear to feel his pain," Carly said as she turned away.

The interior of the Guildhall provided visitors with insight into its various uses throughout the centuries, and plaques detailed the royalty that had passed through or stayed within the building.

From the Guildhall, the shuttle drove to Ford Hospital. Ford Hospital is an Almshouse built in the early 1520s. As an Almshouse, the Tudor building housed several families. During the Blitz in 1940, the Germans hit the building. The matron at the time, as well as her assistant and six residents, were killed. Carly and Delaney heard children while walking through the building but never saw any apparitions. Eleanor commented that her grandparents fled to Ireland in 1939 before the Luftwaffe began bombing England. Carly thought her accent sounded more British than Irish.

"My father was only three, and the government wanted to move people away from the coasts. It was called *Operation Pied Piper*.

"I didn't realize that, Eleanor. Thank you for sharing. I'm sure it was a terrible time for people in Europe." Carly would have to tell her father about this. He loved studying World War II.

From Ford Hospital, the shuttle stopped at the final destination for the day, Coventry Cathedral. It, too, suffered the effects of Hitler in 1940, devastating Coventry.

The most severe raid, the Luftwaffe's *Moonlight Sonata*, was on the night of November 14th. An estimated 568 people died, and 4,300 homes were destroyed, along with St. Michael's Cathedral.

The ruins of the bombed cathedral took the Spirit Seeker guests to the location first. Several people held paranormal detection devices as they walked through the once-majestic cathedral.

Delaney and Eleanor continued discussing the bombing of Coventry, and Sheree shared an investigation she conducted at Ararat Lunatic Asylum.

"The spirits are old souls, you know. I love traveling to the UK. I don't want anyone tagging along back home, though, right?" Sheree elbowed Delaney's side.

The weather for the event was perfect, despite the forecast calling for rain. The group traveled back to Coombe Abbey, where guests could dine in town or at the hotel.

~

Carly and Delaney returned to their rooms to shower and change. They met downstairs for dinner. White linen tablecloths covered tables set for eight guests. In the center of each table were different styles and colors of topiary arrangements.

They served roasted cornfed chicken supreme with potato au gratin, shredded leek and green bean panache, wild mushrooms, and Madeira sauce.

Carly and Delaney inhaled the delicious aroma as the servers placed the plates in front of them. They dined with a group of paranormal investigators from Leeds. Carly found the experiences of the others endearing. Those sitting at the table listened with interest as Carly explained how Delaney and their friend, Boyd, helped her resolve the hauntings in her home.

"Researching the history of the people who lived in my 1790s home proved to point me to the connection the lives of the first owners had with their ultimate demise," Carly shared.

"Your experiences with the Johns Island missing girls caught my attention. Something similar happened in Leeds. We're trying to solve it now," Elizabeth Drury said.

Elizabeth reminded Carly of Elise Ravenel, who was back home in Charleston. Delaney noted the resemblance. Elise's signature look was her immaculate sense of fashion and long blonde locks worn in a stylish updo.

"I hope you can help the spirits move on," Carly replied.

"Drake Taylor invited us to stop in one day when the museum is closed to investigate," Delaney said, her excitement evident in her voice.

"Lucky! I would go on a tour with him anywhere," Dora MacGuire added, raising her eyebrows suggestively. She was what Carly would describe as "the quiet one". You never knew what they were thinking.

Carly didn't deny that he was attractive, keeping her comments professional. As the only married person at the table, she enjoyed seeing Delaney join the banter with the other single ladies.

Libby Dobbins, an Oxford teacher, and Diana Wellington, another teacher who accompanied Libby, agreed that the conference's guest speakers were worth the price. They shared that they left their teaching jobs before the end of their term to attend the event.

The hotel staff had finished clearing the tables, and one waiter reminded the group that the dining hall would be closing in five minutes. The foursome from Leeds decided to call it a night.

Carly and Delaney said goodnight to them and walked to the elevator.

"I'm bushed! How about you?" Delaney repositioned the small backpack she wore.

"As tired as I am, I want to stay awake awhile and go over the itinerary for the rest of our trip." The elevator door opened, and Carly continued, "If we go to the Foundling Museum in London and Myles Frasier's television studio in Scotland, it will cut into our sightseeing."

"Can we visit Stratford as soon as the conference ends?" Delaney pushed the button for the second floor.

"I'll work on it tonight." The door opened to their floor, and they said 'goodnight' before entering their rooms.

When Delaney opened her door, she caught the train of a long gown swoosh past her as a young lady hurried into her room.

"Excuse me," Delaney said, annoyed by the spirit.

The woman turned, surprised that Delaney saw her.

"Welcome to my world, sweet cheeks," Delaney said, taking off her backpack and tossing it onto the bed.

The apparition transformed from a beautiful young woman clad in Tudor finery to a hollow-eyed, decomposed corpse, strips of cloth and tufts of hair where once golden tresses had been. She reached for the dagger protruding from her stomach. Her piercing scream brought Delaney's hands to her ears.

"For the love of… stop screaming! I'm not going to hurt you," Delaney said over the noise. "You aren't showing me anything I haven't seen before!"

The screaming stopped. The corpse returned to the lovely spectral who had rushed inside earlier. The spirit held her position in a ghostly game of Chicken.

Delaney wondered if the rest of the guests heard the commotion. She inched toward the woman, keeping her eyes on her, but she vanished. "I wonder why she felt the need…" She didn't finish her sentence.

When Delaney turned back toward the bed, the room appeared as it was in 1340. The woman lay across the bed with the form of a man over her, stabbing her with a dagger.

Caught off guard, Delaney screamed. A security guard happened to walk past her door and heard the scream.

He rapped on the door, "May I be of assistance?" he asked.

Delaney cursed, angry at herself for her reaction. She peered through the peephole to see a hotel security guard holding his lanyard. Delaney recognized him from walking through the halls, so she opened the door.

"Yes, I'm sorry I alerted you. I saw-" Delaney paused, searching for a good explanation.

The guard said, "It's all right, Madame. We're used to it," then added, "Do you need my assistance?"

Delaney waved him off, embarrassed at her reaction.

"No, thank you. I'm good."

She closed the door, feeling foolish but thankful for the hotel security.

CHAPTER SEVEN

Carly closed the leather-bound folder holding their remaining tours and hotel information. One last look showed a tight schedule with side trips to the Foundling Museum and Myles Frasier's television studio. The Outlander Tour will occupy most of their remaining free time.

She climbed the spiral staircase to the turret and took a hot bath. Tossing in a few bath salts provided, she undressed as the tub filled. The tile floor felt cool on her feet as she walked to the shelf with towels and washcloths, grabbing one of each. She rifled through her makeup bag for a hair clip, climbed into the hot water, and relaxed into the bubbles.

Carly leaned her head back against the cool porcelain and closed her eyes. Her mind wandered from one thing to another. She imagined Vivi and Frederick playing with their cousins and riding on the hay wagon with her dad. She thought of Austin coming home to an empty house each day. *There are plenty of baseball games to watch without interruption.*

Soaking in the warm water caused her to doze off for a moment.

A young dark-haired woman stood alone in the doorway of a stone cottage. A handsome, sturdy man came up behind her, pulling her into his chest, wrapping his arms around her, and rubbing her breasts. Her head fell back, enjoying his caresses. A loud shot rang out, and the woman felt the man fall forward, knocking her onto the hard earthen floor.

Carly's head jerked before she slid down into the water. The woman's face was familiar. She reached for her washcloth and rubbed her face. She finished the rest of her bath and pulled the drain plug. Carly grabbed a towel from the nearby chair and watched as the water swirled down the drain.

Dr. Curry's odd conversation crept back into her thoughts. *"I can help you." How can he help me? What does he mean by 'when you're ready?' Ready for what?* The odd conversation left her puzzled.

Carly checked the ornate table clock in the bathroom. It was only 3:30 p.m. in Charleston. Austin didn't leave the office on Thursdays until 5. She wanted to hear his voice before she pulled the bed curtains closed. Trying to stay awake proved impossible, and Carly drifted into a deep sleep without calling her husband.

Delaney hurried to dress and slid her notes into her backpack. Anxious to talk to Carly, she texted her to meet at the Centre Court dining room. She chose a table close to the front of the room, and Carly walked in behind her.

Delaney pulled her down to her seat. She waited all night to tell Carly about her encounter. "I had a visitor last night."

"A visitor, eh? Living or dead?"

Delaney pointed her finger at Carly and said, "Touche. It seems I only get the dead ones after dark."

Carly laughed, but she knew Delaney wasn't spending all her nights alone. Boyd and she were once very close and remained so.

"Who did you see?"

Delaney describes her encounter with the Tudor lady, explaining how the ghost appeared surprised when she spoke to her in modern vernacular.

"She was murdered in your bed?"

"It seems that way, or at least the room was the crime scene. The spirit wasn't used to guests seeing her because she got nasty."

Carly suggested the spirits in Coombe Abbey were residual hauntings, living or dying repeatedly.

"The women I saw on the stairs interacted with me after I acknowledged them. I'm sure they've been doing the same things every day since they died here."

"Well, we have excellent security. I drew a guard at my door when I screamed. He acted like it happened a lot," Delaney added. "How did you sleep?"

Carly recounted the dream she'd had while in the tub. "A man and woman stood in the doorway of a stone cottage, and the man was shot from behind. The odd thing about the woman is that she looked familiar."

"Is she the same woman you saw in Savannah?"

Carly thought back to the woman at Bethesda. "No, she didn't look thin and sickly. Different scenery, too."

Katherine announced to the attendees that the breakfast buffet was ready. Carly and Delaney merged into line behind the Saids.

"Looks like this will be our last hurrah at the breakfast buffet. Tomorrow, we get tea with jam and bread, just like the song says," Delaney said as she reached for a plate.

Carly walked back to their table. A server brought her a cup and set a small carafe of coffee on the table. She thanked the server and took her phone from her backpack. There were no messages, but she would text her mother. Being away from the children weighed on Carly's mind.

Delaney joined her. "I love the food, but what I wouldn't give for a bowl of grits," she said, biting into her toast.

Carly finished her text. "I texted Mom, letting her know I'm fine and enjoying the trip." She sipped coffee and set her cup off to the side.

Delaney knew something was off with Carly. "What's wrong? Did you hear from Austin?"

"No, I didn't expect to hear from him with the time difference. He isn't much for texting. I miss the kids."

"I'm sure you do but think of this as an adventure for them. Your folks have been planning time with their grandchildren on the farm for months."

"I know, you're right. I should kick back and enjoy our time together." Carly exhaled. "I don't know what I would have done without you."

Delaney didn't require further explanation. She knew what Carly meant. "I wouldn't have left you alone to recover. We're a team, sweetie. We're Velma and Daphne, Thelma and Louise, Lavern and Shirley."

Before she could go on with more examples, Carly swatted at her. "I agree. We're a team, forever." She made a heart with her hands in front of her chest.

A few minutes before Drake Taylor's presentation, they finished eating breakfast. Carly checked her program booklet for the location. The Cloisters Meeting Room was one of the largest and would serve as the setting for the remainder of the conference. Carly and Delaney scanned the available seats and noticed Jordan Fentress motioning for them to join him, Katherine, and Graham at their table. Carly nodded, and Delaney followed her.

Drake began his program by explaining the history of the London Foundling Home and the museum. Carly's mind wandered to her dream and the apparition of the woman Drake mentioned.

How do the woman and the ghostly image at the Foundling Museum connect to my visions and dreams? His reaction to Bethesda also piqued her interest.

Delaney whispered to Carly, bringing her back to the presentation, "Hey, are you okay?"

Carly took a sip of water. "I'm just thinking about the possible connection to the spirits at Bethesda."

After Drake's presentation, guests asked questions about the museum's ghosts and if he could share any personal paranormal experiences. He hesitated but shared the events leading up to the conference, as well as the connection to Carly, and the investigations he had conducted with his team.

Carly's face burned as the current of conversations within the room started, eyes turning toward her. Drake shot Carly an apologetic glance and continued answering the questions.

She nodded, whispering to Delaney, "Well, now we *must* go to the Foundling Home. It's not a coincidence he's at the conference or the connection to the Orphan home in Savannah."

Delaney and Carly gathered their bags and walked to the podium, where Drake folded his notes and slid them inside his lightweight linen blazer.

"I hope I didn't embarrass you. It was churlish of me to blurt your involvement without first warning you." He motioned for Carly and Delaney to walk away from the crowd.

"It's all right. It took me by surprise, though," Carly admitted.

"The whole thing surprised me as well. I didn't have the reference in my talking points."

Delaney added, "Thanks for the invite to the Foundling Home. I hope we can learn the connection to the departed souls at Bethesda."

Delaney took the notes from her backpack and spread them across the top of the podium. She placed the wire coat hangers used as divining rods inside it. She slid her hands down the sides of her sundress. Carly brought her bottled water from the back of the room.

"You're going to knock it out of the park. Just remember, you're sharing your experiences and Appalachian techniques."

Delaney thanked her for the water and added, "I think my nerves will calm down once I start." She took a seat behind the podium.

Graham updated everyone on the afternoon schedule. "Following Delaney's presentation, there will be a forty-five-minute session dedicated to the guests getting books signed, talking with our speakers, and taking photos with their favorite presenters."

Delaney walked up to the podium and began sharing her lifelong experiences with the spirits around her. She explained how she and her investigation partners help homeowners and museums in Charleston, South Carolina, by communicating with spirits to assist them in moving on. The connection to Carly and the spirits in her home became apparent in her discussion. Delaney moved to the portion of her presentation where she discussed her family history and how she grew up with grandparents who taught her the art of their ancestors from Scotland.

Several audience members were from Scotland and Ireland, finding her ancestors endearing. When she brought out the divining rods, Myles Frasier smiled with delight.

Delaney described the trips she and her grandma took to the mountains of Tennessee, where their ancestors lived after immigrating from Scotland in the early 1700s. She explained that the rods helped locate graves without proper headstones. Her uncles followed behind with homemade crosses to mark the graves.

"I learned from my Pappaw how to find water with the rods. As a young girl, I accompanied him to determine where a farmer should dig his well. Pappaw called them dowsing rods."

The audience found her talk interesting, raising their hands to ask questions about locating graves. Byron Harris shared that his family was also proficient in using dowsing rods.

Delaney demonstrated how the rods move independently of each other. One of the Leeds teachers, Elizabeth, asked if she could try, and others asked to try their hand at the rods.

Katherine stood, signaling the 5-minute reminder to end the presentation. Delaney forgot about her nervousness and received a round of applause when she finished.

Myles made his way up to the podium as Delaney placed her notes and divining rods back into her backpack.

"I enjoyed your presentation," he said. "I hope you'll bring them when you visit the studio."

Delaney thanked him and said, "I'd love to."

As Myles and Delaney continued to discuss their mutual connection to dowsing rods within their families, Carly waited outside the Cloisters. She took out her phone and checked her messages. To her surprise, there were two. She read the first one from her mother, who'd included a picture of Freddy and Vivi in the creek with her brother and her sister's children. The message said, *We're having fun with the cousins. Love you, Mommy.* She smiled at the picture, texting back and adding heart emojis. The second text message was from Austin. *Hope you're having fun. Love you, A.*

Before she could answer his text, Delaney joined her. "Are you ready to go to the meet and greet?"

Carly noticed everyone had moved into the next room. "You knocked it out of the ballpark, girlfriend. I'm proud of you," Carly said as they walked down the corridor.

"I think it went better than my last conference. I enjoyed myself," Delaney remarked.

The final panel discussion of the day took place during the noon meal. After dinner, Katherine and Jordan discussed the tour opportunities for the attendees. Ghost investigation trips into town and on-site would begin at dusk. Katherine expressed her thanks to all the guests of honor for their beautiful presentations during the conference.

Jordan reminded the attendees of next year's conference being held in the United States. "We are in the process of lining up our guest speakers for the conference and hope that everyone will join us next year, where we will be discussing the Lizzie Borden Case and the Salem Witch Trials."

Carly poked Delaney. "I've never been to Massachusetts. We should plan to attend."

Delaney leaned closer and said, "I think we ought to plan a trip every year…I'm all in for next year."

Jordan reminded the attendees to sign up for the ghost tour at dusk. Carly and Delaney decided to take an Uber to Stratford-upon-Avon to see William Shakespeare's home. Both went upstairs to change into shorts and T-shirts while waiting for the Uber to arrive. As they descended the stairs, Carly noticed a young man holding a small sign with the Uber company logo.

"Hey, there's our guy," Carly said.

The young man asked if she had called for a drive into Stratford-upon-Avon. After confirming the cost of driving there and back, the three went outside. For the next thirty-five minutes, Delaney and Carly talked with the driver, Will. He told them he lived in Coventry and started driving for Uber to earn money for his tuition at Harlaxton. Carly explained they were attending the Paracon and where they lived in the United States.

Once they arrived in Stratford, they agreed to meet Will at 6:00 p.m. at The Jestor, where the tour was to begin. The tour started at 1 p.m., in ten minutes. Carly had previously purchased the tickets online from her room. They walked to the line to embark on the Hop-on, Hop-off Bus Tour. Both were eager to ride the double-decker bus. Carly snapped a selfie with Delaney as they took their seats on the top of the bus.

The group visited the Guild Hall, Clopton Bridge, Holy Trinity

Church, and a Christmas Shop. Carly purchased small gifts for the children, and Delaney found something for her son, daughter-in-law, and granddaughter. The tour concluded with a visit to the home of Shakespeare, the school he attended, and a stop to take pictures at the Shakespeare statue in the center of town.

When the tour ended, Carly and Delaney walked to the market area, where they spent the afternoon enjoying a stroll along the River Avon. Delaney suggested finding a pub for supper since getting their food might take a while. Carly searched for a nearby pub and found The Old Thatch Inn, where they ate soup and sandwiches.

As they ate, Carly checked her phone. Delaney noticed her brows furrowed and asked, "Something wrong?"

Carly answered without looking up, "It's a text from work reminding me of Jeffery Sullivan's meet and greet."

"I'll bet you two will get along fine once you get to know him," Delaney said, trying to change Carly's mood.

"I suppose so. Chad got used to me after his co-anchor left."

"I want the scoop on him once you two are working together," Delaney said with a wink.

CHAPTER EIGHT

The conference concluded after breakfast on Sunday morning. Carly and Delaney ate with Sheree Carver and Eleanor Murphy.

"This has been the best conference I've ever attended," Sheree announced. Eleanor echoed her sentiments. "I enjoyed both of your presentations and hope we attend a conference together again."

"Thank you," Carly said.

Jordan Fentress and Katherine Hawkins-Cooke approached the podium to close The Spirit-Seekers Paracon UK.

"This conference has brought speakers and guests from six countries together to share experiences and knowledge in paranormal phenomena and time travel," Katherine said. "I'd like to thank Jordan Fentress of Spirit Seekers USA for joining us this year."

The attendees and speakers applauded as Katherine continued. "I offer my deepest thanks to the staff of Coombe Abbey for a wonderful four days."

Katherine moved aside to allow Jordan access to the podium's microphone. "I join Katherine in thanking all of you who traveled from your own countries to be with us for this amazing conference." He asked the guest speakers to join them at the front of the meeting room. Carly, Delaney, and the others stood together amid a raucous round of applause. Drake Taylor moved behind Carly and Delaney.

He leaned down and whispered to Carly, "It's a pleasure meeting you this week."

Carly felt goosebumps form on her arms as his warm breath tickled her ear. She felt her face flush and turned. "Yes, it... uh." Carly stammered without finishing her sentence. For a moment, her mind flashed a scene from the dream she had had a few nights before of the woman and man standing at the door of a stone cottage.

She swayed into Delaney, prompting Delaney to turn to Carly and whisper, "You okay?"

Embarrassed by her reaction to Drake, Carly smiled and nodded to Delaney.

After the presenters had returned to their seats, Katherine asked everyone to smile and move closer as the server took the GoPro to get a picture of the conference attendees. Before dismissing the conference, she asked the presenters to meet at the stairway in front of the hotel at eleven o'clock for a formal picture.

Delaney checked her watch to see the time—10:25—which was enough time to tell the attendees goodbye, exchange emails and business cards, and take her own pictures before everyone left.

Carly followed Delaney's lead. After saying goodbye to Sheree Carver, she and Delaney hurried to their rooms to prepare for the formal conference photograph.

At eleven o'clock, Mr. Guillum, manager of Coombe Abbey, positioned everyone on the stone stairway. Myles Frasier changed into his kilt while everyone else wore formal attire. Carly and Delaney stood beside Alston Curry and Byron Harris on the bottom step. After five formal pictures and the traditional silly one, Katherine thanked them for attending and gave each a small gift bag from her and Graham.

Myles reminded Delaney and Carly about stopping by the television studio if they had time in their itinerary.

"Delaney, we could give the dowsing rods a go if you're game?" he said, the slight cleft in his chin more visible when he smiled.

Delaney nodded. "I'm game!"

Carly added, "We'll try our best to get there. Thank you again for inviting us to join your show." Myles shook Delaney's hand before going upstairs to get his luggage.

Drake waited until Myles stepped away before approaching Carly. "I'll have Tuesday open all day for you and Delaney to visit the Foundling Home Museum. Here's my number and the museum's address," he said, holding out a slip of paper.

Carly took the paper from him and thanked him. Delaney smiled as he walked to the elevator.

"What just happened here?" she asked, sounding like an inquisition about to take place.

Carly seemed confused by Delaney's question. "I don't know what you mean. Maybe you should clue me in."

Delaney pulled Carly away from the other speakers who were still milling about. "I'll clue you in, Miss Oblivious. Drake Taylor has it bad for you."

Carly started to object, but Delaney cut her off. "I have watched him when he's around you. It's plain as the nose on your face."

Carly bristled. "Look, he is freaked out by the woman he saw at the museum the other night. It has something to do with the woman I saw at Bethesda." She lowered her voice. "I feel a connection of some kind to him, but I love Austin. I don't have the hots for this guy."

Delaney threw up her hands. "Okay, I overreacted. I'm a little jealous he forgot I'm your sidekick."

"Girl, you sell yourself short. I saw the exchange between you and Myles Frasier."

"He's cute, and his legs look good in his kilt." Delaney raised her eyebrows. "I've always wondered if what they say about men who wear kilts is true."

"Maybe one day you'll find out." Carly grinned, causing the corners of her mouth to raise.

~

When Carly returned to her room, she removed the tissue paper from the bag she received from Katherine to find bath salts with the Coombe Abbey Hotel logo, two small jars of jam, and packets of Coombe Abbey specialty tea. After texting Delaney, she found out that they'd received the same.

She hurried to put the items in her carry-on and then quickly checked her room for anything she had forgotten to pack. She checked her watch. It was already bedtime at home. She texted Austin and waited to see if he would reply.

She put her phone in the pocket of her yoga pants, gathered her things, and placed them next to the door. Then, she dialed the extension to Delaney's room.

"Hey, are you packed and ready to head downstairs?"

"I started to call you to ask the same thing. I'm ready to go."

After loading their suitcases onto the luggage cart, they rode the elevator down to the ground floor. When the elevator doors opened, Drake wheeled his cart out of the other elevator.

"I think we're the last of the guests to leave the conference," he said, walking with them.

"It looks that way. It's hard to leave such a beautiful hotel," Carly said.

Delaney added, "We'll see you Tuesday. I'm anxious to check out the museum."

Carly adjusted her backpack . "I hope I'll see the woman you saw the other night. What are the odds she is the same woman from my dream?"

"It's possible. The spirits wanted us to meet, that's for certain." He opened the door for Carly and Delaney to wait outside for their Uber.

"Thank you for the invitation. I'll text you when we're on our way," Carly confirmed.

"I look forward to seeing you and Delaney," Drake extended his hand to each of them.

The Uber driver pulled up to the door and rolled down the window. "Carly Tabor and Delaney Warrick?" he asked.

"Yes," they said in unison. In a few moments, he had loaded all the suitcases and carry-on bags into his trunk and returned to the car.

Carly and Delaney said goodbye to Drake and closed the car door. As the driver crossed the bridge leading to the road, Carly's phone vibrated, alerting her to a text. It was Austin.

I hope you and Delaney are having a great time. Remember, leave the spooks in the UK. Lol, Love you, A.

Austin referred to her ghostly encounters as 'spooks' when she dealt with Ben Hastings and the Pettigrews. His last comment took the smile from her face.

Delaney noticed the face Carly made from the corner of her eye. "Something wrong at home?"

"Austin hopes we're having a great time, but not to bring anything home with me."

"Sweetie, I'm sure he meant it as a joke." Delaney wanted to reassure Carly, but Carly only half believed what she said.

The ride to the Hilton Hotel took two hours. Heath, the Uber driver, wasn't as talkative as the driver who took them to Stratford. He spoke little but engaged in polite conversation when asked questions about something they noticed along the way.

At 3:15 p.m., they checked in at the Hilton Metropole. To keep within their budget, they decided to share a room for the rest of the trip. Their room featured double beds and a spacious bathroom.

After their stately rooms at Coombe Abbey, their lodging at the Hilton felt like upscale hotels in the States.

With their conference behind them, Carly and Delaney could focus on sightseeing. Their first stop would be visiting Windsor Castle and Stonehenge on Monday morning. They would have to hurry to meet the tour at 2 p.m. that would set off for Buckingham Palace. On Tuesday, they would visit Drake at the Foundling Museum.

The street bustled with tourists rushing to their next stop, double-decker buses, and impatient drivers. An older couple walked in front of Carly and Delaney, slowing their pace.

"Seeing older couples enjoying their time together makes me sad that Mark and I didn't get the chance to grow old together," Delaney said, remembering her late husband.

"How long has it been?" Carly asked.

"Almost twenty-three years ago, in 2001 right before the attack on the World Trade Center."

"I didn't realize you lost him at so young an age. He was in his early forties?"

"Yes, Mark turned forty-two, and I was just thirty-five. How did I get so old?" Delaney laughed.

Carly stopped walking. "You're not old. Why, I would think you're more my age than yours."

Delaney pulled her arm to continue into The Mayfair Chippy, a quaint pub that boasted the best fish and chips in London. The wait for an outside table took twenty-five minutes. The different aromas coming from the kitchen made Carly's mouth water. "I didn't realize how hungry I am. Some of the local food isn't my thing, however authentic fish and chips are worth the wait."

Delaney brought up the Foundling Museum. "I hope we're able to connect with someone there. Maybe there's a connection with the Foundling Hospital and Bethesda."

Carly thought back to her meeting with Drake earlier in the week. He said the woman clarified that he needed to go to the conference.

"Earth to Carly," Delaney said, waving her hand before Carly's face.

"The meeting with Drake the other night makes me wonder why the apparition wanted him to find me."

"It's kind of him to open the museum when he could rest from the conference. He seems nice and wants to discover why the woman wanted him to connect with you."

Carly agreed. Somehow, the woman appearing right before the conference seemed more than a coincidence.

The following morning, they left the hotel before six o'clock. At 6:30 a.m., the bus departed from Victoria Coach Station and headed to Salisbury. From there, Carly and Delaney switched to another tour bus, arriving at Stonehenge before nine o'clock. The large crowds the tour guide had warned about had yet to show up, so they walked out to the stones with their tour group.

The ropes to keep large groups from entering the area were still down. Carly and Delaney could walk about the ancient stones within the inner circle and take pictures.

"Can you believe the scale of the stones?" Delaney asked.

"One can't appreciate their magnitude without seeing them firsthand," Carly said, taking a picture of Delaney beside one of the giants.

The sunny weather made the trip even more enjoyable, although the temperature soared near 80 degrees. After spending two hours at the site, the tour group continued to the medieval village of Lacock to enjoy lunch at a fourteenth-century pub.

They returned to Victoria Station in time to walk to see the last tour of the day at the Tower of London and have dinner along the River Thames. The warm temperatures and the absence of rain delighted Carly. Delaney leaned her head back on the bus seat. "It's hard work playing tourist. I'm one tired puppy," she said.

"Let's soak it all in, girlfriend. We may never pass this way again, as the song goes." Carly felt the sun beaming through the bus window, warming her face.

"Tomorrow, we must leave early to walk to the Foundling Museum. Let's relax the rest of the evening," Carly suggested.

CHAPTER NINE

Carly's phone alarm woke her at six o'clock. She heard Delaney in the bathroom, the blow dryer's sound filling the otherwise quiet room. Carly went to the window, pulling back the drapes. She noticed the heavy traffic on the street below, filled with commuters and visitors.

"I hope you slept well," Delaney said, opening the door.

"I did. I must've conked out as soon as my head hit the pillow. I don't even remember dreaming," Carly said.

Delaney's head peeked around the half-opened door. "I dreamed about Jarrod. He and Chelsea are staying at my house while I'm gone."

Delaney's son, Jarrod, a pharmacist, and his wife, a teacher, moved back to Charleston after living in southern California for eight years. Their daughter, Sutton, now three, is the apple of Delaney's eye.

"Are you adjusting to having a toddler in the house?"

"It's the best! She calls me Mammy. I see a little of me in her, which makes me laugh. Poor Jarrod and Chelsea!" Delaney's infectious laugh echoed in the room.

"I'll have to bring the kids over to see her when they return from visiting my parents," Carly said.

After breakfast, they walked to the Foundling Museum, which was less than a mile from the hotel. Carly texted Drake to let him know they were almost there. She hurried to keep up with Delaney. Leading ghost tours in downtown Charleston helped her stay in shape.

Carly used the GPS on her phone to get them to the Foundling Museum by nine o'clock. An impressive three-story brick building boasted a bust of Thomas Corum, the founder and benefactor of the Foundling Home. To the right and left of the entrance, two stone cherubs looked down at visitors entering the museum.

Carly remarked that the building resembled the buildings at Bethesda. "Last night, I looked at the online brochure and read that the building had been built on the site of the original 1740 building, using many of the architectural styles found in the original house."

Before Delaney could answer, Drake opened the door. "Good morning, ladies," he said.

"Good morning to you." Delaney walked past Drake, taking in the large room filled with paintings on the walls and several rows of chairs. The ornate plaster ceiling gave the impression of being an upscale art gallery rather than an orphanage museum. Carly and Drake joined her in the large room. Carly smelled polished wood and noticed the enlarged photos on the walls of children's uniforms and the tiny beds in their dormitories, which tugged at her heartstrings.

A feeling of overwhelming sadness came over Carly. Twin teardrops from the corners of her eyes slid down her cheeks, and she wiped them away.

"This is where our visitors begin the tour. The Foundling Hospital, which continues today as the children's charity Coram, was designed to care for and educate England's most vulnerable citizens. The artists, William Hogarth and George Frideric Handel, played a pivotal role in bringing Coram's vision to life. Together, they transformed the Hospital into the UK's first public art gallery and one of London's most fashionable venues. Hogarth encouraged leading artists to donate their work, and Handel held benefit concerts featuring The Messiah in the hospital's chapel," Drake explained.

"So, this building sits on the site of the original hospital and orphanage?" Carly inquired.

"Yes, on the upper floor, there are exhibits containing artifacts and items from the days of the orphanage. We'll go there first, then I'll bring you back to my office, where I encountered the woman's apparition."

After looking at the impressive gold-framed paintings adorning the walls, they walked back into the large vestibule. The stairway, a work of art for the period, led Carly, Delaney, and Drake to the second floor. The rooms to the left and right of the landing highlighted different aspects of the Foundling Home's history from its first years in the 1700s.

The first room, to the right of the stairs, allowed visitors to read panels explaining the meaning of a foundling, and artifacts from the orphanage's earliest days. Behind glass showcases were dozens of tokens or tags left with the infants upon admission to the orphanage.

Delaney read the information aloud.

"Between the 1740s and 1760s, mothers leaving their babies at the Foundling Hospital would also leave a small object as a means of identification. The hope was that they would one day be able to reclaim their child."

Drake continued, "Children were renamed on admission, so the token would help prove their relationship. Each object was kept in the archives, not given to the child. The Foundling Museum Collection comprises approximately 400 tokens, with many thousands more paper and textile items stored in the archives. It gives us an extraordinary glimpse into eighteenth-century society and individual lives."

"How did the orphanage personnel keep everything straight without confusing who was who?" Carly asked.

"When a mother left a token with her child, folded inside the completed admissions paper, or 'billet', it was never opened unless a parent returned to claim their child. In the nineteenth century, the Governors of the Foundling Hospital decided to display some of the tokens. No one thought to note which token belonged to which child," Drake explained.

"But how did you come to understand the tokens?" Delaney asked.

"It wasn't easy. Thanks to meticulous research, we can now reconnect some tokens to individuals. These 'reunited' tokens tell us stories of parents forced to give up their babies and the future lives of their children. Research is ongoing, but we will likely never unlock the stories behind all of the tokens," he said.

Carly couldn't help but feel the ache of a parent who left their child with strangers. She thought of Freddy Richards, left by his mother at the Charleston Orphan Asylum in 1795. "The haunting in my home dates to the late 1700s and involved an orphan from the Orphan Asylum in Charleston, South Carolina."

"Yes, that's right. You mentioned this poor waif in your presentation. Good on your father for snapping the photograph with his image in it," Drake said.

Carly kept the photograph in her office, the ghostly image of Freddy Richards crossing time and space to show up in Carly's future nursery photograph.

Delaney moved into the next room as if a magnet had drawn her inside. A large mural covered the wall, depicting the room as if it were a photograph taken in the 1800s. On all sides, there were cots with pillows and wool blankets tucked in. The room was void of decoration or personalization; it looked more like a barracks. A single cot from the period stood alone in front of the mural, and on either side were artifacts and clothing worn by those who lived there.

A sobbing child's cries filled the room, audible to only Delaney and Carly.

Carly and Drake remained quiet as they watched Delaney interact with the space around the cot. Carly saw the image come into view. A little girl, no more than three, sat on the cot with a small scrap of material clutched in her hands. Tears streamed down her face, and her nose ran because no one wiped it.

Delaney spoke in a comforting voice. The little one reminded her of her granddaughter.

"Mommy is on the other side of the light. Run along now," Delaney said in soft tones.

Carly knelt beside Delaney, and the little girl reached out her hands to Carly.

Carly stood, backing away. "No, I'm not your mommy." The child hurried to Carly, and she felt the force of the child against her. Carly looked to Delaney for help.

Delaney bent toward Carly's legs, where the child clung for dear life.

"Carly, tell her to follow you to the light and walk away."

Carly did as Delaney instructed. The child released her and evaporated before their eyes.

"I don't remember anything like that happening before. I felt the girl's hands grabbing my slacks."

Drake walked over to the cot. "I've heard things in this room but have never seen anything. I'm even more in awe of you both, seeing what you do."

"I hope she found the light. Austin will have a fit if someone follows me back to Charleston."

Delaney replied, "I don't feel anyone here. She must've moved on, sweetie."

Drake didn't comment on Carly's husband. Instead, he suggested they go to his office downstairs. Carly took a last look at the cot to make sure the little girl didn't remain. She exhaled and left the room.

Drake led them to a room at the end of a corridor beyond the exhibit rooms. His office looked as if he had stepped back into the eighteenth century. The desk must've been the original belonging to an early administrator. The two leather chairs, facing each other, were from the 1800s and were in remarkable condition. An Oriental rug, in shades of red, gold, and green, covered the wood floor. On the wall were oil paintings of Thomas Corum and a facsimile of the original charter given to him by King George II to establish the Foundling Home. Also hanging on the wall were paintings of George Frideric Handel and a woman whose nameplate, Carly and Delaney couldn't read due to the years of tarnish. She looked to be from the mid-1700s by her attire, and her features gave her a stern appearance. Her eyes told another story. Carly found her countenance intriguing.

Drake let them look around the office. "This is where the woman appeared to me, in the doorway." He stood at the entrance to another room adjoining his office, turned on the light, and led them inside. The room measured 20 feet x 20 feet, which is ample for a records room. Inside were glass-enclosed display cases and wooden cabinets almost six feet high. A dozen shelves filled with crates, boxes, and long, flat cases lined one of the walls.

"This is where we house all of the Foundling Hospital records. The paper items upstairs are reproductions. We keep the originals inside this room. Once the door closes, it seals the room, protecting the contents from temperature fluctuations."

Carly's eyes widened as she took in the records stored within the room. They waited for Drake to give them an idea of where to begin. "Do you have any documents connecting Bethesda to the Foundling Home?" Carly asked.

Drake walked over to one of the tall wooden cabinets. Inside were drawers holding papers from the 1770s to the 1790s. "I came into the room after my encounter with the apparition. Thinking the task was overwhelming, I sat down on the floor and looked at the endless possibilities of places to look. Then, as if someone or something read my thoughts, the door to this cabinet opened."

"That's freaky," Delaney said.

"What did you find?" Carly asked, the excitement building inside her.

He grabbed three pairs of exam gloves from the dispenser on the wall.

"I located a letter from a Mr. Nathaniel Duncan to a Miss Louisa Albertson."

Drake handed Delaney and Carly a pair of latex gloves and walked to one of the tall cabinets.

"That's a great idea," Carly said, noticing the placement of the gloves inside the room.

He opened a drawer inside the cabinet and lifted out a yellowed sheet of paper. He took it to the credenza and placed it under the antique lamp. Carly and Delaney moved closer to read the faded ink.

He waited a moment as they read the letter. "What do you think?"

Delaney cocked her head. "I'm not sure. What kind of arrangement is he referring to?"

Carly read the letter aloud. "*Miss Albertson, all souls arrived, according to our arrangement, on the twenty-first March. Mr. Thaddeus Broward will be back with a reply in my stead. Please send word to Mr. Broward and me regarding the name of the vessel and the number I will receive in December. I will send messages to Charleston and Boston as soon as I receive your response. I am your most humble servant, Mr. Nathaniel Duncan."*

"Can you make out the date?" Carly asked, moving closer to Drake. She breathed in a faint scent of his cologne.

He held the letter up to the light. "I think it says 1794. The ink appears somewhat degraded."

"Mr. Duncan must've been the administrator at Bethesda at this time. We didn't look at the records when we were there," Carly said, disappointed.

"The Summerfields told us we are welcome any time to look through the archives," Delaney added.

"There are other records related to Bethesda Orphanage inside the drawer. Perhaps you'll find the answers you're looking for. You're welcome to take pictures of anything you think might help."

Carly reached inside her bag for her phone. "Thank you. I'm anxious to dive in."

The trio combed the records for anything related to the late 1700s. Reflecting on the woman she saw with her children at Bethesda, Carly surmised that the clothing dated back to the colonial period. Carly's knowledge of Bethesda didn't go beyond what Brooke Anderson and the Summerfields shared.

Delaney adjusted her glasses to read the script inside the ledger more clearly. Dated 1794-1795, the ink had faded in some of the entries, but she used one of the magnifying glasses left on the credenza to read them.

"Hey, Carly, I found the ledgers for the admissions to the Foundling Home in 1794-1795 that mention Bethesda."

Carly and Drake turned from the papers they had in front of them. Carly handed Drake the paper she was reading and joined Delaney at the credenza.

"Here's where the administrator listed the names of the children sent to Bethesda," Delaney said. "Didn't both orphanages start about the same time?"

"Drake, didn't you tell us Reverend Whitefield received his charter about the same time as Thomas Corum?"

"Yes, I found the letter from George Whitefield asking to visit the Foundling Home. It happened during his trip to England to accept his charter from King George," he said.

"I find their compassion for orphan children interesting," Carly added.

She took pictures of journal entries as Delaney turned the pages. "I can't imagine the children's sadness, leaving the Foundling Home, thinking their mothers might come for them, only to find they were never coming back."

It was almost noon when Carly finished examining the journals and correspondence with a connection to George Whitfield and orphans sent to Bethesda. Most of the entries listed the date and name of the foundlings and the persons who left them in the care of the Foundling Hospital. The unanswered questions remained about the arrangement between Miss Albertson and Mr. Duncan. It warranted a search within the archives upon returning to Bethesda. Most of the entries listed the date of admission, the name, and the person who left the child or children in the care of the Foundling Hospital.

Drake returned the files to their drawers, threw his gloves into the wastebasket, and turned to Carly. "I know you have other plans today, but do you have time for something to eat first?"

She checked her watch, then asked Delaney, "Do you think we can still make our tour this afternoon?"

Delaney smiled, "When haven't we made time for a meal?"

Drake laughed at Delaney's comment. "Very well, it sounds like there's enough time to walk around the corner to The Lamb. I think you'll both enjoy the atmosphere."

"I'm ready if you are," Carly said as she and Delaney threw their gloves into the wastebasket and exited the room.

They followed Drake to the elevator. "We'll skip the stairs. The elevator is quicker."

He held open the door as Carly and Delaney walked outside to the gate. Carly noticed a pink child's glove attached to the iron fence.

She started to lift the glove and hesitated. She was overcome by a vision. Carly saw the front of the Foundling Hospital, an imposing view with its massive stone facade, three stories, and rows of windows. There was a woman. She pulled a woolen cloak closer to her body and leaned over to adjust a young boy's oversized coat around his shoulders. The girl, a year or two older, moved closer to her mother. Her cap covered her flaxen-colored curls, with only one curl poking out from the side of the cap. A more petite girl, a toddler, hid behind her mother's skirt.

"Carly?" Delaney's voice brought her out of the vision.

"I...I think I experienced a ghost showing me something from her life."

Drake missed the encounter with his back to the women as he locked the door to the Foundling Museum. He then walked over to the gate. "These get the visitors every time," Drake said about the mittens.

"I thought they were real and tried to lift them from the fence. That's when I envisioned a mother and children walking to the front gate," Carly said.

"You spaced out," Delaney replied. "What kind of vision?"

Carly leaned against the fence, her knees weak from the experience. "The children walked up the street with their mother. I saw the front of the building and then felt the children lean against my skirt."

Delaney looked at Drake, then at Carly. "You mean the woman's skirt, don't you?"

"It was like the vision of the man and woman in the cottage. I saw her again on the ship. The woman took over my thoughts. It sounds absurd, but that's the only way I can describe it."

Drake shook his head. "I don't think it sounds absurd at all. Remember, I saw her upstairs."

The visions confused Carly, but something about them registered with her. "Delaney, I saw the same woman and children at Bethesda."

CHAPTER TEN

After lunch at The Lamb, Drake, Carly, and Delaney went outside and said their goodbyes. "I want to thank you again for your gracious tour of the museum. Allowing us to go to the archives is more than I'd hoped." Carly extended her hand to Drake, but instead, the two embraced.

The gesture, unplanned, surprised them both. Drake released Carly while Delaney threw caution to the wind with an embrace of her own.

"Where we're from, it's customary to hug. It's who we are," Delaney said in her genuine Southern drawl.

He raked his hand through his dark-cropped hair. "Your customs are endearing to us stiff shirts," Drake replied. He changed the topic to avoid any further awkwardness. "So, where are you off to from here?"

"We are headed to Wales. Carly planned the whole trip," Delaney added.

"I took the train to Wales years ago with my mother. My father's ancestors are Welsh. Father passed away in a car accident before I was born, and Mother left Wales and remarried after my second birthday. Collin Taylor adopted me."

"I'm sorry about your father," Carly said.

"It's all good. Enjoy your adventures, and if I can help you further, don't hesitate to call me."

"You've helped us already. Thank you."

Carly's spirits lifted at the information she learned from the Foundling Home records.

At six o'clock, an Uber drove them to Paddington, where they took the two-and-a-half-hour train to Cardiff, Wales. They relaxed as the train traveled through the picturesque countryside.

As they approached Cardiff, the port town, Carly leafed through the information she had printed at home about Aberdare.

"We'll switch trains from Cardiff to Aberdare. The distance is twenty-two miles to the Marquis Inn. It should only take us an hour from here."

Cardiff, the capital and largest city, boasted a significant television and film production center, a world-renowned museum, and a vibrant cultural scene. Its rich history dated to around 6000 B.C.

Delaney browsed through the information. "The Brecon Beacons sounds interesting. I love the mountains." She turned to another destination Carly marked. "Oh, now this is what I'm talking about!"

Carly smiled as Delaney turned to Llancaiach Fawr, a Tudor manor house built around 1530 and known for its paranormal activity. "I'm drawn to the site for some reason. I know you'll like it."

Delaney nodded. "You know me well."

The mountains dominated the scenery as the train pulled into Aberdare station. Carly and Delaney waited for most of the passengers to disembark. Once outside, they boarded the bus for the ten-minute drive to their Bed and Breakfast, The Marquis Inn.

"Let's check in and go over our plan for tomorrow," Delaney said, pulling her backpack on.

Carly followed Delaney inside. The woman standing behind the counter looked over the top of her thick reading glasses.

"Welcome to The Marquis Inn. Do you have a reservation?" she asked.

Carly read the nametag pinned to the pocket of her shirt: Elin Hughes. "Hello, I made reservations under Carly Tabor. I reserved one room."

"Yes, here you are. One room, twin beds, and a view of the mountains."

"It's beautiful here. We can't wait to explore the area tomorrow," Carly said, handing over her credit card.

"If you need transportation, the train is the best way to get around unless you have a vehicle of your own."

"I've purchased tickets to tour Llancaiach Fawr in the morning," said Carly. "I don't have a rental car, so the train must do."

Elin Hughes, a woman in her early sixties, had short, brown hair cut in a stylish bob. Her eyes resembled twin emeralds, a most unusual shade of green. She stood in front of a wooden sign with her name and the title 'Owner and Operator' displayed.

The Bed and Breakfast had been a venture she and her now-deceased husband started over twenty-five years ago. Having survived the 2020 Pandemic, the establishment came back with record reservations and reviews.

Elin grabbed a set of room keys from the box below the counter and joined Carly and Delaney.

"If you'll follow me, I'll show you to your room."

Delaney and Carly carried their bags to their room on the second floor. The decor was sparse but clean, and there was plenty of space. The twin beds, with a nightstand between them, added to the home-like feel. The beds had matching paisley coverlets and coordinating pillows as accents.

"I hope you enjoy your stay with us. If you need anything, call the front desk."

"Thank you," Delaney said.

"I feel like I'm back home with my sister, Cate." Carly walked over to the bed she chose and plopped down.

Delaney tossed her backpack onto the small loveseat and sat on the edge of her bed. "I wish I'd had a sister growing up. I had an older brother, Neil. He died in Saigon during the Tet Offensive in 1968."

"Oh, I'm sorry. I never knew you lost a brother in the Vietnam War. My father's younger brother went, but he came home." Carly sat across from her on the bed. She felt the sadness Delaney shared, being both an empath and a sensitive.

"I think of you as my kid sister, so I feel blessed," Delaney said, patting Carly on the leg.

"Well, sister, we should open our patio door and go outside to enjoy the mountain view." Carly rose and clasped Delaney's hand.

The view from the balcony displayed the buildings around the Bed and Breakfast, but off in the distance, they saw the beautiful rise to the Brecon Beacons mountains. Carly's eyes scanned the scenery, feeling she already knew the location.

"Tomorrow, we're going to explore the area around Llancaiach Fawr."

"It sounds fun. Why not rent a car and go where we want?" Delaney suggested.

The idea led them back to the front desk. Elin Hughes now wore a sweatshirt and jeans. Her Welsh accent intrigued Southerner Delaney. Carly enjoyed listening to the different dialects spoken while visiting the UK.

"Well, now, what can I do for you?" Elin said, putting on her reading glasses.

"Ms. Hughes, we've decided to cancel our train tickets and rent a car tonight," Delaney said.

"Oh, I doubt you'll get a car this late. The nearest facility is twenty-five miles away. It's peak tourist season, you know?" Her answer, albeit blunt, didn't mean to insult her guests.

"You're right. We didn't give our plan enough thought. Oh well, nothing ventured, nothing gained," Carly replied.

Elin asked them to wait a moment, and she walked into a small room behind the front desk. Carly peeked around the desk to see where she went.

She returned after speaking to someone in the other room, "I might be able to help you. My daughter loves going into the mountains. Alis lives with me now."

She lowered her voice to a whisper, "Her no-good husband, soon-to-be-former, left her, and now she helps me run the place."

"You mean she could take us there?" Delaney asked.

"Oh, we couldn't impose on you or her," Carly interjected, giving Delaney the side-eye.

"It isn't an imposition if I offer, right?" Her eyebrows arched, and a smile turned up on the corners of her mouth.

"Alis, will you come here?" Elin asked, looking over her shoulder.

Delaney and Carly stood speechless, and Alis joined them, still chewing the bite of an apple. She tossed the core into the rubbish basket.

She resembled an athlete with long legs and a trim, muscular physique. At forty, her wavy, blonde hair, pulled up in a clip, accentuated her slender neck. Her tanned face gave the impression that she spent time outdoors or used artificial means to achieve the desired effect. Still, she looked younger than her age.

"Hello," she said.

"Alis, these are the women who want to have a look around the scenery after touring Llancaiach. They need a lift."

"If you have other plans, we can take the train," Carly offered Alis a way out of the situation.

Alis assessed the women, then said, "Neither looks like they want to kill me. All right, I'll play chauffeur."

Carly and Delaney introduced themselves and thanked Alis for agreeing to drive them.

Following the formalities, Alis asked, "What time do I need to meet you?"

Carly said, "If we leave by seven, we will have plenty of time to walk around the grounds before our tour at nine."

"Meet me in the dining room at six. I'll have coffee and a hearty Welsh breakfast for you."

"That's very kind, thank you," Carly said.

"Yes, thank you for your trouble, Alis. We'll buy your gas in the morning," Delaney said.

"No, not necessary. I have a full tank of petrol. Besides, I need a diversion. Tomorrow at six."

Alis emerged from the kitchen with the last covered dish, placing it on the table next to a plate of crisp bacon. A coffee, cream, and sugar carafe rounded off the breakfast, awaiting Carly and Delaney.

"It smells delicious." Carly pulled up her chair to the pedestal-style table. Delaney chose the seat next to Elin.

"This is our first home-cooked meal since we left South Carolina," she said.

"Alis does all the cooking now. She's a magician in the kitchen." The proud mother winked at her daughter.

"I hope you like it," Alis said as she removed the lids.

Carly eyed the dishes full of unfamiliar food. "It smells delicious, what is it?"

Elin snickered behind her napkin. "Eggs, sausage, back bacon, laverbread, and cockles."

"I recognized the eggs, sausage, and bacon. The bread looks delicious," Delaney said.

"Laverbread isn't bread. It's a type of seaweed harvested off the coast. It's boiled to a paste, then rolled in oats to make a patty. I fry mine in bacon fat."

The mention of seaweed caused Carly's expression to change, but she quickly wiped the worried look from her face, not wanting to offend her hostess.

"Oh, I see. It reminds me of collard greens," Delaney said.

"We call it Welsh caviar," Alis said. "Don't let the seaweed hold you back."

"What are cockles?" Carly asked, afraid of the answer.

"You call them clams. We fix them a variety of ways, but I prefer stir fry with onion and garlic."

Carly and Delaney passed their plates and sampled everything on the table. After Elin offered the blessing for the food, Carly whispered to Delaney, "When in Rome," she said, popping a cockle into her mouth.

A newer model black Land Rover Defender pulled up to the front of the house. Carly smiled. "I owned a Land Rover for many years. I like yours."

"Thank you. I've used it a lot since moving back." Alis waved to her mother as Carly and Delaney climbed inside. Then, she pulled onto the road and turned up the radio.

"I like you even more," Carly said, approving of her choice of music: classic rock.

"So, what do you both do when you aren't visiting our fine country?" Alis asked.

Delaney gave a brief overview of her life in Charleston, high-lighting her son, daughter-in-law, and granddaughter. She explained her part-time work leading tours in Charleston and investigating paranormal cases with her significant other, Boyd.

Carly answered, "I'm married to Austin, a Pediatric Neurologist, and we have two children, Frederick and Viviene. I work as a co-anchor on our local television station."

"You both have interesting lives. Are you into the paranormal scene, too?" Alis asked.

Carly glanced in the rearview mirror at Delaney. "Actually, we both are *sensitives,* as the saying goes. 'We see dead people'."

"We came to Warwickshire for a paranormal conference where we were presenters at Coombe Abbey," Delaney said.

"Coombe Abbey is a lovely location. I saw it when I visited Bath years ago," Alis said, then added, "The spirit world is interesting, but I prefer to avoid it. The real world's scary enough."

The view from the winding road to Llancaiach Fawr looked out over green fields that were sectioned by fieldstone walls. Sheep were grazing on the hillsides. In the distance, abandoned iron ore mining sites offered a glimpse into the days when iron ore and coal mines employed men throughout the county.

Quaint stone cottages dotted Rhymney Valley as they approached the manor. Carly rolled down the window for a better view of the large house and immaculate gardens. She breathed in the air, which smelled clean and carried a scent of heather and wildflowers from a nearby garden.

"We arrived with time to spare," Alis announced as she pulled into the gravel parking lot.

Carly checked her watch. It was eight-thirty. "Our tour starts in thirty minutes. I want to walk around the grounds before we go inside."

Delaney and Alis followed Carly as she strolled along the stone paths. Carly walked past the spirits gathering in the garden. She didn't engage, noticing they were oblivious to her.

As they made their way towards the house, Delaney noticed them turning to look at her. She nodded to them and continued walking with Alis, who was unaware of the interaction that had just occurred.

"You'll love the tour. The guides dress in period costumes and speak in old Welsh."

"Carly organized our side trips. I'm just here for the adventure."

Carly joined the women at the front entrance. "Perfect timing. Let's go inside."

Chapter Eleven

The historical guides addressed the guests in the native dialect of the Tudor era, and a docent dressed in short britches, knee boots, and a linen shirt shared the fascinating history of the manor house. Llanchaiach Fawr, built during a turbulent period in Welsh and British history, is considered one of Wales's best-preserved, semi-fortified manors. Its first known owner, Dafydd ap Richard, was the lord of the manor in 1549.

Another docent, a young woman wearing a long rust-colored gown, continued, "The original defensive design featured a single entrance, four-foot-thick walls, and spiral stone staircases connecting the floors. Sturdy wooden doors with iron bolts secured the manor, which may have initially included up to fourteen staircases—one for each room. When the doors shut firmly, the manor effectively divided into two sections, with the inner east wing as a self-contained refuge in case of an attack."

The tour began in an open vestibule, where the guide welcomed the guests and led them to the kitchen. He pointed out the large fireplace with a small fire burning inside. A young boy sat to the side, turning a handle that rotated the fowl cooking on the spit.

Carly tilted her head to acknowledge the boy, unnoticed by the rest of the tour. He made a nod to her and wiped the sweat from his forehead.

Delaney moved behind Carly and whispered, "I feel he's been doing this for a long time." Delaney knew there would be apparitions on this trip, just not this many.

Next to the stairs, a housemaid stood with her arms crossed over her ample figure. Almost all the guests ignored this unseen servant. A child, no more than three years old, glanced at her. Seeing the stern look on the maid's face, the child buried her face in her father's shoulder. The rest of the group remained oblivious to the maid's presence. Carly shot the housemaid an equally stern look, which elicited a huff from the servant.

The young man portraying a seventeenth-century servant continued to describe the history of the home. "The house is furnished to reflect 1645, during the English Civil War."

A guide dressed as a butler explained that the furnishings were accurate reproductions, with some originals, such as a mid-seventeenth-century cast-iron fire screen displayed at the St. Fagans National History Museum.

"This setting marks when King Charles I visited Colonel Edward Prichard and attempted to persuade him not to change his allegiance, which he ultimately did, allowing the house to represent both sides of the conflict throughout that year."

Alis added, "Wait until you see the upstairs." She stepped aside to allow Carly and Delaney to access the open hallway. In front of them, a staircase led to the landing, where a tall window overlooked the grounds, offering a glimpse of the distant mountains.

As Delaney reached the top step, two spirits of young boys rushed past her, causing her to lose her balance. The guide paused, taken aback by the muffled sound that escaped her lips.

Carly stepped aside as the boys rushed past, noticing Alis's confused expression at their reactions to something she didn't see. The guide continued the tour, allowing the rest of the group to join him.

The second floor housed four bedrooms and a large room above the kitchen that was designated for the surrounding area's court proceedings.

Once everyone assembled in the central hallway, another historical interpreter stepped from one of the bedrooms. She shared a story about the children who lived in the manor house. Carly and Delaney exchanged knowing glances as the interpreter discussed the hauntings of the young boys who passed away in the adjoining room. As she led the tour inside one of the bedrooms, Carly felt a pull toward the opposite end of the hallway.

She heard shouting from the courtroom, and visualized a man bound in heavy chains standing with two strong arms holding him in place.

The room featured a trestle-style table draped in a woven gold and crimson tapestry. Two inkwells with feathered quills lay on a metal trough, a wooden writer's desk stacked with papers, and a wrought iron candle holder filled a portion of the oversized table. Behind the table, two high-back chairs faced the shackled man, and a pair of six-candle holders lit the otherwise dark room. A short, bow-legged man kept a watchful eye on a metal lockbox and money scale at the end of the table. The magistrate appeared behind a curtained entrance, carrying his leather-bound record book.

Carly found herself sitting on one of the long benches designated for spectators. Surrounding her were men dressed in various styles, indicating that some belonged to the gentry class while others were farmers. She listened to the magistrate speaking in Welsh and understood the language, remaining quiet and observant of the proceedings.

The magistrate addressed the spectators, providing an account of the crime for which the accused was being tried. The bound man looked defiant at his accuser, and Carly felt his hot eyes burning into her.

"What do you say, Gethen Bowen, of the charge brought against you?" the magistrate asked, breaking the man's stare.

"I'm innocent of the crime. The wench is a lying bronten."

The term brought Carly off the bench. "He's the liar. I saw him behind the rocks, his gun still smoking from the shot. I'm not a bronten." She spat the term from her lips, insulted and outraged.

Shouts of support for Gethen Bowen hurled insults at Carly, causing the magistrate to bring down his fist against the table, quieting the outburst from Carly and others around her.

"Mistress, you will mind your tongue. It isn't your place to speak to the court." His voice boomed inside the noisy room, sending a ripple of murmurs from the onlookers.

Carly turned to look for anyone who supported her. A lone woman sat with her husband, forlorn expressions on their faces. She pleaded with someone to speak up, anyone, on her behalf. No one dared speak out against Gethen Bowen for fear of retribution.

Another voice caught Carly unaware, and she turned to see Alis and Delaney in the doorway. At first, they seemed unfamiliar to her. Delaney crossed the room, and Carly appeared startled by their appearance.

"Sweetie, are you okay? We heard your voice from the other room."

She shook her head in disbelief. "I don't know what happened. Moments ago, I saw a man brought in on charges before the magistrate."

Delaney and Alis glanced at one another.

"What did you hear me say?" Carly asked, bewildered.

"You were shouting, '*Ef yw'r celwyddog. Dydw I ddim yn bronten*'. It translates to, "He's the liar; I'm not a bronten," Alis said.

"Bronten? What does it mean, Alis?" Carly asked.

"It means, pardon my language, *slut*."

Carly gasped. "He called me that vile name, and no one offered to defend me."

Alis tried to lighten the moment. "It's common for people to have odd experiences here. It makes sense you would, too. You have the spirit gift."

"I suppose you're right. I'm ready to get out of here. Let's finish the tour," Carly said, shaken from the experience and feeling miffed at the derogatory term the man had called her. She followed Delaney and Alis as they descended the stairs to the first floor to join the group.

The tour finished in the kitchen, where it had begun. The guests lingered to ask the interpreters questions, but Carly, Delaney, and Alis thanked the guide and made their way to the parking lot.

"What did you think of the tour?" Alis asked as everyone clicked their seatbelts.

"It's a lovely manor house, I enjoyed it," Delaney said.

"I've not had a more interactive tour, that's for certain," said Carly.

Alis pulled out of the gravel lot and stopped before entering the highway. "Where do you want to go next?"

Carly pulled up her phone where she'd jotted down a few notes the night before. "Something tells me to find Ffos y Gerddinen."

"I haven't heard of that name before. Can I go back and ask the gentleman at the gift shop? Maybe he knows of it."

Delaney waited until Alis closed the door. "When did you learn the native dialect?"

"It just came out. It's the oddest thing. I understood the people in the vision upstairs in the courtroom. The woman got into my head again." Delaney put a stick of chewing gum in her mouth and offered a piece to Carly.

Alis returned. "You amaze me. The man inside said Ffos y Gerddinen is an eighteenth-century name for a town five minutes away from here- Nelson."

"I guess we're going to Nelson," Delaney said, nudging Carly's elbow from behind her seat with her foot.

Carly took several pictures with her phone of the emerald green hills and sheep grazing along the stone-walled fences. The scenery looked familiar, and she felt she'd walked along the same road.

"Alis, do you mind pulling off ahead? I've seen this before."

Delaney moved over to see the road in front of them. "What about this looks familiar?

"The hillside. In my dream, it's where the woman and her husband lived."

Alis pulled the Land Rover off the road before Carly bolted out the door. She walked across the road to the opposite side, where the hills formed a natural valley below.

Carly looked over her shoulder to see Delaney hurrying to catch up. "Over there, where it levels out. That's where the house stood, and I saw the man walking inside." She took pictures in quick succession as Delaney gazed at the rolling hills, covered in heather and stones, around them.

"I know what you're thinking, and it's trespassing," Delaney announced. Carly walked further down the road, looking for an end to the stone wall. She let out a sigh and turned back.

"You're right. I can't forget we're tourists."

Before they reached Alis, waiting beside her vehicle, Carly turned and panned the scene again. She closed her eyes and saw the couple again, hearing a gun and feeling the man's body falling onto her. She turned to Alis and Delaney, "The man died here. Gethen Bowen murdered him."

Mrs. Hughes made a delicious dinner of Welsh Cawl soup, Bara brith, and fruit bread. The dinner conversation kept to the day's itinerary without mentioning Carly's encounters with the spirit world. Carly asked Alis not to share the encounters with her mother, and she agreed.

After the meal, Carly and Delaney offered to help with the cleanup, but Alis said, "There are no guests in Mother's kitchen. She is very particular."

Elin Hughes swatted her napkin at Alis. "I prefer my guests to take a stroll outside or relax on the balcony in your room to enjoy the mountain views."

"Thank you for a delicious meal. I'll finish packing. The Uber is supposed to pick us up at four-thirty in the morning to drive to Cardiff and catch the train."

"Oh, I see. You'll have a long travel day," she said, glancing at Arlis.

"Mother's right. You will arrive at least two or three o'clock."

"Last night, I changed our flight back to the States from Heathrow to Edinburgh. The flight will cost us less, so I booked it," Carly said.

"We wish you safe travels. Will you want breakfast in the morning?" Alis asked.

"No, thank you. We'll get a bite on the train," Delaney said, speaking for both of them.

They finished packing, made themselves a cup of hot tea, and relaxed on the balcony. The chirping birds from the nearby tree answered his mate.

"Have you decided whether or not you want to tell me about what happened today at the Manor house?" Delaney asked.

Carly took a sip from her cup and began her story. "After I walked into the courtroom, I became part of something that happened in the room centuries earlier. Two men restrained a shackled man, and a magistrate appeared from behind a curtained area."

Delaney waited to ask her first question.

"Did the magistrate say what crime the man had committed?"

"Yes, Gethen Bowen murdered a man. He turned to me and called me a bronten, which I understood. That's when you and Alis found me."

Delaney leaned back in her chair.

"I'm baffled. Is it like when the girls helped you see what happened with Van Ness?"

"No, I'm experiencing what the woman saw, but through my own eyes. We know something links the woman to Bethesda. Why is she there if her children aren't orphans?" Carly exhaled, frustrated that she couldn't explain what caused the visions.

"You have the information from Drake Taylor at the Foundling Home. Maybe we'll find a connection there," Delaney walked over to the balcony's edge, admiring the lush green hillside beyond.

"Even with all the craziness we've experienced, I've had the time of my life." Delaney nudged Carly in the side, "And, for the record, you aren't a bronten."

Carly laughed. "Me too, and there will be time to tape the program on Thursday before we fly home."

The added trip didn't give them time to go sightseeing as they wished, but he train ride to Edinburgh provided excellent scenery.

"We should turn in early tonight. First, I'll text Austin and let him know we changed our flight plans."

"My family knows our plans, but we skip texting. Boyd sent a text when we got to Coombe Abbey, but that's it."

"I paid extra to call home while on the trip. We agreed only to call if we had an emergency or to call my folks," Carly said.

She sent Austin a text. With the time difference, she knew better than to wait for a reply. She turned off the light and drifted off to the sounds of night birds lulling her to sleep.

～

The train arrived at the station at 2:05 p.m. Delaney checked the map and found the hotel nearby, and Carly requested an Uber to take them and their luggage there. They had a light lunch on the train and enjoyed watching grazing sheep which dotted the farmland.

"As soon as we get checked in, let's find a place to eat," Delaney said. "I promised to text Myles Frasier when we arrived so we can get directions to the television studio."

Chapter Twelve

"If we tape the program early tomorrow, we still have enough time to go to Edinburgh Castle," Carly said, getting her credit card out of her wallet.

The hotel registration desk didn't have a line, so Carly registered while Delaney contacted Myles. After getting to their room, they went upstairs to get ready for dinner.

The Thistle House boasted clean rooms and an in-house Scottish bar. Delaney and Carly's rooms offered a view of Edinburgh Castle and the Haymarket Train Station. They sat in a back booth and watched the various patrons inside the establishment.

"We should sample some fine Scottish whiskey while we're here." Delaney perused the menu.

"Just promise me you won't start doing the Whip and Nae Nae," Carly said, laughing at the memory.

"No worries, I might throw my back out."

The waiter took their order and brought their complimentary shot of Whiskey. As they sampled their drinks, Delaney and Carly checked their phones.

"Myles texted me and said to get to the station by eight. There will be another guest taping with us," said Delaney.

"Oh? I suppose I didn't consider the possibility of more guests. Did he say who?"

Delaney reread the message. "No, the message just said another guest, no name."

Carly continued reading her messages. "Austin reminded me about meeting me at the baggage claim after we arrive home."

The waiter returned with their fish and chips and soft drinks. Carly double-checked her phone for tour reservations.

"If we want to see the castle, it must be early tomorrow. We tape the show at eight and hopefully finish by ten. Our tickets to Midhope Castle say one o'clock."

"Perfect. The rest of the time here will include shopping and enjoying our trip."

The early dinner gave Carly and Delaney time to discuss the trip's highlights and walk the historic Royal Mile, popping into shops along the way. Street performers entertained with bagpipes, men performed their acts on stilts, and even a man with an owl caught their attention. The owl swooped down, missing Delaney's head as he returned to his handler. Carly's thoughts drifted to the children with her parents and Austin alone at their house, probably watching a baseball game and drinking a beer.

They finished walking the Royal Mile at the entrance of Edinburgh Castle. The tour lived up to its reputation in the tour book. Both Carly and Delaney ranked it as one of their favorite sites in Scotland.

At ten o'clock the following morning, Myles met Carly and Delaney in the front lobby of STV, the television station in Edinburgh. The studio streamed hundreds of programs on public television.

"I'm happy to see you both again. Thank you for adding me to your travel plans to Scotland."

Delaney accepted his hug, while Carly opted for a handshake. They followed him onto the set. "It fits my budget, nothing fancy," he said.

The set included an oval coffee table, a sofa, and matching wing-back leather chairs.

"I think it feels home-like," Delaney said.

Before Carly commented, a familiar voice joined them from the doorway. "Hello, Carly, hello, Delaney."

"Drake? I didn't expect to see you today," Carly admitted.

"Myles asked me to join the show. I hope you don't mind sharing the program?"

Carly's face flushed. "Of course not. The more, the merrier."

Delaney hugged Drake, adding, "It's good to see you again, stiff shirt."

Drake chuckled as he recalled his comment about being a *stiff shirt* when she and Carly were leaving the Foundling Museum.

A make-up assistant emerged from the adjoining room with a tray of powder, applicators, and tissues. Myles explained that Jama would apply some powder to eliminate shine under the lights. He reviewed the talking points and stated that each would take a moment to share their paranormal experiences. Delaney and Carly sat on the sofa, while Myles and Drake took the chairs.

Myles kept the vibe low-key, more like old friends sitting around the room catching up since their last visit. Carly enjoyed listening to Drake's experiences as a paranormal investigator and the experiences of ghost hunting in London.

Myles brought out his dowsing rods, giving a quick demonstration. Delaney took a hand at it while sharing life in Appalachian North Carolina. "The scenery in Scotland reminds me of the places I grew up and visited as a child."

Carly shared her experiences with the paranormal growing up in rural Kansas. She talked about the connection she'd felt with children, mainly.

"Children appeared to me during my childhood. My siblings didn't believe I saw the dearly departed."

The program took an hour to record and had only one retake. At the end of the program, Myles shared the air date for the episode and thanked them for making the trip to Edinburgh. Myles and Delaney left the set together, leaving Drake and Carly alone.

"I've thought of our shared encounter since you left on Tuesday. Our experiences with the mystery ghost woman are quite remarkable," Drake said.

"I've thought about it, too. Speaking of strange, we visited Llanca-iach Fawr Manor yesterday. I found myself sitting in a trial from the eighteenth century."

Carly felt at ease sharing the experience with him and continued the exchange between herself and the prisoner. "As odd as it sounds, I know I was there."

"What a fascinating story. I hope you'll keep me posted on the connection between the Foundling Home and Bethesda."

Drake and Carly joined Myles and Delaney at the studio's entrance. Carly thanked Myles for the invitation to appear on his paranormal program.

"I enjoyed taking part in the show. Is there a way to send a link so we can watch at home?" Carly inquired.

"Yes, of course. As soon as the edits wrap up, I'll email the program link to both of you." Myles handed Carly a piece of paper.

"Would you mind jotting down your emails?"

Carly wrote their emails on paper while Delaney chatted with Drake.

"Are you headed back to London, Drake?" Delaney asked as they left the studio.

"I'm meeting a bloke from my university days in about an hour. He's a history professor at the University of Edinburgh. What's next for you and Carly?"

"We're going to take the Outlander tour to Inverness and Clava Cairns. We're supposed to see Culloden, too," she said.

Myles walked Carly outside to join the others.

Drake extended his hand to Carly, "I'll look forward to hearing from you when you have news of Bethesda," Drake said.

"I might need more information on the Foundling Home if you don't mind?" Carly asked.

"I'm available whenever you need me," he said, then added, "I hope you'll both have a safe flight home."

They parted as the Uber driver stopped to pick up Carly and Delaney. As they pulled away, Carly glanced back at Drake. His dark hair and slender build bore an uncanny resemblance to the man in her vision.

The Uber driver drove the ten minutes to drop the women off at the designated bus tour loading area.

The highlights of the nine-hour Outlander tour included the standing stones at Clava Cairns and the Culloden Battlefield. Carly and Delancy took most of the photographs on this stage of their adventure.

"Let's plan to return to Scotland and make a trip to Skye," Delaney suggested as she reclined her seat.

"I'm excited to see the standing stones. Maybe we'll go through to Jamie," Carly said, referring to the handsome Scotsman in the series, *Outlander*.

The drive on the road to Inverness traveled through the Highlands, with historical places that their guide alerted them to for optimum pictures. Carly held her phone next to Delaney's as they both took photos from the bus window.

"When will you and Austin drive to Kansas to pick up the kids?"

"Sunday morning, we'll drive out, spend a day or so visiting family, then return home on Thursday."

"I plan on helping Jarrod and Chelsea finish moving into their new place and spoiling Sutton," Delaney said.

The narrow road to Clava Cairns wound through the countryside of farmland and small homes. Finally, the bus pulled into the gravel parking lot. They had an hour to spend walking around the ancient site, taking pictures of the burial cairns, which were stone piles stacked upon one another with a central burial chamber at their core.

Carly and Delaney took turns taking photographs of one another in front of the tall stones, reenacting poses from the television show. They listened as their guide explained the site's age, which was almost 4,000 years old. He also warned about taking a souvenir stone from the Cairns. He recounted the tale of a tourist who put a stone in his pocket and returned home after his vacation. Tragedy struck his family, one by one, and the taker of the stone mailed it back to the site, apologizing for his deed.

The group ended the hour with a quick lunch at a nearby pub, The Clachnaharry Inn. The Caledonian Canal flowed beside the establishment, and visitors walked along its banks. A waitress snapped a quick picture of Delaney and Carly posing in front of the canal.

They arrived at Culloden Moor in Inverness, the site of the last battle of the Jacobite Rising, on April 16, 1746. The tour began at the Visitor's Center, where the group purchased souvenirs inside the Gift Shop. Carly found woolen tartan caps for her father and Austin, and a Celtic ring for herself. She picked up a tartan scarf for her mother. She purchased a Highland Coo for Vivi, who loved animals, and a sweatshirt with "Battle of Culloden - Inverness" on the front for Frederick.

They quickly put their purchases inside the bags they bought from the shop, then followed their guide onto the battlefield. The sounds were deafening to both Carly and Delaney. The spirits of the various clans who fell that day continued to fight the British, unseen by those walking along the paths.

An overwhelming heaviness washed over both Delaney and Carly as a light rain began to fall.

"It's a slaughter. They had no chance against the British weaponry," Carly said, the carnage playing out before her eyes.

Delaney stepped back, almost stepping on a brave Highlander from the Clan McDonald. "Let's take some pictures of the cottage," she said, moving away from the body.

She and Carly walked the stone path through tall grass, clover blooming in pink and white, and small clumps of heather. Carly looked for the thistle plants, but none were in bloom yet.

Leanach Cottage, a single-story thatched dwelling, was one of the last survivors of a once-common local structure. It was likely constructed in the early eighteenth century, situated on the Culloden estate.

Once inside, Carly saw men lying on straw mats everywhere on the floor. The cottage served as a field hospital for the wounded British outside its walls. The moans of the men were overshadowed by the sounds coming from outside the walls.

Carly and Delaney moved out of the room, unable to bear the scene any longer. A couple waited to enter as they left the building. The woman asked, "I bet the inside is amazing," she said to Carly.

"Yes, amazing," Carly echoed, her expression one of sadness.

They walked along the path, stones marking the various clans that had fought and died in the battle that fateful day. Carly took photographs of each one, as did Delaney. A lone piper walked in the distance. At first, they thought a reenactor performed for the visitors, but soon they realized the bagpiper came from a different time, repeating the same mournful song for the last two hundred years.

After walking the entire site, heavy rain began to fall on everyone touring the battlefield. Carly and Delaney pulled out their umbrellas from their backpacks and hurried back inside the visitor center.

Everyone boarded the tour bus for a trip into Inverness for dinner at the Mustard Seed, on Fraser Street. The establishment, set in a former church, offered views of the River Ness. Carly and Delaney were thankful the rain stopped so they could dine outside and watch the people walking by.

"It's a lovely place to visit. I hate to leave," Carly said, sipping a drink of her hot tea.

"I know, not enough time to see everything, but we've experienced a lot."

They dined on the soup of the day, which featured carrots and coriander, along with fresh bread.

After spending an hour eating their dinner and listening to the birds chirping in the nearby trees, it was time to board their bus and return to their hotel in Edinburgh.

The ride back to the city gave them time to relax and review the pictures they had taken that day. In Carly's photos, a faint image of Highlanders on the battlefield appeared. Delaney captured an EVP on her phone, having recorded the sounds she heard inside the cottage.

"I'm anxious to upload this to my computer at home," Delaney said.

"Did you get the bagpiper on the battlefield?" Carly asked.

"I'll have to listen to each part I videoed," Delaney replied.

The tour bus arrived at the designated lot at nine-thirty p.m. A taxi drove them back to their hotel. At ten, they returned to their room to pack for an early departure.

"I called the Uber driver to take us to the airport at seven. Our flight leaves at nine-thirty, and we have a two-hour layover in Newark."

Delaney wrinkled her nose. "Not exactly my favorite place to stop off, but at least we don't have to change planes but once."

"Looks like we'll arrive in Charleston at eleven forty-six p.m." Carly looked at her phone. "I'll text Austin when we arrive in Newark. He'll know to get to the airport by eleven."

They finished packing, and Carly checked her phone alarm. She fell asleep to the sound of Delaney snoring next to her.

Delaney's nails dug into Carly's arm as the plane bounced from heavy turbulence over the Atlantic. The jolting seemed to last for an eternity as the aircraft passed through a heavy thunderstorm, accompanied by thunder and a fantastic lightning show. When the plane finally landed in Newark, Carly and Delaney turned on their phones to check text messages.

"Austin will meet me at the baggage claim. Where is Boyd supposed to meet you?"

"Same place." Delaney put her phone away.

They found a place to grab supper and ate a sub sandwich while waiting to board the plane to Charleston. Carly called Austin's phone, but it went straight to voicemail. She left a message and finished eating her sandwich.

They walked back to the terminal, where they checked the times on the flight board. Their flight would arrive earlier than expected, at eleven-thirty p.m. Carly rechecked her phone. Still no message yet, but a severe weather alert for Charleston County appeared on her screen.

"Oh, great. Looks like we'll fly into another storm," Carly shared. "Charleston County is under a severe thunderstorm watch until two a.m."

"I just texted Boyd. I'm turning off my phone to save battery," Delaney said, putting her phone back into her backpack.

The announcement for first-class boarding came over the intercom. Carly and Delaney leaned against the wall as they waited for their turn, feeling the effects once again of jet lag. Once everyone had boarded the plane, the captain announced that the aircraft might encounter turbulence due to severe weather in the Charleston area. Delaney closed her eyes as the flight attendant reviewed safety procedures. Carly felt Delaney's grip tighten on her forearm as the plane taxied down the runway. She smiled and put her other hand over Delaney's.

Once the plane reached maximum altitude, Delaney relaxed and put in her AirPods to listen to a podcast. Carly felt unsettled. Perhaps the weather caused the uneasiness, but whatever the reason, she couldn't shake the feeling.

At eleven-thirty, the plane started its descent over Charleston. Lightning flashed across the sky and into the dimly lit plane. The aircraft touched down in a driving rain. The rain pelted the plane's windows, and thunder rumbled after each flash of lightning.

Delaney checked for Boyd's message, and one appeared. "The rain slowed me down, but I'm at baggage claim."

Carly turned her phone on again. "I have two missed calls with messages and a text message from Austin," she said. She read his text: *I had a meeting earlier. I'll shower, change, and return to meet you at the baggage terminal.*

She felt relieved. "It's all good."

She forgot to listen to the voice messages, and they walked to the baggage claim to retrieve their luggage.

Delaney saw Boyd standing by the corral and waved to get his attention. Carly waved, expecting Austin to be nearby.

Carly asked, "Where's Austin?" He wasn't standing with Boyd or anywhere in the area.

Boyd hugged and kissed Delaney, then said, "I got here at eleven. He hasn't arrived yet."

Carly remembered the two voicemail messages. "I'll bet Austin called me, and he's running late." She mentioned the voice messages and listened to the first one. "Oh, no," she said, the color drained from her face.

"What's wrong, sweetie?" Delaney asked.

Carly advanced the second message. "Oh, Austin," she exclaimed. "Boyd, will you take me to Roper? The calls are from Dr. Grennell in the ER. Austin's in surgery. There's been an accident."

Boyd grabbed their suitcases from the carousel. "Of course, we'll take you, honey," Boyd said as he tried to hold his emotions in check for Carly's sake.

Carly's thoughts ran wild as they hurried from the baggage claim to the front of the airport. Boyd turned to Carly, "I'll hurry and bring my car around. Wait here."

The rain hadn't let up as Carly and Delaney stood under the protective awning. Carly handed her phone to Delaney.

Delany listened to the voice messages. "Do you think you should call the number back to tell them you're on the way?"

"Austin is already in surgery. We need to hurry." Carly's heart raced, and she couldn't control the tears any longer, scared of what awaited her at the hospital.

Delaney asked again, "Do you know the doctor who left the voice messages?"

"Yes, I know Rick Grennell. He's an ER physician and a friend of Austin's."

Boyd pulled up beside Carly and Delaney. He loaded the luggage while they got in and buckled their seatbelts. He pulled out with their flashers on as he quickly merged onto the highway from the airport. Carly sat in front with Boyd, and Delaney leaned over the seat.

"Would you like me to call anyone to let them know Austin's in surgery? Maybe let his folks know?"

Carly couldn't think straight. Her mind conjured up horrible scenes of the accident. "I should call Kent. I'll let him tell Myra."

Carly found the strength to compose herself as she called Austin's parents. Kent Tabor answered in half-awake confusion at the late call. "Carly? Is everything all right?"

"Kent, Austin is in surgery. He was in an accident earlier." Carly's lungs were tight, and her voice cracked.

"Accident? What happened?" Kent asked.

In the background, Myra Tabor questioned her husband, "What's wrong? Is it one of the children?"

Carly heard the panic in their voices. "I'm sorry to call without knowing more details. I just returned from a trip, and the ER doctor at Roper left messages for me."

Kent sat on the edge of the bed, listening to Carly relay the messages. "Do we need to get a flight to Charleston tonight?"

"Let me get to the hospital and speak to Dr. Grennell. We're almost to the ER entrance now."

"All right, honey. Please, call us when you find out what is going on," Kent said.

At twelve-thirty, Carly, Delaney, and Boyd arrived at the Roper Emergency Room. They went to the admission desk to gather information about Austin and find out where to wait to speak to the surgeon. The admission clerk checked the computer for any admissions of Austin Tabor that evening.

"Oh, Dr. Tabor. Yes, I heard he had been in an accident earlier. They brought them both through the ER and then to surgery."

Delaney and Boyd looked at one another, unsure if Carly had heard the nurse. Delaney mouthed, "Both?"

The attendant instructed Carly to go to the east waiting room on the seventh floor. They hurried to the elevator and rode in silence. When the door opened, Carly rushed to the nurse's station while Boyd and Delaney followed close behind.

"Did the ambulance bring two crash victims to the ER?" Boyd whispered.

"Yes, but maybe they meant the other driver." Delaney took Boyd's hand in hers.

When they caught up to Carly, a surgical nurse met them at the nurses' station. "Which one of you is Mrs. Tabor?"

Carly stepped forward, "I'm Carly, Austin's wife. What happened?"

The nurse's demeanor changed to a more personal tone. "I worked with Dr. Tabor as his assistant during many surgeries. I'm Lisa Wyley." She asked Carly to follow her into the waiting area, where she could explain the extent of his injuries.

Austin sustained significant trauma in a car accident earlier this evening. From the officer who came to the ER, Austin's vehicle crossed Cannon Street, and another car hit him head-on, probably from hydroplaning and losing control."

Carly's chest tightened as Nurse Wyley continued.

"He came into the ER this evening at ten o'clock with a fractured skull, lacerated liver, punctured lung, and several broken ribs."

Carly's eyes pooled with tears. "He operated on hundreds of children, many were accident victims."

Nurse Wyley shared more about the extent of his injuries. "Dr. Notari is an excellent Neurosurgeon. He's relieving the pressure on Austin's brain by removing the fractured portion of his skull to prevent the brain from pushing against it. His condition is serious, Mrs. Tabor."

Carly felt the hot tears running from her face and down her neck. "How much longer will he be in surgery?"

The nurse cleared her throat. "Dr. Notari is doing everything he can. Another team will work on the injury to his liver."

She patted Carly's hand, continuing, "Do you have any questions?"

Carly shook her head and tried to process the extent of Austin's injuries. "No, none that I can think of."

"All right. I'll go back inside but return when I have more news." She put her hand on Carly's shoulder. "If you have a minister or priest, the hospital can call him if you'd like."

Boyd put his arm around Carly. Delaney wiped tears as she reached out and handed Carly the box of tissues.

"I have to call my parents and my in-laws." She exhaled the pent-up anxiety and said, "Excuse me."

While Carly relayed the news to her parents, she asked that they not tell the children yet. She advised them to wait until she knew more before coming to Charleston. She called Austin's parents, repeating the extent of his injuries. After her initial call, Myra had insisted they leave on the first available flight. They were already on the route to the airport.

Boyd texted Tucker McGee, his former partner, and friend to Carly and Austin. Delaney phoned her son to explain the reason for her delay. Carly put her phone inside her purse and sat beside Delaney. The clock kept a cadence with Carly's heart. Two-thirty. Carly paced from her chair to the hallway, waiting for the nurse to return with information.

She checked her phone, rereading Austin's text to her. Who was the other person brought into the hospital with Austin? She sipped on a cup of coffee that one of the nurses had given her as she waited. The nurses and doctors continued to walk through the doors marked "Restricted-Authorized Personnel Only."

The sound of the intercom calling for Dr. Sepheri jolted Carly from a moment of sleep. Delaney and Boyd were sitting together on the couch, whispering. She wasn't sure how long they'd been back. "I'm glad you're here," Carly said to Delaney.

"We just sat down. Do you need anything?"

"No, thank you."

She rose from her chair to stretch her legs. Nurse Wyley emerged from the operating suite.

Carly exhaled, her heart beating faster as she awaited the news about Austin's surgery.

"Carly, Austin is out of surgery. He suffered significant trauma to his brain. Dr. Notari finished the surgery to relieve the pressure. Dr. Corey is repairing the laceration to his liver, and a tube was previously inserted into his chest to prevent his lung from collapsing. He received several units of blood during surgery because of internal bleeding."

Carly nodded as she processed the extent of Austin's injuries.

"Dr. Notari will come out in a few minutes to talk with you," Nurse Wyley said.

"When can I see him?"

"After he is out of surgery, he'll spend time being monitored in recovery. You'll need to go to the sixth-floor ICU after you speak with the doctor."

"Thank you for everything," Carly said, her voice weary.

"Sweetie, can I get you something to drink or eat?"

"No, thank you. But if you and Boyd want to grab something, go ahead. I'm fine."

Within a few moments, Dr. Notari came into the waiting room, his mask hanging off one ear. He introduced himself and sat next to Carly.

"When Austin came into the ER, his heart had stopped beating several times, and the staff resuscitated him. EMTs also told the ER doctor Austin wasn't breathing when rescued from the wreckage. He received a fractured skull in the crash, not to mention a high amount of blood loss due to internal bleeding."

Carly responded as if on autopilot. "I see."

"I removed a portion of the skull to drain the blood and reduce brain swelling. Austin has experienced a severe traumatic brain injury, Mrs. Tabor. He didn't regain consciousness in the ER. His condition is grave."

"When may I see him?"

"As soon as he goes to the ICU, you may see him briefly." He paused and said sympathetically, "I've done everything possible. If you haven't notified your clergy, the hospital chaplain is on call."

Carly heard the words, and a sickening feeling overtook her. For a moment, she thought she might vomit.

"We have a minister at First Baptist. I'll call him. Austin's parents are on their way from Kansas."

Dr. Notari exhaled. "Austin is on a ventilator to help him breathe. I will reassess his brain activity after he arrives in the ICU."

"Thank you. I don't know what to ask. I'm numb."

Dr. Notari hugged Carly. He didn't leave, bringing the elephant up in the room.

"I'm sorry, Mrs. Tabor. There is something else I need to discuss with you."

The sound of Carly's heart beating competed with Dr. Notari's voice.

"I'm sorry to report that Austin's passenger passed away during surgery. Her identification listed her residence as Biloxi, Mississippi."

Carly straightened her shoulders. "Passenger? I'm afraid I'm unable to help you. Austin was coming to pick me up at the airport."

Dr. Notari took a scrap of paper from his pocket. "Her driver's license says her name is Cora D. Burton. Does the name sound familiar to you?"

Carly tried to think of his coworkers, former colleagues, and anyone who rang a bell. Then, she remembered.

"Austin's first wife… her name is Cora."

Chapter Thirteen

Dr. Notari broached the subject delicately. "Mrs. Tabor, I'm only asking because her family deserves to know she has passed away."

The walls closed around Carly. The thought of her husband and his ex-wife together made no sense. "Where are my husband's belongings?"

"The emergency room has Ms. Burton's and your husband's effects. I'll call the ER and have someone bring his things to you."

Carly walked with the doctor to the waiting room door. "My mother and father-in-law will know more about Ms. Burton. I know they contacted her after she and my husband divorced."

"Thank you for your help in the matter. I'll have the nurse call the waiting room when you can see Austin."

Carly rubbed the back of her neck, and the tension made her body ache. Her legs felt weak, and she collapsed in the chair.

"It's six o'clock. You both need to go home and get some rest. I'll be fine. It might be a few hours before I see Austin."

Delaney balked, but Carly won. "Okay. I'll go home long enough to shower. Do you want me to bring a change of clothes for you?"

Carly took her house key from her bag and handed it to Delaney. "Go to our house and shower. It's closer. Boyd can drop off my luggage."

"We'll hurry back." Delaney held Carly close. "I'll bring a change of clothes and a few things you might need."

"Thank you for being here. I love you both," Carly said.

Boyd and Delaney hurried to the elevator.

Carly went to the restroom to put cool water on her face. She kept hearing the doctor repeat that Austin and his ex-wife were together. *Why were you with your ex-wife?*

When she returned to the waiting room, a nurse came in with a small white bag in her hand.

"Mrs. Tabor?" the nurse asked.

"Yes, I'm Dr. Tabor's wife." The nurse handed the bag to Carly. "This is everything removed from Dr. Tabor's pockets."

Carly took the bag. "Thank you."

The nurse left, and Carly numbly returned to her chair. The sun's reflection through the tinted window felt warm on Carly's back, starkly contrasting with the air conditioning blowing against her from the other side of the room.

The nurses' station was busy with the shift change. A nurse's aide came to the waiting room to offer Carly something to drink. In a few moments, she returned with a cup of ice and a can of Sprite.

Carly thanked her and took several long sips from the straw. She hadn't eaten in hours and felt light-headed. She rummaged in her backpack and found a leftover candy bar from the airport in Newark. As she ate, she reached into the bag and pulled out Austin's cell phone. A small crack ran across the top of the screen. *It must've cracked during the accident.*

She took a charger from her backpack and plugged it into the nearby outlet. In a few moments, Austin's phone came on. She went to his text messages and saw her last message from the airport. She scrolled up and saw the name *Cora*.

After reading a series of messages, she started to cry. *How could you do this to me?*

The ICU nurse entered the waiting room and found Carly dozing, Austin's cell phone in her lap. The clock in the waiting room displayed eight a.m.

"Mrs. Tabor," the nurse said quietly as she touched Carly's arm. "I'll take you to the ICU."

Carly jerked, dropping Austin's phone. She picked up his phone, the bag, and her backpack, then followed the nurse to the elevator. When the door opened to the ICU, Carly noticed the patients separated by a curtain and the machines that kept them alive. Sounds were coming from everywhere, and Carly's eyes took a second to adjust to the brightness.

As Carly walked past the various men, women, and teenagers hooked to a variety of machines and ventilators, she felt her heart beating faster against her chest. When she reached Austin, Carly couldn't contain the fear and anxiety she'd felt since arriving eight hours earlier. Hot tears rolled down her cheeks. The nurse explained the extensive swelling of Austin's face and eyes. Carly moved apprehensively to the bedside and touched Austin's hand.

The nurse checked his vitals and entered them into the computer. Then, she joined Carly at the bedside.

"Austin, I'm here," she whispered. "It's me, Carly."

Carly squeezed his hand but felt no response. Dr. Notari entered the room, and the nurse left, pulling the curtain closed.

"Carly, I performed another assessment of Austin's brain function.

I'm sorry, the initial results aren't what I'd hoped to see after relieving the swelling during surgery."

"It's early. Isn't it common for brain swelling to take a while to improve? Austin used to come back to assess his patient, and the patient improved."

"In some cases, yes. Austin was unresponsive in the ER, and his brain isn't responding as it should after relieving the pressure. I'll re-evaluate him before I leave this evening. I'm not going to give you false hope. His prognosis is grim."

Carly grabbed the bed rail for support. "His parents texted me earlier, and they will arrive from the airport soon."

"The rule is one visitor for ten minutes every hour. I'll ask the nurse to bend the rule out of courtesy to Dr. Tabor."

He waited outside the room for Carly. She leaned down to kiss Austin's hand. "I love you, Austin. Hang on, please."

On the other side of the bed, Cora Burton's spirit held Austin's hand. Carly pointed her finger at the apparition, who looked into her eyes, pleading for forgiveness. "Get away from *my* husband. This is all *your* fault." Carly raised her voice. "He was coming to get me." She collapsed into the chair beside his bed, sobbing. Cora disappeared from the room.

A nurse pulled the curtain aside, "Is everything all right, Mrs. Tabor?" she asked, looking around the small area for another visitor.

Carly raised her head. "I'm sorry." She excused herself and walked down the hall to text Myra the directions to the ICU waiting room. Delaney, Boyd, Tucker, and Sylvie McGee gathered in the corner of the room, whispering. When Carly saw them, she hugged them and thanked them for coming. She told them about the latest update on Austin's condition.

Kent and Myra Tabor entered the waiting room as Carly delivered the news to her friends. Carly embraced Myra and said, "I'm sorry to see you under these circumstances."

She took Austin's parents back to the nurse's station, and the three followed the nurse into Austin's cubicle. They were both overcome with emotion at the sight of Austin in his current condition. Carly stayed back so his parents could have a private moment with him. Kent Tabor knew the hope of seeing Austin recovering and going home would not come to fruition. As a physician, he knew the lack of brain activity meant his son couldn't survive without life support. He leaned over his son and kissed his cheek.

Kent led Carly out of the room while Myra held Austin's hand and spoke softly. He put his hands on Carly's shoulders and pulled her into him. They both wept, knowing Austin was alive only because of the ventilator. Carly hadn't eaten since earlier the previous day. Kent coaxed her away from Austin's bedside long enough for her to go down to the cafeteria for a sandwich. He hugged Carly and assured her, "I'll text you if anything changes."

"Shall I bring you and Myra a sandwich?" Carly asked before walking out of the room.

"No, we're good. We ate on the plane. Thanks."

Carly stood outside as Kent and Myra shared a private moment with Austin. She saw Delaney at the entrance to the ICU, and she joined her by the elevator while waiting for Myra.

"Sweetie, there are lots of people here for Austin. They wanted to let you know they are praying for him."

"Please thank them. I'll update everyone after I meet again with Dr. Notari." Carly squeezed Delaney's hand. "Please pray, it doesn't look good."

The minister from the First Baptist Church, Tom Newlin, met with Carly and her in-laws. He prayed for Austin and spent time ministering to Carly. A nurse stepped into the room, excusing herself.

"The medical team is on their way to discuss Austin's latest brain function results.

Carly, Kent, and Myra waited for the medical team led by Dr. Notari to join them. Three other doctors followed him into the already crowded area beside Austin's bed.

Tom promised to put Austin on the prayer chain at their church and hugged Carly before leaving.

Carly didn't recognize two of the team, but both introduced themselves. Dr. Reema Hassan, Cardiologist, and Dr. Michael Bernstein, Pulmonologist. The other, Dr. Sharon Shroer, a neurologist, was someone she'd seen at a recent Christmas party given by the hospital.

Dr. Notari displayed Austin's latest brain activity scan, which he administered an hour before. "Carly, the scan confirms what we hoped wasn't the case."

He looked at the team behind him. "We agree that Austin's brain isn't showing activity when I checked his reflexes. His lungs and heart aren't functioning without the ventilator. Austin injured his brain stem during the accident, which paralyzed him. He hasn't regained consciousness."

Dr. Notari sat down in the chair beside Carly, his voice measured and compassionate. "The last test on Austin's brain shows no activity. When we examined his eyes, his pupils were fixed and didn't respond to the light. He is alive because machines are doing what he can no longer do."

He lifted his eyes to Kent Tabor, "If Austin is removed from life support, he will expire within the hour."

The pulmonologist, Dr. Bernstein, continued, "We did a trial run to assess his breathing without the ventilator. His breathing stopped, and his heart started to flatline. He is unable to maintain his breathing and regular heart rate when off the machine."

The words cut through to Carly's core. A muffled cry erupted into an uncontrollable sob. Dr. Notari put his arm around Carly, consoling her. "I'm so sorry. I wish there were something else I could do for Austin." Austin's parents held each other and wept, pulling Carly into their embrace.

"How long do we have to make a decision?" Carly said, her voice was breaking with emotion.

"The machines will continue to keep Austin alive. You have time to decide how to proceed and go to a Higher Power for a miracle."

Dr. Notari led the team members out of the room. Dr. Shroer whispered her sincere sympathies to the Tabors and Carly.

Carly remembered Austin's wishes on his driver's license. "Austin is an organ donor. He wanted to help others." She went over to his bedside, bringing his hand to her lips. "I don't want to let you go. I love you." Carly felt as if her heart might break.

She left the ICU and joined the Tabors in the small family waiting room. She recalled a conversation the two had shared after he came home from operating on a young teen. He watched the parents agonize over their child, who would never wake up. He had said, "Please, don't ever keep me alive in that condition."

"You need to sleep, Carly. Myra and I will stay this shift with Austin. Why don't you let Delaney take you back to the house for a shower and a nap?"

"I can't leave. I have a bag and will freshen up in the restroom."

Kent and Myra knew objecting would do no good. Carly wasn't leaving Austin.

The number of friends waiting for news about Austin's prognosis trickled down to close friends and immediate family. She agonized over the decision and spoke with Austin's parents about his brain showing no activity. Carly had the final say in the matter and told the nurse to let Dr. Notari know about her decision to remove Austin from life support.

Within an hour, an organ procurement representative contacted the families of patients waiting for an organ transplant. Carly went to the chapel, where she spent the next hour alone. She prayed her decision was the right one.

At three o'clock, after meeting with the organ donor procurement coordinator, Carly asked if each of Austin's friends in the waiting room could say goodbye to him. First, the Tabors were given time alone with Austin.

Carly gathered her strength as she walked to the waiting room to tell their friends Austin had been declared brain dead, and they could each have a moment to say their goodbyes.

She walked each to the room and waited outside the cubicle. After everyone had their chance to speak to Austin, they gathered in the conference room, where they would remain to give Carly support.

Finally, Carly entered the room where the nurse was waiting for her. She explained what would happen next. "Austin will remain on life support until he is in the surgery suite. Take the time you need, and when you're ready, we will give Dr. Tabor an honor walk. Several of his staff wanted to be here." She turned before exiting the room, "I'll let your family and friends know what will happen and when."

Carly exhaled her anxiety slowly, "Thank you for all you've done. I want more time with Austin, please."

After the nurse left, Carly took Austin's hand. "I don't know how to do this. We were supposed to grow old together, enjoying our grand-children." Tears flowed onto Austin's hand, and her throat constricted, making a whisper.

For a moment, Carly saw a similar scene in her mind. The room changed to a scene from eighteenth-century Wales. A husband reached his hand up to his wife's as his eyes closed with his last breath. *What's going on?* She looked back at Austin, and the room changed once again to the present. She continued her last moments with him. "You've broken my heart twice tonight," she said as she leaned down to kiss his face. " I love you."

Friends, doctors, nurses, and the family of Austin Tabor openly wept as his hospital bed passed by them. Carly and Myra held hands as they walked as far as the operating room door. A nurse led Carly and those who came to support Austin to a private room away from the surgery area. Delaney wrapped her arms around Carly and cried with her.

Carly and the Tabors spoke in private after the funeral director came to take Austin's body to the funeral home. On top of the loss of their son, Kent and Myra learned he and their former daughter-in-law had resumed an affair over the last two years. The news added to their despair. Kent spoke to the hospital about where Cora's husband and parents lived and their contact information. He, too, had unanswered questions.

Carly phoned her parents to provide them with the news that Austin had passed away and the circumstances surrounding his becoming an organ donor before his death. Curt and Paula Evans would tell the children their daddy was in the hospital, and they would fly home as soon as they could get a flight.

Carly's brother and sister-in-law had agreed to drive their van, carrying Frederick and Vivi's bikes back to Charleston. They would arrive within the week.

Boyd and Delaney waited to see Carly before leaving the hospital.

"I'm so sorry, sweetie," Delaney said as she hugged Carly. "I love you and I'm here for you."

"We love you, honey," Boyd said with his deep southern drawl.

"We're here for you and the kids." Boyd tried to keep his composure, but he wiped tears as he hugged Carly.

The Tabors and Carly drove back to her house. After being awake for two days, her body yearned to sleep. She wanted to take care of Austin's parents, but they insisted she shower while Myra went into the kitchen to make something to eat.

Carly relented and went upstairs to her bathroom. Her body moved on autopilot. She turned on the shower and saw Austin's clothes from the day before draped over the back of the chair. She picked up his shirt and held the fabric to her nose, breathing in his scent. She caught the faint smell of Cora's perfume and threw the shirt on the floor. "Damn you, Austin. Why did you do this to us?"

She closed the shower door and released her sadness, betrayal, and anger as the water drowned out her cries.

A half-hour later, Myra knocked on the bathroom door. "Carly, honey, I've made us something to eat. We'll wait for you to join us."

Carly exhaled. Myra Tabor was a force that Carly didn't have the energy to fight. In truth, having her in-laws in the house kept her from spiraling into despair. She brushed out her hair and pulled it into a ponytail. She pulled a sweatshirt over her head and found a pair of yoga pants to wear. She walked barefoot downstairs and joined Kent and Myra, who were seated at the table.

A tossed salad and leftover rotisserie chicken seemed like a feast to Carly, and she thanked her for making supper for them. No one wanted to talk, but Myra needed to speak to Carly before people stopped to pay their respects.

"Honey, I didn't know about Cora and Austin. I wouldn't have approved, of course. I'm sorry it happened."

Carly felt tears pooling in her eyes. "I didn't think you knew. Their text messages leave nothing to the imagination. I feel betrayed."

Kent reached over and took Carly's hand. "We will help you and the children in any way we can. We love you, Carly."

Carly had a funeral to plan and the dreaded task of telling Freddy and Viviene. She needed the Tabor's support, as well as that of her family and friends. Regardless of the terrible hurt she felt, she knew Kent and Myra were grieving, too.

~

Carly turned the covers down on their bed. She pulled Austin's pillow close, breathing in and closing her eyes. She saw Austin, whole, handsome, and tan. They walked along Folly Beach, hand in hand. He bent down and kissed her. The memory vanished from her mind.

Carly turned to face the windows, the moonlight casting a glow across the room. She caught a glimpse of Austin's spirit standing at the foot of the bed, his face illuminated by the glow of the moonlight.

"Austin." Carly threw the covers back and reached for him, only to find herself alone again. The house creaked and groaned, making its usual sounds throughout the long night, as if it, too, mourned for Austin.

~

Carly woke after nine o'clock. The funeral director had left a message on her phone to discuss Austin's funeral arrangements. She went upstairs to her office to find the number of their attorney, Harv Ball, and inform him of Austin's passing. After Carly's near-death experience, she and Austin agreed they should write a will. Austin's wishes were cremation, while Carly chose a traditional casket burial.

She made a call to Harv Ball, a descendant of the Charleston Ball family, and their attorney for thirteen years. He offered his deepest condolences to Carly and the children.

She made an appointment to meet with him later in the week. After her brief call, she showered and dressed before joining the Tabors downstairs.

"Good morning. I'm sorry if we woke you," Myra said, making another cup of coffee. "Can I fix you a cup?"

Carly put her arms around Myra. "I don't want you to wait on me. You're our...my guest."

Kent took his coffee and walked out to the lower piazza. Carly looked out to see her father-in-law with his head in his hands. She turned away from his private moment and joined Myra at the table.

"I'm going to meet the funeral director at ten to discuss Austin's funeral arrangements," Carly said.

"Kent and I will go with you. You shouldn't go alone."

Stuart Funeral Home, located on the corner of Calhoun and Smith Streets, was within walking distance of Roper Hospital. The funeral home assistant welcomed them inside, leading them to a conference room where the funeral director, Marty Knight, offered his condolences to Carly and the Tabors. He had a file on his desk marked Austin and Carly Tabor. The familiar nausea overtook Carly, but she willed the sensation away.

Marty waited for everyone to sit, then continued, "As you know, Austin prepaid for cremation services. Do you want to honor his wish, or do you want to do something else?" Marty asked.

Myra and Kent sat stoically while Carly and Marty discussed Austin's funeral arrangements. Marty guided Carly into a room where she chose an urn. He then explained that the family could see Austin again before the cremation took place. "I want to prepare you for what Austin will look like," he said before they walked down the hall to the viewing room.

Carly, Myra, and Kent entered a small chapel room with Marty and found Austin lying under a white sheet pulled up to his chin. The sheet hid any signs of organ donation surgery. Despite the swelling and bruising on his face and the sterile bandages around his head, he looked at peace.

Marty offered them the room with Austin for as long as they needed. Carly touched Austin's cheek, cold and lifeless. She felt her knees go weak, like a newborn colt. Myra put her arm around Carly's waist to steady her.

She bent down to place a gentle kiss on his cheek. "Goodbye, Austin. I love you." Overwhelmed by her profound grief at losing her husband, she reached for Kent, who was standing behind her.

Carly's heart ached at the task ahead of telling the children about their father.

Despite his objections to spirits following Carly around, Austin's spirit still lingered. Carly saw his form standing behind his parents as they held one another, grief-stricken.

She closed her eyes, hoping against all hope that this was just a bad dream.

An hour later, they emerged. Carly returned to the office with Marty to write the death certificate and obituary. "By law, I will need to wait until tomorrow to go ahead with the cremation. When you have decided on the time and place you wish to have Austin's service, I will put it in the obituary."

Carly paused to think. Her family and Austin's sister would arrive within the next 24 hours. "I want to schedule his service for Tuesday, June 11th. We'll hold the funeral at our church, First Baptist, on Church Street. I'll call our pastor to arrange everything."

"Let me do that for you, Carly," Marty offered.

She agreed and said, "Thank you. It's one less thing."

With the funeral arrangements in the works, Carly went home to plan the service.

~

Later in the afternoon, Delaney accompanied Carly to the airport to pick up the Evanses, Freddy, and Vivi.

As they waited for the passengers to disembark from the plane, Delaney said, "Sweetie, I'm here for you. I've been in your shoes with Jarrod."

Carly remembered Delaney's son, Jarrod, who lost his father during his first year of high school. "Thank you. I'm sorry we share yet another tie that binds us."

Carly saw her parents and the children walking from the gateway. Freddy and Vivi ran to their mother, pulling her down to them. Curt and Paula waited for Carly to stand.

They held one another, tears flowing, as the children sensed something more than daddy in the hospital. Carly tried to keep the death of their father from the children until they arrived at the house. On the drive home, she and Delaney asked about their time with their cousins. The ploy worked for a time, but Carly's dark circles and appearance didn't fool Freddy.

Once inside the house, Carly explained that Daddy couldn't come home with them. "Daddy had an accident in the car. He was hurt badly, and the doctors tried to make him better."

"When can we see Dad?" Freddy asked, fear in his eyes.

Carly struggled to find the words to explain to the children. "Daddy, uh, went to Heaven. When we get to Heaven, he'll be waiting for us."

The grandparents comforted the children as they tried to comprehend the death of their father. Carly held them both, and tried to comfort them.

Freddy ran upstairs, and slammed his door shut. Carly started to go after him, but Curt stood.

"Let me go upstairs, Carly," he said.

Carly smiled. "Thank you, Dad."

Delaney went into the kitchen to give Carly and her family privacy.

June 10, 2025

Harv Ball stood behind a massive cherry credenza, which he used as his desk. Under six feet tall with a deep tan and almond-shaped brown eyes, Harv was what most ladies considered handsome. Marlin fishing and weekly golf outings were regular excursions for the lawyer, even at seventy-two. He extended his hand, but instead, hugged Carly—something she had begun accepting willingly after Austin's death.

"Come on in, Carly. I'm sorry we're meeting under these somber circumstances," he said with a sympathetic southern drawl. "Can I pour you something to drink?" He pointed to the credenza, where he had a fully stocked liquor cabinet inside.

"No, thank you, Harv." She sat in one of the leather chairs in front of his desk. "I wanted to get this out of the way as soon as possible."

"Yes, of course. I have Austin's last will here," he said, opening the gray legal folder. "We'll need to meet with others, as Austin mentions several people in his will. Are his parents and sister in town yet?"

Carly explained that Austin's service would take place on Friday. The Tabors arrived before Austin passed away. His sister arrived earlier in the day and took the children to the Aquarium. She asked who else needed to attend.

"The immediate family and someone from the hospital should discuss funds to go into a trust for children whose families need assistance during their child's hospital stay or funeral expenses."

Carly smiled, reflecting on Austin's love for the children he treated over the years. "Austin's compassion and understanding of parents' stress during a medical crises is something he wrestled with."

"I'll contact Roper Hospital and call you to schedule a meeting to read the will. We can do it before everyone leaves Charleston."

"Thank you, Harv. The sooner, the better."

Carly heard her phone inside her purse. She said goodbye and went outside to check her messages. An unfamiliar number without a name displayed on the screen alerted her.

She read the text. *Hello, Carly. I found information about Gethen Bowen while searching historical records. I hope you and Delaney made it home safely. We'll chat soon. Drake Taylor.*

She scrolled to the following message from Channel 5. She had forgotten about Jeffery Sullivan's party. She didn't want to think about Channel 5 or how to muster up the fortitude to return to the newscast.

That prompted her to remember another party for Chad Flannery on Saturday. She put her head on the headrest and sighed—*one more thing. I'll go for Chad, both times, he came to the hospital for me.*

Time seemed to stand in a perpetual time warp. Whenever she closed her eyes, she relived the moment she saw Austin in the ICU and Cora's ghost standing beside the bed. She put her phone away and drove back to her house from Broad Street. Austin's sister, Ainsleigh, and her husband, Ryan, sat on the floor in the den with Freddy and Vivi. They were playing a game, and she heard laughter for the first time in days.

Chapter Fourteen

June 11, 2025

Carly watched the last of Austin's mourners leave the chapel. His partner, Dr. Frank Elston, and Ainsleigh's eulogies were touching and a testament to Austin's character. Carly ground her teeth when she thought of the affair. It seemed everyone avoided the knowledge that he didn't die alone from the accident. She let the hospital handle contacting Cora's husband. The matter was dead to her, just like Cora. Or was it?

She walked to the front of the church to remove the picture of Austin beside his urn. Freddy and Vivi stood at the back of the church with their grandparents. Neither said a word as they watched their mother return with the items in her hands.

After Carly returned home, she took off the black suit and threw it in the dirty clothes hamper. She noticed Austin's clothes were still hanging on the chair. Myra must've picked them up after Carly threw them on the floor the night she came back from the hospital. She'd not noticed before. The house echoed sounds from below, in the kitchen, and other rooms where family and friends gathered. Carly was thankful for the distractions—Freddy and Viviene needed their family now more than ever. They were managing their grief better than Carly imagined. Nevertheless, she would find a grief counselor for the children. Carly's sister-in-law encouraged her to find a grief support group to attend. She promised her she would find one in town.

The following morning, she prepared to attend Chad's retirement party at Henry's. Her father-in-law wrote her a prescription for an anxiety medication at the hospital when Austin passed. She'd been reluctant to use it but felt that today she'd need something to get through the happy occasion. She and Delaney raised eyebrows when they walked into the reserved room. No one expected to see her so soon after Austin's death. Chad and Josie were the first to greet them, and Chad wrapped his arms around her, whispering how much her coming meant to him. She kissed his cheek, then hugged Josie.

"He's all yours, Josie. Enjoy the time together in the new motorhome," Carly said, smiling for the first time in days without forcing it.

She felt a hand on her shoulder and turned to see Jeff Sullivan. "Jeff, hello," Carly said, surprised to see him.

"I'm sorry for your loss. If there's anything I can do, don't hesitate to ask." Jeff's sincerity touched Carly.

"Thank you. I appreciate it. I plan to come in next week to start back to work."

The statement caught Jeff off guard. "Take the time you need. I can't do too much damage."

Carly hadn't given it much thought. She'd been busy with funeral preparations and other responsibilities. "Who's filling in for me?"

Jeff pointed to a young reporter Bauer had hired several years ago to host the early morning news program. "Erin's handling the pressure like a champ. She'll fill in for as long as you need," he said.

Carly liked Erin Finney and helped her learn the ropes when she filled in during Carly's maternity leave with Vivi.

By the time Chad thanked everyone who came to celebrate his retirement, Carly didn't expect him to mention her as one of his best memories of Channel 5. She put her hand to her lips and blew him a kiss.

Mutual respect and affection were evident throughout each evening's television program. Channel 5 ranked the highest in Chad and Carly's time slot. Jeff Sullivan had big shoes to fill, and he was aware of it.

On the ride home, Carly thanked Delaney for going with her. "I'll get through this with your help."

"I'm here for you. You aren't going to go through this alone." Delaney knew the pain Carly felt, and she wanted to support Carly and her children.

After Delaney pulled out of the driveway, Carly walked inside. The children were in bed, and everyone gathered in the kitchen. The smell of coffee greeted Carly as she closed the door.

"How was the party?" Paula asked.

"Everyone from the station came, even Jeff Sullivan. I think Chad appreciated it."

"I hope you'll take family leave, honey," Myra said.

Carly bristled. The thought of staying at home in a house full of Austin's things and his memory caused the old anxiety demon to raise its head. Carly conquered this part of her life after months of therapy following her kidnapping ten years ago. She knew she'd need to start grief counseling, as she promised.

"I'd like to go back to work when the children go back to school, actually," Carly said, putting up her hand to silence the objections about to launch from everyone in the room.

"You need time to process everything, not to mention be at home for Freddy and Vivi," Kent offered. His deep baritone echoed in the otherwise quiet room.

Carly's father spoke up, having kept quiet up to this point. "You can come back to the farm with us. The country air would do you good."

"Thank you, Daddy. I need to stay with the status quo for now." She hugged her father, feeling his strength and love for her.

Carly's siblings had already left for home following the memorial service.

Austin hadn't mentioned any of Carly's siblings in his will, so they didn't need to remain for the reading. The Tabors and Evanses would stay until Tuesday.

~

June 17, 2025

Harv Ball waited for everyone to arrive at ten o'clock before starting the reading of Austin's will.

Austin's parents and sister sat opposite Carly and the Evanses, J.D. Turhune, from Roper Hospital, and Karen Wright, the director of Magnolia Cemetery in Charleston. Harv sat at the head of the table with Austin's will open in front of him.

"This is the reading of Austin Lee Tabor's will. He requested that I give this letter to his wife, Carly Tabor." Harv handed the sealed envelope to Carly. "He asked that you read it privately, after the will. I don't know what it contains, but he brought it to my office on June 6th."

Carly found the timing uncanny as she held the envelope, seeing her name written in Austin's messy doctor's script. *He delivered this to Harv the day before his accident.*

Harv continued. "To my wife, Carly, I leave my investments in stock, bonds, and an account in my name at the First Federal Bank in

Denver, Colorado." Harv looked at the ledger, which listed the final amounts of the investments. "The total of these investments came to $5.5 million dollars at the close of business yesterday."

Carly gasped. "I had no idea about the account in Denver."

"In 1997, Austin invested in a company that produced waterproof cell phone cases. Along with four college roommates, he became one of the original investors in a venture started by a former college roommate. Over the next decade, the company thrived and grew into Turtle Shell Enterprises, a billion-dollar business based in Denver that manufactures hard cases for various styles of cell phones. Last year, Austin sold his shares to another investor, earning $3.75 million from his initial one-thousand-dollar investment, which he deposited into several HYSA accounts."

Kent and Myra exchanged glances, proud of their son's business sense. Harv continued. "I bequeath $100,000 each to my beloved children, Austin Frederick and Viviene Jo, to receive their portion when they reach their twenty-first birthdays. I bequeath my vintage Porsche to my mother, Myra Tabor. To my father, Kent Tabor, I bequeath my Kansas City Chiefs season tickets.

To my sister, Ainsleigh Tabor Ralston, I bequeath $20,000 for her enjoyment and benefit. To my mother and father-in-law, Curtis and Paula Evans, I bequeath $15,000."

Harv continued to the funds mentioned for Roper Hospital. John Turhune, administrator of Roper Hospital, thanked Carly for Austin's generous gift of $50,000.

Harv mentioned Mr. Turhune's acknowledgment of the Austin Tabor Neurology wing on the Pediatric Neurology floor, which is scheduled to open after the hospital board approves the name.

Carly wiped tears at the name and gesture. The final gift came to Magnolia Cemetery.

"I bequeath $10,000 to Karen Wright, the director and administrator at Magnolia Cemetery, for the upkeep and care of the graves of Abigail

Lawson and Frederick Richards. I request that floral arrangements decorate the graves with changing seasons."

After attending to the final details, Harv thanked everyone for their attendance. He handed Carly an envelope containing a cashier's check made out to her. Leaning closer, he whispered in her ear, "Take this to your bank and deposit it until you decide what to do with it. You're a wealthy woman now, Carly. Be sure to protect your funds carefully."

Stunned by the financial secrets Austin had hidden, she shook her head in disbelief. "I had no idea," she said. "We had life insurance policies, but I wasn't aware of everything else."

Once outside, Carly put the letter from Austin and the financial papers inside her purse. Paula walked with her arm through Carly's.

She kept her voice low, "Carly, the money Austin left your father and me touched us."

Carly smiled at the generous gesture. "He loved you both."

The following day, Carly's parents left for Kansas. She walked with them to their rental car. "Thank you for being here for me and the kids. I can't wait to hear more about their time with you and Dad."

Paula hugged Carly. "You know we will always do whatever we can to help you. We love you, Freddy, and Vivi."

"As soon as I get my head together, I'll decide what to do with our house."

"You're always welcome to come home," Curt said. "You can build a nice house on Pop and Granny Eddleman's acreage."

"Thank you, Dad. I'll give it some thought. I love you."

The Tabors waited for Carly's parents to say goodbye, then carried their suitcases to their rental car. "We're only a phone call away if you need anything. We'll plan to see you, Freddy, and Vivi for Thanksgiving."

She watched them drive away and felt the weight of the future, now without Austin, on her shoulders.

~

For the first time in weeks, Carly and her children were alone. She tried to keep a strong appearance for the children but found it impossible. The shower became her grieving space.

Vivi spent the evening lying in Austin's recliner. She turned to Carly, who sat on the couch reading the latest condolence cards from the mail. "Mommy, why did Daddy go to Heaven and leave us? Didn't he want to be with us anymore?"

Carly's breath caught in her throat. She willed herself not to break down. "Oh, Vivi, Daddy wanted to be with us. Remember, he had an accident in the car and couldn't get better."

Freddy moved beside Carly on the couch, putting his head in her lap. Carly traced his jawline with her finger.

"Daddy loved you both more than anything. He didn't want to leave us, but we know we'll see him again one day."

Chapter Fifteen

In the days that followed, Carly took the children to their grief counseling appointments. They slowly resumed sports activities during the month following Austin's death. She returned to Channel 5 in the first week of July, and to her surprise, Jeff showed compassion and support for her difficult return.

Each evening, after Freddy and Vivi went to bed, she finished the paperwork needed to receive life insurance premiums and file death certificates with Social Security and other entities. She placed the urn holding Austin's ashes on their bedroom fireplace mantle after the memorial service. The unopened letter from him also rested there. She didn't know why she had waited so long to read it. Perhaps it was anger over the affair or the hurt she felt when she read the text messages between Austin and Cora.

She didn't show the messages she found on Austin's phone to Delaney. Out of respect for Carly's privacy, Delaney hadn't asked about the affair. Carly needed to tell Delaney. The grief counselor from her church helped her deal with the loss of a spouse. She felt the knowledge of his affair kept her from completely healing.

She poured a shot of Scottish whiskey she'd shipped from Edinburgh for a special occasion. She decided this was an occasion and opened the envelope while drinking from the bottle. The liquor burned a trail from her throat to her stomach, making her wonder why people tossed it back like a glass of sweet tea. Nonetheless, it couldn't make her feel any worse than she already did. She curled up on the sofa in the den and opened Austin's letter, dated May 28, 2025. She took a drink and read aloud: *Carly, you already know I'm dead since you're reading this letter. You know me, blunt is the best way to put it. First, I'm sorry for the pain my death caused you and our children.*

Carly looked up from the letter and got another drink. "Oh, Austin, you have no idea. Imagine my pain when I read the messages between you and your darling Cora." She swirled the amber liquid in the glass and toasted to an invisible drinking partner.

She continued reading. *What I'm about to tell you will be hurtful, and I'm sorry for what I've done to our marriage. In March of 2023, two years ago, my ex-wife, Cora, came to Charleston on her way to a conference in Asheville. I found myself in a mid-life crisis affair, knowing full well it would tear our marriage apart if you ever found out. I've continued to see Cora, but I've come to my senses and will end our affair.* Another drink. "Wrong again, my love. The secret's out… Cora's husband would no doubt kill you if you weren't already dead." Carly heard the words coming from her mouth, and it surprised her. She loved Austin despite his affair. At least he confessed, albeit he waited until his death to admit it. She thought for a moment about the timing. *He wrote the letter after I left for Europe, and Harv said he delivered the letter the day before the accident. If he ended the affair, why did Cora end up in his car?* Carly continued reading. *You won't have to worry about finances. I've made sure you and the children will be financially independent. There is one more thing. I'm sorry I didn't support your ability to see the spooks. Maybe you'll see me now that I am one.*

"I'll give this one to you, your quirky sense of humor almost made me laugh. I'm afraid you'll have to wait your turn, though. There's already a full house of spooks in my head, Austin."

She took another drink, finding it burned less than the first few. She finished reading the rest of the letter.

I'll love you throughout eternity and want you to live without worrying about the financial burden of raising Freddy and Vivi. The affair ended long before you received this letter. I don't know why I'm telling you now, but something makes me believe you'll know either way. Please forgive me, not because I need it, but so you can move on. I hope you'll find happiness again with another. I love you. Always, Austin.

Carly felt a tear slide down her cheek. She also felt a chill in the room. "I can't move on, Austin! You betrayed me." She belched loudly. "It's hard to forgive a ghost." She stuffed the letter into the pocket of her pajama pants. She caught the image of Austin's form as it faded from the room.

Around midnight, the sound of Carly's phone jolted her out of semi-consciousness. A text from Brooke Armstrong announced the birth of her baby boy earlier that evening. She replied, *I'm so happy for you, Brooke. Congratulations and love, Carly.*

She leaned back, her eyes heavy from the liquor. She closed them. Her head fell back against the recliner. She dreamed that the painters and contractors worked around her. Rich Trevenour, the head of the construction company working on her and Austin's 'diamond-in-the-rough,' stuck his head into the den.

"I'm sorry to bother you, but another man left the job site today." He seemed perturbed but remained respectful.

"Quit? What happened?" Carly didn't know about the previous man quitting.

"Hammers flying across the room, noises coming from the walls, seeing things that aren't there. My crew is scared half to death."

Carly knew about the odd noises she'd heard while working alone in the house. "I'm sorry, Rich. I don't know what to say."

Just then, Carly heard a child crying, which was getting louder in the room. Vivi!

She'd fallen asleep, and Vivi's crying woke her.

Carly hurried upstairs, unsure how long she'd dozed off. Vivi sat up in bed, crying for her mother.

"Sweetheart, Mommy's here." Carly slid into the bed beside Vivi.

"I want Daddy," she wailed. Soon, Freddy appeared in the doorway, having heard the commotion.

Carly felt the tears rolling down her face. "I know. I miss Daddy, too."

She pulled Freddy into the bed beside her and Vivi. She comforted the children until they settled and fell back to sleep, then went downstairs to turn off the lights.

When she reached the bottom of the stairs, she encountered young Freddy Richards, who was no longer the forlorn waif she had encountered regularly as a spirit years earlier in her home. He looked small and afraid. He was holding the hand of another child, a blonde-headed girl. A petite woman stood behind them in the shadows. The trio blocked her from moving off the bottom step.

"Freddy?" Carly whispered in disbelief.

She reached out to touch them, but they vanished. Carly reached for the banister.

Emotion overtook her, a daily occurrence since Austin's death. She gave in to the overwhelming loss that engulfed her and crumpled to the floor. She wept for her children, having to grow up without their father, and her anger over his affair. She wept for Freddy Richards, dying at the hands of Benjamin Hastings in her house two centuries ago. Perhaps selling the house would sever her connection to the past and prevent Austin's spirit from appearing to her.

As the days passed, the children began to adjust to having Carly take on both mother and father roles. Carly enrolled the children for the new school year and spoke to the headmaster about utilizing the school counselor when needed.

Freddy announced he wanted to go by *Frederick*, entered the sixth grade, and Vivi started second grade. The name change shouldn't have come as a surprise to Carly. Freddy wanted to shed the babyish name, as he called it, and become the 'man of the house'. The school notified the teachers of the change. She also shared the decision with Delaney and the grandparents.

With the children back in school, she would use her free mornings to resume working on the Bethesda haunting and grave discovery from May. Getting back into a routine helped Carly manage being over-whelmed by the paperwork and grief that had been consuming her.

On the morning of August 12th, Larry Deveroux called to say that the DNA results from the Bethesda Twelve remains had arrived, and Deveroux wanted to meet with Carly to discuss them. She texted him back to let him know her available days. Within a few moments, Larry confirmed the meeting on Friday, August 16th, at the library on Calhoun Street.

She also contacted the Summerfields to apologize for the delay in returning to Bethesda, explained the reason, and promised to return soon after speaking to Larry Deveroux.

Hospital bills and paperwork pertaining to Austin's death seemed to arrive daily. The absence of Austin and the children back in school made the house feel like a prison of sorts. *How will I manage to take care of all this on my own? You were supposed to take care of us. Everything here reminds me of you and us.*

A text from Drake Taylor piqued her interest, and news that he had found information about Gethen Bowen sparked her excitement. Since returning from the paranormal conference, Carly's visions and thoughts of the woman had happened only a few times. She started to have flashbacks of Austin's last day in the hospital.

The odd vision she had at Austin's hospital bedside of Cora Burton left her unsettled. Thankfully, their encounter ended with her not appearing again to Carly.

Carly remembered the information she'd brought back from her trip and put it on her desk in her office. She'd not gone upstairs since.

She grabbed her phone and walked upstairs to the third floor. She felt the resistance as the humidity caused the door to stick. She made a mental note to bring the dehumidifier out of the cellar upstairs.

Once inside, she noticed the odor, caused by the attic being sealed off from the rest of the house by the closed door, which reminded her of when they had bought the home. It smelled old. Carly turned on the air conditioning units to circulate air.

She sat at her desk and opened the folder of the Foundling Hospital. She'd texted Delaney earlier in the week to send the pictures she took from their *Outlander* Day trip, and she sent her pictures from Wales and Coombe Abbey. Looking at the pictures lifted her spirits and made her feel less sad.

Her curiosity got the best of her, and she decided to call Drake Taylor instead of texting. She looked at the clock on her computer. It was already five o'clock in London. She entered the number from his text and waited for him to answer. She started to end the call, getting cold feet. She felt as if she were doing something wrong. As she began to end the call, she heard his voice.

"Carly? How wonderful to hear from you!" His voice sounded as she remembered.

"Drake, it's good to hear your voice. How are you?"

Carly heard voices in the background. "I'm sorry if I've called you at an inconvenient time."

"No, no, it's fine. We're closing for the day," he said. "Let me go upstairs to my office and get my files."

Carly heard him close the door to his office. "I wanted to explain why I didn't respond to your text after I returned home," Carly began, her throat tightening. "My husband was in an accident on the way to the airport and passed away from his injuries the following day."

"I'm so sorry for your loss, Carly. Please don't feel obligated to talk now. There's no hurry."

An awkward silence followed. "Carly, do you want me to continue our call later?"

She willed herself not to break down this time.

"No, I'm fine. I want to discuss Gethen Bowen with you. Your text said you'd found information relating to him."

"I did, and I also discovered why he appeared before the magistrate at Llancaiach Fawr. Court records showed Bowen killed a man from the village of Ffos y Gerdidden. I'm sure I mispronounced it." Drake's information confirmed what she'd suspected.

"Delaney and I went to Ffos y Gerdidden. I can't explain it, but something told me to go there." Carly's memory of visiting the site and her vision of what had taken place there seemed to merge into one.

"I saw a man and woman embracing inside the doorway of a stone cottage. A shot rang out, and the man fell to the floor, bringing the woman with him." Carly remembered something else-- a name. She heard the man say, "Caroline," as the woman held him to her breast.

"Do you believe the woman, Caroline, in the vision and the woman at the Foundling Home are the same?"

"Yes. I didn't remember the man calling out Caroline until just now. How strange is that?"

Carly rubbed her eyes, confused at the sudden revelation. "Drake, I saw the same woman on the ship and also at Bethesda. They are the same."

"It's fascinating, and I look forward to hearing what you learn from the DNA results," Drake said.

"Oh, I forgot to tell you. The results of the Bethesda Twelve have returned. I'm meeting the coroner to discuss the findings." Carly looked at the time. She had to pick up Frederick and Vivi from school and take them with her to Channel 5.

"I'm sorry to cut our conversation short. It's time for me to pick up the children from school. Thank you for doing the research for me," Carly said.

"You're most welcome. We'll talk again soon, I hope," Drake said, adding, "Good night."

A smile spread across her face. "We will. Good night, Drake."

She turned off the air conditioning units and hurried downstairs to pick up the kids. She'd have enough time to grab a bite for the children and get to Channel 5 to prepare for the newscast.

Austin and Vivi carried their Happy Meals back to the break room at Channel 5 while Carly hurried to get her hair and makeup done for the six o'clock news.

Jeff Sullivan turned as she breezed past him for her chair. "No need to rush," he said, the words dripping with sarcasm.

Carly feigned an obligatory smile. "You don't have children, do you?"

Feeling the awkward exchange, Liz Green said, "Carly, you have the sweetest kids. I love when they come to work with you." She gave Jeff a side-eyed glance.

"I'm trying to find a nanny. I didn't realize how much Austin helped with our kids," Carly said.

Jeff took off his cape and folded it neatly. He put it on the chair and touched Carly's shoulder. "I think you do a wonderful job juggling everything, and no, I don't have children."

Bauer walked into the room, bringing the exchange to a close. "Carly, stop by my office when you finish up here."

Carly looked at Liz in the mirror. She rolled her eyes and continued adding loose curls to Carly's hair.

"I'll see you in a few minutes," she said to Bauer as he closed the door behind him.

Liz applied Carly's makeup and finished spraying her hair. She removed the makeup cape from around Carly. "All finished and beautiful as always."

Carly thanked Liz and walked down the hall to Bauer's office. She took a deep breath and tapped on the half-closed door.

Chapter Sixteen

Carly would have crossed herself had she been Catholic. She closed the door and took a seat in Bauer's office. Bauer took a drink of Dr. Pepper and excused the belch that followed.

"Carly, let me first say I know things are tough for you, juggling work and caring for the children."

She braced herself for the 'but'.

"But you've shown up late repeatedly, and you've taken off weeks for vacation and then bereavement leave. It disadvantages your co-anchor and the rest of the team."

"I'm sorry, Bauer. Since school began, I haven't had anyone to pick up the children and sit with them until I'm home at eight." Her tone sounded more defensive than apologetic.

"You know, I don't mind you bringing them once in a while, but you can't use Channel 5 as your childcare," he said, then added, "I'm sorry."

Carly nodded. "I understand. It won't happen again." She felt like a child reprimanded by her parents.

Bauer started to stand and walk her to the door, but she walked out and closed the door behind her.

She leaned against the door, willing the tears not to come. Taking a deep breath, she composed herself and walked down the hall into the studio.

Jeff said, "I'm sorry about the comment I made earlier. Is everything okay?"

Carly didn't want to discuss her reprimand from Bauer. She accepted his apology and said, "I'm fine. Some days suck, you know?"

The six o'clock newscast went off without a hitch. Carly appeared to have gotten her groove back, joking with Jeff at the appropriate times. The hour passed quickly, and she signed off with her usual "Good night, Charleston." She waited until the camera went off to remove her microphone. She waited for Addie to unhook her pack from the back of her dress and started for the door.

Jeff unhooked his microphone pack connected to his belt and hurried to catch up with Carly at the studio door. "Carly, if you need anything," he said, leaning closer, "I want to help."

She breathed in his cologne, and a heady feeling overtook her. She missed Austin's cologne and his warm breath on her face when he whispered his desire for her. Carly came back to reality. She stepped away from Jeff and replied, "I'm not ready for anything now."

She left Jeff at the door and walked to the break room to get Frederick and Vivi. They hurried outside, getting into Carly's vehicle to drive home. Carly turned on Bluetooth and called Delaney.

"Hi. Can you talk?" Carly asked. She merged onto Savannah Highway, turned off Bluetooth, and held her phone up to her ear.

Delaney sounded winded, "Of course, Boyd and I just walked in from playing Pickleball. What's going on?"

"Larry Deveroux contacted me about the DNA results from Bethesda. He'd like to meet and go over everything."

"Count me in. Did you find a nanny for the kids yet?"

Carly looked in the rearview mirror, seeing Frederick and Vivi watching programs on their devices. "No, and I'm getting flak from Bauer."

"I'm sorry, sweetie. Have you thought about working part-time at the station?"

Carly hadn't thought of working fewer hours on Channel 5. It might make her life less complicated. Besides, she paid off the mortgage with one of Austin's life insurance policies.

Due to Austin's other life insurance policy and his investments, Carly didn't need to work. She hadn't received all the money due to her yet but expected it soon. The thought of working at home appealed to her. Besides her close friends, she had no family in Charleston to help with the children.

"I make ends meet with far less, and I'm not a millionaire. Think about it," Delaney said.

Carly would give anything to have her life back before June 7. She wrestled with the grief she felt, coming to terms with her anger over Austin's affair.

Since Carly's revelation of the woman's name, there hadn't been time to share the news with Delaney. She wanted to tell her in person, not over the phone.

"Hey, why don't we meet tomorrow for dessert and coffee at that new pie shop down by the college?"

"I wish I could today, but I promised Boyd I'd meet him at Mama Kim's for a late lunch."

"It's okay. Tell Boyd hello for me."

Carly went into the kitchen and checked her phone. As she ate her sandwich, she scrolled down the messages. She noticed a message from Harv Ball. *I wonder what he wants?*

She called his office and waited for the receptionist to put her call through to Harv. After several minutes of listening to the annoying elevator music, she heard him pick up the phone.

"Carly, so good to hear from you. Thank you for your quick response." Harv's baritone voice sounded comforting and fatherly.

"You're welcome, Harv. What's going on?" Carly's pulse quickened.

"Well, the SLED officer returned my call, and it seems the toxicology from the driver at the accident had a high level of amphetamines in his system, namely Meth. The police report at the initial phase of investigating the accident said Austin's vehicle crossed over the center line."

Carly tried to follow where Harv was going with all of this. "I don't understand. I thought it was a closed case because of the standing water causing the cars to lose control."

"Initially, yes. But there is a street camera pointing at the intersection. At the time of the crash, the police didn't use it, for whatever reason, but since the toxicology results came back, I asked to see the video from that night."

"And did it show something different from what you thought?"

"Yes, Austin crossed into the oncoming traffic, but he corrected and returned to his lane for five seconds, according to the video." Harv cleared his throat. "Carly, the oncoming vehicle crossed into his lane, striking him head-on."

Carly felt her heart race. "Harv, what does all of this mean?"

"It means the driver, high on Methamphetamine, caused the accident. His toxicology report confirms what the video shows."

Carly fell back into her chair. "Now what happens?"

"The police arrested the driver, Cody Addison, as soon as he left the hospital. The solicitor charged him with manslaughter. His actions cost Austin and Cora Burton their lives."

The mention of Cora's name brought back the underlying anger she'd tried to repress. Her jaw tightened.

"I'll let you handle it. The thought of a trial is more than I can comprehend now."

"I'll contact you when I know more. Take care of yourself, Carly."

Her shoulders sagged, and she kneaded the knotted muscles in her neck. Her phone rang again, this time with the number displayed as unknown.

"Mrs. Tabor, this is Jamesetta Summerfield from Bethesda Academy."

Carly looked at the clock above the sink. She had to pick up Frederick and Vivi in thirty minutes.

"Yes, so nice to hear from you. Please, call me Carly."

"I wanted to speak with you regarding information I found in Bethesda's early records after speaking to Larry Deveroux."

Carly knew the time constraints didn't allow for a detailed conversation. "I'm going to pick up my children from school in a few minutes. I'd love to hear about your discovery." She walked over to the hall table to pick up her keys and backpack.

"If you're free tomorrow, I'm available to talk," Jamesetta offered.

"All right, I don't work weekends. I'll call you at ten if that works."

"I look forward to it. Thank you, Carly," she said.

Carly put her phone inside her bag and hurried out the door to pick up the children.

~

The principal at First Baptist School walked out with Frederick and Vivi. Carly waved and waited for the children to get in her vehicle. Mr. Drew walked around to Carly's window.

"Hi, Carly. I didn't have time to call you, but I've had Frederick in the office with me this afternoon."

His tone led Carly to understand that it wasn't a pleasant visit to the principal's office. There were other cars in line behind her, and Mr. Drew looked back at the different vehicles waiting to pick up their children.

"If you could pull over into the parking lot, I'd like to speak with you inside," he said.

Carly noticed Frederick's cheeks flushed, and his eyes looked red as if he'd been crying. "Yes, of course."

Carly pulled into a parking spot, shut off the car, and turned back to face Frederick. "Do you want to tell me what Mr. Drew wants to talk to me about?"

Frederick stalled, then said, "I got in a fight."

Carly sighed and grabbed her bag. "What's gotten into you? You've never gotten into trouble at school. Come on." She waited for Vivi and Frederick to follow her into the building.

Ms. Julie, the secretary, smiled at Carly. Ms. Julie, who had worked at the school for twelve years, knew the Tabors from both church and school. Carly kept her voice low, "Mr. Drew asked to speak to me."

Ms. Julie nodded, "Yes, y'all can come back to his office."

Carly, Vivi, and Frederick walked through the door and down a small hallway to Mr. Drew's office. His door was open, and he walked around his desk to meet Carly.

"Come on in, let's talk," he said, moving aside to allow them to enter.

"Frederick tells me he got into a fight today. I'm sorry."

Mr. Drew went back to his chair. "Yes, Frederick and Micah Ryders were pushing and shoving one another. According to Mrs. Lyons, Frederick knocked Micah to the ground."

Carly's jaw tightened. "Why did you push Micah down? He's your friend."

Frederick straightened, his eyes filling with tears. "He said Dad was a cheater, and you're weird because you talk to ghosts."

Carly's heart skipped a beat, and she felt her face flush. "I'm sorry, Frederick. Fighting isn't the answer."

"I spoke to both boys, and Micah apologized for saying unkind things to Frederick." He looked at Frederick, "Frederick chose not to apologize for pushing Micah to the ground."

Tears welled in Frederick's eyes. Carly thought about what the children had already endured, losing their father. "Mr. Drew, Frederick knows this is not acceptable behavior." She turned to Frederick, putting her hand on his. "Frederick will call Micah and apologize for pushing him."

"Frederick, I will let you handle this with your mother. I understand that your emotions influenced your actions. In the future, come to me before you take matters into your own hands, okay, buddy?" He smiled at Frederick and, to Carly, said, "Thank you for coming."

"Thank you, Mr. Drew. I'm sorry this happened. It won't happen again." She stood and shook Mr. Drew's hand.

Before Carly reached her vehicle, she heard her phone ping. It was Jeff Sullivan. *Hi Carly. Just a heads-up. Bauer walked by to chat. He wants to talk to you.*

Carly cursed under her breath and texted, *I'm on my way.*

It was already four-thirty. She didn't have time to run home to fix a quick bite for Frederick and Vivi.

"We'll have to grab dinner on the way home tonight. I'm sorry, guys, I'm late for work."

Chapter Seventeen

Frederick and Vivi took their iPads and went to the break room. Carly rushed to the makeup room. She looked at her reflection in the mirror, her face flushed and circles under her eyes.

"Hey, you might want to hustle. We're on in ten." Jeff Sullivan said, standing in the doorway.

Liz Greene came over to Carly with the curling iron and hairspray.

"You can start putting on your makeup while I work on your hair. We'll make it."

Carly applied a generous amount of concealer as Jeff paced in the hallway. Liz looked over her shoulder, then back to styling Carly's hair.

"What's his deal?" Liz whispered.

"He's a perfectionist. I make him a nervous wreck when I cut it close, like today."

Carly hurried with the foundation, blush, and lipstick.

"Here, let me do your eyes."

Liz applied eye shadow and her lash extensions.

Jeff looked back at Carly and then walked over to have the production assistant clip his microphone on. The anchors for the five o'clock news left the set, and Jeff hurried to take his seat.

Carly's assistant, Addie, hurried to attach her microphone pack and clip it to her lapel with fifty-nine seconds to spare.

The camera's red light blinked as the producer counted down with his finger. Carly gave a quick smile and nodded to Jeff.

The newscast began, and no one watching at home knew the frantic pace before the newscast.

At the first commercial break, Jeff leaned over to Carly and said, "Let me lead off with the next story. You don't have to do it."

Carly hadn't looked ahead at the stories for their newscast. She had the lead following the break about the driver of the car that hit Austin. "Thank you."

When the commercial break ended, Jeff read the story off the teleprompter. Carly saw Austin's picture and felt her throat tighten. She swallowed back the urge to cry. Austin's dark hair and suntanned complexion portrayed his good looks, but the following picture showed the mangled car and a man in handcuffs walking into the courtroom. When the story ended, she delivered the next segment without missing a beat. In the following commercial break, Liz came out with makeup to touch up Carly.

"Hang in there, girl." Liz brushed the powder from Carly's jacket and gave her shoulder a sympathetic squeeze.

Carly nodded, "I thought I might lose it during that segment, but I made it through. Will it ever get easier?"

"No, you learn to manage it," Liz said as she walked away.

As Carly ended the broadcast, she saw Austin in the reflection of the control room's glass window. When she turned, he vanished.

"You okay?" Jeff asked as he took off his battery and mic.

"Yeah, I'm fine." A cold chill ran up Carly's arms.

Jeff smiled, helping Carly with her mic. "Yes, you're definitely fine."

Carly didn't know what to make of Jeff's not-so-subtle flirting.

"I know it's last minute, but how about dinner tonight? My treat," Jeff said.

He walked with her to her cubicle to retrieve her backpack from the file cabinet. The late-night anchors were in the break room, so Jeff and Carly had the area to themselves.

"I have the kids with me, and I didn't get a chance to feed them supper." She remembered the awkward meeting with Mr. Drew earlier, which caused her to run late.

"Great! I found a great pizzeria near my condo. Whattaya say?" he asked with a boyish smile and Boston accent.

"Well, I *do* have to feed the kids, and they love pizza." She gave a sideways grin. "But it's my treat. You saved my ass earlier with your text."

He scratched his chin and said, "I'd save your ass and anything else if you'd let me."

Carly started to reprimand Jeff for his forward comment, but he retracted it. "I'm sorry. I'll watch it."

They both laughed at the inside joke as they walked down to the break room together.

Frederick and Vivi were unsure of Carly's co-worker. They saw Carly laughing and having a good time. Soon, they, too, warmed up to Jeff Sullivan. He shared that he had nieces and nephews their age and talked sports with Frederick. Vivi laughed at his silly antics when he blew the end of the straw paper at her.

Austin and Carly often walked with Frederick and Vivi to D'Allesandro's Pizza on King Street, which was conveniently located near their home. They ate and played on their iPads as Carly and Jeff made small talk.

"I haven't eaten inside a restaurant since..." Carly paused, "In a long time."

Jeff looked across the table at the kids, lowering his voice. "How are they doing?"

"It's still hard on them, especially at night," Carly shared, keeping the reason for her late arrival at the station—a meeting with the principal—to herself.

"Glad I persuaded you to join me for supper. It gets old eating alone."

"I know the kids love getting out of the house… it does get old."

"You should do this more often with me," Jeff said, suggestively raising his eyebrows.

"Maybe, once I figure out who I'll hire as a nanny for them," she said, looking at the kids.

"Okay, just remember the offer stands."

Jeff paid the check before Carly could reach her purse. She thanked him, and they walked outside.

Carly, Frederick, and Vivi thanked Jeff for a fun evening before heading to their vehicle. Carly waited for Jeff to pull out of his parking space, then she followed.

Once they arrived home, Frederick followed Carly and Vivi into the den, dreading the punishment awaiting him.

"Vivi, why don't you go upstairs and take your shower first? Frederick and I need to talk."

Vivi hugged Carly, "Thank you for taking us to eat pizza."

It surprised Carly. "You're welcome, honey. We need to do it more often."

After they were alone, Carly sat beside Frederick on the couch. "Frederick, it's too late to call Micah tonight. Before school tomorrow, I'd like you to apologize to him."

Frederick lowered his eyes, his jaw set. "He said Dad cheated. What did he mean?"

Carly cursed Austin under her breath. The words stung; she shouldn't have to explain Austin's affair to a ten-year-old. "Daddy loved us very much. When you're older, I'll explain it to you. It is hard to understand."

Frederick raised his head to look directly into Carly's eyes. "Mom, do you talk to ghosts?"

Carly remembered her promises to Austin: Don't bring the 'spooks' home, and don't involve the children in the paranormal. She inhaled and said, "I do, but not like you see on TV shows."

"But I thought there's no such thing as ghosts." Frederick's expression changed to one of confusion and perhaps fear at his mother's admission.

"Buddy, you know about Heaven, where Jesus, God, and the angels live. Daddy is there, too." Carly tried to answer his question without scaring him.

"And the Devil lives down there," He pointed to the floor. "I don't want to go there."

Carly smiled, "No, we don't." She knew Frederick needed to hear her deny Micah's charge against her. Instead, she told him the truth.

"Sometimes I help people move on to where they'll spend eternity."

"So, you talk to dead people?" Frederick asked, his voice a whisper. "Do you talk to Dad?"

"No, I haven't talked to your dad." Carly hugged Frederick. It wasn't exactly the truth, but she avoided explaining. "You don't have to worry about ghosts."

"Is that why you went with Aunt Delaney on the trip?"

"Yes, she helps people, too."

Carly's broken promise to Austin caused her pangs of guilt, but she didn't want to lie to Frederick, either.

Frederick laid his head on Carly's shoulder, his face hidden from her. "Mom, do you think we made Dad mad that we went to supper with Mr. Sullivan?"

Carly experienced mixed feelings about going, and now Frederick questioned her decision.

"Buddy, I don't know what people in Heaven see back here on Earth, but I think he would understand if someone wanted to show us kindness."

The explanation seemed to pacify Frederick's worry about enjoying a night out. He turned to his mother, tears in his eyes. "I miss Dad and wish he could've taken us to get pizza."

The sadness overtook them both. "I miss Dad too, Buddy." Carly pulled Frederick close, and they wept together.

August 16th, 2025

Delaney picked up Carly after she dropped off the kids at school. The two friends hadn't seen each other since Carly's meeting with Bauer. Delaney was taken aback by the news of Frederick's fight at school and Carly's admission of her abilities to Frederick.

"You did the only thing you could, sweetie," Delaney reassured.

"I know, you're right. I'd hoped to keep the kids innocent of what Austin did, as well as never tell them I see the dearly departed."

"He's tough like his momma. You did the right thing."

Austin's life insurance check arrived earlier in the week, and Carly told Delaney she'd stopped by her financial advisor's office to manage the funds.

"I'm tossing around the idea of selling my house." Carly waited for the reaction.

Delaney shot a surprised look at Carly. "Sell? I thought you loved your house."

"I did; I mean, I do. It's too big for me, Delaney, not to mention the upkeep."

"Well, you certainly can afford it. Just don't rush into it now. You shouldn't make any business decisions for at least a year."

Carly's mouth scrunched. "You're right. It's too soon to sell the only home my kids have ever known."

Delaney pulled into the Charleston Public Library, finding a spot near the back entrance.

They walked inside, heading to the lower level, where Larry Deveroux waited. Two sets of stapled pages lay on a research table across from him.

"Carly, Delaney, good to see you both," he said, standing.

"Hi, Larry. Thank you for meeting us here. What's the scoop on the Bethesda Twelve?" Carly asked, referring to the bones found at Bethesda Day School.

"It's amazing what forensic science can tell us." Larry took out a collection of colored graphs with a map of the world. He handed them copies of each, along with the papers on the table. The company over-seeing the DNA specimens highlighted several regions on the map of the United Kingdom.

"This looks pretty intense," Delaney said.

Carly studied the map, noticing the countries of Wales, Scotland, and England in fluorescent colors.

Larry explained, "The bones went to a forensic anthropology facility in upstate New York, as well as a lab in Switzerland. Both returned results that confirmed the race and sex of the bones, as well as the location where the deceased came from."

Carly looked closer at the results. "It's remarkable, Larry. Will it even date the bones?"

"Yes, all the deceased were alive during the eighteenth century. The lab utilized carbon-14 dating, as well as stable isotopes derived from both bones and dental remains. The time includes the period during which Bethesda operated as an orphanage in the late 1700s."

"The scientific terms are confusing at best," Carly said as she scanned the findings.

Larry took a map of the excavated burial site from his briefcase. "There were a variety of grave goods included with the burials. These items were also instrumental in dating the period from the area, along with the bones."

"Your own Dr. Brooke Armstrong, here in Charleston, worked on enslaved remains found on Anson Street. Using the same techniques, the remains proved to be from the same family and region in Sri Lanka. We used her original research for our case in Savannah."

"I had no idea Brooke participated in such ground-breaking research not far from my home," Carly remarked.

"I saw enslaved spirits when we visited the site. Were any of the bones of African descent?" Delaney inquired.

"No, none were from Africa. However, the team located an infant's remains among the bones collected." Larry said.

"I saw an infant in one of the women's arms," Carly said.

"One of the women in the collection most likely died in childbirth or soon after, along with the child."

Carly thought back to the vision of the woman on the ship. She looked pregnant.

Delaney tried to make sense of the numbers and graphs.

"The information is hard to understand. For those of us who didn't excel in biology, tell us in simple terms what we're looking at."

"Of course, from the bones collected for analysis, all were from the United Kingdom. The three were from Wales, and the rest from England."

"Wales?" Carly gasped.

"Yes, and one adult female in her twenties," Larry said as he read the notes on the page. "The woman, infant, and one of the children have the same family DNA."

The rest of what Larry read didn't register with Carly. Her thoughts swirled. The woman at the cottage, in the museum, at the gravesite—it was the same woman.

"Larry, the woman in her twenties, from Wales- I've seen her in multiple visions, and she has appeared to me."

"Are you sure?" Delaney asked.

"Yes, I'm sure, and I know her name- Caroline." Carly's heart was racing.

CHAPTER EIGHTEEN

Carly and Delaney went back to Carly's house after Larry's bombshell results from the carbon dating and DNA results.

Carly fixed them both a glass of tea and sat at the table.

Delaney put the papers down. "You said you knew her name was Caroline. When did you figure it out?"

"The other night, I dreamed about her and the man at the cottage. As he fell onto her, I heard him call out her name before he died. He said, 'Caroline'."

"It's amazing that you remembered that from a dream."

"Delaney, what's more amazing is we share a name." Carly brought her hand to her heart.

"What? I don't understand."

"When I was born, Mom couldn't decide on a 'C' name. Granny told her she must name me Caroline Emily."

Carly's eyes sparkled as she told the story the way she heard Granny tell it. "I dreamed you had another dark-haired baby girl, and her name was Caroline Emily."

"Wow. What the heck?" Delaney said, shaking Carly's arm.

"I know, but no one really knows that's my given name. Mom appeased Granny, but insisted everyone call me Carly, a combination of the two."

"So, they both got their way. Don't you find it interesting that she dreamed about the name Caroline?"

"I do. I wanted to tell you about my dream after I remembered it, but you and Boyd had plans. I didn't want to tell you over the phone."

"No, I'm not mad. I find it interesting you share the same name."

"Chalk it up to coincidence. I do feel like we share so many commonalities, though."

Delaney took a drink. "I'm confused about why she and her children started appearing to you, not to mention how they ended up at Bethesda?"

"I had another strange dream. The other night, I fell asleep, and Rich Trevenour, the contractor we used in renovating the house, and I were discussing the odd things happening while he worked here."

"Odd to remember that now. I remember Rich. I get the feeling there's more to the story," Delaney added.

"The dream went from poltergeist occurrences to me seeing ghosts."

"That's when you reached out to me. It seems like a lifetime ago," Delaney said. "What about Freddy?"

"I saw Freddy Richards with an older girl and someone standing in the shadows. At first, I didn't think it was him."

"I can imagine it was a shock seeing him again. We helped him move on."

"I thought so, too. I felt like he wanted to show me something."

"I won't lie; Freddy Richards in the house again can't be good, but strange you dreamed about him and Rich." Delaney pulled the afghan from behind her and threw it over her shoulders, suddenly feeling a cold chill.

Carly pulled her knees under her, turning to face Delaney. "I've also seen Austin."

"Oh, sweetie." Delaney reached over and patted Carly's arm. "It doesn't surprise me, the way he passed."

Carly bristled. "It's more like what he did to me and his guilty conscience. I'm angry, Delaney. I can't forget it."

Delaney tried to comfort her. "Of course. It's so traumatic."

The tears fell, and Carly found herself telling Delaney about Jeff Sullivan taking her and the kids to dinner. "I saw Austin's reflection in the control room window the other night. Subconsciously, I think the only reason I went was because I wanted to hurt Austin."

Delaney listened, letting Carly continue. "It wasn't until Frederick asked me about his dad being upset that we went out for pizza with Jeff that I felt I had cheated on Austin."

She grabbed a tissue and blew her nose.

"I think what you're feeling is part of the grieving process. I went through the anger when Mark died suddenly."

"I'm sorry, Delaney. You're also a widow. You never let your grief show."

"You should have seen me, all alone, with Jarrod starting his first year of high school." Delaney's eyes filled with tears. "I cried and moped around for months."

"I'm glad you and Boyd found each other. He's good for you," Carly said.

"Speaking of Boyd, I should get moving. We're driving down to Edisto tonight for an investigation."

"Thanks for letting me vent. We need to make a trip to Savannah. I told Jamesetta I'd get back with her."

Delaney took out her phone and checked her calendar. "I don't have to babysit this week. I can go on Saturday if that works for you."

"I'll ask Elise Ravenel's daughter to come over to watch the kids."

"Sounds good." Delaney took her copy of the DNA results from the table and hugged Carly before walking out the door.

After she left, Carly checked the time. She had a couple of hours to spare before she needed to pick up the kids from school, so she called Drake Taylor. Her prepaid calling promotion would end at the end of the month, and she felt guilty using it to call Drake. Austin had only been gone a couple of months. She must be a horrible person. Regardless, she wanted to talk to him.

"Hello, Drake, it's Carly." Her voice echoed in the otherwise quiet house.

"Carly, what a pleasant surprise."

Carly didn't hear any chatter in the background, so he must have had the office to himself. "I hope I'm not calling at a bad time."

"No, I'm finished for the day. I'm on my way home."

Carly smiled. His voice sounded calm, almost sensual. Her cheeks flushed. "I spoke to the coroner this morning. He brought a copy of the forensic results on the bones from Bethesda."

"Great news, I hope?" Drake said.

"Actually, yes. It's better than I expected. If you have time, I'd love to tell you about it."

"I'm all yours."

Carly explained the different tests and laboratories that analyzed the twelve sets of remains. "Forensic anthropology has come a long way. The results tell the region where the deceased originated."

"I'm intrigued. Go on," Drake prompted.

"Well, of the twelve, two of the deceased were teenagers and one, a female, mid to late twenties, from Wales."

"Wales, you say. Were any others from Wales?"

"Yes, a young girl, somewhere between the ages of six and eight, and a small infant, perhaps a newborn. All three shared family DNA."

No one spoke for a few seconds before Carly continued. "I believe we've seen the same woman, Drake. You saw her at the museum, and

I've seen her in visions and apparitions both in Wales and England, as well as in Bethesda."

"I find it remarkable we've encountered the same woman, but why?"

Carly shared another revelation with Drake. "The other night, I had a dream about her and the man murdered in the cottage. He called her Caroline."

"Carly, that's astounding. Now you have a name."

"Yes, it's huge. Caroline's remains are one of the remains found at Bethesda."

"So, we're looking for the name *Caroline* in the Foundling Home records that match the same woman at Bethesda?"

"Yes, I'm going there next. I plan to search the original records of orphans and workers at Bethesda."

Drake reminded Carly of the letter found in the museum's artifacts room. "If you find the arrival of orphans on the same date as the letter, perhaps you'll find Caroline."

Carly checked the time. She had to change clothes and pick up Frederick and Vivi. "I'll have to continue our conversation later. I need to pick up the kids and go to the television studio."

"No worries, Carly. I look forward to speaking with you whenever the opportunity arises. Take care."

She ended the call and hurried upstairs to get ready for the evening's newscast.

"Hello, Jamesetta. I wanted to chat with you regarding the forensic information I received from Larry Deveroux."

"Good to hear from you, Carly. As a matter of fact, Mr. Deveroux called us last night, and he just left the house after meeting with Darrick and me."

"Oh, then you're both up to date with everything."

"Yes, but the information we received overwhelmed us. I can't wrap my head around all the things he shared."

"I'm amazed as well. Would you still be okay with me coming and perusing the records?" Carly asked.

"Did you have a day in mind? We're back at school, as you know."

"Delaney and I cleared Friday off our schedules. Will that work with you?"

Jamesetta paused and then confirmed that Friday would work. Carly thanked her and ended the call. She telephoned Grace Ravenelle to see if she'd pick up the kids and take them back to Carly's house on Friday. With a sitter confirmed, she and Delaney could spend the day in Savannah.

Frederick and Vivi were in the den, watching television, while she made notes about her visions and the information she had received regarding the remains of The Bethesda Twelve. None of the male children were related to the woman, and two females and the infant came from Wales. *Why did Freddy Richards and a young girl appear to me? Also, who stood in the shadows where I couldn't see a face?* Something gnawed at Carly. She put her head in her hands, rubbing her temples. Her head jerked up. *That's it! I know who Caroline is."*

She almost ran up the stairs to the third floor, Frederick and Vivi on her heels. Carly turned to see their worried faces. "It's okay. I just remembered something, and I need to find it in my office."

Frederick rolled his eyes at his sister. "Come on, let's go back downstairs."

Vivi smiled at Carly and followed her brother back downstairs. Once they were in the den, Carly finished going to the third floor. She felt the afternoon heat slam into her body as soon as she opened the door. *Now, where are those notes?* Carly went to the file cabinet and began searching for the files labeled *Charleston Orphan Asylum.* In short order, she retrieved the file folder containing the copies from the historical society, dated 2013. She remembered Harlan Greene's notes and highlighted information Carly checked regarding Celeste Pettigrew and the work at the asylum. She leafed through the pages of inmates throughout the 1790s. Her finger slid down the names until she came to Frederick Richards. *He was admitted on September 25, 1794, at the age of 3, by his mother, Susannah Richards. Runaway: January 19, 1799.*

Carly felt as if she'd been sucker punched in her gut. She searched further down the page, but no other Richards matching the date appeared. She sat on the floor, wiping the sweat off her face as the heat became oppressive. *I don't understand. How is Freddy connected to all of this? I felt confident that Freddy's mother was Caroline Richards.*

Defeated, Carly returned the file to the cabinet. She wiped the perspiration from her face with the hem of her shirt. *Well, nothing ventured, nothing gained.* She closed the door to the upstairs apartment and joined the children in the den.

Carly relaxed in the receiving room, sipping a glass of sweet tea. The antique mantle clock struck midnight. She thought back to the 1799 murder of Andrew and Celeste Pettigrew in this very room. The hauntings of the Pettigrews and their murderer, Ben Hastings seemed distant memories. She had a sense of accomplishment in discovering the murder after two hundred years, along with the unknown murder of Freddy Richards. *Why did you come back, Freddy? You went to Heaven. I don't understand.* Carly felt the wine relaxing her, making her eyes feel like lead weights. She massaged the back of her neck, kneading the muscles and trying to relieve the tension she felt. Soon, she drifted into a deep sleep.

Behind the house were two headstones, one with fresh dirt mounded over the ground. She placed fresh bouquets of dainty daffodils on each, crouching down to remove the wilted flowers. Tears fell from her eyes, soaking the front of her chemise. Her stomach lurched, and she vomited the breakfast she'd just finished. How would she feed another mouth without a man to tend the fields? She wiped her mouth and the tears, stood, and let out a scream which echoed across the fields. "Damn you to hell, Gethen Bowen."

The Grandfather clock in the hallway struck two o'clock. Carly rubbed her eyes and searched for her phone to light the room. Disoriented, she remembered drinking wine before dozing off. She must have dreamed about the woman at the cottage in Wales. Her mind raced forward to the urn upstairs holding Austin's ashes. Austin's parents discussed having a burial service in Kansas when Carly was ready. He'd been gone for almost two months. She'd think about it later when she could plan for time off from work—no sense asking Bauer so soon after her bereavement leave and taking off from the news tonight. For now, Austin would remain inside the closet next to his favorite Kansas sports attire. She couldn't bear to look at the urn. He hadn't moved on, as she told Frederick.

Carly went upstairs to her bedroom and changed into her pajamas. She felt a presence in the room, and she refused to give in to the urge to turn on the light. Instead, she crawled into her bed and pulled the covers over her head. She turned over on her side to ignore the spirit in the room, knowing full well it was Austin.

"Did you bring a copy of the letter from London?" Delaney asked as she put on her sunglasses.

Carly mentally checked off the items she had brought with her. "Yes, it's in with the other copies I made from the Foundling Museum."

"Was Bauer miffed when you took off tonight?"

Carly cleared her throat. "Well, he wasn't happy. I told him I was using the bereavement day I had left."

"Well played. You should have taken more time off than you did." Delaney put the visor down as the sun shone in her eyes.

As they drove down I-95, the heat from the hot August asphalt at eight o'clock a.m. created the optical illusion of waves crossing the road. Carly turned the air conditioning up a notch.

"It looks like we should get to Bethesda in about twenty-five minutes. It doesn't seem like the drive takes two hours," Delaney said, reading the MapQuest information on her phone.

"Did Larry give a date for the reburial of the bones at Bethesda?" Carly asked.

"I don't think he said. I'm sure the historic preservationists will expect a monument with names or something to observe the small graveyard."

In the time it took Carly to navigate through Savannah to Bethesda Academy, they had wolfed down their grilled chicken wraps and chips, which Carly had packed.

As they entered Bethesda through the curved wrought iron and brick entrance, Carly said, "You know, I was certain that Freddy Richards's mother was Caroline Richards, so I felt disappointed when the records revealed Susannah instead."

"I'm sure there's a reason Freddy's spirit visited you the other night. Maybe the connection between Bethesda and the Orphan Asylum in Charleston has something to do with it, and it isn't a bad thing."

Carly passed the academy, noticing a group of young men entering the building. She and Delaney returned the wave to them and continued to the front of the dormitory to meet Jamesetta.

"I spoke to Drake about Caroline. I'm hoping he can search for information about her and the man who died from the gunshot. I dreamed about her again."

Delaney arched her eyebrows, not a word spoken. Carly smiled, knowing what Delaney meant without her saying it.

"It's all platonic. I'm still trying to deal with Austin and my emotions from losing him. Twice."

Her intended meaning didn't escape Delaney. "Sweetie, you're dealing with anger and grief together. You have every right to talk to

Drake," she said, softening her tone. "Besides, *you* aren't betraying your marriage vows."

Carly wiped away the tear that slid from the corner of one eye. "Touche. I mentioned Drake to Dr. Durban during our virtual visit the other day."

"Oh? And what did she say?"

"She mentioned that I might be replacing the male companionship I lost when Austin died with Drake. I explained to her the connection we have through Caroline.

"Does she know you're, uh, that you see spirits?" Delaney said cautiously.

"Yes, and she doesn't comment about it. She listens and then tries to make sense of it." Carly looked away, focusing on the large tree in front of the dormitory. "I've thought about seeing someone else who doesn't know I'm a sensitive."

Carly became a patient of Dr. Janet Durban after her kidnapping and the subsequent death of Joella McGee. She dealt with the fear of being alone with her guilt, putting Joella in danger the night of the vigil for Cadence Davis. Austin suggested she continue going to therapy, even when Carly felt she'd conquered her *demons,* as she put it. Carly tried to put the paranormal behind her, even though she and Delaney attended Paranormal conferences on request over the years. Her story had its *fifteen minutes of fame* for months after the James Van Ness serial killer story died down. She became famous in paranormal research circles after the murder of James Van Ness in prison, and the story came full circle again.

Carly stopped going with Boyd and Delaney on investigations. It wasn't until she started having dreams and visions of Caroline and other spirits that she opened that part of her life again.

"Grief counseling is good for you. But if Dr. Durban makes you feel uncomfortable, try someone new."

Carly patted Delaney's knee before turning off the ignition. "I will. I'm taking things one day at a time."

Jamesetta met them on the front steps of the dormitory. "Welcome, ladies."

Carly reached into the back seat and grabbed the leather bag. "Thanks for making time for us today," she said.

Jamesetta led Carly and Delaney down a narrow hallway to a small office. "This was once Reverend Whitefield's personal space."

The room had a single window opening to the side of the building, with the Moon River flowing beyond. An ancient desk, small but worthy of its owner, faced the window.

Jamesetta pointed out that the desk belonged to Reverend Whitefield and had remained in the room throughout the various administrations of Bethesda Academy over the last two hundred years.

Three small glass-doored bookcases lined the wall adjacent to Reverend Whitefield's desk. These contained the volumes of books in which the orphans who arrived at Bethesda were recorded. Jamesetta pointed to other volumes containing the transfer of inmates, as they were called, to various families upon adoption and the removals to other orphan asylums north of Savannah.

Carly and Delaney surveyed the task before them. It would take several hours to go through each volume. Carly reached inside her bag to find a copy of the letter she had brought from London from Nathaniel Duncan, Esq., to Miss Louisa Albertson.

"Jamesetta, we found this letter in the archives at the London Foundling Museum," Carly said, handing the copy to Jamesetta. "It is from a Mr. Nathaniel Duncan, from Bethesda."

Jamesetta read the letter. "Very interesting. Did Bethesda bring orphans from the London Foundling Home to adopt out here in the colony?"

"From what we gathered, there must've been an ongoing arrangement between the two," Delaney interjected.

"We're hoping to find an entry of orphans from London around the same time as the letter states. Correspondences between Mr. Duncan and the Foundling Hospital might tell us more about Miss Albertson and the arrangements." Carly took the letter back from Jamesetta.

"I have things to do around here, but please help yourself with the books. Some of the ink has faded," said Jamesetta.

"Can we make copies?" Delaney asked.

"No, but I ask that you let me make the copies for you. Other than that, if you have any questions, holler."

"Thank you. We will." Carly turned and started with the first volume. She handed Delaney one, and they started the search.

Chapter Nineteen

Carly stood, stretching her legs. Delaney held onto the side of the desk as she stood. They had spent the last two hours painstakingly going through pages of early orphan records. The early volumes, dating from 1745 to 1760, were returned to their original location. Another stack contained orphan records, building information, and records of servants who came to Bethesda to construct two dormitories after a fire in 1764.

"How about a restroom break? I need to give my knees a stretch." Delaney walked to the doorway.

"You go ahead. I'm going to peruse the next stack," Carly said, returning to the stack of books.

She reached for the next volume, which held the names of the inmates who arrived between 1770 and 1790. The ledger contained the names of the vessels on which the orphans arrived, as well as their names and ages. As with the ledgers from the Charleston Orphan Asylum, some entries also included the name of the person who left the child, along with their relationship to the child.

The name London Foundling Hospital appeared more regularly

during this period. A smallpox outbreak took the lives of twenty-seven people over several months, according to the record. From April 1793 through October 1793, orphans were listed as deceased due to smallpox.

Carly saw a notation that included the initials ND. *Could this be Nathaniel Duncan?* Carly hurried to the next page as Delaney returned.

"Find anything interesting?" Delaney asked.

"I think so. Look at this," Carly said, pointing to the notation with the initials ND.

"Do you think it's our Mr. Duncan?"

"It appears to fit the same time as the letter." She turned the page to find a list of ten orphans, all of whom had been admitted on the same date, December 15, 1794.

Delaney read the names over her shoulder. "Looks like the ship *Mary Galley* brought the orphans from the Foundling Hospital."

Carly scanned the list of names. "I don't see an Albertson on the list as the one who sponsored the orphans. Oh, here is a Mistress Prothro. Not our Miss Albertson."

They kept searching through the records. The next book revealed something important. Delaney scanned the list of entries and then found a name: Frederick Richards.

"Carly! Here, I found Freddy Richards." Delaney spun around from her chair, eyes as big as saucers.

"What? Our Freddy?" Carly leaned across the desk to see the names written in neat script. *August 17, 1794~ Elizabeth Richards, 6; Frederick Richards, 3; Eira Richards, 1 year 8 months.*

Arrived aboard the Mary Galley today with their mother, Mistress Richards, who has arranged for transport to South Carolina.

"Could this be the same Freddy? Did you know he had two sisters?" Delaney asked.

"No, I didn't find anything about a sister in the orphan records at Charleston. Did his mother take the others but leave Freddy behind?" Carly couldn't fathom the mother leaving him.

"Didn't you find his mother dropped him off in September of 1794? It listed the mother's name as Susannah Richards." Delaney wrote the name on the top of a sheet of notepad she'd brought with her.

"Something isn't adding up. Let's have Jamesetta copy this for us. We'll keep searching." Carly said, then went to the doorway to call Jamesetta.

Jamesetta appeared, wiping her hands on a towel. She'd been preparing a casserole for the boys who boarded at the dormitory. "Did you find something interesting?"

Carly handed her the ledger to copy. "If you could make a couple of copies of this page, I'd appreciate it."

"I'll be right back."

Delaney found a volume including inmate adoption and deaths for the years 1790-1800. Carly checked her phone for the time. It was two o'clock. She wanted to get back on the road to avoid the late-afternoon traffic. "Let's finish looking through the books we have on the table, then we'll have to come back another day."

Delaney sat down and read the entries. She had read the first six pages when Jamesetta returned with the copies. "Hold on, Jamesetta. I think I found the Bethesda Twelve."

"Read what you found," Carly said, excited at the possibility of good news.

"It says here that a typhoid outbreak, brought by the ship *Mary Galley, took the lives of twelve passengers, as well as six inmates. The passengers were given a Christian burial in a common grave on the sixth of September instant.*"

"I believe that means the current year, 1794. Go on," Carly said.

"The names are hard to decipher. It appears that John Davidson, aged 6 years; Tabitha Woodbridge, aged 16 years; Sarah Strange, aged 4; Eleanor Dodds, aged 16; Elizabeth Richards, aged 6; Caroline Richards, aged twenty-seven years," Delaney said. She stopped reading.

"Her name *was* Caroline. I knew it." Carly sat back in the chair, overcome with emotion. She and Delaney fist bumped.

After a moment, Delaney continued. "James Creighton, aged six years; infant girl, Catrin Richards, aged two days; Alice Arthur, aged three years; Alston Lee, aged twelve years; Samuel Lee, aged nine years; and Thomas Olson, aged thirty-one years."

"The baby, Catrin, Caroline, and her daughter, Elizabeth, all died from typhoid fever. That left Freddy and his younger sister, Eira, without their mother."

Jamesetta brought her hands together in a loud clap. "You did it. I'll hurry and make the copies of this for you." She turned with the book in hand, leaving Carly and Delaney overjoyed with the revelation.

"Well, that tells us what happened to them, but who brought Freddy to Charleston, and what happened to Eira?" Carly asked.

"We have some time—let's look for information about Miss Albertson." Delaney searched the volumes left for any mention of the woman's name.

After another hour, they searched through the remaining books for the relevant period. None mentioned Miss Albertson. They did locate a volume pertaining to Nathaniel Duncan's dissolution of employment. Carly wrote down the date and planned to look at the Newspaper.com account she still had. If Mr. Duncan's association with Bethesda resulted in termination, the newspaper might have a story related to it.

At four-thirty, Carly and Delaney finished returning all the volumes they had read to the bookcases. Jamesetta walked with them to Carly's SUV.

"We plan on having all the bones returned to the burial grounds on the property. I don't know how to proceed, but perhaps there is room where Freddy Richards is buried to include the remains of his mother and sisters?" Jamesetta asked.

"That's a wonderful idea. I'm sure there will be red tape, but I'll speak to my friend, Brooke Armstrong, as well as Larry Deveroux. Thank you again, Jamesetta.”

Carly accepted Jamesetta's hug. “I don't think you and Darrick will have any more issues with the spirits. I think Caroline needed me to find her.”

They drove away from Bethesda Academy, feeling great accomplishment and good fortune in locating the information. “Thank the Lord above for record-keeping. And to think that place caught on fire more than once.”

“That's right, and that personal room of Reverend Whitefield survived both fires,” Carly said.

On the ride back to Charleston, Delaney and Carly discussed possible scenarios regarding Susannah Richards's identity. Also, Carly's dream of Caroline at the two graves began to resurface.

“I couldn't make out the names on the headstones, but she put flowers on both of them. I think she was carrying the child who died within days after birth at Bethesda.”

“Caroline will show you, I'm sure.”

“There's more to the story, Delaney. I believe the baby belonged to the man Gethen Bowen murdered.”

Carly called Grace after they left Savannah. “Hi, Grace. How's everything going?”

Grace gave Carly the lowdown on the afternoon, letting the kids talk to her. “Auntie Delaney and I will be there after dinner. I left Grace money for pizza.”

“Tell the kiddos hi for me,” Delaney said.

Carly put the phone on speaker so they could talk to Delaney. “I'll see you all in about two hours. Save me a piece of pizza,” she said.

“Grace, I left the pizza money on the bar. Go ahead and get two; we'll eat when we get there.”

Carly turned off her phone. “Well, it sounds like everything is going well. I'm so glad Grace likes to babysit.”

"You'll have to call Larry tomorrow and give him the 411 on the names we found today. I still can't believe we found them so easily," Delaney said.

"I'm sure he will want to toot the horn of the Chatham County coroner's office using the latest DNA testing. It's a huge nod to Brooke Anderson's prior research."

Delaney agreed. "I hope the remains of Freddy, Caroline, and her children can rest together."

Carly thought about Austin's wishes in his will. "I think Austin would advocate for it, and I'm sure he would want to have one large headstone for all."

The funds set aside for Magnolia Cemetery provided for the upkeep of Freddy Richards and Abigail Lawson's graves. The gift from Austin's will covered the cost of a proper burial and headstone. After speaking with Larry and Brooke about it, she would make a point of mentioning it to the cemetery manager.

"Proving the woman is Freddy Richards's mother is another matter. I don't want to dampen your enthusiasm, but it might not happen," Delaney said.

"I know. Proving Caroline, Elizabeth, and the infant to Freddy Richards hinges on my ability to see the spirits of the dead."

"If it's any consolation, we know who they are, and you can pay your respects to them anytime at Bethesda."

"I have to find out what happened to Eira."

Carly watched Frederick's soccer team take the field. Vivi and a friend sat beside her, eating snacks and watching the game. She looked around at the spectators: dads advising from the sidelines, moms in yoga pants and baseball caps providing water bottles on cue, coaches yelling instructions to players. Carly smiled. Her attire matched theirs. Austin loved watching Frederick play whatever sport he participated in. She tried not to let herself fall into despair for what wasn't but instead focused on what was right now. As the weeks passed, Carly found herself having fewer breakdowns and sharing more with her new therapist, Dr. Ross Hunter.

A warm breeze caught the dry leaves and lifted them magically into the air, reminding Carly of the simpler things she'd lately become oblivious to. Frederick scored a goal and instantly looked at Carly, smiling ear to ear. "Good job, Buddy!" she called out. Vivi clapped and whooped as well. Carly felt her phone vibrating in her pants pocket. She looked at the message—*Good morning, Carly. Wonderful news. At your convenience, I'd like to discuss information regarding Gethen Bowen with you. Regards, Drake.*

Carly returned a quick text to acknowledge Drake's message and explained she would telephone this afternoon. Her imagination ran wild, wondering what Drake found. She also wanted to update him on her recent trip to Bethesda. Her information was still lying on her desk upstairs. Between work and the children's schedules, Carly hadn't made it to the historical society to look through the orphan asylum records. The remains of the Bethesda Twelve stay for now in the possession of the Chatham County Coroner's office. Jamesetta and Darrick Summerfield were also waiting for information on the reinternment at the Bethesda graveyard.

As soon as the game ended, Carly gathered up the chairs and Frederick's soccer gear. She engaged in small talk with other parents, then loaded up the kids and gear and drove to their favorite pizza parlor.

As the server walked them to their booth, a familiar face turned and waved to them. Jeff Sullivan had just sat down and was finishing his drink order.

"Hi, who won the match?" he asked Frederick.

Frederick looked at Carly as if he needed permission—his grin displaying the dimples he'd inherited from Carly. "We did. I scored two goals."

"That's awesome, kiddo," Jeff said, giving Frederick a high-five. "Did you play today, young lady?" he asked Vivi.

Vivi shook her head, too shy to speak. Carly answered, "No, Vivi isn't into soccer. She's Frederick's cheerleader."

Jeff started to turn back to his table when Frederick asked Carly if he could join them. Putting her on the spot, she nodded. "Jeff, why don't you join us if you're eating alone?"

"Are you sure I won't horn in on your fun?" he asked.

"Of course not. We insist." Carly grabbed his arm and pulled him up, laughing as she did. She surveyed Jeff's attire—khaki shorts, a well-worn Boston Red Sox t-shirt, and his Red Sox baseball cap. "Cute," she said, approving of his physique and tanned legs.

Jeff winked, grabbed his cap off the table, and followed them to their booth. Within minutes, the waitress returned with a large pizza, breadsticks, and drinks. The foursome talked over their pizza, this time, Carly's treat. Jeff brought up sailing, one of his favorite pastimes.

"I looked at a boat this morning. I'm buying it later this week," Jeff said.

"Congrats, I'm sure you'll enjoy taking it out on the intercoastal."

"After I get accustomed to her, I'll give the first voyage to the Tabor family. Sound good to you?"

Carly saw the excitement in Frederick's eyes. He looked at her and asked, "Can we, Mom?"

Vivi echoed her brother's question, smiling at Jeff as she did. Carly agreed, then asked, "What are you going to name her?"

"I haven't decided. Maybe y'all can help me with a good one." Jeff waited for Carly to notice his proper use of *y'all.*

Carly noticed and said, "Well played, Sullivan."

Jeff walked with Carly and the kids to their SUV. "I'll see you Monday. Will I see you guys, too?" he asked.

Frederick and Vivi spoke up simultaneously. "Yeah, we'll be there. We don't have a sitter."

Jeff eyed Carly's reaction. She exhaled at the comment, feeling the anxiety of not having reliable childcare.

"I have a great sitter when I'm in a pinch or need to be somewhere for a few hours, but not every day."

"I'm sure you'll find someone. Have a good weekend," Jeff said.

Carly and the kids said goodbye and drove the short distance back to the house on King Street. While the kids went into the den to watch television, Carly went upstairs to call Drake.

Chapter Twenty

Carly turned on the window air units as if it had become a ritual act. She would need to purchase a small air conditioning unit for the upstairs if she decided to keep the house.

The files from the Charleston Orphan House were on the first order of business before she called Drake. Carly could've overlooked Eira's name in her initial search for Freddy. She leafed through the pages Harlan Greene copied for her over ten years ago. She found the page where Frederick Richards, aged 3, appeared. After searching through all twenty pages of minutes from the Orphan Asylum, Carly gave up. Susannah Richards didn't make sense. She leafed through the two copies from Bethesda. It appeared the Foundling Museum and Bethesda had arrangements to deliver orphans to the colonies and later the United States. Carly pondered Caroline Richards, who had three children and a newborn listed in the ledger at Bethesda. Why did she go to the orphanage house in Savannah with the children from the Foundling Hospital? Was she running away from something in England or Wales? Carly might never know why Caroline Richards came to Savannah, but now that she had an identity, along with the girls, the visions and dreams should end.

Carly put Drake's number into her phone. It was after eight o'clock, London time. He answered on the first ring.

"Hello, Carly. I've anxiously awaited your call."

Hearing Drake's voice brought a smile to Carly's face. "Hello, my mind has conjured up all sorts of things after reading your text."

Drake laughed aloud at the comment. "I've taken a few days of vacation since the museum has closed for renovation. The heating and cooling system needed an overhaul, so I took advantage of the time to do some research for you."

"That's so kind of you. Thank you," Carly said, taken aback by Drake's thoughtfulness.

"My pleasure. I haven't visited Wales in years, but it seemed like the perfect opportunity."

"You said you found information about Gethen Bowen?"

"I contacted the director of Llancaiach Fawr, Owen Humphries. I asked about the early records when court proceedings happened there."

"How exciting, go on," Carly said, intrigued.

"He gave me quite a history lesson on the feuds and fights between the commoners who lived around the manor house. He initially gave me the name of Gethen Bowen. He is well-versed in murder trials of the 1700s."

Carly inserted a "how interesting" every few sentences. She listened as Drake explained how he had amassed his wealth of information.

"Which brings me to the case involving the young man from your dreams. Mr. Humphries directed my search to the criminal court records at the National Archives housed in Cardiff. I took the train back to Cardiff, where I procured the assistance of a historian. The files of criminal cases were heard twice a year by the Assize court. Most of the records are on parchment, which is beneficial for us. The ink on paper degrades, but parchment holds on to the ink much longer."

"If you incurred any expense, please let me reimburse you," Carly interjected.

"No need. I found a historian with an understanding of Welsh records. She translated the court document from the original proceedings. I will send you a copy."

Carly couldn't believe her good fortune in having someone with boots on the ground, so to speak, locating the information for her. "Did the transcript mention the man's name that Gethen Bowen murdered?"

"Yes, Stefan Madoc, husband of Caroline."

Carly gasped. "It says Caroline as well. Oh, Drake! What a break for us. What else does it say?"

"I will paraphrase the legal terms of the day. The charge brought against Gethen Bowen is murder. He shot Stefan in the back, just as you saw it, Carly."

Goosebumps covered Carly's arms. "I felt his weight fall against me. How is that possible?"

"It's remarkable. It seems Gethen owned the adjoining acreage to the farm where Stefan lived with his wife, Caroline Richards Madoc. Stefan is not present, for obvious reasons, but Caroline testifies to her account of the murder. . ." Drake was interrupted by Carly.

"He attacked Caroline. He forced himself on her, unaware she had married Stefan."

"How did you know?" Drake asked, slack-jawed from Carly's accuracy.

"I don't know. It's as if I already knew what you were going to say."

Carly continued to share her knowledge of the trial with Drake. "After he called me a bronten, I took the stand. He thought that by killing Stefan, I would have to marry him. He'd take my land."

"You mean Caroline, right?" Drake asked.

Carly didn't follow. "What do you mean?"

"You said *I* would have to marry Bowen."

For a moment, Carly said nothing. She felt that Caroline's experience had become her own. "Drake, what just happened?"

"I don't know, but you recounted the court transcript word for word," he said.

Carly became anxious, feeling as if Caroline had taken over her mind. "Caroline had to find her first husband's brother to take over the land. She couldn't work on the land and pay her taxes, especially now. She would soon give birth to another baby."

"Your ability to cross the veil amazes me, Carly. What did you find at Bethesda?"

Carly told Drake about the ship arriving in Savannah with a group of orphans from the London Foundling Hospital, just as Ms. Albertson's letter stated. She told him about the deaths of the orphans, Caroline, her oldest daughter, and newborn daughter, Catrin. Freddy and his little sister, Eira, survived. Freddy went to the Charleston Orphan Asylum, where Susannah Richards claimed to be his mother. Eira is not mentioned anywhere in the records.

"I think I know the identity of Susannah Richards. Our Miss Albertson changed her name from Louisa to Susannah. I believe she is the one who took Freddy to Charleston," Drake said.

"Of course, that makes perfect sense. Someone had to bring Freddy to the orphan asylum, and Miss Albertson might also have arrangements with other orphanages in America besides Bethesda."

"Your experiences remind me of Alexandria Diaz. Her time travel experience intrigued me. I'm not sure if you believe in such things, but you are familiar with the details of Caroline's life. It's as if you have lived her life."

The thought never occurred to her. "I wrestle enough with my sensitive abilities. I can't fathom time travel."

"I find it interesting, nonetheless. Spirit Seekers put on a great conference, didn't they?"

Carly started to feel excited about the shared joy of the conference, but anxiety over Austin's affair, and his death took her back to a dark place.

"Uh, Drake, I need to go downstairs and start dinner. I'm sure the kids are getting hungry. I can't thank you enough for the time and research you've done for me."

"I'm happy to help you, and I apologize for taking you away from the children for such a long phone conversation."

"No, it's all right. I want to talk more about this, just another time."

Carly heard the kids upstairs. "I'll call you soon. Take care, Drake."

"Good night, Carly. I'll look forward to it."

She was turning off the air conditioners when Frederick and Vivi entered upstairs. "Sorry, guys. I had to make a phone call."

"It's okay, we're hungry. Vivi wanted me to find you," Frederick said apologetically.

Vivi piped up, "No, I didn't. You did."

Carly playfully rubbed the top of Vivi's dark curls. "I'm hungry, too. Let's go downstairs and figure out what to eat." Carly closed the door and followed them downstairs.

The night sounds of Charleston provided a welcome distraction for Carly. She savored a hot cup of tea, relishing in the sense of normalcy that she had missed. It had been two months since Austin's death. The pressure for Carly to demonstrate her ability to cope with her deep grief had finally worn her down. Just two months ago, it felt as if her entire world came crashing to an end.

Between taking over Austin's investments, life insurance payouts, and now an upcoming court case against the man who caused the dreadful accident, she needed to escape from it all. If not for the children, Carly admitted to herself, she would most likely withdraw from everyone and everything. As strange as it seemed, Caroline might have saved her from spiraling into the same dark place she inhabited after her kidnapping. Had she and Caroline become the same person over the last two months? She thought back to Drake's comment. She wondered if time travel was possible. *Stop it, Carly. You know you haven't traveled in time, but what have I experienced then? How did I know about the murder of Stefan Madoc? I was there.*

Carly took another drink of wine. She twined a lock of hair around her finger, thinking about Freddy Richards. Why didn't Freddy and Eira stay together after Caroline, Elizabeth, and the baby's deaths? What happened to Eira? Louisa Albertson used Caroline's identity by changing her name to Susannah Richards when she took Freddy to Charleston. Still, something told Carly that Miss Louisa Albertson and Mr. Nathaniel Duncan were part of something more sinister involving the orphans.

The memory of the paranormal convention came into mind. There were so many speakers with unique stories and abilities. Drake Taylor's encounter with Caroline, as well as her picture and profile, caught his eye in the conference booklet. It all seemed to connect. Why did she choose to go to Wales and pick the very location of Caroline's cottage and the trial at Llancaiach Fawr? Was time travel so far-fetched? Carly refused to believe in reincarnation, as her strong Christian upbringing prevented her from considering it. She accepted her ability to see and communicate with departed souls. Helping those souls move on and others receive their just desserts somehow was satisfying to Carly's soul.

Oh, Granny, how I wish you were here. You could help me. You always knew I had the gift because you had it, too. Is that why I spent so much time with you and Pop?

Carly turned up the wine glass, draining its contents. She went inside, locked the door, and went upstairs. She walked to the end of the hall and looked in on Vivi. The eyelet canopy over her bed moved with the ceiling fan. Vivi lay sleeping with the bear made from one of Austin's shirts.

She closed the door and moved to Frederick's room. His iPad lay beside him, still playing the video of their last vacation as a family to the Smoky Mountains. Carly bent down to kiss Frederick on the forehead. She turned off the device and set it on his dresser. She remembered the last time she and Austin tucked the children in, the night before they went with her parents to Kansas.

She felt her throat tighten, and tears pooled in her eyes. *I'm not going to cry again. Not here.* Carly closed the door and went into her room to prepare for bed. In the hallway, the apparition of Austin turned and disappeared into thin air.

Carly let Frederick and Vivi out at their school and continued along Meeting Street to the Charleston Historical Society. She pulled into the parking garage and found a spot on the second level. She walked the two minutes to her destination just as one of the staff members unlocked the doors.

"Good morning," Carly chirped. She took her messenger bag from her shoulder and walked over to the information desk. "Hi, I'm looking for more information on the Charleston Orphan Asylum. Harlan Greene helped me with information initially, but now that he has retired, I'm not sure where to look."

Jamie Wills put her glasses on top of her head. "What can I help you with?"

Carly took out of her bag a copy of the Orphan House Minutes. Harlan Greene had found the records for her in 2013. "I've searched the entries in the book, but I'm having trouble locating an orphan named Eira Richards."

"Okay, let's see what you have, and we'll try to locate the name you're looking for." Jamie left the desk and led Carly to the area where the museum kept the historical files from the Orphan Asylum. "So, do you know when Eira Richards came to the Orphan Asylum?"

"Yes, I have the actual date. Eira's brother, Frederick Richards, was an inmate in 1794, and later murdered along with Andrew and Celeste Pettigrew, in my house," Carly shared.

Jamie turned, excited, "Wait, I know you. You're Carly Tabor!"

"Yes, the one and only," Carly said, sarcastically, used to the public recognizing her from Channel 5 News.

"I worked with Harlan during that period. Your story is now a legend around Charleston."

Carly smiled, "I guess it took on a life of its own, so to speak."

"I'm glad you found out what happened to the little boy. I've always had an interest in ghosts and such. I moved to the right place."

"You certainly did." Carly cleared her throat and waited for Jamie to help with her search.

"Well, let's take a look at the name and date you have," she said, taking the paper from Carly.

"The book you have lists all the admissions to the Orphan Asylum during the period in question. Could the name be spelled differently, such as a shortened version or something different altogether?"

"Frederick, or Freddy Richards as we knew him, had a younger sister, Eira Richards, aged 1 year and ten months. There is no mention of her admission to his. The woman, Susannah Richards, was an impostor. His real mother passed away at Bethesda Orphan House in 1794, the month before he arrived at the Charleston Orphan Asylum."

Jamie pulled the file drawer holding the records. She donned a pair of white cloth gloves before taking the individual ledgers from the drawer.

"The monthly minutes include the names, ages, and condition of the orphans, or inmates as they were called, during the meeting of the board. If an inmate passed away, the manager would make a note in the minutes."

"I noticed Freddy had a notation beside his name in the list of orphans when admitted, runaway, January 1799. I searched for Eira in the remaining entries from 1794 through 1799. There are no girls admitted with the spelling Eira or any version close to it." Carly looked up from her papers. "I think Susannah Richards took Eira to another orphanage."

"In 1794, there were not many orphanages operating in the United States. Besides the Orphan Asylum here in Charleston and the Bethesda Orphan House in Savannah, there were only a few that operated as true orphanages. Most were poor houses that accepted orphaned children and the indigent, and institutions to care for young girls to the age of 10."

"I expected more orphanages with the Revolutionary War taking the lives of the young fathers in the colonies. With yellow fever, cholera, and typhoid outbreaks occurring frequently, I would have thought more places to care for orphaned children would be a necessity."

"I can do a search of the eastern United States for the period 1740 through 1800 for institutions and asylums for children. It should come up with all the places during that period where orphans were cared for."

Jamie used one of the computers that were set up for patrons. In a matter of seconds, the printer provided the information.

Carly commented, "It's amazing how much time one Google search can save a person."

Jamie handed Carly the printout of all the locations and dates of operation of the various orphanages listed. "You can go online and search for the digital minutes of each of these institutions. Some might be hard to get, but I'm sure there are still records for the Boston Female Asylum. It had a connection to Benjamin Franklin and Abigail Adams, it says."

"Thank you for helping me. I'll get to work on it. I think there is more going on with the number of orphans coming into Savannah and Charleston by way of the London Foundling Hospital," Carly said as she put the copied pages inside her bag.

"Glad I could help. Is there anything else you need?" Jamie asked.

"No, not today. I think I'll go home and start searching before I have to pick up my kids from school. Thank you again," she said.

Carly left the Historical Society armed with another day's work. She had several unanswered questions: Why didn't Caroline Madoc disclose her marriage? What happened to Eira Richards? And why did Nathaniel Duncan get removed as director of the Bethesda Orphan House?

She was sure the latter were connected. She hurried back to the house to start searching Newspapers.com for information regarding the Bethesda Orphan House and Mr. Nathaniel Duncan. Researching the Orphan Houses would entail more time.

Chapter Twenty-One

Carly's phone rang as she left to pick up the kids from school. It was Chad Flannery. "Chad, hey! What's going on?"

"Hi Carly, this is Josie. Chad's phone has your number, so I used his to call you. Is this a bad time?"

Carly put her phone on Bluetooth and pulled out of her driveway. "No, it's fine. Is everything okay with you and Chad?"

"Yes, we're getting ready to head out west tomorrow. I wanted to call you first. I may have a housekeeper and nanny for you."

Carly's heart skipped a beat. "Really? Oh, my goodness. Thank you for thinking of me."

"Well, we were talking about you and the kids last night, and Chad mentioned his older sister, Dorothy. She goes by Dottie."

"Okay, tell me about her."

"Dottie Childress is what I would call a June Cleaver. She always keeps her house immaculate and has dinner on the table by four o'clock each evening for Jerald."

"They sure don't make them like that anymore," Carly laughed.

"I know, and Jerald passed away from ALS last spring. She doesn't like living alone or dealing with all the bills and upkeep on the house."

"I know how she feels." Carly was empathetic to Dottie's situation.

"I'm sure you have a full plate, Carly," Josie said, then added, "We're keeping you and the kids in our prayers. That's why Chad feels Dottie needs you as much as you need a Dottie in your life."

"I certainly have room for a live-in housekeeper and nanny. I've thought about downsizing and selling." Carly turned onto Meeting Street, wanting to finish the conversation before the kids got in the SUV.

"Would you like her number? Chad filled her in last night when we took her out for dinner."

"Yes, I would. Dottie drives, doesn't she?" Carly asked.

"Yes, she has a nice car that Jerald bought her two years ago."

"All right, give me her number, and I'll call her tomorrow morning. I'm on my way to work after I get the kids."

Josie gave Carly the phone number for Dottie Childress. Carly thanked her and told her to have a great time with Chad on their new motor home's maiden voyage.

She finished her call as Frederick and Vivi climbed into the back seat. "How was your day?" Carly asked, feeling upbeat after her conversation with Josie.

"Mom, can I go home with Braden tomorrow? He's having a party after school for his birthday at the Sportsplex, and everyone is staying the night."

Carly mentally scanned her day tomorrow, Friday. "I think it should be fine. I'll grab a card on the way home tonight for him and slip some cash inside."

"Thanks, Mom." Carly saw a massive grin on her son's face.

"I guess it's just us chicks tomorrow night, Vivi."

"Can we play Barbies?"

"Of course, as long as I don't have to be Ken."

"Okay." Vivi looked over at her brother as if she had one-upped his adventure.

Carly parked her SUV in the Channel 5 lot. "Okay, I brought subs and chips for y'all tonight. There are water bottles in the fridge in the breakroom."

Carly lifted her bag and the sack with the kids' supper and hurried inside.

Jeff Sullivan joined Carly in the makeup room as she donned her robe and waited for Liz to work her magic. Carly noticed Jeff's nose was a little red.

"You've been out on the boat, haven't you?" Carly questioned.

"Yeah, I think the Charleston sun is a skosh more intense than in Boston," he answered.

Chris, the second makeup artist, dabbed moisturizer on his nose before applying the makeup. "We'll get your Rudolph nose all covered in no time," she teased.

Carly stifled a laugh while Jeff rolled his eyes. "Very funny."

"What did you name her?" Carly asked.

"The boat? I named her Sullivan's Witch."

Carly didn't comment for a second, letting the name sink in. "I'm going to have to let it grow on me," she said.

"It's okay, I like it." Jeff faced forward in his chair as Chris finished applying his makeup.

Carly reached for the evening news script. Jeff hesitated before speaking.

"There's a story about the guy who hit Austin tonight."

Carly tensed. "I'll let you read it if you don't mind."

"Carly, there will be pictures of the other passenger." Jeff removed his cape and looked over at Carly, whose jaw tightened.

Carly waited for Liz to finish applying her eyelash extensions before responding. "I didn't expect her photo, but since she died due to the other driver's actions, it makes sense."

No, she wouldn't be okay. The thought of the people in Charleston connecting the dots troubled Carly. By now, most of the newsroom, her acquaintances, and everyone who worked with Austin were aware of Cora and the affair. She exhaled, trying to relieve the anxiety that had overwhelmed her.

As they walked out together, Jeff took Carly's arm and pulled her back. "I'm sorry, Carly. I wanted to tell you now before you saw her picture on the teleprompter."

Carly side-hugged Jeff. "You're a class act, Jeff. Thank you."

The story about Austin and Cora Burton led off the newscast. Pictures showed smiling faces, and Carly felt angered that someone had used her Facebook pictures without her permission.

She felt the eyes of the production crew on her as Jeff read the script off the teleprompter. "Dr. Austin Tabor and his passenger, Cora D. Burton of Mississippi, were driving north onto I-26 when a 2017 Honda Accord, driven by twenty-two-year-old Cody Addison of Charleston, crossed the center median, hitting Dr. Tabor's 2022 Lexus. Toxicology reports showed Addison had high levels of meth and alcohol in his system at the time of the crash. Both Austin Tabor and Cora Burton died from their injuries. SLED Officer Cory Phelps spoke to Channel 5 before Addison's arraignment."

Carly tried to tune out the video clip, not wanting to break down on air. When the clip ended, she felt Jeff nudge her under the table. She quickly composed herself and continued with the next story.

∼

The six o'clock newscast wrapped up. Carly finished talking to the producer and walked into the breakroom to get the kids. She saw the large screen television showing the newscast. She saw Vivi had been crying, and Frederick's expression told Carly they had seen the segment on their father and Cora.

She went to Vivi and gave her a hug and a kiss. "Come on, kids, let's go home." She picked up their backpacks and bent over to Frederick, "We'll talk about what you saw on the way home."

On her way out the back door, she didn't stop to talk to Jeff or any of her coworkers. The children remained silent until Carly broached the subject of the news story once they were inside their vehicle.

"I'm sorry you saw the story about Daddy. It's okay to be sad, and if you want to talk about it, we can."

"Who was that girl with Dad?" Frederick said, his voice was full of anger.

"Before Dad met me, he had been married to Cora. They were divorced when Dad and I met." Carly felt a knot form in her stomach.

"Why did that man hurt Daddy?" Vivi started to cry again.

"Honey, when people take drugs, it makes them do dangerous things. I'm sure he wishes he hadn't taken drugs."

"Is that why you're mad at Dad?" Frederick's eleven-year-old mind comprehended more than Carly knew.

"Buddy, it's hard to explain. I love Dad and I miss him very much." Carly hoped this would satisfy his curiosity.

"Micah was right. Dad cheated."

The words stung Carly. She wanted to throw Austin under the bus. She tried to call him every name that came to mind. But she didn't.

"When you're older, I will answer your questions better. I know for sure Dad loved us, and he was sorry for what he did."

Carly's answer answered his question, and regardless, it didn't change what Frederick and Vivi saw on the television.

"Being angry is okay, kids. I'm working on forgiving. Jesus forgives us, so we also must forgive." In her rearview mirror, Carly saw Frederick and Vivi look at one another.

"I know. I'll ask God to forgive me for being mad at Cora and Dad."

Carly's tears fell. She couldn't hold them in any longer. She had promised Frederick earlier that she would stop at the pharmacy before going home. She dried her eyes, and they went inside to pick out a card for Braden.

Frederick and Vivi were in bed when Carly had a moment to decompress from the conversation with the children. Her thoughts went in a hundred different directions. She called her mother, hoping that hearing her calming voice would settle her.

"Hi, hope it isn't too late for a call," Carly said.

"It's good to hear from you. How are you doing, honey?" Paula asked.

"It's been a day. The kids saw a story on the news about Austin and Cora. I don't think I handled it very well." Carly felt her throat tighten as she tried to explain the earlier events.

After Carly had talked for several minutes, Paula spoke. "You're handling things the way you should. Frederick is more mature than you think."

"Cate called me last week to check in. I even heard from Connor in a text." Carly's siblings had made time each week to check in with her.

"Cate's and Connor's children want Frederick and Vivi to visit during their next break," Paula said.

"I know, they had a wonderful time. Thank you for giving them such good memories." A wave of panic bubbled up in Carly's stomach.

"Mom, can I ask you something?"

"You know you can."

"Do you have the *gift* like Granny and me?"

Paula was silent for what seemed like an eternity to Carly. "I shouldn't have told you about Granny. Has something happened?"

"It's nothing. I've had some dreams, and I just wondered if you and Granny ever talked about spirits and the like," Carly said, not wanting to upset her mother.

"Granny didn't talk about those things with me. She knew I didn't want any part of it." Paula didn't elaborate any further.

Carly got the message. She changed the subject. "I might have a lead on a housekeeper and nanny for the kids."

"Oh? That sounds promising."

"Chad Flannery's older sister lost her husband last year to ALS. He thinks she is perfect for the job, and I think I'll call her about it tomorrow."

"I hope it works out. Keep us posted, honey."

"Thanks, Mom. I'll let you go. I love you."

"I love you. Daddy says hello."

Carly ended the call and went into the kitchen to make a snack. She turned on the kitchen television for noise. The ten o'clock news caught her attention. Melissa Hutchins and Vance Charles were delivering the story about Cody Addison's arraignment. Carly turned to the television as Cora's picture came on the screen. Carly remembered seeing her in Austin's room before he passed away. She didn't look apologetic; she looked like a woman about to begin her sentence for eternity. She saw Austin again on the screen, his blue eyes reaching her very soul. Carly counted on Austin to be her rock. He was amazing through everything—until June 7th. *Now you're a cheat. Your son said it.* Even with tears clouding her vision, she sat through the segment. Her love for Austin and her feelings of betrayal caused her to regret the sentiment she now felt. She finished her snack and wiped the counter clean.

Carly turned off the television and the downstairs lights before heading upstairs to take a shower and prepare for bed. She undressed and stepped into the shower. The hot water soothed her tense muscles beneath the cascading spray. She found that tears always came when she felt that no one could see her raw emotions.

After she dried off and donned her nightgown, she climbed into bed. While she relaxed, she thought about her Granny and the special bond they shared. She wished she could tell Granny about her experiences.

CHAPTER TWENTY-TWO

Carly finished doing the laundry and took her phone into the den. She entered Dottie's phone number and waited for her to answer. The voice that answered made Carly think of Phoebe Figalilly from *Nanny and the Professor*, instead of Euphegenia Doubtfire from *Mrs. Doubtfire*.

"Hello," she said.

"Hello, Dottie. My name is Carly Tabor. I believe Chad mentioned me and the children to you?" Carly twirled a loose tendril of hair around her finger.

"Yes, Mrs. Tabor, thank you for calling. I understand you need a sitter and housekeeper." She sounded younger than Carly imagined.

"Yes, Ma'am. I have two children: Frederick is eleven, and Viviene will soon be seven. My house is large, and there are stairs."

"I see. The stairs shouldn't cause problems. What exactly do you have in mind?" Dottie asked.

"I understand you recently sold your house and will have to move. If you come to work for me, I have a spare room on the second floor or an apartment on the third floor."

Dottie said, "Oh, my, you do have a big house."

Carly laughed. "Yes, it was a dream of my husband and me to have a historic home. I am considering selling it and purchasing something on one level."

"I'm sorry for your loss. I lost my husband eighteen months ago. I decided to sell because I didn't want the headache of all that goes with upkeep. It's hard to live alone."

"I don't have any pets, although the children have asked for a dog. I'll probably cave at some point." Carly tried to think of anything else to tell Dottie. "Oh, as you know, I work at Channel 5. I leave for work around three for the evening news, which means I need someone to pick up Frederick and Vivi from school."

"I'm sure I can manage. If you decide I'm a good fit for you, I'm available to start in two weeks. I need to arrange for the things I have to go into storage."

Carly thought about the apartment. "If you have special items you want to keep, I'm sure movers would bring your bedroom furniture and your favorite chair and couch, since I do have an unfinished apartment."

"That's very kind. I appreciate the offer."

Carly felt a burden lifted from her shoulders. "I'd like to meet on Saturday if you can come into town. I'll text you the address."

"Yes, I'm available on Saturday. I'm pretty good at getting around town, especially on King Street. I'm looking forward to meeting Frederick and Viviene, too," Dottie said.

Carly shifted the conversation to the amount she would pay Dottie, taking into consideration the room and board. Dottie agreed to the salary and thought the apartment would suit her needs.

"I have two sons, one married a girl from Maryland after college, and they work for the government in Washington, D.C. I see them several times a year. My other son, well, he has *a friend* and doesn't come home often."

Carly understood her meaning and said, "Well, my family all lives in the Midwest, so it sounds like we'll do just fine. I'll see you at two, if that works."

Carly entered her office and examined the space. She had an antique rolltop desk, a gift from Austin on their first anniversary, two filing cabinets, and her computer and printer both sitting atop an antique credenza. She and Boyd could move things down to the receiving room, converting it into an office with most of the existing furniture. She looked at the size of the task and thought better of it. Movers could do it more easily and quickly. The thought of someone else using the apartment made Carly happy. Dottie could make the space her own, and Carly could have someone to help with the children and the house.

She set to work researching Bethesda Orphanage in newspapers on Newspapers.com from 1790 to 1799. This time frame would give her a wide berth on any news mentioning the orphan house.

After several hours of searching, she found an advertisement that announced the arrival of indentured servants from London in 1794. It listed Nathaniel Duncan, Esq., and Thaddeus Broward, Esq.

Carly took off her glasses and moved away from the screen. She thumbed through the copies she had at hand from the London Foundling Hospital. In the letter dated 1794 from Nathaniel Duncan, he mentions *'that all souls have arrived, as per our arrangement'*. At the end of the letter, *'I will send correspondence to Charleston and Boston as soon as your reply arrives.'*

Carly said aloud, "So, Duncan and Albertson used a middleman, Thaddeus Broward, to carry the letters back and forth, along with the orphans and indentured servants."

"Did Caroline indenture herself?" Carly said as she tapped the pen on the credenza. *No, Caroline came to America for another reason.*

Why did you leave Wales, travel to the Foundling Hospital, and sail to America?

She reread the letter. *Boston. Could an orphanage in Boston hold the key to where Eira Richards went after Louisa took Freddy to Charleston?*

A surge of hope coursed through Carly, giving her a new sense of direction. She hurried to the notes from the Historical Society. Jamie Wills gave her the names of all the various almshouses, Orphan Asylums, and Female Asylums known in the United States at the time Caroline Richards arrived at Bethesda.

The printed information listed orphanages in America from 1754 to 1829. Carly read through the seven pages, finding Baltimore, Philadelphia, New York City, Boston, New Orleans, Savannah, and Charleston, each having *an establishment for orphans, indigents, outdoor relief, and almshouses.*

In the letter between Albertson and Duncan, Carly noticed Boston and Charleston as the cities where the London Foundling Hospital and the Bethesda orphans were transported once arriving in America. Carly surmised that orphans were chosen based on their age or circumstances and whether they remained at Bethesda or went north.

She typed in *Boston Orphan Asylum.* The earliest records dated to the late 1750s, and donations from prominent Bostonians, including Benjamin Franklin, were included. Later, in the 1790s, the Boston Orphan Asylum became the Boston Female Asylum. In 1800, First Lady Abigail Adams became involved, and the Boston Female Asylum became the Boston Female Orphan Asylum. Carly found a host of links under WorldCat through the LDS library.

Under the *Boston Society for the Care of Girls: Asylum Records (1790-1866),* Carly noted that the microreproduction of original records was housed at the State House in Boston, with copies at the Massachusetts State Historical Library. The file contained the minutes of board meetings, records of orphans entering and leaving the asylum, financial documentation, as well as some baptisms and deaths, and a list of the asylum's supporters.

Another annotation on microfilm contained the names of children and adolescents placed under indenture, along with the names of those to whom they were indentured.

Carly's stomach rumbled in the otherwise quiet office. She checked her phone. She had two hours before she needed to shower and change before picking up the children. Grace Ravenel planned to arrive by two forty-five p.m. so that Carly could get to the news station in plenty of time.

She ran downstairs, hurriedly made a protein smoothie and drank it, and texted Delaney the news about what she'd found online. Within twenty minutes, she returned to her desk to search for more information.

The records from the Boston Female Asylum, the Boston Orphan Asylum, and the Boston Female Orphan Asylum weren't available online, requiring a trip to the Massachusetts Historical Society. As she searched the website, she found several volumes of information regarding the Boston Female Asylum in the library.

I don't have time to go to Boston. Maybe I can take the kids on a trip during Fall Break. It might make Bauer give me the boot, too. Carly scowled at her options. She loved working at Channel 5, but having a business from home sounded increasingly appealing. Other women she knew worked remotely and maintained part-time status in their different positions. She doubted Bauer would accept part-time status unless she covered the weekend news. The thoughts of managing the house also weighed heavily on her mind. She could sell the house and move anywhere with the money Austin left her. A heaviness overcame her at the thought of Austin, leading her to feel the weight of his loss while raising the children alone. Determined not to cry, she knew that tears wouldn't restore her life before the accident. With a heavy sigh, she recalled the gut punch of Austin's betrayal.

Carly heard the clock in the hallway strike two. She turned off the computer and air conditioner units and went to her bedroom. For now, Eira Richards's whereabouts remained a mystery.

Vivi and Grace were eating popsicles on the lower piazza when Carly pulled into the parking area. She walked over to join them. "Did Frederick get the card on the table?"

Grace nodded, "Yes, he said to tell you he needed to get picked up tomorrow by five."

Carly thanked Grace for ensuring he arrived at the Sportsplex on time. "I have your money inside. I'll go inside and grab it for you."

When she returned, Vivi had her arms around Grace's waist in an embrace. Carly handed the cash to Grace and said, "I appreciate your stepping in to help me with the kids. I think I've found a housekeeper and nanny."

"Oh, that's great. Thank you for the gift card, too," Grace said, referring to the gift card to Mama Kim's restaurant near the university.

"You're welcome. You've been a godsend the last few weeks." Carly hugged Grace. "Please tell Elise hello for me."

Vivi and Carly walked inside. Vivi kicked off her flip-flops and followed Carly into the kitchen.

"Mommy, who did you get to watch us now?" Vivi asked, swiveling back and forth on the stool.

"Well, I want to invite her to stop by. Her name is Dottie."

Vivi giggled. "Dottie? That's a funny name."

Carly smiled. "It's short for Dorothy, I bet."

Vivi nodded, "Like Vivi and Viviene."

"That's right. If Dottie agrees, she'll move in here and live with us." Carly waited for Vivi's reaction.

"Will she have her room, like us?"

"She'll move upstairs to the apartment. That way, Dottie will have her own space."

Carly changed the subject. "Hey, where do you want to go eat tomorrow?" Carly warmed up the leftover pizza that Grace and Vivi had eaten for supper.

Vivi cocked her head, attempting to act like she was deep in thought. "The Oyster House."

Vivi loved seafood, like Carly. The lunch portions were perfect for her. "Okay, you've got a deal," Carly said, leaning across the bar to take Vivi's face, kissing her forehead.

Carly awoke to the moonlight illuminating her bedroom. She sat up in bed and saw Austin standing near the fireplace. At first, he appeared translucent. Carly's eyes watched as his form solidified, and he sat in a nearby chair.

"Austin," Carly whispered, not wanting to wake the children. "You've come back to me." Carly threw back the bedcovers and walked over to where Austin sat. As she reached out to touch his face, Cora appeared behind him.

"You?" Carly spat. "Get out of my house." Carly's voice, no longer a whisper, caused Vivi to stir and call out.

"Mommy?"

Carly looked to see both apparitions unmoved. "Leave." Her tone demanded action.

Vivi ran into her room as Austin and Cora vanished. "I had a bad dream," she said.

Carly wrapped her arm around Vivi and led her back to bed. "I had a bad dream, too. I'm sorry I frightened you."

Vivi started to cry. "I miss Daddy."

"I know, sweetie. I miss him, too." Carly hugged Vivi and smoothed her tousled hair. She crawled into bed beside Vivi and waited until she fell asleep, then crept back to her room.

The confrontation with Austin and Cora left Carly restless. She felt unseen eyes watching her. She checked her phone—two-thirty. She huffed loud enough that she thought she might wake Vivi again. The urge to punish Austin, even though she still grieved for him, overtook her. She got out of bed and took the urn downstairs to the receiving room. She looked for a place to put the urn other than her closet. She decided the receiving room mantle would do for now. The walk downstairs put her mood in perspective.

"There." She moved back to approve the urn's new spot. "This will do until I can take you back to Kansas near your grandfather and grandmother."

As she reached to turn off the lamp on the entry hall table, she noticed their wedding photo. Had Austin brought it downstairs after she moved the urn out of the bedroom? Stranger things had happened in the house over the years, why should this surprise her? She picked up the photograph and felt the weight of a hand on her shoulder. Without turning to face him, she said, "Good night, Austin."

Chapter Twenty-Three

September 2025

Carly awoke before dawn from having an unusual dream. She turned onto her side to check the bedside clock and groaned when it displayed five thirty on a Saturday morning. She wished she could sleep in for once. The dream lingered in her mind: a much younger version of her grandmother holding a little girl's hand as they walked together, placing flowers on several graves. Carly felt a sense of familiarity with the dream, recalling how she had walked through the same cemetery with her grandmother when she was a child. However, this wasn't her usual experience. The little girl wanted to hurry home. Something frightened her in the cemetery. Carly recognized the little girl, and it was her mother.

For a moment, Carly tried to remember what had happened before she awoke. She didn't remember feeling afraid with Granny when they visited the cemeteries. She recalled her conversation with her mom about seeing spirits, and Paula wanted to change the subject.

Carly wondered, *"Does every generation on Granny's side communicate and see spirits?"*

"Don't bring the spooks home with you." Carly smiled at the memory of Austin's term for the spirits. She reflected on the letter Harv had given her; Austin's last words, so to speak. He referred to himself as a '*spook*'.

Flashes of the departed souls she encountered during her lifetime paraded in her mind, as if wanting to stay relevant in her memory. All were trapped or lingered because of unfinished business or unknown whereabouts. Carly felt her eyes burn with the onset of tears, remembering each of them. Austin appeared last. She rubbed tears from her eyes. *The sooner you receive a proper burial, the better for everyone. I can't move on with you sitting in the living room, literally and figuratively.*

Frederick called out from the kitchen, "Mom, we're out of cereal."

Carly snapped into action. "Hang on, I'm coming." Hurrying into a pair of yoga pants and a Channel 5 News t-shirt, she finished getting ready in the bathroom. After she brushed her teeth and swished water and spit into the basin, she pulled her hair into a ponytail and dashed down the stairs.

Vivi joined Carly and Frederick, her hair in a mass of tangles. Carly bent down to put a kiss on the top of her head as she hurried to her stool at the counter.

"It looks like you had a rough night, Vivi. What sounds good for breakfast?" Carly asked.

Frederick swirled around on his stool, shaking the empty box of cereal. "She won't have cereal," he said, clearly annoyed with his mother's neglect of the weekly grocery shopping.

"Hey, cut me some slack, Bud. It's been a busy week." She bent down to peruse the freezer for choices. She pulled out a box of frozen waffles and held them up for approval.

"Yeah, that's good," Frederick said, nonplussed.

Vivi wrinkled her nose up at the choice. Carly put two waffles in the toaster for Frederick. She raised her eyebrows, cocking her head to the side.

"So, Miss Twist," the nickname she'd called Vivi since she was a toddler, "What sounds good to you?"

Vivi appeared deep in thought at her mother's question. "I want muffins."

While Carly scavenged in the cabinet for a box of blueberry muffins, her phone rang. She paused to look at the incoming call and put it on speaker.

"Hey, girl, what's going on?" she said, mouthing to the kids that it's Delaney.

Frederick and Vivi called out hello in unison to her.

"Hello, munchkins," Delaney said jovially. "If you're busy, I can call back."

Carly dumped the box of muffin mix into a bowl and continued with the preparation as she talked to Delaney.

"It's fine, I'll multitask as we talk," Carly said.

"Did you find out anything on Caroline?"

Carly filled the last muffin tin. "I did, in fact," she said.

Carly shared the information she found regarding Albertson and Duncan's middleman, Thaddeus Broward, and how orphans were sent from England to various orphanages and asylums throughout the colonies, especially Charleston and Boston.

"So, you think Eira Richards ended up in Boston?"

"I believe Miss Albertson disguised her identity as Susannah Richards when she dropped off Freddy, and I'll bet you she also did the same when she left Eira."

Delaney remained silent for a moment before continuing. "I don't understand why she didn't leave both children at the same place."

Carly took the muffins out of the oven for Vivi and put two on a plate for her. She poured a glass of milk as she continued. "Well, I think it appears the whole lot of them were traffickers, if that term applies to their time."

The kids took their food over to the table and turned on the television. They paid little attention to Delaney and Carly's discussion. Carly switched the phone over from speaker mode for more privacy.

"Will you take a trip to Boston anytime soon?"

Carly snickered, then said, "It won't be until later this month, if I do." She took the phone into the receiving room. "Frederick and Vivi have Fall Break starting the week before Halloween. I'm not sure if going to Boston will work out with kids."

"What about taking Grace along to watch them?" Delaney asked.

Carly didn't want to ask her, as she was attending college full-time and no doubt had made plans of her own during her short break. "I might have a nanny to bring along."

"Oh, really? Did Chad's sister pass muster?"

Carly peeked into the kitchen, where Frederick and Vivi were oblivious to her conversation. "Dottie is coming over at two o'clock today to meet the kids and me. I hope they like her. She's already said yes to employment with me."

"I'm so glad you found her. I know it's a huge weight off your shoulders."

Carly agreed. The feelings of grief and anxiety over the care of the children caused her to question remaining in Charleston. If she lost her job, she'd have to move back to Kansas to have help with Frederick and Vivi.

"Let me know how it goes today." Delaney paused, then said, "Any word from Drake?"

"No, not since I told you about our conversation." Carly lowered her voice to keep the kids from hearing, "Austin's appeared a couple of times."

"I hoped he wouldn't."

Carly pulled the receiving room door closed to keep the kids from overhearing her. "He's appeared alone and with *her*."

"Cora? What the hell?"

Carly exhaled. "I know, right? I've felt Austin's presence here since I brought his ashes home with me."

Delaney quipped, "You need to tell him to practice what he preached- don't bring the spooks home with you."

They both shared a laugh, even if it was inappropriate. Delaney continued, no longer joking. "Did you decide to take his ashes to Kansas for burial?"

The thought of planning for a headstone and burial seemed daunting. It needed to happen, and the paranormal happenings involving him could stop.

"I thought I'd call Austin's folks and ask if they could handle ordering a stone and arranging for the burial. I know several family members and friends couldn't make it to the service here." She twined a tendril of hair that had escaped from her ponytail. "Maybe the kids and I could spend Thanksgiving with my family this year. We could take Austin's ashes for a memorial service."

"I'm sorry you have to deal with this all over again."

"It's hardest on Frederick and Vivi, and I hate to put them through it again." Carly heard one of the kids outside the door. "I'll call you later. I need to go."

"No worries. Jarrod and Chelsea are taking me out to a late lunch. Boyd's on an overnight investigation with Tucker."

"Thank you for everything, bestie."

"We're like Lucy and Ethel. You're welcome."

Carly joined Frederick in the hallway. "Mom, Vivi spilled her milk."

Carly shoved her phone in her pocket and hurried into the kitchen to clean up the mess.

∼

"She's here!" Vivi exclaimed. Frederick reached around her to pull back the plantation shutters, giving him a better view.

Dottie Childress didn't resemble a babysitter. She looked like Auntie Delaney —not old, but not young like the girls Carly had used in the past.

Carly hurried to toss her sandals into the entry closet before Dottie rang the doorbell at the street entrance. "Mind your manners, okay?" she said, walking past the kids on her way to answer the door.

"Mrs. Childress, come in."

Dottie smiled and thanked Carly as she stepped inside the small entry. "In the future, you're welcome to come and go through the lower piazza door."

She led Dottie into the hallway. "It's so good to meet you." Frederick and Vivi appeared from their vantage point in the den. "This is Frederick and Vivi," Carly said.

Dottie leaned down to hold out her hand to Vivi, "I'm pleased to meet you, Vivi. What a lovely name."

Vivi grinned, showing two missing teeth. "My real name is Viviene, but everyone calls me Vivi."

Dottie released Vivi's hand and turned to Frederick. Unsure what to do with an eleven-year-old, she said, "Hello, Frederick. I'm pleased to meet you."

He hesitated, then held out his hand. "Nice to meet you."

Carly released the breath she held. "Mrs. Childress, can I get you a refreshment?"

"No, thank you. I stopped by the McDonald's for the dollar meal and a Coke." She added, "Please, call me Dottie."

Carly led her into the den. "This is where the kids spend a lot of time. We use it as a family room."

"You have a beautiful home, Mrs. Tabor."

Carly thanked her, adding, "You may call me Carly. Would you prefer the children call you Mrs. Childress?"

Dottie laughed, "Growing up, we always called our elders by their surnames, Mr. this and Ms. that. I like Ms. Dottie."

"Well, then, it's settled. You'll be Ms. Dottie."

For the next hour, Carly took Dottie on an extensive tour of the house. Dottie admired the centuries-old fireplaces in each room and Carly's decor. Finally, they climbed the stairs to the third floor. The heat hit them as she opened the door. The window units hadn't thoroughly cooled the room. "It gets a little warm up here in the summer. You're welcome to use the fourth bedroom if this isn't to your liking."

"I've lived in the heat and humidity all my life. I'm sure a couple of floor fans will help circulate the air." Dottie walked around and looked out the floor-to-ceiling windows. "Some darkening shades will do wonders along with closing the shutters."

Carly took note. "Of course. I want you to feel at home here."

Dottie turned and nodded, "If everyone agrees, I'm happy to take on the house and your family."

"Yes, we want to have you move in as soon as you're ready," Carly said, then remembered another part of the house to show Dottie. "If you'll follow me downstairs, I'll show you the cellar."

Vivi waited until Carly and Dottie went downstairs. She turned to Frederick, "I like Ms. Dottie."

Frederick took a water bottle from the refrigerator and took a swig. "Yeah, she seems all right."

Dottie waited until she and Carly were back upstairs before commenting.

"Cellars always give me chill bumps."

Carly and the children smiled. "Yes, I understand," Carly said, and she latched the door.

"I'll make arrangements for the movers to bring my things this week, as the new owners will take possession of my house on Thursday after the closing."

"If you'd like, Wednesday evening is fine with me."

Carly and Dottie walked to the door. She turned to tell the children goodbye. "I think we'll get along just fine."

Carly arranged for Boyd and Tucker to come over on Tuesday after work to help her move her belongings from the apartment to her makeshift office in the receiving room. After Vivi and Frederick went to bed, she began the task of boxing up her things upstairs. Carly felt excited about having a smaller office area downstairs.

She carried the final box of awards and pictures downstairs and collapsed into one of the chairs. She closed her eyes for a moment, feeling the cool air relax her. A vision overtook her.

A gust of wind blew her hair into her face, while the spray of the salt stung her eyes. She pulled the children away from the side of the ship, afraid one might fall overboard in the choppy sea. Caroline saw the faint outline of land in the distance. Georgia was a debtor's colony. She'd only stay until Arwin Richards came for her and the children.

She placed her hands on her swollen stomach, feeling the baby stretch inside her. She hadn't told Arwin about his brother's death yet. As she pondered her situation, she witnessed two burly sailors tossing another bundle, wrapped in a blanket and secured with knots in three places, overboard. She tried to shield the children from the distressing sight, but it was to no avail. Such incidents occurred more frequently as the voyage dragged on. Her attention was then drawn to a loud shout from above. A young sailor called from the crow's nest, "Land ahead!"

CHAPTER TWENTY-FOUR

Bauer Donahue sipped the last of his Dr. Pepper. He and Jeff Sullivan shared a laugh over a recent fishing trip they shared. Carly tapped on the door, then went inside. The two men stood when Carly entered, and she sat in the empty chair next to Jeff.

"Carly, I want to fly something by you both- it's nothing set in stone." Bauer tossed the empty Dr. Pepper can into the trash.

Jeff looked at Carly, and her eyebrows arched, waiting for Bauer to continue.

"The ratings came in for the last quarter. Your time slot is down from the previous quarter." He sniffed, trying to broach the subject without upsetting either Carly or Jeff.

Jeff spoke up before Carly could say anything. "You know, we switched anchors in mid-stream, so to speak. Everyone loved Chad Flannery."

Bauer's eyes shifted from Carly to Jeff. "Actually, you're as popular in the feedback as Chad in his final year."

Carly got the drift, without Bauer writing it on the wall for her. "Oh, I'm the drag on the ratings?"

"You've been out with Austin's passing, and also the extended trip prior." His tanned fingers massaged his temples. "I think the ratings were better in your time slot with Erin and Jeff co-anchoring."

Carly sat stunned, for once, nothing came to mind to say. "I see. Well, I watched Jeff and Erin together a couple of nights." She turned to Jeff, "You two have great chemistry."

Jeff piped up, "So do we. I think we have the beginnings of a great connection on air."

"Thanks, Jeff. I think what Bauer is trying to say is that I'm losing the appeal to the viewers. It's okay."

"I don't want you off the camera, Carly. I think in this season of your life, with the children and navigating the loss of your husband..." He stopped, seeing Carly wasn't buying his B.S."

"Honestly, the thought crossed my mind to ask if I could go back to being an investigative reporter or even work from home." Carly waited to see Bauer's expression.

Jeff let out a loud sigh and leaned against the wall. "Come on, we've only been co-anchoring for six months, for goodness' sake."

The cumbersome feeling made the walls close in, and Carly could see Jeff's eye twitching. She inhaled sharply, taking one for the team, so to speak.

"Bauer, I hired a nanny three weeks ago. If you think a weekend anchor or even early news solves the ratings issue..." Carly didn't finish, as she saw Bauer's expression.

"Erin is doing the early morning newscast with Kyle Warren. The two of you could switch time slots, for now."

For now? Did Bauer want to fire me, but didn't have the balls to do it? Carly tapped her fingernails on the wooden arm of the chair.

Jeff finally spoke. "Bauer, Erin, and I work well together, but I think..."

Bauer cut him off. "Let's go with this arrangement and hopefully the ratings will climb during the next quarter."

Even though Carly wrestled with the idea of asking for time off, she'd just hired a nanny. She still felt the gut punch of being demoted, as it were.

"Carly, the public loves you. I think they want consistency in their nightly newscast. They had it with you and Chad," Bauer said.

Carly knew bringing the children to the station didn't go over well with Bauer, even though he tried to cut Carly slack. "When will the switch happen?" she asked.

"Monday. I'll let you have the rest of the week together, and you can tell the audience you'll be switching to mornings."

Carly smiled, "Thank you. I'll keep it private, thank the viewers, and tell them I'll be on mornings at six."

Jeff remained speechless. He appeared blindsided by the announcement. "I'm sorry, Carly. I've enjoyed getting to know you and the kids."

"Thanks, I've enjoyed working with you, even if you are a Yankee."

They both laughed. Bauer stood, signaling the end to the meeting.

"Thank you both for your professionalism on and off the air."

Jeff and Carly walked together to the parking lot. "Well, that was awkward," Carly announced when they reached her SUV.

"I'm at a loss, for once. I didn't see it coming." He stood by her door and waited for her window to come down.

A gentle breeze blew Carly's hair into her face. She pushed her sunglasses up onto her head. "I'm okay. I'll miss doing the news with you, but this way I'll be home in the evening and can pick up the kids from school. It's a better schedule, with young kids."

Jeff leaned in the window, wanting to keep the conversation between them, as others walked to their vehicles. "I'd like to take you out sometime, if and when you feel like it."

Carly felt her stomach lurch, not sure how to respond. "Uh, well, okay. I don't see anything wrong with two friends going out for dinner."

He crossed his chest. "Purely platonic, cross my heart."

"I don't think I'm ready to *date,* but I have fun with you. You're growing on me."

Jeff backed away from the window. "Growing on you, like mold?"

Carly smiled. "No, like someone I enjoy being around."

"Okay, okay. I'll take that as a compliment. I'm glad we have the rest of the week."

Carly's mood became serious. "I'm going to miss the crew and you. I'll tell the kids and Dottie tonight."

Carly rolled up her window as Jeff got in his Mustang convertible. He waited for her to pull out of the lot. She waved and merged onto Highway 17. The drive home allowed her time to digest the meeting with Bauer. Long story short, she was demoted in the world of news broadcasting. Carly felt a moment of sadness overtake her. Her eyes filled with tears, but she willed herself not to break down. *Now is the perfect time to explore remote job opportunities. I could conduct investigations, provide consulting services, and deliver public speaking presentations at conferences...there's no shortage of options if I want to travel.*

Carly's outlook changed in a matter of minutes. She turned on the text-to-speech option on her phone to send a text to Delaney.

Hey, it's Carly. I got demoted tonight after I signed off on the news. Ratings aren't what they were, and it's apparently my fault. Long story, but I'm being booted to the morning show. Erin will take my spot with Jeff. We'll talk later. Love ya.

She drove the rest of the way home without the radio. Tomorrow, she'd think about her future with Channel 5. Bauer might have given her the nudge to pursue a different career path.

～

Carly walked inside, tossing her keys into the silver bowl on the entry table. Dottie called her from the den. "We're in the den. Supper's in the microwave."

Vivi hurried into the kitchen, wrapping her arms around Carly's waist. "You're late." Her voice carried a hint of anxiety.

"Oh, I had a meeting after work, and I got a late start home. It's okay." Carly bent down to hold Vivi in her arms and kiss the top of her soft hair.

Since Austin's death, anytime Carly arrives late, Vivi exhibits signs of anxiety, waiting for her to return. The therapist for the children reassured Carly that this behavior is expected.

Dottie and Frederick joined them in the kitchen. "Mom, can I go home with Parker tomorrow? He wants me to go to Wednesday Night church with him."

Carly ensured the children remained involved in sports and church activities. "I don't see why not. I can pick you up when it's over." She carried her plate over to the table.

Dottie sat beside Carly with her bowl of leftover soup. "I saved mine so you wouldn't have to eat alone," she said.

Carly smiled at the gesture. "You didn't have to wait on me to eat. I appreciate your company, though."

Dottie passed Carly a napkin. "I like the company as well. I'm getting comfortable and settled."

Carly wanted to discuss the changes to her hours at the station with Dottie. Frederick and Vivi went back into the den, leaving Carly and Dottie to speak in private.

"I'm changing time slots at the station."

Dottie looked up from her bowl, "Oh? I thought you and the new anchor hit it off?"

Carly saw no reason to hide anything from Dottie. She continued. "Well, actually, I'm getting moved to the morning show because of ratings." Carly shoveled a spoonful of soup into her mouth.

"How can your ratings drop because of you? Everyone loves you," Dottie said incredulously.

"I've taken off a lot of time, not to mention arriving late and having to use the break room as childcare. I'm probably lucky he didn't fire me."

"I'm here now, and there's no reason for you to do those things with me helping."

Carly patted Dottie's arm. "I know you coming to us is a godsend, but this might not be the end of the world for me."

Carly finished her soup and carried her bowl to the sink. "I've thought about working from home for a while now. I've thought about holding more conferences and maybe doing a podcast from home."

Dottie joined Carly at the sink. "Here, let me. Sit at the bar and tell me your plans." She filled the sink with water and dish soap as Carly continued.

"I have money in my retirement account. Austin left me in good financial shape. I've thought about selling the house and moving to a smaller home on one level."

"Oh, my. Where will you go, back home to your folks?"

Carly hadn't thought that far. "Mom and Dad would love it, but I don't know how the kids would feel."

Dottie didn't comment. Carly sensed her uneasiness with the subject. "I don't foresee us moving to Kansas, at least not anytime soon. I haven't even said anything to the kids."

Dottie turned to Carly, "I'll understand when the time comes. There are Senior living places all over Charleston for people my age, should I need a place to go."

Carly shook her head. "No, you will go with us to our next home. Besides, you're not ready for a retirement home. You're not much older than me!"

Dottie laughed. "I'm sixty-five, and my husband took care of every-thing. I never thought I'd be a widow. I thought I'd go first."

The part about *never thinking I'd be a widow* resonated with Carly. "I know what you mean. I'm forty-two, and Austin always kept my compass pointing North."

Talking with Dottie helped with the demotion and uncertainty ahead. She threw caution to the wind and shared more with her. "You know about my *ability,* don't you?"

Dottie lowered her voice to keep the children from hearing her, "If you mean you talk to ghosts, yes. I'll admit it gives me the willies, but you didn't ask for it."

"That's true, and I am in the middle of something that could take me to Boston for the kids' fall break. I'm thinking about speaking to Bauer about leaving Channel 5."

Dottie's jaw dropped. "Do you think you're jumping the gun? You're thinking in the short term, but you must think about the long term."

"I can't explain it, but I've been thinking about it before he spoke to me."

Before they finished their discussion, Carly received a text notification. Delaney received her message and wanted to talk.

"Thank you for listening to my dilemma."

Dottie squeezed Carly's arm. "I'm glad to be needed again."

Carly put her phone in her pocket and started drying the dishes in the drainer. Dottie wiped her hands and went upstairs to her apartment after they exchanged good nights.

It was already nine o'clock. Vivi lay on the couch, asleep with the afghan pulled over her. Frederick had taken his shower earlier and sat in the recliner, watching a kids' program on television.

Vivi stirred at the sound of Carly's voice. "Come on, kiddos. Time for bed." She walked over to the couch and helped Vivi up, folding the afghan and putting it back on the arm of the sofa.

Carly walked upstairs with Frederick and Vivi and tucked them in. She left the hall light on and went back downstairs to her office. She took her phone from her pocket and texted Delaney. "Is this a good time to call?"

Instead of a text, Delaney called her. "Hey, what's going on at Channel 5?"

Carly tucked her legs underneath her in the chair. "Hello to you, too," she laughed, then said, "I got put on morning show anchor duties. Erin is taking my six o'clock slot."

Delaney's voice rose with surprise. "Morning show? Who watches that?"

Carly closed her eyes, the strain of the day caused a headache to pound. "I know, it's the worst. I think I'm going to turn in my two-week notice. I've thought about doing something from home, and Bauer just nudged me in that direction with the meeting tonight."

"I know how much working at six o'clock means to you. How'd Jeff react?"

Carly recounted the meeting and how he went to bat for her. She also explained the drop in ratings, pointing to a decline in interest in Carly as the co-anchor.

"I think I need to spend more time on my paranormal gifts, helping others, and offering my speaking services at conferences and such."

"It sounds like you've thought about this before tonight. You'll make it just fine, financially speaking."

Carly shared her exchange with Jeff in the parking lot. "I told him I'd like to go out sometime. Do you think I'm horrible for it?"

"Did you say yes because you want to get back at Austin, or because you want male company?"

Carly started to deny everything Delaney insinuated, but in reality, she was guilty of a little of both. "I don't feel a romantic connection to anyone. I still feel the love I had for Austin. I also find I want him to know how much his affair hurt me."

"I think it's only human, even though it's only been a few months.

We all grieve differently, and your circumstance in learning about his affair throws a monkey wrench into everything."

"I think I'll send a message to the people from our conference. I've thought a lot about earning money in speaking fees and subscriptions to a paranormal blog."

The pronouncement took Delaney a moment to process. "Sweetie, the time away from the demands of work will open up time for you to solve the Bethesda Twelve connection to your visions and hauntings."

Carly changed the subject on that note. "I had another vision of Caroline and the children on the ship. I heard the name of her first husband's brother. Do you think I'm a time traveler?"

"You mean like *Outlander* time travel?" she asked, surprised.

"I sometimes feel like I've become Caroline. I feel her thoughts and know things and conversations."

"Have you contacted Alexandria Diaz? Her presentation at Coombe Abbey sounded very convincing."

Carly kept the files from the conference and the Bethesda Twelve on her desk. "I kept all the business cards and papers from the conference. I want to talk to several of the speakers again."

"Have you talked to Drake?" Delaney asked, raising her eyebrows.

Carly's face lit up. "As a matter of fact, I'm going to call him. I want to talk to him about Caroline."

She started to say something else when the picture of her and Austin fell to the floor and shattered.

CHAPTER TWENTY-FIVE

Carly tapped on the door. "Do you have a minute, Bauer?"

"Sure, come in. Do you plan to announce the move to mornings at the end of the newscast?" he asked, standing as Carly walked in and closed the door behind her.

Wow…nothing like getting right to the point. She felt her heart beating in her ears. She knew red blotches covered her cheeks and neck like they always did when she was nervous or upset.

"Actually, there's something else I wanted to speak to you about." She exhaled. "Whew, this isn't going to be as easy as I thought."

Bauer's brows furrowed. "We've always shot from the hip, so let me have it."

Carly smiled, thinking back to all the conversations he thought he'd had the upper hand, when in fact, Carly had Bauer eating from her hand.

"I've had time to think about what I need to do for myself and the kids. Right now, I need to step away from Channel 5." She felt her throat tighten and felt like she'd swallowed cotton.

"Damn. Didn't see that one coming." Bauer gulped from a bottle of water on his desk. "Is there anything I can do to change your mind?"

Carly wanted to look away from Bauer's intense stare, but she looked him directly in the eye. "No, I've decided tonight I'm telling our viewers I'm resigning. Please consider this as my two-week notice. If you'd like, I will remain on the morning show during that time so you can find a replacement."

"Yes, I'll need you through next week. I can move Darby Jacobson from the weekend to mornings. She wants more hours, and this will make her happy."

"Well, if that works, I'll use whatever time I have left and end next Friday after the morning show."

"You've done a hell of a job over the past eleven years for Channel 5." Bauer came from behind his desk and reached out to hug Carly, something uncharacteristic of him.

Carly accepted his hug, "Thank you for all you've done for me, Bauer. I'll miss Channel 5 and everyone I've had the pleasure to work with."

She heard Jeff Sullivan's voice outside Bauer's office with Erin Finney, Carly's replacement. She waited for a moment, then gathered her emotions and left Bauer's office.

Jeff held the door open for Erin, and the two went into the newsroom. Carly entered the makeup room, grabbed a cape, and sat in her usual chair. Liz came from the wardrobe closet, unaware that Carly had entered.

"You're early!" Liz said, putting her arm around Carly's shoulder.

"I wanted to talk to Bauer before the news. Tonight's my last night on the six o'clock, you know."

Liz nodded as she applied concealer under Carly's eyes. "I won't get to do your makeup for the early news. I'm sorry."

Carly turned in the chair to face Liz. "I'm leaving Channel 5 at the end of next week."

Liz's look of surprise caused Carly's eyes to fill with tears. "I need to spend more time at home with Frederick and Vivi."

"No need to explain. Your kids need you." Liz patted Carly's back. "We go way back, girl. I'll miss you something terrible."

Jeff walked in and plopped down in his chair. "Did I interrupt a girl moment?" he said in his usual joking manner.

"No, I told Liz tonight is it for me at six o'clock. I'm leaving next Friday," Carly said without making eye contact in the mirror.

"So, you decided not to stay, huh? I'm going to miss you and the kiddos."

Carly laughed, "I'm sure they will miss everyone here, including you."

After the news, the producers ran a montage of the past eleven years featuring Carly, from her early investigative reporting through her years with Chad Flannery, culminating in her time with Jeff Sullivan. She couldn't stop the tears from flowing, and all her staff over the years, along with Bauer Donahue, joined her on set.

"Thank you, all, for making this feel like home. I'll remember you fondly as I move on to my next adventure."

The studio lights dimmed, and Carly made the rounds, hugging each person. Chip Burlinger, Executive Producer, and Doug Lukas, her cameraman for the last eleven years, were the last to bid her farewell.

"I feel like Dorothy leaving Oz," Carly said, giving each a hug.

"We've been through a lot, Tabor," Doug said. "I wish you all the best."

"Thank you, both, for everything." Carly kissed Doug's cheek and hugged Chip, the anti-hugger who made an exception for Carly.

Carly went to her locker and removed her purse. She found an empty box on one of the shelves and cleaned off her desk. Jeff walked in as she finished putting her pictures and nameplate into the box.

"Do you need any help?" Jeff asked.

Carly closed the drawers to the desk. "No, thanks. I've taken a few things home each night. Eleven years of memories packed in this box. Unbelievable."

Jeff walked in closer, leaning down to Carly's ear. His warm breath and scent of his cologne caused Carly to flush. She didn't move.

"Remember what I said, I want to see you outside of work."

Carly stood up, feeling uncertain about what might happen next. "I remember," she replied.

Jeff hesitated, then wrapped his arms around her. "Take care of yourself."

"Thank you, Jeff. I'll look forward to watching you and Erin on the news."

He insisted on carrying her box to her vehicle. He watched Carly drive out of the parking lot.

As Carly pulled into her driveway, she saw a curious couple standing in front of her house on the mounting block. The stone block, originally on her home's lot, was used during the eighteenth and nineteenth centuries for ladies to dismount from their carriages. The stone step survived its early days due to the preservation efforts in Charleston but served no other purpose. Tourists liked the stone block for a quick photograph in front of Carly's home.

The couple waved, and Carly returned the gesture and went inside. She'd grown accustomed to sightseers on her street, and especially after her fifteen minutes of fame with her paranormal dealings. Inside, Dottie carried a steaming dish over to the kitchen table.

"Hey, I'm home." Carly put her purse on the hall table and continued into the kitchen. "Whatever you're making smells delicious."

Dottie returned to the counter to retrieve another bowl. "Well, I thought we'd have one of your favorites: shrimp and grits, along with Carolina Rice."

Carly's eyes lit up at the sight. "You're the best, Ms. Dottie. Thank you for taking such good care of us."

Frederick and Vivi hurried down the stairs and into the kitchen, hugging their mom and talking at the same time. "Did you quit your job tonight?" Frederick asked.

Vivi chimed in. "Can you stay home with Ms. Dottie now?"

Carly tried to answer both questions simultaneously. "I'll work next week on the morning show, then I'll stay home for a while. I'm not exactly sure what I'll do next."

Before anyone could ask another question, Dottie pointed to the children. "You two go wash for dinner. I'll pour your drinks. Two lemonades?"

"Yes!" Frederick and Vivi answered exuberantly.

Carly washed her hands and dried them with a paper towel. "I rented a van for next week. I'm surprising the kids with a trip to Boston, and if you're willing, nanny duties for some of the time."

"That's why you hired me, plus housework. I'm at your service," Dottie said, putting ice in the glasses.

"Great. I found an Airbnb outside the city limits and found a great children's museum nearby."

Frederick and Vivi took their place at the table. Austin's seat became Carly's, and Dottie sat in Carly's. Everyone took the hand of the person beside them, and Frederick offered the blessing. Carly wanted to bring her family traditions to her home now that the children were getting older.

After the prayer, Carly dipped a portion of the shrimp and grits onto the children's plates. "Next Saturday starts your fall break. I'm taking us on a trip."

Frederick's eyes widened. "Where are we going?"

Vivi looked apprehensive about the *trip*. She still became anxious when she thought of the last trip Carly took.

"I'm taking us to Boston. We'll stay in an Airbnb in Medford. There's a lot of history during the Revolutionary War and several great museums." Carly passed the rice to Dottie.

Frederick had recently developed an interest in history, and Carly planned day trips to Lexington, Concord, and downtown sites. Vivi, still silent, didn't seem at all excited.

"Vivi, there's a Children's Museum and Aquarium, and I've purchased tickets for us. You'll love it," Carly said. The mention of an aquarium appeased Vivi.

"Do I have to sleep with her?" Frederick pointed his finger at Vivi.

Carly gave Frederick the 'mom look'. "We'll each have a bed. You and Vivi will have to share a room, though."

A truce reached, they continued with the amenities of the house and getting a rental car from the airport.

For the rest of the meal, the conversation centered around the places Carly planned to take them. She also shared that she'd spend a day searching for information about Eira Richards in the orphan records. As interesting as research sounded to Carly, the children were unamused.

The children and Dottie went upstairs to get ready for bed, and after tucking in Frederick and Vivi, Carly went downstairs to her office. The file containing everything from her trip to the UK sat on top of her desk. She found the small paper bag containing business cards and note cards from the conference.

Alexandria Diaz's card listed her contact information. Carly checked the time- ten o'clock. She counted back the three hours to Pacific time, where Alexandria lived. She put in the number and waited.

"Hello," a woman's voice says.

"Alexandria, this is Carly Tabor. We met at the Spirit Seekers Conference in June."

"Yes, of course. It's good to hear from you."

"I meant to reach out to you sooner. Do you have a minute to talk?" Carly asked.

She spent the next twenty minutes sharing the incidents involving Caroline Richards, the murder of her second husband, Stefan Madoc, and the DNA results on the Bethesda Twelve.

"I'm intrigued by the experiences you've shared with me. It's truly fascinating."

Carly felt a letdown coming. "Do you think I'm experiencing traveling in time to the eighteenth century?"

"I'm not sure it's time travel, but you've experienced Caroline's life events as if you are Caroline," Alexandria explained.

"Some days I think I'm losing my mind. The visions are so real, and I experienced a murder trial in Wales," Carly shared.

She waited for Alexandria to say something, anything at all. Finally, she spoke.

"I suppose it's possible for someone to experience time travel in bits instead of a whole period, like I experienced." Alexandria continued, "I traveled back in time, for days, consecutively."

As they continued their discussion, Dr. Alston Curry's business card drew Carly's attention away from Alexandria for a moment. She turned the card over and read an inscription she'd missed before. *When you're ready, I'm here to help. Alston Curry*

"If you're free, I'd love to see you again," Alexandria said.

Carly missed part of the conversation. "I'm sorry. What did you say?"

"Byron Harris and I are speaking at a paranormal conference in

Arizona. There's still time to contact the administrators if you'd like to speak at a session."

Carly declined but thanked Alexandria. "I'm planning on speaking at the conference in the summer with Spirit Seekers. Will you attend?"

"Yes, several from Spirit Seekers Paracon will attend, including me."

"All right, I'll see you in Massachusetts. Please tell Byron hello for me, and Delaney."

Carly flipped through her conference notes. The message on the back of Alson Curry's business card kept coming back in her mind. *How could he help me? I don't need help making objects move or ESP.* Carly put the business cards back in the bag and picked up the booklet from the conference. She leafed through the pages of the speaker biographies. Drake Taylor's bio caught her attention. His dark hair and emerald, green eyes resonated with her. His features, chiseled and somewhat regal, added to his attractiveness. The deep green of his eyes reached into her soul. She'd wanted to contact him a couple of weeks ago, but the changes at Channel 5 kept her mind on other things. She knew the time difference meant Drake more than likely still slept. After Dottie left to take the kids to school, she'd call him.

A text from Delaney drew her away from thoughts about Drake. *Hey, I'm sorry I won't get to join y'all on the Boston trip. I'm watching Sutton while her parents fly to Cancun for the week.*

Carly texted back. *No worries, enjoy your time with Sutton. I'll catch you up when we return. We'll talk tomorrow.*

She set her phone on her desk and reclined for a moment in her chair. Her eyes grew heavy, and she found herself in a vivid dream.

"Please, send word to Arwin Richards. He'll come for the children."

"Mistress Richards, you've just the two children now. The babe and young Elizabeth entered their eternal rest early this morning," Orpha, the wife of Thaddeus Brown, said.

"Bring me the children," Caroline said, weak, struggling to form the words.

Young Frederick, three, and Eira, eighteen months, stood at the foot of the bed with Orpha Brown. Caroline held out a thin, discolored hand.

" Rwy'n dy garu di. Duw ewch gyda chi," Caroline said in Welsh, which means, I love you. God go with you.

Carly's chin fell to her chest, causing her head to jerk up. She looked around the room. The ghost of Freddy Richards stood in the corner, clutching the small blue and white checked baby quilt Carly had placed in his coffin in 2014.

She started to walk toward him, but the scent of Austin's cologne filled the room, and Freddy vanished. Emotion overtook her, and she began to cry. She remembered kissing him goodbye as she prepared to go through TSA. It was the last time she'd seen him whole, without the swelling of a broken body from the crash. His last text to her, still on her phone, read, *Love you, Austin.* But how could he text that he loved her and have Cora with him? She wanted to throw something to hurt him like he'd hurt her. Then she saw him standing in the doorway. His mouth, his sensual lips moved, but she couldn't make out the words. He moved toward her, inching closer to her chair. Carly's body froze, unable to stand. She remained transfixed on his face, the words becoming louder. She understood now. *Please, take me home.*

CHAPTER TWENTY-SIX

October 20th, 2025
Medford, Massachusetts

The drive from the airport to the Airbnb in Medford offered picturesque views and foliage in brilliant yellows, crimson, and vibrant orange. Upon arrival at the house, everyone grabbed their luggage and waited for Carly to punch in the code to unlock the door. Carly led the way inside, into a beautifully decorated open kitchen and dining area. The home drew excited whoops from the children, while Dottie and Carly uttered several "Oh, my goodness!" and "What an amazing kitchen!"

The children noticed the enormous television mounted on the wall and the game room area off the kitchen, complete with another television, as well as air hockey and ping pong tables. A spacious laundry room and an enclosed sunroom rounded out the downstairs area.

Upstairs, Carly found a large bedroom with two double beds, where Frederick and Vivi put their luggage. Down the hall, two bedrooms featured Queen beds and plenty of windows. Carly and Dottie shared a bathroom, as did the children.

"I may want to buy this for a week or two during the summers in Charleston," Carly teased.

"How did you find this place? It's lovely." Dottie gave her stamp of approval.

"Actually, Jeff Sullivan recommended it when I mentioned in passing I wanted to come to Boston."

"I love it here," Vivi squealed, running into the hallway and hugging Carly.

"I'm glad, sweet pea. I love it too."

After everyone unpacked, they drove to a nearby supermarket to get groceries and supplies for the week. The town of Medford boasted a rich history dating back to the seventeenth century. Carly marveled at the houses from the colonial period. Living in a historic house made her appreciate other historical homes from different regions.

"We're so close to places where our country began, kids. If you want, we can drive to Bunker Hill, Lexington, and Concord..." Before Carly could continue, her phone rang.

"Did you get settled in yet?" Jeff Sullivan asked.

"Yes, and we love it. We're driving around; just got groceries and heading home to eat dinner."

"I'm glad to hear it. I miss the old stompin' grounds. This time of year is beautiful."

"I miss the seasons, too. Thank you again for your suggestions," Carly said, trying to concentrate on the road while talking.

"Let's do dinner and cruise on *Sullivan's Witch* when y'all come home."

Carly grinned. "Did I just hear a southern drawl coming from you?"

"I'm working on it. You might take on the Boston accent while you're visiting."

Carly gave the accent a shot, bringing snickers from the back seat.

"Okay, we'll take you up on the cruise and dinner. Have a good night, Jeff."

"Thanks, you too. Stay safe and enjoy your vacation."

Carly planned morning outings each day with the kids and used the afternoons for their downtime. The trip to the historic sites took place from Monday through Thursday. Carly planned Friday and Saturday as research days, while Dottie supervised the kids until her return. The house next to the Airbnb had a boy of Frederick's age. They made friends the first day and played basketball in their driveway while Dottie kept a close eye on them.

On Friday morning, Carly drove into Boston, ready to delve into the historical books and documents. Her first stop, the Massachusetts Historical Society, at 1154 Boylston Street, took longer than she'd planned. Traffic backups in downtown Boston forced her to use the GPS reroute to get around the delay. She arrived at the Historical Society twenty-five minutes after it opened to visitors. She Googled information about the Historical Society and read that the Massachusetts Historical Society was the oldest historical society in the United States, founded on January 24th, 1791. The Colonial Revival building, constructed of limestone and red Roman brick, was designed by Edmund Wheelwright and completed in 1899. The building rose above Boylston Street, making a grand statement. The vast collections held inside the building included the Adams Family Papers, Thomas Jefferson Papers, as well as an original copy of the Declaration of Independence.

With her love for American History, Carly knew the Historical Society could easily take weeks to view its vast holdings. She didn't have the luxury of time on this trip. She marveled at the rich wood paneling and marble floors. She found the reference desk, and Dan

Hinchen, reference librarian, greeted Carly as she approached with a notebook and digital recorder.

"Good morning," Dan said. "How may I help you this morning?"

Carly took out her notes. "I'm looking for specific books related to the Boston Female Asylum. I'm searching for a particular inmate."

Dan took the paper and looked over it. "Of course, I'll be able to help you locate the collection we have here on site."

In a matter of minutes, he led Carly to the room where the micro-film collection was located. "We have several volumes pertaining to the first Female Asylum as well as subsequent years. Is there a particular year you're interested in seeing?" Dan asked.

"Yes, I'm looking for 1794."

"That would include the first and second years of the Asylum, as it began in 1793." Dan brought out the film Carly asked for. It included two volumes of the book, Orphan Children Admitted Into The Boston Female Asylum, 1793-1850. He also brought out Boston Society For The Care of Girls: Asylum Records 1793-1860.

"Thank you. Both volumes should have the name of the child I'm searching for."

Dan nodded. "Excellent resources. We have others if you're unable to locate the child in either of these minutes and records." Before leaving, he turned, "If you need assistance, Darby Alexander is sitting just outside at the desk." He pointed through the door to a small desk and a petite college-aged woman, who was engaged with another patron.

"Thank you, I'm sure I'll find her. I feel confident today," Carly said, her excitement evident.

She copied the information in her notebook, in case she'd need to return online. The screen brought up the first pages of the book, and it took Carly a moment to read the script. She took a pair of readers from her bag and adjusted them to see the entries.

Reading the minutes took longer because Carly remembered that a lowercase f was often replaced with an s in the writing of the time. She read the names, dates, and person responsible for admitting the child to the care of the asylum. She scanned the list of baptisms and financial records for 1793.

After an hour, she checked the notes she'd taken when researching online. She needed to find November of 1794, as that date marked Freddy Richards's admission to the Charleston Orphan Asylum on September 25th, plus at least two months to travel from Charleston, South Carolina, to Boston, Massachusetts, along the King's Highway, a distance of 1,300 miles. Most of the way was an unpaved dirt path, a widened version of existing Native American trails.

Carly remembered studying about President George Washington's travels on the King's Highway to tour the South after he became president from March to June 1791. The couple murdered in her home, Andrew and Celeste Pettigrew, were introduced to President Washington while he visited McGrady's Tavern in Charleston. He also stayed at Celeste Pettigrew's father's, Dr. Peter Fasoux, home. She thought about Alexandria Diaz and her travel through time. Carly wished for the ability to travel back and warn Celeste and Andrew about Jacob Hinman's plan, saving them and Freddy Richards. Carly said under her breath, "Maybe I did travel in time, just a different continent." The thought seemed too far-fetched, even for Carly to believe.

After giving her eyes a much-needed rest, she continued on to Volume II. She flipped through every page until she reached January 1794. Miss Albertson would have wanted to get to Boston as quickly as possible, especially while traveling with an infant. Carly searched the entries again, looking for different spellings of the name Eira. *Could Miss Albertson have changed the child's name since she used a fictitious name when she admitted Freddy?*

Is this turning into a wild goose chase? Carly sighed and took a moment to gather her thoughts. *If I wanted to travel from one orphan asylum to another while minimizing travel time, I certainly wouldn't choose to journey overland for two months with a small child. I would take a ship up the coast.*

She quickly searched for a list of ships arriving in Boston in 1794. Her efforts yielded a list of vessels from several locations in Ireland, Scotland, and one from the West Indies. Notably, a ship was coming from Charleston to Boston. Carly then searched for the length of time it took to sail from Charleston, South Carolina, to Boston, Massachusetts.

The information that came up included a detailed explanation of various factors that could either shorten or extend the sailing time. It typically took between eight and fourteen days to make the journey, unless the ship encountered the doldrums, which could significantly delay its arrival.

The time it took to get to Boston was only two weeks. Carly regained her confidence and started to backtrack her search. She hurried to the beginning of the entries in October. She moved the cursor ever so slightly, not to miss anything. "Yes!" Carly exclaimed. She looked around, embarrassed by her outburst.

Her patience paid off. The document was written neatly with the date, October 5, 1794, and the name *Eira Richards. Happy tears slid down her cheeks. This child, once lost to the records of Bethesda, was found 231 years later.* Carly continued reading the rest of the line. *Deposited on this day, by Susannah Richards, mother.*

Carly felt immense satisfaction in locating Eira yet also felt a sense of sadness. How tragic to endure separation from her mother and older sister in death, then, to face separation from her sole relative, Freddy. How could Ms. Albertson exhibit such cruelty? Why did Bethesda's administrators not honor Caroline's dying request?

The next question weighed on her mind. What became of Eira Richards? The arrangement between Mr. Duncan and Ms. Albertson involved bringing orphans from the Foundling Home in London to the colonies for profit.

She printed the page for her records, then forged ahead. For the next two hours, Carly scanned the entries for mention of Eira. She reached for her phone to check the time. Her stomach already told her she needed to eat something. Carly went inside her bag for a protein bar; it sufficed until supper.

By three o'clock, she'd exhausted the microfilm volumes from the Female Asylums entries and minutes of the care of the inmates. One volume, "Boston Society for the Care of Girls: Asylum Record, 1794-1860," caught her attention. She went to the young girl, Darcy, at the information desk. In short order, the microfilm volume was loaded into the microfilm reader. The book consisted of three reels, and it contained baptisms, names of orphans entering and leaving the asylum, as well as deaths of inmates.

Carly looked away from the screen. She'd not given in to the thought of Eira not surviving in adulthood. *You're here, somewhere, and I'll find out what happened to you.*

The museum closed at five o'clock. She'd remain another hour and return tomorrow if nothing turned up today.

She read through the transcribed pages, an added luxury by the Genealogical Society in Salt Lake City, Utah. It sped up her reading and allowed her to skim the entries.

The name Eira Richards practically jumped from the page. *Eira Richards, aged 1 year and 8 months, to Robert Clarke, Esq. and consort, November 17th, 1794.*

"Thank you, Lord," Carly said, printing the page. She sent a text to Delaney. "Wonderful news. I'll call tonight."

She thanked Darby and asked if she could search for the name Robert Clarke in the family papers held at the historical society. Within minutes, she found the family's papers.

"Would you like me to print out what we have on site?" Darby asked.

"Yes, please." Carly waited as Darby retrieved the paper. "Thank you, I'll see you tomorrow!"

Chapter Twenty-Seven

Frederick and Vivi finished eating their dinner and sat on the cozy sofa with Carly. They wanted to know what she did at the historical society while they played games with Dottie and watched television.

"It sounds like you enjoyed a day just hanging out here. I, on the other hand, stared at a microfilm screen all day."

Vivi scrunched her nose, "What's a microfilm? It sounds like a microwave." She giggled at herself.

Carly explained the process as best she could to a six-year-old.

"It sounds horrid," Vivi said.

Hearing her use such a grown-up word surprised Carly. "Where'd you hear that word? And no, I learned a lot today."

"Granny says it," Vivi said, nonchalantly.

Carly's expression turned serious. "Granny? You mean Memes?" The kids didn't have a grandparent they referred to as 'Granny'.

"No, Graannny," Vivi said, drawing out the name to emphasize who she referred to.

The only person called Granny was Carly's Grandmother Eddleman, and she died before the birth of Carly's children.

"I saw her when Memes took me for a walk to where she grew up," Vivi said.

The blood drained from Carly's face, and Frederick looked at Vivi in disbelief.

"You're making it up, Vivi! You didn't see anyone." Frederick looked at Carly. "Mom, she's trying to be like you."

The sudden panic Carly felt robbed her of her voice for a second. When she came back with a reply, it didn't sound convincing. "Vivi, I'm sure it just sounded like you heard someone."

"She stayed outside on the porch swing. She isn't scary, Mommy."

"You're freaking me out, Vivi. Mom, make her stop it." Frederick went into the kitchen area with Dottie.

Carly put her hand under Vivi's chin, lifting her face to hers. "Vivi, do you see anyone else, I mean, like Granny?"

Vivi's eyes widened, and she hesitated. Carly put her arm around her, wanting to protect her from whatever she felt now.

"No, just Granny. I don't see her at home, just at Memes's house."

Carly knew her daughter shared the gift, but she hoped she wouldn't see anyone else. "It's all right that you saw Granny. She loved me very much, and I loved her."

For the rest of the evening, no one spoke of Vivi's revelation. Frederick watched a movie and went upstairs to take his shower while Carly and Dottie cleaned up the kitchen.

Vivi played with a doll she'd bought at a gift shop at one of the Revolutionary War sites. Carly peeked in to check on her, then turned back to Dottie, "I guess you heard what Vivi said."

Dottie continued washing the dishes without looking at her, but answered Carly, "Yes, I heard what she said. You handled it as best as you could."

"Austin would lose his crap if he heard her say she saw my Granny," Carly said.

"I don't see how this is anyone's fault. Neither you nor Vivi asked for this. Besides, she found comfort in seeing your Granny." Dottie's voice, although reassuring, didn't change the fact that Carly's six-year-old daughter shared her ability.

"So, tell me what you learned today at the museum," Dottie said, changing the subject.

Carly brought her papers into the kitchen to share the information on Eira Richards. "Tomorrow, I want to go back to the museum and search for Eira in the Census records or anything else I can find before we leave Sunday morning."

"I'll take Vivi upstairs and draw her a bath, if you want to call Delaney."

Carly waited until Vivi and Dottie were out of earshot, then called Delaney. She picked up on the first ring.

"Hey, perfect timing. My hand just reached for the phone to call you," Delaney said.

"I'm glad I caught you. I hope it's not a bad time to call."

"No, Sutton just left with Jarrod and Chelsea. I'm all ears."

"I found Eira Richards. Ms. Albertson sailed up the coast with her to the Female Asylum in Boston the first week of October. The record book says Robert Clarke and his consort adopted her in November of 1794."

"You're amazing! How did you know the right month and where to look?"

Carly went over the notes she'd taken prior to leaving, and with a little help from Caroline, she said half-jokingly. "I'm going tomorrow to the Historical Society to find more information on Eira and the Clarke family. Maybe something needs to be resolved with her. Why else has Caroline haunted me?"

"Do you know when the remains of Caroline and the others will get reinterred?"

"I expect it will take place soon. I want to attend the service for Caroline, Elizabeth, and the baby."

Delaney made small talk about a house on the market, a street over from her home. They discussed Carly's prospects for employment now that she'd resigned from Channel 5.

"Austin appeared to me before we left on our trip. He told me he wants to go home."

"Home, like Kansas?"

"Yes, I think he wants to have a proper burial. I told him I couldn't move on, and he couldn't either."

"Mark is buried at Mt. Pleasant nearby. His people are there." Delaney sighed. "I don't think I could entertain another man here with Mark in the house."

They found the topic comical, despite its seriousness. Carly cleared her throat. "Something else happened that I wanted to share with you."

"Something good, I hope." The lilt in Delaney's voice brought a smile to Carly's face.

"Well, it's probably not what you'd call good, per se." Carly continued, "Tonight, Vivi shared somewhat out of the blue that she has seen my Granny Eddleman."

Delaney gasped. "Vivi said that to you? When did it happen?"

Carly explained the events where Granny appeared to Vivi while she and Frederick stayed with Carly's folks. "I'm sure she doesn't see Austin or Freddy, like me. I promised Austin."

Delaney interrupted, "You didn't do anything to cause this. None of us asked for this. I hope she isn't afraid."

Carly felt thankful for Vivi's innocence. "I remember as a child of her age seeing ghosts at the graveyard with Granny. No one else in the family believed me."

"I think my mother and Grandma expected I'd share their abilities, but I never felt afraid," Delaney said.

"I didn't either, until we bought our house. Benjamin Hastings terrified me. Thank the Lord he moved on."

Vivi and Frederick came downstairs, both wanting a snack. The cabinet door opened and closed, prompting Carly to say, "I'll find some popcorn. Hold on."

Delaney said, "Tell the kids Auntie Lanie loves them. I'll see you when y'all get home. Safe travels."

"I'll tell them. Good night."

Carly stared at the ceiling, wide awake and unable to shake Vivi's insight into the spirit of her great-grandmother. The revelation regarding Eira Richards and the increasing appearance of Austin kept her mind racing. She rolled onto her side and glanced at her phone; it displayed five o'clock. Closing her eyes, she willed herself back to sleep.

"I've sent word to Trefor's brother in South Carolina. He'll have the money I need to pay the taxes on the land," said Caroline.

"If you don't return before spring, Gethen Bowen will buy the land once you can't pay the taxes," Catherine replied. She gazed out the window of the stone cottage, her eyes fixed on two graves. Each had an inscribed headstone marking the resting place of Trefor Richards and Stefan Madoc.

Her sister, Catherine, took her hand. "Trefor wanted this land for you and the children, and Stefan died defending it," she said softly.

Caroline placed her hand on her stomach; her pregnancy was just beginning to show.

"When do you leave?" Catherine asked.

Caroline continued spinning the wool into thread. "Dafydd, Stefan's father, will take us to London. He will speak to the court on my behalf."

Catherine reached into the wooden basket beside her and handed Caroline more wool.

"Sister, if the court in London agrees to wait six months before seizing the property, will you have enough time to return with the money?"

Caroline huffed. "I've given it much thought. We'll find a ship sailing to South Carolina. Arwin told us he had a land grant in South Carolina. When I reach the port, I'll inquire as to his whereabouts."

"And what will you tell him when he sees you with your belly pushed out from your skirt?"

Caroline stopped spinning and raised her eyes. "He didn't know Trefor died of the fever or that I married another. He'd already left for the colonies."

"What if he says no?" Catherine asked. "Traveling with the small ones and another coming, have you thought of this?"

"Dafydd will return and protect our land until I sail home with the money." Caroline raised her chin, "I have to go. There's no other way."

Carly rubbed her eyes, the alarm on her phone still playing. She managed to shut it off before the rest of the house heard it. Carly remembered the dream. Or was it a dream? Why do I see Caroline's life so clearly? Her experiences are as clear as mine.

"Breakfast is ready!" Dottie said, standing at the bottom of the stairs.

Carly heard Vivi and Frederick's voices coming from the kitchen. "On my way!" she said.

A different lady sat behind the information desk than had been there the day before. Carly pulled a Post-it note from her purse that listed the name Robert Clarke.

She waited until the lady looked up from her phone.

"Good morning, how may I help you?" she said.

Carly asked for help finding the Robert Clarke family papers. "I'm especially interested in the years 1794 and after."

Connie, the lady behind the desk, searched the online holdings for Robert Clarke, Boston, Massachusetts. "I have several items. They are with the Bromfield-Clarke papers."

"Excellent!" Carly said, curbing her enthusiasm as best she could.

"The collection consists of the records of Boston import merchants Robert Clarke and Sons, including correspondence, financial records, and commonplace books," Connie read from the screen, then added, "Robert Clarke (1729-1800) was born in Boston, Mass., on 1 May 1729, the son of William Clarke and Elizabeth Appleton Clarke. He graduated from Harvard College in 1749. As a Boston merchant and agent of the East India Company, he operated his business as Robert Clarke and Sons with his sons Edward, Richard, and Nathaniel. One of Massachusetts' largest tea importers before the Revolutionary War, Clarke's shop on King Street drew large protests on 3 Nov. 1773 after he refused to resign his East India commission, and his tea was among that thrown into Boston Harbor on 16 Dec. 1773."

"Oh, my goodness. The Clarke family held prominence for several reasons, including the patriots' cause," said Carly.

"Indeed. It also states that he married Abigail Brumlow on May 3, 1750, and the couple had three sons and five daughters. Is there anything else you'd like copied?" Connie asked.

"Yes, actually, I'd like to see the census records or baptismal records for the Clarke sons' families."

Connie searched for any record of Edward, Richard, and Nathaniel. "I found records of the baptisms of the Clarke family from 1729-1850 at Christ Church. This is the Old North Church, the oldest standing church building in Boston."

"If you bring up those records, I can search for the name of a child, Eira Clarke."

"Of course. Give me a minute, and I'll print out what we have."

Carly thanked Connie and took the papers into the reading area. The children of Robert and Abigail Clarke were baptized at Christ Church, and none were named Eira. Also disappointing to find that all received their baptisms prior to 1794.

She searched for Edward Clarke and his family, scanning for a child named Eira. After exhausting the list of family papers from Edward, Carly moved on to Richard. The rumble of her stomach caused her to take a break. She took a protein bar from her purse and rested her eyes for a moment. Only one son remained, then Carly would begin on the women in the family.

"Ma'am, I found something you might find interesting." Connie handed her several printed pages. "I took the liberty of searching for a couple of things since I'm not busy. I'll let you look at this."

Carly put her glasses on. The neat script listed the baptisms at Christ Church for the twelve months of 1794. On December 12, she found an entry for Mary Eira, daughter of Nathaniel and Elizabeth Clarke. Sponsors~ Richard Clarke and Felicity Clarke.

"Thank you," Carly said. "I can't believe you found her."

The grandfather, Robert Clarke, went to the orphanage for Eira, but obviously not to raise her as their own. His son and daughter-in-law became Eira's parents.

For the next hour, Carly searched for census information and found Mary Eira Clarke listed in the 1800 Census. Her name and age were neatly written below those of her father, aged 37, and her mother, 35. Mary Eira~ 8.

She copied the page and continued her search. The Clarke family papers were extensive, but she didn't find anything else of significance.

At two o'clock, Connie returned. "I ran a search for a marriage license for Mary Eira Clarke. I found it and made a copy for you." She handed Carly the paper.

November 27th, 1812~ The intention of marriage between Mr. John Preston, of Boston, State of Massachusetts, and Miss Mary Eira Clarke, of Boston, State of Massachusetts.

"Well, this is wonderful, thank you!" Carly's voice rose several octaves.

"I'm glad I could help. We have other information on the Clarke family if you're interested. I also took the liberty of making a copy of the couple's marriage announcement in the newspaper."

The nineteenth-century newspaper announced the wedding on November 29th at Christ Church. Mary Eira and John Preston, it said, were to take residence in Philadelphia, Pennsylvania, on December 1st.

"Thank you for your help today." Carly put the copies into her bag.

"You're welcome. You may want to review the file I sent you, which includes miniatures and portraits of the Clarke family. Perhaps you'll find the child among them."

"I didn't think about ever seeing an image of Eira. Thank you." Carly opened the PDF file containing images from the Clarke family. There were portraits of Robert and Abigail Clarke, painted by Gilbert Stuart. Stuart painted several prominent Bostonian families, as well as President George Washington.

The Clarkes were a handsome couple, although Abigail looked rather stern, Carly thought. Stuart also painted portraits of the Clarkes' sons and several of the children. Next on the screen were portraits of Nathaniel and Elizabeth Clarke. Nathaniel's dark hair and piercing eyes caught Carly's attention. Elizabeth's petite features depicted a frail woman with high cheekbones and gray eyes. The following slide made Carly gasp: Mary E. Clarke, a young girl with dark curls and brown eyes. Something about the child looked familiar. Carly recalled seeing the same dark eyes in Freddy Richards and Caroline. A familiarity also caught Carly's attention. *I know you, or at least I feel we're connected somehow.* Seeing Eira's face drew her back to the visions of Caroline and her children at the Foundling Home, on the ship across the Atlantic, and again at Bethesda.

As far-fetched as it sounds, could I have lived as Caroline in Wales?

Chapter Twenty-Eight

Carly gazed out the window as the plane gained altitude. She kept seeing Eira's face and felt the odd sensation that accompanied it. She'd called Delaney on her way back to the Airbnb, wanting to share the information she'd located. Delaney's reaction matched Carly's. She glanced over at Dottie and Frederick, both listening to their phones, and their eyes were closed. Vivi held her doll, eyes closed, resting on Carly's arm.

Carly closed her eyes and rested her head on the back of her seat. She felt herself drifting off, seeing Austin's face at the airport as he waved goodbye to her and Delaney.

The warm trail of a lone tear instinctively caused her hand to wipe it away. She heard his voice, "Take me home, Carly."

Carly jerked, and her eyes sprang open. The sudden movement caused Vivi to stir. "It's okay, honey. Go back to sleep."

"You know, it makes sense that Eira, Mary, or whatever she went by, seems familiar to you," Delaney said. "You've seen her in the visions with Caroline."

Carly paddled her feet to move her float closer to Delaney's. "I guess you're right. There's something more… I can't explain it."

"Have you heard anything from the Bethesda Twelve's interment?"

"No, nothing other than the Savannah local station is covering the event," Carly said, climbing onto her raft.

The sunlight reflected off the water, prompting Delaney to pull her sunglasses from her head and put them back on her face. "This whole Caroline haunting your thoughts makes me wonder about all the weird connections."

Carly turned, dangling her tanned legs into the water. "Weird in what way?"

"Caroline's spirit has never appeared to me."

The words took on a different meaning to Carly. "You saw her and the others at Bethesda, didn't you?"

Delaney stammered, "Well, not like you see her. She didn't seem clear to me, like the others."

Carly's phone rang, ending the conversation. Carly jumped off her raft and quickly crossed the pool to the ladder. She dried herself off and checked her phone.

Jeff Sullivan's number was displayed on the screen. "Hey, Jeff. What's up?" Carly asked.

Delaney lay back on her raft and put her earbuds back in.

"How did you like Boston?" Jeff asked.

"We loved it. Frederick and Vivi enjoyed the historical parts, and I needed another week to explore."

"Well, good. I wish I could've tagged along. I'm a little homesick," Jeff admitted.

"I can see why. Thank you for suggesting the Airbnb," she said. "How's everything going at Channel 5?"

"I miss working with you. Other than that, it's good."

Carly smiled. "I still think I did the right thing, even though I'm unemployed at the moment."

"Give yourself some time, kiddo," he said, sounding more like her brother, Connor.

"I'm going to pursue the conference circuit, doing more paranormal speaking engagements."

"Keep a date open for me. I haven't forgotten you agreed to go out again," Jeff said.

"I will, Jeff. Thanks for checking up on me."

"Anytime. Tell the rugrats hi, and we'll talk again soon."

Carly put her phone on the table. "I know what you're thinking, and you're wrong."

Delaney had gotten out of the pool while Carly talked to Jeff. She'd placed two glasses of iced tea on the table.

Carly took a sip, and Delaney put up her hands in mock surrender. "Now, simmer down. I don't see anything wrong with you having a night out."

"You're right, there isn't. But I felt guilty when I went before. It's still too soon."

Delaney let out an overly dramatic sigh. "Sweetie, no one is calling you the merry widow. You're angry at Austin, and you're grieving."

"Sometimes, I don't know what I feel or who I am," Carly confessed, her voice betraying her usual self-assurance.

Delaney softened. "Look, I know you're worried about the visions and hauntings. For whatever reason, Caroline isn't connecting with me."

"Maybe now that I've found out what happened to Eira, the connection to Caroline will stop."

Delaney nodded, "Yes, it's possible she wanted to know as well. I still don't understand why Ms. Albertson took Freddy and Eira to different orphanages."

"The Clarke family had means and connections in the colonies and England. If Nathaniel and Elizabeth wanted a child, they must've contacted Mr. Duncan or even Ms. Albertson."

"Do you think they arranged indentures and adoptions?" Delaney asked.

"When Drake and I spoke about the letter Ms. Albertson sent to Mr. Duncan, it seemed there were prior arrangements for orphans to come to Georgia."

"It makes me wonder about the older orphans. Weren't a couple of the Bethesda Twelve teenage girls?" Delaney asked.

"Yes, two, I believe."

"Do you think Duncan and Albertson were trafficking young girls for prostitution?" Delaney raised an eyebrow, emphasizing her point.

"I never thought about it, but it's possible. Didn't Miss Albertson lose her position at the Foundling Home soon after the deaths?" Carly asked.

"The Foundling Home and Bethesda severed their ties sometime around the year 1800. The arrangement to sell teenage orphan girls likely led to that decision."

Carly lay her head back on the lounge chair. "I seem to remember reading something on Newspaper.com about two men involved with Bethesda who were charged with a crime. I don't remember now."

"Maybe Drake can look up the information in the records regarding Louisa Albertson at the Foundling Museum." Delaney smiled like a cat holding a mouse.

Carly sat up to catch Delaney's expression. "I guess it wouldn't hurt to ask him."

She rolled onto her side and glanced at the clock on the bedside table. Still blurry-eyed and needing to use the restroom, she hurried to take care of her business before crawling back between the warm sheets. Pulling the comforter up to her chin, she settled in and let her mind drift to the dream she left—this time, it took her to Wales.

She stood in the magistrate's office, ready to pay taxes on the property she owned, but her husband had passed away the previous year. Trefor Richards, resting in the glen behind her cottage, had no outstanding debts, yet here she was, pleading for the right to remain on the land. It had been barely two months since her marriage to Stefan Madoc, and now he, too, lay in the small graveyard next to her first husband.

"Your deceased husband's brother is the rightful heir to the farm. You have six months from today, August 11th, to bring Arwin Richards to this court. He will need to decide to either sell the farm or hold it in conservatorship until the child, Frederick Richards, reaches legal age."

A surge of protest rose within her, desperate to plead for the land to remain in her care until Frederick was old enough to inherit it.

She remembered the exchange between herself and Gethen Bowen. And now, he is in line to bid for her land if she can't bring Arwin back to Wales.

How he convinced the magistrate of his innocence in Stefan's murder, she couldn't say, but she saw him crossing the rippling stream near her cottage. He wanted Caroline for the water and extra land for his sheep. When she wouldn't marry him, he killed Stefan. He'd called her a bronten before the court and her neighbors.

She began to sob loudly. Her only chance to keep the land was to sail to the States to find Arwin.

Carly awoke to Vivi patting her cheek. "Mommy, don't cry."

The sound of Vivi's soft voice brought Carly out of the strange dream. "Mommy just had a bad dream. It's okay, baby."

She hugged Vivi tightly, not wanting to frighten her. "Did you dream about Daddy?" Vivi's bottom lip quivered.

"No, just a bad dream. But it's over now. Thank you for being here." Carly kissed her cheek.

"We didn't want to wake Ms. Dottie."

Carly lifted the clock from the table. Six o'clock. She'd go downstairs and start fixing breakfast and lunches for Frederick and Vivi. She heard Dottie coming down the stairs to the hallway.

"Good morning," she called as she continued downstairs.

Vivi jumped off the bed and scurried downstairs after Ms. Dottie. Carly rubbed her eyes. *I don't know why I'm still dreaming about Caroline, unless the dreams are a product of my past.* An uneasiness crept inside, causing Carly to question everything happening to her. *For whatever reason, Caroline's haunting my dreams. Why isn't Caroline appearing to me like all the others?*

She went into Frederick's room, but he'd already joined Dottie and Vivi in the kitchen. She grabbed her clothes from the chest of drawers in her room and changed before joining them downstairs.

Dottie took the children to school, and Carly entered her office with a steaming cup of coffee and an apple turnover in hand. She turned on her computer and reached for the file labeled "Spirit Seekers 2025 Conference." Inside the folder were business cards, a program booklet, and notes from the various presentations.

As she sifted through the materials, Carly found Dr. Alston Curry's business card and placed it on the small silver tray beside her computer. The words of Dr. Curry echoed in her mind: *When you're ready, call me.*

Continuing to leaf through the business cards and notes, she came across Dr. Curry's card, which had a folded piece of paper attached with a paper clip. She opened the note, intrigued by the contents.

Carly, I believe we've met at the conference for a specific reason.

*When you're ready to reach out to me, I'd be delighted to speak
with you.*

Kind regards,

Dr. Alston Curry.

Professor of Parapsychology, University of Glasgow

University Avenue Glasgow, G12 8QQ +44(0)141 330 2000

Carly took a bite of her turnover, chewing thoughtfully as she held the
note in her other hand. She recalled Dr. Curry's presentation on the
ability to move objects through telepathy and the phenomenon of
poltergeists. His presentation, as she recalled, seemed more like a
college lecture than a paranormal spiel on parapsychology.

She wanted to speak with Drake. She checked her phone, added six
hours to eight o'clock a.m., and decided that two o'clock p.m. would be
a good time to catch him.

She entered Drake Taylor's number into her phone and waited. He
answered on the second ring. "Carly, so nice to hear your voice on this
dreary day in London."

"I hope I'm not interrupting anything."

"No, not at all. In fact, I've discovered a couple of things since we
last spoke, and I'm bursting to share them with you."

Carly felt the excitement through the phone. "I'm excited to share
information with you as well. You first, though," she said.

Drake rustled papers in the background, then continued. "I did some
digging into the various correspondences we have in our possession
between the Foundling Home and Bethesda Orphan Asylum. What I
found will surprise you."

Carly inched to the edge of her seat, hanging on his every word.
"You have my attention. Go on."

"Before the note we found when you and Delaney visited in June, I
discovered two more letters from Mr. Duncan to Ms. Albertson. In both

letters, he specifically requested girls who were approaching the age where they would be bound out for indentured servitude."

Carly felt a sense of déjà vu from the conversation she had recently had with Delaney.

"I understand. What typically happened if a girl didn't find a home before reaching a certain age?"

"If a young girl turned sixteen and had not found a permanent home, she could become an indentured servant here, or in several cases, be sent to the colonies, or later, the United States."

"How many girls were sent to Bethesda, in particular?"

"In the two letters, Mr. Albertson requested four but also asked for other orphans of various ages."

"I discovered that Miss Albertson took Caroline's two surviving children to separate orphan asylums."

"I see. I assume you unearthed this information through your paranormal abilities?" Drake asked.

"Partly," Carly replied. "I also discovered that Louisa Albertson disguised herself as someone named Susannah Richards. It was she who left Frederick in Charleston and his sister, Eira, at the Female Asylum in Boston a couple of weeks later."

"Amazing. From what I've researched, the whole arrangement is a bit dodgy, if you ask me," Drake said.

"Dodgy?"

"Oh, beg your pardon. It means not on the up and up."

Carly laughed. "I'm not familiar with it, but you're right."

"As I mentioned, Miss Albertson found herself in a wee bit of trouble, due to her dealings," Drake explained. "I discovered her termination from the London Foundling Hospital in 1801. The London Daily Times reported that the matron of the Foundling Hospital, Miss Louisa Albertson of London, and Mr. Nathaniel Duncan, Esq. of the Bethesda Orphan Asylum in the United States, were dismissed from their positions due to inappropriate actions involving orphans."

"Delaney brought up the idea of selling the teen girls into houses of prostitution," Carly prompted.

"The newspaper doesn't provide further details, but after Miss Albertson's termination, there were no more transports of orphans to Georgia," Drake continued, shuffling papers on his desk.

"Caroline didn't know about the arrangement. I'm certain of it. I can't understand why she would end up at the Foundling Home," Carly said.

"We may never know," Drake replied.

Carly paused for a moment. "What happened to Gethen Bowen? Did he ever face any consequences for killing Stefan Madoc?"

"I'm not sure. His testimony contradicted Caroline's, and no one else witnessed Gethen Bowen near the Richards's cottage."

"Since Caroline didn't return, the murder charge likely fell through. It seems Gethen Bowen got away with murder," Drake surmised.

Carly shook her head. "We may never know. I'm confident Caroline's family never learned of her demise."

Chapter Twenty-Nine

November 20th, 2025

Dottie and Carly flipped through various realtor magazines spread out on the table. Carly couldn't shake her interest in selling the King Street house, a thought that had been on her mind ever since she picked up the real estate magazines from the bank two days earlier.

"It's ridiculous how much houses cost these days," Dottie commented as she turned the page.

"I know. I've got so much on my plate right now. Maybe I should put the idea of moving on hold."

The upcoming six-month anniversary of Austin's death weighed heavily on her mind. Earlier that week, Harv Ball had called to inform her that the young driver who had hit Austin and Cora had recently pled guilty to avoid a trial and likely manslaughter charges. Carly thanked Harv for letting her know. The thought of going to a courtroom and facing Cora's husband and family caused her anxiety to rise. She often experienced her heart racing and sudden feelings of panic whenever she thought about an impending court appearance.

Her previous therapist, Dr. Jane Durban, had prescribed her medication for anxiety, which she had just started taking earlier that week. Carly had chosen not to share her visions and encounters with her new therapist, Dr. Hunter. She believed that no one in the medical field would understand how she felt. Why bother?

Fortunately, she could confide everything to Delaney, whom she had come to call her "soul sister." She had only recently felt comfortable enough with Dottie to share some of her experiences with her.

"Why don't you table the idea of selling, at least until after the school year ends. This is the only home Vivi and Frederick have known."

Carly reached out and grasped Dottie's hand. "In my heart, I know you're right. I didn't consider how selling might adversely affect the children."

Not wanting Carly to dwell on sad thoughts, Dottie changed the subject. "I've been reading up on Salem and the Witch Trials. Is the conference you're attending close by?"

"I think Danvers is over an hour away from Fall River. It's one of the day trips and investigation sights," Carly replied.

A call from Delaney ended the conversation. "Hey, are you busy?" she asked.

Carly took her phone and went into her office. "No, just looking at the real estate magazines. What's up?"

"Has Larry Deveroux or the Summerfields contacted you about the Bethesda Twelve interment?"

"I don't think so. Let me check my messages," Carly said, bringing up the voice and text messages on her phone.

"The reason I asked is because I got one from Larry this morning."

Carly saw his text at the same time. "Yes, he texted something this morning. I must've missed it."

Carly read the text: *This is Larry Deveroux. On the twenty-second, the Savannah Historical Preservation Society and the Georgia Histor-*

ical Society will be on hand to witness the reinterment of the twelve remains discovered at Bethesda Academy in the Fall of 2024. I will try to attend and hope you will as well. Thank you, Carly, for your help in solving the mystery of identities. Yours, Larry.

Delaney's excitement grew while waiting for Carly to finish reading the text. "Is that not the bee's knees?"

"I'd say so. What time? Did I miss that?"

Delaney read her message. "Mine says at eleven a.m. on November 22nd at Bethesda Academy."

Carly looked at the desk calendar. "That's the day after tomorrow. Will you be able to go?"

"Wild horses won't keep me away. I'll pick you up at seven. I'll even bring the coffee and breakfast goodies."

Carly smiled. "I'm excited and anxious at the same time. Okay, I'll text Larry back and let him know we'll attend. Thank you."

"You're welcome, sweetie. How did your appointment go with the new therapist?"

"It went all right, I guess. I didn't share anything about Caroline."

"You don't feel comfortable sharing it with him?"

Carly pulled a strand of hair between her fingers. "No, I'll look like a mental case. I'm thinking about weaning myself away from therapy."

"Oh, I thought it helped with Austin and everything," Delaney said, her voice apprehensive.

"I'm forty-three years old. It's time I started handling my problems myself."

Frederick and Vivi ate breakfast early so they could spend time with Carly before Delaney picked her up.

"Auntie Lanie and I may not be home before you two today. Please help Ms. Dottie by starting your homework after you get back, capiche?"

They giggled at Carly's usual phrase when she wanted to avoid any backtalk. "Yes, we *capiche,*" Vivi replied, still laughing.

Carly patted Vivi's head while Frederick turned to his phone. Carly tapped his hand and said, "Hey, no devices at the table, sir."

He rolled his eyes and put his phone in his pocket. As Carly finished her coffee, she noticed the changes in Frederick since Austin's death. He had matured significantly in the six months since his world had turned upside down. At eleven, he felt he had assumed the role of the pseudo-man of the house. Soon, he would turn twelve; it would be another birthday celebration without Austin.

Delaney tapped on the side door and then entered the entry hall. "Hey, everybody!" her voice echoed throughout the downstairs.

"I'm almost ready," Carly said, taking her coffee cup to the sink.

"Good morning," Dottie said. "Do you want a cup of coffee before you two head out?"

"No, thank you. I brought us a goody bag in the car," she said.

Carly went to Frederick and Vivi, giving both kisses on their cheeks and a quick hug. Frederick, at least, still let Carly hug him.

"I'll see you tonight, love you." Carly followed Delaney out to her car.

The weather promised to delight the guests assembled at Bethesda Academy. Typical for November in Savannah, the blue skies and near seventy degrees made for a perfect day to hold the reburial of the Bethesda Twelve.

Carly and Delaney thanked the woman who handed them both a program. Larry Deveroux saw them and left the group he was standing with to join Carly and Delaney.

"I'm glad you both could make it." Larry shook both of their hands.

Carly looked at the twelve pine coffins lined up before her. She could hear the sounds coming from the area, which had once been the site of a hasty mass burial.

Her gaze fell upon the most miniature coffin that held the remains of Caroline's baby, Catrin, only days old. The sight tugged at Carly's heart.

Carly wished Caroline had shared her actual last name, even though she understood why she didn't.

Turning to Larry, she asked, "May I have a moment with them?"

Carly glanced back at Delaney. "I feel like my heart is breaking. I'll only be a moment," she said softly.

Larry blotted his forehead with his handkerchief, "Yes, of course. We have a few minutes before the program starts." He joined the women from the historical society.

Delaney stepped back and gave Carly some space, choosing not to follow her.

The voices of Caroline and Elizabeth filled her ears with low chatter. She saw Caroline holding Elizabeth's hand, Catrin resting in her other arm. Carly felt the slight weight of the infant and Elizabeth's bony fingers.

She took a step back, seeing the coffins once again. "I found Eira. She was raised in a good home. I'm so sorry this happened to you." Carly whispered over Caroline's coffin. "Freddy is at rest. Everything is settled now." Carly jumped, feeling Delaney's arm around her shoulders.

"The program's about to start. Let's take our seats." Delaney and Carly joined the others under the white event tent covering the graves and the surrounding fifty chairs.

Darrick and Jamesetta Summerfield spotted Carly and Delaney sitting back a few rows from them. They waved, and Jamesetta put her hand to her heart and mouthed a thank you.

Carly and Delaney both nodded as the speaker took to the podium.

The chronological details regarding the Bethesda Twelve were presented, simplifying the forensic language and most of the terminology associated with the technology used to confirm the identities of the remains. Each name was read aloud, followed by a small bell tolling in memory of them. Carly took a tissue from her purse to dab her eyes, and Delaney gently patted her knee. She listened as Darrick Summerfield recounted the account of the deaths, which was a surprising find in one of the journals belonging to the Bethesda administrator in 1794. Eleven deaths were attributed to a typhoid outbreak from a ship, while one was due to scurvy. It was astonishing to find this information after more than two hundred years.

Larry Deveroux delivered a brief speech and included Carly and Delaney in his acknowledgments. After the final speaker from the Savannah Historical Society finished, several men began to assemble at the grave sites. A single white rose was placed on top of each coffin before the procession to lower them into the ground.

Following the burials, Carly and Delaney had a short conversation with Darrick and Jamesetta.

"Thank you both for all the hard work you put into uncovering the stories of the twelve who died," Jamesetta said, embracing both Carly and Delaney.

"I hope this puts an end to all the paranormal occurrences here, at least involving them," she added, gesturing over her shoulder.

"I can't promise anything about the rest of the spirits here," Delaney said with a smile.

"I'm grateful they received a proper burial and that their names were read aloud for everyone to hear." Carly's anxiety began to settle.

"Darrick made a photocopy of the journal page for both of you," Jamesetta said as she took the papers from her handbag and handed them to Delaney and then to Carly.

"Thank you," Carly said.

As Carly and Delaney walked toward the car, Carly paused to take a final look at the graves, now twelve mounds of red clay. She felt sure that Caroline could find peace, knowing where her children would go after her death. Austin's words echoed in her mind: *"You're the champion of lost children, Carly."*

The Summerfields had promised to honor the graves of the Bethesda Twelve. Carly should have felt a sense of closure, but some-thing didn't feel right. This didn't seem like the end.

Chapter Thirty

Thanksgiving Break~ November 24th, 2025

Carly checked the children's luggage, ensuring they had enough clothes for their trip to her parents' house for Thanksgiving. She carefully placed Austin's urn into her carry-on.

She walked into the den where she found Dottie relaxing in Austin's chair, filling in a crossword puzzle.

"I'm glad you decided to join Chad and Josie for Thanksgiving. Will you make sure to turn on the alarm system when you leave on Wednesday night?"

"Yes, of course. I'll be all right rattling around in this big house until then. You don't need to worry." Dottie placed the crossword puzzle on the coffee table. "I want to hug the kids before you leave." She went down the hall to join the kids in the kitchen.

Carly rolled the luggage into the entry hall and took a quick look at her makeup in the hallway mirror. The carry-on with Austin's ashes caught her eye on the floor. She had taken Austin's remains and placed them inside a small cardboard box. She'd contacted and obtained all the necessary documents and papers for carrying cremated remains on a flight. Everything she needed was inside the carry-on, along with the box.

Kent and Myra Tabor arranged for the memorial service at their church, the day after Thanksgiving, on the 28th. Friends of Austin's who were unable to come to his funeral in Charleston were notified about the arrangements.

Carly knew this would upset Frederick and Vivi all over again, but she knew this would give closure to Austin's family, having his remains back in Kansas. With a trial no longer looming in the future, burying Austin's ashes would start the healing process for everyone.

Delaney pulled into the driveway. She helped Carly load all the luggage into Carly's SUV. She would drive them to the airport, then switch back to her car when she returned to Carly's house afterwards.

"Tell Curt and Paula hello for me," Delaney said as she helped Carly get the luggage out at the curb.

"I will. Thanks for everything," Carly said, hugging Delaney.

"Have a safe flight and enjoy this time with all the Evanses and Tabors. Don't worry about anything, okay?"

Carly nodded. "Okay. Have a happy Thanksgiving with Jarrod's family and Boyd."

Carly and the kids wheeled their luggage into the airport, backpacks in place. Carly held on tight to her carry-on as they stepped up to the airline counter to check in their bags.

The miles of fields and farms brought back fond memories for Carly. She recalled the country roads where her grandfather and other men, now gone, drove tractors pulling hay wagons full of teens to wiener roasts and bonfires. As she passed her high school, she noticed that the building seemed smaller than she remembered from her teenage years. Memories of cheerleading at basketball games flooded her mind, along with thoughts of the friends she had attended school with—Carly and her classmates had spent all twelve grades together, but now they were scattered across the state and country.

"We're almost to Memes and Pap's house," Carly said, feeling anxious to see her whole family. The last time they were all together was six months ago at Austin's funeral.

"I can't wait to drive the tractor with Pap," Frederick said as he put his phone on the seat.

"Mommy, are Blaire and Briann coming to Meme's house?" Vivi asked. The twin girls, daughters of Connor and his wife, Beth, were a year older than Vivi.

"Of course, and so will Braden. You two had a good time helping Pap, didn't you, Frederick?"

Frederick smiled, remembering the fun the two had together.

Out of nowhere, a sadness washed over Carly, spoiling the excitement of everyone seeing one another again. It would only be a matter of time before the children also thought about the last day they spent at their grandparents' house.

A somber tone came over the happy car, only moments before. Frederick broke the silence.

"Do I have to go to the cemetery?"

Carly didn't see that one coming. Her throat felt like she'd swallowed a ball of cotton. "Don't you want to go see where Dad's family is buried?"

He looked out the window, not answering the question. His silence caused Carly to glance in the rearview mirror at her son. She saw his hand wipe a tear from his cheek.

"We don't have to think about it today. We'll help Memes get the house ready for Thanksgiving." She caught his eye and winked.

Frederick smiled. The matter was resolved, for the moment.

Vivi noticed a cemetery outside her window. She smiled as the car went past it. Carly saw her reaction and understood her smile.

A bitter wind blew as Carly opened the trunk to retrieve the luggage. Her dad came out of the metal pole barn at the side of the driveway. He reached out his hands to lift Vivi, who ran to jump into his arms. It felt good to be at home again.

"Here, let me get those. Go on in the house and get out of the cold."

Carly motioned for the kids to go inside while she stayed to help unload the car.

"I've missed you, Dad," Carly said, hugging Curt. His Carhart jacket scratched her cheek.

"I've missed you, Punkin," he said, calling her by the nickname he'd given her as a toddler.

She smiled at hearing the name again. "I think coming home will do us all some good."

Curt Evans was a few inches taller than his daughter. His hair, now a blend of dark brown and silver, was still styled as it had been in his younger days. At seventy, he looked no older than fifty. Both he and his wife, Paula Evans, seemed to defy the effects of aging. Curt's dark complexion and kind green eyes were traits he passed down to Carly and her two siblings.

Her mother, a blonde who never let a three-week color and highlight appointment go by, still walked daily and helped her husband with the farm. This routine kept her in shape and made her look younger than her age of sixty-eight.

Paula Evans stood at the kitchen counter, doling out fresh snickerdoodle cookies, a favorite of Carly's and the children. She walked into the living room to hug Carly.

"I'm so happy to have you and the kids here for Thanksgiving. Connor and Cate will arrive later this evening," she said.

"It's been a while since we've all spent Thanksgiving at home. I can't wait to see everyone," Carly replied, hugging her mom.

After Carly put the luggage away in her room, she came downstairs to help her mom arrange the card tables and chairs in the large family room adjacent to the dining room. Later in the afternoon, the rest of the Evans family, including the children and grandchildren, arrived, significantly increasing the noise level. Frederick and Vivi put on their coats and went outside to play with their cousins, giving the adults some time to visit and relax before dinner.

Carly shared the news of her departure from Channel 5, which elicited mixed reactions. "I needed a change. Working from home and speaking at conferences allows me to set my schedule," she explained.

Connor was the first to respond, saying, "You're good at what you do, even if I don't fully understand it. But since you're financially secure now, you might as well do what you want."

Cate, who had always doubted Carly's abilities, chimed in, "You might have cut off your nose to spite your face, Carls. You can't survive for the next fifteen years or so on just the money Austin left you."

"Austin invested wisely, and I believe we'll get along just fine, especially with the additional income I'll earn from speaking engagements and consultations," Carly said confidently, prompting her mother to join the conversation.

"Beth, could you please write down everyone's names on a piece of paper? We can draw names for Christmas after dinner," she said.

Beth looked at Carly and smiled. "Of course! I know our kids are eager to draw names."

Carly excused herself and walked down the hall to the restroom, where she took a moment to collect herself. She anticipated some negative comments from Cate. Although they were close in age, the two had never bonded as Carly had hoped. This could have been due to her close relationship with her parents or perhaps the fact that she and her grand-mother shared a special connection. Granny Eddleman openly favored Carly over the others.

When Carly returned, all the children were gathered in the family room, excited for dinner. Paula paid the pizza delivery girl, who brought a variety of pizzas for the occasion. Six boxes of pizza were spread out on the counter, along with salad and an assortment of desserts.

The mood in the room lifted as the family gathering began. Frederick and Vivi were laughing and enjoying their time with their cousins. Austin's family was next in line for the Thanksgiving celebration. Carly would stay the weekend with Kent and Myra Tabor, celebrating the holiday with Austin's parents and sister. His memorial service would conclude her time in Kansas.

The Thanksgiving dinner exceeded everyone's expectations. The traditional turkey, dressing, and all the fixings filled the room with a delicious aroma. After the meal, the children put on their coats and went outside with Curt, Connor, and Cate's husband, Reese, leaving the cleanup duties to the women—a tradition in the family.

Carly wanted to walk down the hill to her grandparents' house, now vacant but well-maintained. She hoped to feel Granny Eddleman's spirit and perhaps uncover an explanation for her strange connection to the spirits of Caroline and her children.

The conversation between Paula, Cate, Beth, and Carly centered on their children's activities, including sports, dance, and church events. Carly proudly shared Frederick's soccer skills and Vivi's artistic talents. Cate and Carly compared how much their daughters were alike, even suggesting that Carly let the kids visit her house for a few days next summer when they come to see their grandparents. It seemed that everyone enjoyed their time together, as such gatherings now happened less frequently, now that their children were growing and engaging in their activities.

Before dark, the vehicles were loaded with leftovers and bags as Connor and Cate, along with their families, said goodbye. Each had over an hour's drive to return home, and the freshly fallen snow had left a coating on the roads.

Carly hugged Beth, whispering a 'thank you' in her ear. She nodded, understanding, and kissed Carly on her cheek.

"We love you and the kids, Carly. If you ever need anything, we're here," Beth said.

"Thank you. We love you, too." Carly hugged Connor, echoing what she had told Beth earlier.

A few moments later, Cate and Reese were saying their goodbyes to Carly and the Evans family. Cate held Carly close, upholding the family tradition of hugging whenever they were leaving, arriving, or after an argument. "If I hurt you, I'm sorry, Carls. I only want the best for you."

Carly kissed Cate on the cheek. "Thank you. I love you, and I'm sorry I snapped at you."

Cate and Reese, along with the children, waved goodbye as their van drove down the long driveway.

Carly spent the morning helping Paula carry Christmas decorations upstairs, another Evans tradition -putting out the Christmas decorations the day after Thanksgiving. Frederick and Vivi went into town with Curt to buy a few lights to decorate the outside of the house. It gave Carly and Paula time alone.

"So, what's been bothering you since you got here?" Paula asked, leaning over the large tote filled with decorations.

Carly knew better than to try to hide anything from her mother.

"Well, there's this woman who's been hanging around since before Austin passed away."

Paula's expression changed. "I take it she isn't alive anymore."

"No, she isn't. She is Freddy Richards's mother." Carly sat beside her mother on the floor.

Paula paused her work of unpacking the decorations and focused on Carly. "Okay, how did she get connected to you?"

Carly chose her words carefully. "It all began at Bethesda Academy in Savannah, when Larry Deveroux called Delaney and me about bones discovered at the site of the Academy in Savannah."

"Yes, I remember you texting something about going to Savannah for an investigation. Do you still see her?"

"She followed me to England and Wales, or maybe I followed her. I'm not sure, but sometimes I think I am her, or I was her."

Paula's eyes widened. "Oh, honey. Have you talked to your therapist about this?"

Carly sighed. "Mom, this isn't something my mind conjured up because of my past trauma. I've seen her children, her husband, and even found myself in a 1790s Welsh courthouse."

"I don't know what to say. Is she trying to harm you or the children?" Paula's voice sounded more afraid than surprised.

"No, nothing like that. From everything I've experienced, she is a loving wife and mother who died before she could save her land."

"I thought Austin's memorial service had something to do with it. I don't understand how you see and hear what you do."

"Do you mind if I take a walk? It might not be until next summer before I return. I need to clear my head before we leave for Kansas City."

"No, it's alright. I have plenty to do with this mess," Paula laughed.

"I won't be long. Thanks for listening." Carly leaned over and kissed her cheek.

Chapter Thirty-One

arly zipped up her jacket then slipped on a pair of her mom's snow boots. The air felt colder than it did earlier. It stung her nostrils and made her eyes water. As she walked down the driveway, her boots crunched in the light snow that covered the gravel. The walk to Granny and Pop's house took less than five minutes. She cut across the field, now lying fallow, stepping over misshapen dried corn stalks and clumps of dirt beneath her feet.

A murder of curious crows cawed above her, circling as if warning her to go back. She'd taken this same route hundreds of times as a child; sometimes with a basket of wild blackberries that she and Granny picked, or a doll wrapped in a blanket to give to Granny to sew her a new dress.

Today, she longed for Granny's presence. The comforting arms that cradled her when she hurt her knee. Feeling her presence would be so soothing right now.

The clouds overhead darkened with the promise of snow. The cold wind stung her eyes and caused her nose to run. She reached into her coat and found a tissue.

As she approached the two-story clapboard farmhouse, she noticed that the original porch floor had been replaced with a new one. The original porch swing moved with a gust of wind. Carly's mother didn't want to sell the house. She wanted to keep it in the family in case someone needed a temporary place to stay. Cate and Reese had lived there for a few months after a tornado damaged their house. No one had lived in the farmhouse for at least four or five years.

Carly reached up to the doorframe where the spare key was hidden. She rolled her eyes, thinking that her parents really needed to install a security camera or at least a deadbolt lock on the door.

Carly turned the key and stepped into the family room, which was empty, void of the love she once felt inside. She remembered the wall to the left of the doorway, which once displayed gilded frames of long-gone faces. Braided rugs covered the floor, and knick-knacks were displayed on Pop's shelves.

She remembered where Granny and Pop kept their long, maple dining room table and tall-backed chairs, as well as the wooden bowl that always held fresh fruit in the center.

Carly faintly smelled the aroma of the woodstove, now gone. She walked through each room downstairs, recalling Christmases and other gatherings that had been held every year at Pop and Granny Eddleman's house. For a moment, she thought she heard a shuffle upstairs. Without hesitation, she called out, "Granny, I'm home." She turned to the stairway, running her fingers along the banister that she and her cousins used to slide down. The familiar creak of the fourth step caught her attention. Granny always knew if one of the kids tried to sneak down to the icebox for a late-night snack.

When she reached the second-floor landing, a wave of emotion washed over her. "Granny, I miss you so much. I wish you could tell me what's happening to me with Caroline." Carly sat in the middle of the floor that had once been Granny and Pop's bedroom. She pulled her knees up to her chest and wrapped her arms around them. "Granny,

I feel so lost and confused without Austin. Am I losing my mind?" The large white iron bed, which creaked when she fell back onto it, used to occupy the space where she now sat. Tears began to fall, driven by her uncertainty about everything that had happened since seeing Caroline at Bethesda and the upcoming memorial service for Austin.

Suddenly, Granny slowly materialized in the room, a careworn expression on her face. "Granny?" Carly whispered. The form took shape, and Carly recognized Granny as she looked in life.

Carly wiped her eyes and sniffed loudly. She felt the warm touch of Granny's hand on her face, brushing back the hair from her eyes. "What's happening to me, Granny? Have I lived another life—Caroline's life?"

In her mind, she heard Granny's voice say, *"Everything will turn out fine. You're ready. Let him help you, Carly."*

"I love you, Granny. I miss you so."

As Granny Eddleman began to fade from Carly's sight, she called out, "No, wait, Granny. I need to ask you about Vivi."

Carly looked around the room. Granny left as suddenly as she appeared. *Who is "he?" Was it Alston Curry? How did Granny know about Alston Curry's note?*

After a few moments, Carly rose and brushed off the seat of her pants. No longer feeling Granny in the room, she smiled. "Thank you, Granny. I know what I need to do."

By the time Carly walked into the family room, Paula had already finished putting up the tree. "I almost sent your dad out to find you. Everything okay?"

Carly hugged her mom. "Yes, I had a good visit. I'm glad you and Dad have kept Granny and Pop's house in good shape."

Curt came into the room from the kitchen. "I've been hoping you'd move back."

Carly turned to her dad. "I always loved the house, but it's the people who lived there that made it special."

Frederick and Vivi bounded down the stairs upon hearing Carly's voice. "Mom, look what Pap got us," Frederick said.

He and Vivi each had a pair of cowboy boots. Vivi wore Carly's cowgirl hat from her childhood. "Look, Mommy. Memes gave it to me!" Vivi exclaimed.

"Oh, my goodness. You both look like Uncle Connor and me," Carly said, hugging them both.

"Well, if they're coming back this summer, they'll need boots," Curt said, hoping they would return for an extended visit.

"They'll come back to visit. I promise," Carly said, to whoops from Frederick and Vivi.

Everyone gathered in the kitchen to enjoy Thanksgiving leftovers. The conversation shifted to the new puppies that the Evans' Scottish Terrier is expected to have any day now. This topic brightened Frederick and Vivi's spirits, as they were preparing to leave the following morning for Kansas City to attend their father's upcoming memorial service.

Paula decided to become a breeder a few years prior, and this litter would be the last for Claire and Jamie. Paula, like Carly, loved *Outlander* and named the puppies after the show's main characters.

Vivi took a bite of turkey, then asked, "Mommy, can we have a puppy?"

Carly looked across the table at her mother. "Do you have all the puppies spoken for, like the last litter?"

"No, only four people have put a deposit down. Her ultrasound at the vet on Monday showed eight puppies."

Frederick's eyes brightened. "Can we buy one, Mom?"

Carly loved dogs. She and Austin had a large Golden Retriever named Shasta when they lived in Denver. She passed away before they moved to Charleston. The thought of a puppy for Frederick and Vivi to take care of appealed to Carly. It provided them with both responsibility and companionship.

"Tell you what, it is easier to have two than one, just because they will miss their mommy," Carly said, then added, "I think we can make a deposit for two, if everything works out with the numbers."

Curt tapped his fingers on the table, hatching an idea of his own. "I have a better idea. Since you're not going to fly out for Christmas, how about we bring them to you as your Christmas presents, a little late?"

"Can we, Mom? Memes, is it okay?" Frederick pleaded.

Paula saw the look in both Frederick and Vivi's eyes. She couldn't say no. "It won't be until the end of January or even the first of February before you'd get the puppies."

"We have to buy things and tell Miss Dottie," Vivi said.

Everyone laughed at Vivi's thoughtfulness. It gave the children something to look forward to, and Carly didn't want to let them down.

"It sounds like a done deal. Two months will give us time to come up with two names. If possible, we'd like a boy and a girl."

"We'll see what we can do," Curt said, grinning like a child.

"Do you want anything for the road?" Paula asked. "Driving to Kansas City is a couple of hours, on a good day."

"Thanks, Mom. Maybe a bottle of water for the kids. Myra is expecting us to come hungry and ready to eat at one o'clock."

Paula went inside to grab the water bottles. Curt leaned inside the car window to talk to Carly.

"If you want to move back to Hade and Eva's house, we'd help you update it and make it your own." Curt kept his voice low, so the children didn't hear him.

Paula returned with the water bottles and handed them through the window to Frederick and Vivi. She kissed Carly on her cheek. "I'll let you know when Claire has her puppies."

Frederick and Vivi chatted in the backseat while Carly put in her earbuds to listen to a message on her phone. Delaney had called to wish her a Happy Thanksgiving. Carly quickly sent a text while waiting at a traffic light.

Abilene still held the charm of a small town while offering amenities that attracted city dwellers. Carly thought it was a great place to raise a family.

She played her music to ease the rising anxiety about seeing Austin's family for the first time since his funeral. The gathering wouldn't be the same without Austin talking about football with Kent or doting on Myra. Ainsleigh and her husband were also attending, so Carly and the kids wouldn't be alone with Austin's parents.

Inside her backpack, the urn holding Austin's ashes was wrapped in bubble wrap; she had kept her promise to his ghost. The kids were quietly engaged with their iPads as Carly remembered what Granny said—it had to be Dr. Alston Curry, as Granny had repeated his message almost verbatim.

What if he, too, thinks I've lost my mind? What other explanation is there? I've experienced what someone else has gone through in their life. As far-fetched as it seems, I've taken a trip back in time. If not, then I've lived a prior life. Carly put the thoughts of Caroline out of her mind for the rest of the drive to Kansas City.

Carly remembered the tree-lined street leading up to Austin's parents' house. It reminded her of the street in the movie, *Home Alone*. The homes were older, but well-maintained and upscale.

Ainsleigh and Ryan met Carly and the kids at the front door. Carly hugged Ainsleigh, and nothing was said between them. Ryan embraced Carly, a gesture that seemed awkward to her.

"Happy Thanksgiving, Ryan," Carly said, wanting to end the uncomfortable feeling from his unexpected hug. Myra and Kent were in the kitchen, carrying food from the refrigerator and oven to the table.

Frederick and Vivi ran into the kitchen to hug their grandparents. Kent had his Jayhawk sweatshirt on and looked as if he had aged ten years since Austin's death. It had taken a toll on him, understandably.

Myra looked lovely as ever. The woman aged backwards. She wore a plaid skirt that fell below the knee and an off-white cashmere sweater, accompanied by a paisley silk scarf tied expertly around her neck. She set the turkey on the table, then reached for each of her grandchildren to shower them with kisses.

"Frederick, I swear you've grown a foot since we saw you last," Myra said, rubbing the top of Frederick's head.

"Vivi, you're such a pretty young lady," Myra said, cupping Vivi's chin.

"We missed you, Gigi," Vivi said, hugging Myra tightly around her waist.

Myra saw Carly standing by the table, not wanting to interrupt the reunion between Myra and the children. Kent put his arm around Carly, drawing her to him.

"We're so glad to see you and the kids." Kent gave Carly and the kids hugs.

Carly admired the table, which resembled a Martha Stewart spread. The gold chargers held China plates, with linen napkins placed beside them. A fall floral arrangement graced the center of the table. Kent poured a glass of wine for the adults, while Frederick and Vivi received sparkling grape juice.

Kent said grace before carving the turkey. Carly noticed that either Myra or Kent had removed an extra chair from the table. She observed that everyone was trying to keep their emotions in check. The awkward avoidance of Austin's name made it feel as though everyone was walking on proverbial eggshells during the gathering.

Twice, she noticed Myra dabbing the corner of her eye with her napkin while Ainsleigh tried to carry on a conversation with Frederick and Vivi.

The family managed to get through the meal without anyone breaking down. Carly felt like the kettle was about to blow any second. Kent asked how her job at Channel 5 was going, and Frederick blurted out that she quit her job.

Thanks, Frederick. Carly went through the whole story about her demotion and used the time to schedule speaking engagements and conferences, as well as the burials of the Bethesda Twelve. She told them about Dottie and how she's adjusted to housekeeping and child-care when Carly's away.

Austin's family kept their opinions to themselves. No one wanted to rock the boat, leading to an emotional breakdown.

After dinner, Myra, Carly, and Ainsleigh went into the den to talk while Ryan and Kent hooked up the game system Ryan brought. Frederick and Vivi were engrossed in the game, not noticing that Carly had left the room.

"The service tomorrow starts at eleven. We've taken care of everything. It will be short, but meaningful," Myra said.

"Thank you for seeing to this. Will Austin's friends be able to attend?" Carly asked, unsure of who received the notification.

"Yes, several of his college buddies are coming, as well as his closest high school friends."

Carly updated Myra and Ainsleigh on the young man pleading guilty to driving under the influence, sparing Carly from a trial.

"I'm so glad you don't have to go through a trial," Ainsleigh said, squeezing Carly's hand.

"So am I," Carly replied. "I told Harve to handle it."

Myra spoke cautiously, "Carly, would you mind if I kept some of Austin's ashes?"

The request, although unexpected, didn't rattle Carly. "Of course, yes."

"I wanted to have something made. I saw where a stone in a ring or necklace could contain your loved one's ashes."

"Whatever you want to do, and you as well, Ainsleigh." Carly didn't want to make this any harder on them.

"Thank you. We can take care of that before the service tomorrow," Myra said.

Carly took Austin's room for the night. She felt his presence throughout the house. The feeling was powerful in his bedroom.

Austin's high school graduation portrait hung on the wall, along with pictures of his college graduation, trophies from high school sports achievements, his medical school graduation, and their wedding picture.

She touched the face staring back at her. "I want you to rest in peace. I love you, and regardless of what happened with Cora, I forgive you." Carly kissed the picture, putting it back on the dresser. She slipped into bed, pulling the comforter up around her shoulders. Austin appeared at the foot of the bed, looking at peace with a smile Carly missed. She kept her eyes on him as he faded from view. "Good night, Austin. You're finally home."

CHAPTER THIRTY-TWO

Carly and the children followed Austin's parents, Ainsleigh and Ryan, to the church where the Tabors attended. The parking lot began to fill with Austin's extended family and friends. Carly carried the urn into the church, with Frederick and Vivi following close behind her. The minister greeted the family, extending his condolences to Carly and the children first.

Kent and Myra thanked their minister and continued into the sanctuary, where Carly joined them. A table adorned with roses and fern fronds surrounded the spot where Austin's urn and picture were placed. Frederick and Vivi remained quiet as they sat in the front row with their aunt and uncle. Carly, Kent, and Myra went to the back of the church to greet the mourners.

Many of the attendees were Austin's cousins, aunts, and uncles.

A few college friends introduced themselves, and Carly recognized them. Two of the men were co-investors with Austin in the cellphone case venture. Their wives offered their condolences and then proceeded to their seats.

When the designated time arrived, Carly and her in-laws took their places in the front row, ready for the service to begin. Carly gazed at the large photograph of Austin, his dark azure eyes staring back at her. Memories of all the happy times they had shared flooded her mind, making her acutely aware of Cora and the last time she had seen him.

As the minister spoke, Myra dabbed her eyes, and Ainsleigh tried to soften her sniffles with a handkerchief. Unexpectedly, Carly remained composed until Joyce Myler, a church vocalist, stood to sing "It Is Well With My Soul." The beautiful performance resonated in the rafters, bringing many attendees to tears.

At the end of the service, Carly stood with the rest of the family to shake hands and receive heartfelt hugs of sympathy.

The interment, a private affair, involved driving to Myra and Kent's hometown of Cottonwood Falls. The distance from Kansas City was two hours. Kent wanted to stop for lunch before driving the distance to the cemetery. They pulled into a small hometown restaurant halfway there in Williamsburg. Frederick and Vivi started to complain about being hungry, so the timing worked perfectly.

Lunch gave everyone time to talk about the guests who came to the memorial service, some family members Carly hadn't seen since her and Austin's wedding in 2005. Carly thought about the upcoming 20th anniversary date, and a jolt of sadness coursed through her.

Once the family finished their fried chicken, tenderloins, and various midwestern fare, they continued to the rural cemetery northwest of town in Cottonwood Falls.

The cemetery was nestled in a small valley, situated between a wooded area and the family-owned Tabor farmland. As they walked through the cemetery, the local grave digger and his assistant arrived, bringing the necessary equipment to bury the urn behind the headstone.

For the first time, Carly saw the black granite stone engraved with her name and Austin's. Two entwined wedding rings were placed in the center, with their wedding date below. The sight brought tears to her eyes.

"The stone is beautiful, Myra," Carly said, squeezing her hand for comfort.

On the back of the stone, the words "Our children, Austin Frederick and Viviene Jo" were etched in. Both Frederick and Vivi saw their names and smiled at the tribute.

Some of Austin's ashes were placed in small bags for Myra to use in creating jewelry items, while the rest were placed in the urn, which was then buried.

Kent led the family in "The Lord's Prayer" to conclude the solemn ritual. Austin's remains were buried between his grandparents, alongside the stone that had been purchased for Kent and Myra. Although the most challenging part was now over, Carly felt as if she were having an out-of-body experience. She was aware of everything happening around her, yet she felt transported to another grave at another time, mourning over the graves of two husbands.

She heard Vivi ask about a small marble headstone further down from Austin's, which was topped with a carved lamb. Turning to her, Carly noticed Vivi's attention was drawn to the small stone.

Worried about Vivi's curiosity, Carly explained that the headstone belonged to a child, hoping she wouldn't press her grandparents with questions about it.

Thankfully, Vivi accepted the answer and walked with Ainsleigh through the cemetery toward their car.

The children sat quietly in the backseat, immersed in their devices, while Carly reflected on the service and burial. Bringing Austin to Kansas fulfilled a promise to her dead husband. Now, she affirmed her life would go on, focusing on the well-being of the children and moving through the next chapter of her life as a single parent.

When everyone arrived back at the house, Carly remained downstairs with the rest of the family while Frederick and Vivi went upstairs to pack the freshly laundered clothes Myra had placed on their bed.

The flight to Charleston would leave at six o'clock the following morning. Carly needed to leave to return the rental car and get through TSA two hours prior to the flight. She and the children ended the night early, putting them to bed by eight-thirty.

As Carly came out of Frederick and Vivi's room, Myra met her in the hallway. "Thank you for bringing Austin back home. It's what Kent and I hoped you'd do."

Carly hugged her mother-in-law and said, "It's what Austin wanted, too. I can't explain it, but I know he wanted to come home."

The two women shared a tender moment, then Carly said, "Thank you for everything. The service meant so much, and the stone is beautiful."

For the rest of the evening, Carly felt a peace she'd missed the last seven months. She slept soundly until the phone alarm alerted her at three a.m.

She woke the children and got them out the door in record time. Myra and Kent followed them to the rental car. Kent hugged Carly tighter than he realized.

She winced but never let on.

"Let us know when you arrive back in South Carolina. We love you," he said.

"We love you both," Carly said, amid the hugging and kissing of everyone before she pulled out of the driveway.

❧

Carly and Delaney met for lunch at Poogan's Porch. Christmas shopping finished, they both felt accomplished in getting it done before Christmas Eve.

"I wanted to let you know the conference in Florida, the second week in January, is a go for me," Delaney said.

Carly sent out requests in October for speaking engagements, and the offers to speak came back quicker than she imagined. "Oh, good. I thought I'd use most of the notes from Coombe Abbey and maybe include the Bethesda Twelve."

"I think that's an excellent idea," Delaney said. "By the way, did you ever contact Dr. Curry?"

"That reminds me. Oh, my goodness. I completely forgot to tell you about Granny!" Carly exclaimed.

Delaney leaned over with one eyebrow raised. "Talk about it," she said.

"It happened before we left for Kansas City. I'd felt so confused and anxious. I did what I always did- I went to Granny and Pop's house."

"Your folks still own it?"

"Yes, Mom didn't want to see another family buy it, since our farms connect."

"O.K., go on."

"The house is empty. I went upstairs because I heard what sounded like feet shuffling."

Delaney listened without interrupting.

"I spoke to Granny, as if she could hear me. She started to appear, faint at first." Carly spoke faster, "And then, she became a full apparition. She told me that I'm ready and to let him help me."

Delaney's eyes grew wide. "Isn't that the gist of what Dr. Curry told you at the conference?"

"Yes, almost word for word. The visions and experiences haven't stopped, which makes me question my own sanity."

"You've experienced something for months, even before the graves were found."

Carly thought back to the dreams she told Austin. He assumed it involved children. Her paranormal experiences continued during her visit to England.

"You know, I felt better when Drake confirmed the woman appeared to him. He came to me, remember?"

"Maybe Drake is connected somehow, I'm just not sure how." Delaney nodded at Carly, "Call Alston Curry."

Carly agreed. "I'll do it today." She rolled up her paper napkin and put it on the table. "Are you ready to head home?"

Delaney grabbed her purse. "Let's make like a library and book it."

Carly laughed at Delaney's wit and followed her to pay for the check.

Carly took her packages upstairs and put them inside Austin's closet. His clothes still hung on the hangers. Carly knew the time to donate his things had come. She touched the sleeve of his Jayhawk t-shirt, the one he wore to the airport and hung back on its hanger. She pulled the fabric close to her nose, breathing in the scent of his cologne, still present.

She closed her eyes for a moment, then closed the door. She walked downstairs, meeting Dottie at the bottom, who was holding a laundry basket full of clean clothes.

"Oh, Carly, I didn't realize you came back from shopping. I put my earplugs in to listen to a program and didn't hear you."

"It's okay, I'm going to work in my office," she said.

Dottie continued upstairs to put away the laundry, and Carly went into her office, closing the door behind her.

Carly found a note with a phone number for Alston Curry. She checked the time; it was nearly seven o'clock in Glasgow. Taking a deep breath, she dialed the number and made herself comfortable in the eighteenth century settle, pulling her legs up and covering them with a crocheted throw.

Her eyes widened and her heart pounded as she heard his heavy Scottish brogue. "Good evening," Dr. Curry said.

"Dr. Curry, this is Carly Tabor. We met at.." Carly didn't finish, as Dr. Curry interrupted her.

"Yes, I've expected your call for quite some time, Carly."

Carly felt as she did when he gave her his card and the cryptic message over eight months ago. "I meant to contact you earlier, but I lost my husband after I returned from the conference. I've let things go," Carly said apologetically.

"Dinna fash," he said. "No worries."

"You told me that when I was ready, to call you. Well, I'm ready." Carly exhaled, and the anxiety started to leave her body.

Carly told Dr. Curry everything, from the dreams she had before leaving for the conference to the discovery of The Bethesda Twelve. She continued with the visions and hauntings, the feeling of living Caroline's life, up to her grandmother's ghost telling her to contact him. Throughout the conversation, Dr. Curry inserted phrases such as "I see" or "I expected as much."

Finally, when Carly finished telling him everything she remembered, he spoke.

"I don't feel I'm able to explain what you're experiencing over the phone. I need to show you my research as well as data to confirm my findings."

Carly's mind raced—he didn't think of her as a raving lunatic or someone delusional. Maybe he could help her.

"I'm not sure if I'm able to come to Glasgow with Christmas next week."

He didn't say anything for a moment, then said, "I'm always

receiving grants for my research. I am willing to provide your airfare and accommodation for a few days. What do you think?"

Carly's mind raced. What a generous offer, as well as a promise of helping her. "All right. I'll get a flight after the holiday. If you could, send me a list of accommodations near the university."

"I'll arrange your hotel, and if you would, find the flight and send me the information. The university will pick up the fare."

"Thank you, Dr. Curry, I'm so grateful you can help me."

Carly put her phone on her desk, and a flood of emotions washed over her. The answers were two weeks away. She blew her nose and wiped the tears from her face. She pulled up the airline website and began looking for flights to Glasgow for January 2.

She found a flight, emailed Dr. Curry, and awaited his reply. Within minutes, he returned with the information for her flight, as well as the name of the hotel near the university. "I'll book you a room at the Alamo Guest House, a lovely Victorian Bed and Breakfast. It's only a two-minute walk to the university."

She entered the name and googled Bed and Breakfast. It looked like a castle. Carly replied, "Thank you. It looks lovely."

With everything settled, the next step will be finding the right time to tell the children and Dottie.

CHAPTER THIRTY-THREE

December 15th, 2025

Delaney handed Carly a strand of lights, having untangled the mess moments earlier. "Why don't you do the easy way and order a new tree, prelit?"

Carly started the strand at the top, handing the conglomeration of lights over to Delaney, "I've thought about it, but the kids have experienced enough change this year. I want to keep it the same for them."

"I understand. They'll love it just the way it is." She handed the last of the strands over to Carly.

"Austin always let the kids do the lower ornaments. It's a tradition." Carly stepped back to look at the tree. "I think we have enough lights, don't you?"

Delaney moved to a different spot in the den. "Yep, it looks perfect to me. You almost beat me with decorating."

Carly knew better. Delaney had already decorated for Christmas the day after Thanksgiving, as she always followed tradition.

"I spoke to Dr. Curry. I'm going to Scotland on January 2nd," Carly revealed. She had kept the news a secret for a few days, choosing to share it only now.

Delaney's head snapped around in surprise. "What? You didn't tell me about this huge news until now?"

Feeling guilty, Carly backpedaled. "I'm sorry. I wavered back and forth over the last few days. I almost called to back out of the whole thing."

"So, what did the good doctor have to say about all of the hauntings and appearances into the past?"

Carly laughed. "I unloaded on the poor man. Spilled my guts and left no stone unturned."

Delaney shook her head, joining in with her laughter. "I can see him rubbing his hands together in delight! A new guinea pig."

"Yeah, he did have a moment of euphoria, I'm sure." Carly enjoyed a light-hearted moment remembering Dr. Curry from the conference. "All kidding aside, I believe he knows what I'm experiencing and can help me."

A look of concern covered Delaney. "Sweetie, please be careful. I know he offered months ago to help you, but if something feels wrong..."

Carly interrupted. "I know, and I will. I'm starting to doubt my own experiences. Will he think I'm deranged?"

Delaney offered a reassuring smile. "I have been with you through unbelievable events, and you've seen things most people wouldn't believe."

Dottie and the kids came through the door, interrupting the conversation. Frederick and Vivi, still wearing their backpacks, rushed to hug Delaney.

"Hey, y'all are like wild horses," she said, bending down to hug backpacks and all.

Dottie waved and said hello to Delaney as she hung up coats in the entry closet. "They saw the lights on the tree and almost jumped out of the car while it was still running!"

"Don't worry, we saved the ornaments for you." Carly gave Vivi a swat on her bottom as she hurried into the den, following Frederick.

"When can we decorate, Mom?" Frederick asked, the lights reflecting in his eyes, wide with excitement.

"After supper and homework," Carly said, then added, "Why don't you unpack your backpacks and take your homework to the kitchen?"

"I have supper already started," Dottie said, already in the kitchen.

With only minimal grousing, they did as they were told. Delaney grabbed her coat from the back of the recliner and followed the kids to the entry hall.

"I need to hit the road, Boyd's meeting me at The Oyster House, then we have an appointment with a couple on James Island."

Carly's eyebrows raised, "Oh? A potential investigation?"

"Maybe. A couple we investigated a while back moved to a different house. Seems the spirits moved with them."

"Tell Boyd hey for me. We'll talk later." Carly hugged Delaney.

Carly joined Dottie and the children in the kitchen. Frederick and Vivi chattered about the new puppies coming to live with them in a couple of months. Paula's Scottish Terrier, Claire, had seven puppies. The male and female puppies chosen over FaceTime were black coats like Claire's. Names were changed weekly, but there was still no consensus.

"You have another month until you get them, you might pick names for Memes to start using them, so they know their names."

Dottie and Carly carried the salad and casserole to the table. Frederick and Vivi had moved their homework to the counter, making room for it.

After Vivi said the prayer, Carly put chicken casserole on the plates as they passed them to her. Carly wanted to wait and tell everyone about her upcoming trip closer to the day, but something made her spill the beans.

"I'm going back to Scotland for a few days after Christmas," Carly announced, throwing caution to the wind.

Frederick stopped eating and looked at Carly, his expression telling. "Why? You can't go again." The declaration stated his feelings without wavering.

Vivi looked first at Frederick and then at Carly. "Mommy, can we go this time?"

"Honey, I'm going to meet with Dr. Curry, and it isn't a vacation trip." Carly saw the uncertainty in Vivi's expression.

Dottie remained quiet, although her expression said enough. Frederick took a bite of salad, chomping down on a carrot. The sound bounced off the walls, breaking the awkward silence.

Carly swallowed a gulp of water, continuing. "I'm sorry to leave and not take you both. I hope he can help me with things I'm feeling. He thinks he can help me get better."

Frederick didn't look at her, but said, "Is it because of Dad?"

"No, buddy, this isn't about being sad about Dad. It's hard to explain, but Dr. Curry specializes in what I'm feeling."

"Will you only stay a few days and come back?" Frederick's voice cracked.

It wasn't Carly's leaving that upset Frederick; it was that she wouldn't come back. His therapist told Carly that Frederick is dealing with the fear of losing Carly, too.

"I don't have any plans to stay beyond the 3 days. I have a flight coming back on January 5th."

Carly reached out and took Frederick's hand. "You and Vivi will stay here with Dottie. I'll FaceTime every morning and night."

Vivi smiled. "Okay, Mommy." She continued eating, her uneasiness settled. "I can talk to Granny and Jesus if I get scared."

Dottie and Carly exchanged glances across the table. Carly put an arm around Vivi's shoulder, next to her.

"Yes, always talk to Jesus. If talking to Granny helps, then talk to her, too."

Frederick rolled his eyes. "Vivi, you're coo-coo."

Carly smiled at Vivi and winked.

Dottie left on the morning of the 22nd to spend Christmas in Alexandria, Virginia, with her son and daughter-in-law. Dr. Curry sent the hotel confirmation via email, and the airline emailed her e-ticket receipt. She also received two emails from paranormal conferences inviting her to be a guest speaker.

Carly's visions and dreams about the events in Caroline's life continued. The idea of time travel resurfaced each time she saw Caroline with the children or Stefan.

She didn't know what made her reach out to him, but she picked up her phone. Something about him felt safe, and he, too, had been visited by Caroline.

Carly walked into the hall, calling Frederick and Vivi, who were upstairs. "Hey, if you need me, I'm working in my office."

Both kids shouted simultaneously, "Okay!"

Carly pulled the door closed and settled into the high-backed chair with her phone. She'd saved Drake's number in her phone, and it rang twice before he answered.

"Good morning, Carly," he said, his voice gravelly.

Carly winced. She hadn't considered the time difference in London. "I'm sorry I woke you. I didn't think."

He cleared his throat and replied, "No, I'm just staring at the ceiling. Insomnia again. I'm glad you called."

"I reached out to Dr. Curry after I went home for Thanksgiving last month and had a visit with my Granny's spirit."

"Oh, how interesting. I hope the encounter brought you a sense of peace."

"Yes, she told me to contact Dr. Curry, that he would help me." Carly added, "I'm paraphrasing, but that was the general idea."

"Have you discovered any more information about Caroline, besides what you've told me?"

Carly tried to recall their last conversation. "I've returned to Wales during the encounters. My heart breaks for the loss of two husbands and two children."

Drake's voice softened. "You mean Caroline. Her husbands and children."

"Yes, of course. I suppose my recent loss and the losses Caroline faced have merged in my thoughts," Carly said.

"What did Dr. Curry suggest?"

"I'm going to Glasgow on January 2nd. He wants to see me in person and share his research. I'll stay for a couple of days."

"Will Delaney travel with you this time?" he asked.

"No, I'm flying solo this time," Carly replied.

"Have you arranged lodging? I know of a few great hotels," Drake offered, sounding more awake now.

"What about the Alamo Guest House? Have you heard of it?"

Drake paused. "It's very nice. Dr. Curry is quite the poseur."

"He mentioned grant money, so I suppose it's university funded." Carly continued, "Sometimes I feel like I've time-traveled or lived a completely different life."

"I'm not sure what to believe, having thought both were impossible. However, after listening to Alexandria Diaz's experience, I'm less skeptical."

Carly appreciated Drake's candor. "Listen, I'm not going to drone on about what I'm going through. I guess I just wanted to hear your voice."

"Anytime you want to hear my voice, I'm here for you. Have a jolly rest of your day."

Carly laughed. "I hope you'll get some sleep."

They said goodbye, and Carly went into the kitchen to decide what to fix for supper. She perused the freezer for a frozen meal Dottie prepared and found a large container of chili. As she walked to the microwave to defrost the contents of the bowl, she heard her phone sitting on the counter leave a notification.

Carly put the bowl inside the microwave and picked up her phone. The message was from Jordan Fentress of Spirit Seekers Paracon. Carly read the text.

Hi Carly! This is Jordan of Spirit Seekers reaching out about our 2026 Conference. We moved the date to May 28th through the 31st. We're all set with Boston as the venue, and a couple of day trips to Danvers and Fall River.

I hope you're still on board speaking again this year. I reached out to Delaney in a separate text. Many of the same speakers have agreed to take part, so I hope you and Delaney will join us. Let me know as soon as you're able. I'll send information regarding the venue, lodging, and payment for speaking. Kind regards, Jordan.

Carly flipped the 2026 calendar over to May. She circled the dates and wrote "Spirit Seekers" on them. She texted Jordan, *Count me in!*

This year's Christmas Eve was unlike any in the past. Austin's absence weighed heavily on both Carly and the children. She attempted to take on all the tasks that were typically Austin's while also fulfilling her responsibilities. Carly read "The Night Before Christmas," Austin's favorite part of the holiday excitement. Although Frederick acted too old for the story, Carly noticed him smile as she put in her best effort.

Vivi, on the other hand, still loved watching Santa Claus on the evening weather report.

To conclude the night, Carly read the Nativity story from the family Bible. After tucking both Frederick and Vivi into bed, she returned downstairs to enjoy her traditional Christmas Eve hot toddy. The combination of spiced rum, lemon, honey, and hot water warmed her from the inside and tasted wonderful. She felt a sense of accomplishment as she checked off the boxes for her first solo Christmas Eve as a parent. The twinkling, colored lights on the Christmas tree reminded her of past Christmases she had shared with Austin, both as a young couple and later with their children. Carly knew that Austin would be proud of her for keeping his traditions alive during her favorite holiday.

The next morning, Frederick and Vivi woke up before Carly's six o'clock alarm. She opened one eye, blurry and heavy from the previous night's libation. She rolled over to their eager faces, ready to bound down the stairs to see what wonderful things awaited them under the Christmas tree.

"Give me a minute. Go run a brush through your hair and let me throw some water on my face."

She hurried to get in position at the foot of the stairs to video Frederick and Vivi coming down to open gifts, another of Austin's roles on Christmas morning. Carly reminded them to wait for her as they raced past on their way to the den.

She took multiple pictures of the kids opening their gifts. Frederick went behind the recliner and put two gifts in Carly's lap.

"What's this?" Carly asked, surprised.

"Dottie took us shopping. Merry Christmas," Frederick said, bending down to hug Carly.

Vivi rose from her place on the floor and put her arms around Carly's shoulders. "Merry Christmas, Mommy," Vivi said.

Carly appreciated Dottie making sure the kids went Christmas shopping to buy one another a present and one for her. The job, one of Austin's favorites, fell on Dottie.

Her gifts included a gold pair of hoop earrings with a braided design, and a mother's ring with their birthstones flanking Carly's.

"They're beautiful. But I didn't give Dottie any money for you to shop. I forgot."

"Dottie didn't do it. Meme and Pap gave us money to give to Dottie for your presents." Vivi grinned, showing the two large spaces where her missing teeth once were.

"Vivi, you goober, Pap said not to tell," Frederick said, chastising his sister.

Carly smiled at her parents' kind gesture, the act causing her emotions to overflow, and tears ran down her cheeks.

"I'm sorry, Mommy. I didn't mean to tell." Vivi hugged Carly's neck.

"No, honey, I'm not mad. I'm so thankful for you both." She kissed them both, feeling overwhelmed with gratitude.

CHAPTER THIRTY-FOUR

For the rest of Christmas vacation, Carly spent time with the kids. Dottie returned on December 27th. Carly scheduled a conference in Denver and one in Arizona for 2026. She'd even started a podcast, with Boyd's help, called Spirit Talk. She'd already seen a good following after just a couple of programs.

On the morning of January 2nd, an Uber picked up Carly to go to the airport. Her flight flew to Reagan Airport, then to Glasgow. She arrived at Glasgow airport at five a.m. the next morning.

Freya McGourty, Dr. Curry's assistant, stood in the baggage claim section, holding a small sign that read "Carly".

Carly noticed the pretty redhead immediately. She picked up her bag from the conveyor and walked over to her. "I'm happy to see you. I'm Carly," she said, pointing to the small sign. Both women laughed.

"It's good to see you. We'll take a wee trip on the shuttle to the Alamo Guest House. It's quite lovely," said Freya.

Carly followed her to the shuttle bus that was waiting along the curb. Her mind raced as the shuttle drove the fifteen minutes on the M8, a busy thoroughfare even at five-thirty a.m.

As they arrived at their destination, Carly recalled Drake's term "posure." The B&B exceeded her imagination. The exterior of the building piqued her curiosity about what the inside might look like. The elegant four-story stone structure, built in the 1870s, was a Victorian gem situated in Glasgow's West End, directly across from the University of Glasgow.

Freya walked inside with Carly and mentioned that the bespoke rooms are very posh, each designed to suit a particular guest's desires.

"You can choose whichever room you like. I'm sure whatever you decide will be exquisite," Freya said.

The attendant looked up from her computer screen. "Welcome to The Alamo Guest House. How may I help you?"

"I have a room reserved for the next three days. My name is Carly Tabor."

The attendant smiled. "Yes, one moment." She found Carly's reservation. "You're staying in the Skye room. It overlooks the park and the Kelvingrove Art Gallery. Of course, the university is across the street."

Carly nodded, "Thank you. I'm sure the room is lovely."

A porter met Carly at the desk, and the attendant gave the key to him.

"We'll walk a wee way down the hall to the elevators. You're staying in room 202." The porter wheeled her luggage down to the elevator.

"Thank you." Carly leaned against the elevator wall, feeling the effects of jet lag.

The porter led her down to the end of the hall, using the key to press it against the key reader, which opened the door and allowed Carly to go inside. He wheeled her luggage inside and placed it on a luggage hammock. He turned on the room light and checked the thermostat to ensure the heat setting was set.

"Madam, is there anything else I can do for you?"

Carly placed several coins in his hand. "Thank you, no, everything looks lovely."

As soon as the porter left, Carly began to explore her room. It rivaled the suite at Coombe Abbey, featuring her bathroom with a deep copper tub and a surprisingly large shower equipped with a huge showerhead and a massage nozzle mounted on the wall. Carly admired the two cozy bathrobes hanging on the door.

Next, she entered the bedroom where the corniced ceiling rose to an impressive fourteen feet. An elegant brass and crystal chandelier lit up the entire room. The four-poster bed, dressed in rich shades of gray and burgundy, sat across from stylish marble-topped 'Bombe' oak bedside tables and a dressing table. The matching damask draperies were pulled back to let in light and reveal the beautiful view.

Carly wanted to shower and change into something more presentable than her travel clothes. Although she felt the urge to lie down and take a nap, she knew that if she did, she might sleep through her appointment.

She placed a pair of plaid slacks, a white blouse, and a wool pullover vest on the bed. She chose a pair of black ankle boots and put them beside the bed.

Carly left the hotel and found a pub near the university. She ate a small salad, not wanting her stomach to growl during her meeting. It only took her thirty minutes for lunch, giving her plenty of time to walk over to the university. The morning rain had ceased, giving way to a cold wind and light snow. She zipped up her jacket and crossed the street to the University of Glasgow, which was founded in 1451 and resembled a medieval manor. Climbing the twenty-four steps from the street to the doorway of the main building, she stood in awe, taking in the beautiful architecture.

Suddenly, she heard someone call her name and turned to see Dr. Curry walking toward her.

"Carly! Welcome to Glasgow. I hope your accommodations are satisfactory," he said, appearing less ostentatious than she remembered. He held out his hand to shake hers.

"Thank you. Yes, the room is gorgeous."

"Well, my office is in another building—the West Medical Building. It's just a wee walk from here. Shall we?" Dr. Curry invited Carly to follow him.

"The university is lovely. I love architecture. I've seen it on *Outlander*."

"Oh, yes, the famous series I've heard so much about."

Carly laughed. "I take it Scots aren't as obsessed as Americans are."

They walked to the rear of the main university buildings to the Medical Building. The offices of neuroscience and psychological researchers were in this complex of buildings.

The outside of the building matched the rest of the university. The James Black Building, with its twin turrets, looked impressive. Carly followed Dr. Curry inside.

"My office is one of the nicer ones in the building. I'm not sure how I got it, considering my research isn't bringing in huge amounts of money for the university."

Dr. Curry then walked through a narrow corridor to an office labeled 'Dr. Alston Curry, Ph.D., Parapsychology, Psychokinesis, and DNA Research'.

"After you, Carly." Dr. Curry held the door open.

Carly observed the tall windows, which allowed an abundance of natural light that bathed the room. Four black file cabinets stood on either side of bookshelves which held a wide array of volumes. A television screen was mounted on the wall above the fireplace mantle. Copies of colorful charts and diagrams of brain waves were spread out across a large desk.

Her palms started to feel like wet rags, and her nerves kicked in as soon as she went inside. "I'm a little nervous," Carly confessed.

"There's no need to be nervous, Carly. I want to talk first, then I'll share the science behind my theory." Dr. Curry offered Carly the first glimpse of his compassionate side.

Carly sat across from his expansive antique desk. He offered her a bottle of water, which she accepted and thanked him. He turned on his computer and the television monitor above an antique walnut credenza opposite the door.

He opened several tabs, then moved from behind his desk to where he could see Carly. "I'd like for you to tell me how your sensitive abilities have evolved with your connection to the spirit of Caroline Richards."

She scooted back in her chair and began telling Dr. Curry everything she remembered. "I dreamed about Caroline before I went to Bethesda Orphan Asylum. I saw her on a ship, and her children were with her."

"I see. Did you ever see anyone else, as in a place and time where you found yourself with that spirit?" He scribbled on a piece of yellow legal paper as she spoke.

"Yes, I remember once during an investigation on Johns Island, I had a strange vision or memory." Carly stopped, then said, "Why did you ask me that? I never shared it with anyone, not even Delaney."

Dr. Curry smiled at the memory of Delaney from Spirit Seekers. "Oh, yes, I remember Delaney. She is what we call 'canty'." He blushed, surprising himself for being unprofessional.

Carly covered her mouth to avoid Dr. Curry seeing the large grin on her face. "What does canty mean?"

"Spirited, lively. The life of the party."

"That describes Delaney Warrick to a 't'."

Dr. Curry went back to what Carly shared. "You see, I believe that your experiences over the years are not separate events but are all connected as part of your past."

Carly's eyebrows rose. "*My* past? How so?"

Dr. Curry turned to his computer screen and brought up a slide that appeared to look like DNA. Carly put on her glasses to get a better view.

"Carly, what I'm about to tell you has the potential to alter the way the world views how DNA encompasses more than one's hair color, eye color, potential diseases, and the like."

Carly's mind raced. *What does DNA have to do with Caroline Richards haunting my thoughts and me?*

Dr. Curry moved to a chair beside Carly, bringing with him charts and notes on a legal pad. "I work here under the Psychology wing of the university, however, my role has changed from professor to head of research."

"I don't understand what DNA has to do with the paranormal."

"For the past twenty-five years, my research has shifted from neurological research to Parakinesis studies, the science behind the movement of objects by a force insufficient to explain the motion."

"I've witnessed an object moving without someone in the room…a spirit forced the movement." Carly thought back to the tiny rocking horse and Freddy Richards.

"Yes, that's Parakinesis. But my research changed after reading the findings of psychologist Carl Jung. He introduced me to epigenetics," Dr. Curry said enthusiastically.

"I'm unfamiliar with the term. What is it?"

"The brain is a complex and astonishing organ, and its capabilities are astounding. Epigenetics is the study of how cells control gene activity without altering the DNA sequence. It explores memory in two contexts: genetic memory and central nervous system memory."

Carly's expression shifted from amazement to confusion. "I wish my late husband were here to explain. He was a neurosurgeon."

"Let me simplify the scientific terminology for you. What Jung and others theorized is that some people are born with the memories and experiences that their ancestors have imprinted on their DNA. In other words, we inherit certain memories that are passed down through matrilineal lines. These memories could be incorporated into the genome over long periods."

Carly tried to process everything she had heard in relation to her own experiences. "I want to understand more about how this relates to me."

"The studies were originally conducted with mice. The control specimens were exposed to certain stimuli, unfortunately, which were painful. In their offspring, the memory of the painful experience—whether it was a sensation like an electrical shock or a smell present before the experience—was passed down, and the stimuli caused the same reaction in the mice, even though the offspring themselves had not experienced it."

"So, the experiences of my ancestors could have been imprinted into my DNA? How does that work, I mean, I have thousands of ancestors."

"Yes, that is true. Certain ancestors experienced trauma or something profound that the memory passed into the DNA of eggs in the female, prior to fertilization."

Carly sat for a moment, silent, processing the information Dr. Curry had told her. He showed her the information on the large television screen. He explained that her DNA, which originated from her grandmother, passed through her mother to her, and subsequently to her daughter. Carly recalled the dream of her mother and grandfather together in the barn, so vivid that Carly thought she was the child.

"So instead of hauntings, the experiences are actually memories?"

"Not all the experiences you have are from your ancestors. You can communicate and see another realm, the spirit world, which is another gift you've inherited from your ancestors."

Carly knew Granny Eddleman passed her *gift on* to Carly. However, her mother or Cate showed no signs of having had sensitive experiences. And now, Vivi has shared the same.

Dr. Curry changed the screen to a family tree. Carly immediately recognized her parents and grandparents. She looked at the screen and back at Dr. Curry.

"How did you get this?" Carly asked, feeling as though her privacy had been invaded.

"Before you get upset, let me explain what I've discovered." Dr. Curry enlarged the screen.

"A month or more before we met at Spirit Seekers, I found myself drawn to your profile, almost instantly. Something or someone visited my thoughts, even my dreams, and led me to you. I contacted a long-time associate in the United States whose employment works closely with the Church of Latter-Day Saints research."

"You did this before we even met?" Carly is in disbelief.

"Yes, some, but not all of it. You provided me with the information needed to connect you with Caroline Richards and Cadence Davis."

Carly gasped. "Cadence Davis? What does she have to do with my DNA?"

Dr. Curry displayed the family tree of Caroline Richards Madoc. "As you told me, Caroline Richards married twice, first to Trefor Richards, and second to Stefan Madoc. When I enlisted the aid of a genealogist in Wales, I located the church records and found the Richards family, including Arwin Richards."

Carly's eyes widened with astonishment as she followed the infrared pointer moving down the chart. "I can't believe you found what I learned through the memories and records at home."

"Epigenetics and paranormal together. Now, once you gave me the name of Eira Richards Clarke, I followed her. She married John Preston, and the two left Boston for South Carolina. There, the two welcomed four children to the marital union."

Carly sat amazed. Her work, which had led her to Boston, had found Eira, but Dr. Curry had located the same information and more from Scotland. "I'm surprised she found her way back to South Carolina, where her uncle lived. I'm guessing she never met him."

"No, I doubt the two crossed paths. But I followed two of Eira and John's children, Matilda and Phoebe. Matilda Preston married George Washington Lewis, and they left the South at the beginning of the Civil War, traveling west. They settled in Kansas, where George opened a dry goods business. Matilda is your Grandmother Eddleman's grandmother. Matilda Lewis's daughter, Sarah, married Warren Foster. Sarah Foster married Arthur Goodson. Your Great-grandparents were Sarah and Arthur Goodson."

"My goodness. How in the world?" Carly exclaimed.

"Good connections, Lass." Dr. Curry smiled, proud of his work.

"Now, Sarah and Arthur's daughter, Eva Irene, married Hade (Harrison David) Eddleman, your grandparents. Your mother, Paula, married Curtis Evans. I took the liberty of having a copy of your ancestry through Caroline Richards documented and printed for you."

Carly began to cry. The information overwhelmed her to tears. "I don't know how to thank you. The connection to Caroline...I can't believe we're related."

"Yes, but it gets more amazing. Remember, Eira and John Preston's other daughter, the one who remained in South Carolina? This is her ancestry chart."

Dr. Curry brought up on the screen the chart displaying the family tree of Pheobe Preston. Carly listened, astonished, as Dr. Curry moved through the generations of Pheobe Preston and husband Robert Rhett to Lana Marshall and Darrell Davis, the parents of Cadence Davis.

"Holy cow. I'm distantly related to Cadence. This is mind-blowing."

"You see, the paranormal brought Cadence to you, but your connection to her mother led the two of you to find one another. That explanation, I'm still researching."

"I guess finding Freddy Richards in my cellar wasn't just luck. I needed to help him get justice for Caroline to find me."

"Something like that. Your connection to the Richards family transcends the centuries. Your search for Eira Richards would have been impossible to connect to Caroline had it not been for your paranormal gift."

Carly took another tissue from the box on Dr. Curry's desk. "I suppose I have enough material here to speak at paranormal conferences for years. How can I ever thank you?"

"I hope you'll join me sometime when I present my findings at the Epigenetic Conference in Geneva next fall."

Carly exhaled, "Whew. That sounds amazing. I've always wanted to visit Switzerland."

"I hope you'll do me the honor of dinner this evening. The Ben Nevis is a local pub with great food and Scottish music."

"Thank you, that sounds wonderful. I'll meet you. What time should I arrive?"

"Let's make it early, since you have an early flight in the morning. Say, five o'clock?"

"Perfect. Thank you for everything, Dr. Curry."

"You're welcome, Carly. Please, call me Alston."

"All right, Alston, it is. I'll see you later."

Carly carried the family trees that Dr. Curry had framed and exited the university. She walked across the road to the Alamo Guest House. As she approached the steps, she brought her hand to her mouth. "Drake?"

CHAPTER THIRTY-FIVE

"What are you doing here? What a wonderful surprise!" Carly exclaimed, accepting his embrace, adjusting the two frames between them.

"I can't explain it, but I had to see you." Drake pulled back, "I hope you don't mind."

The thought of meeting Drake on this trip hadn't crossed her mind. Whatever the reason, she felt genuinely happy to see him again.

"Are you staying here?" Carly asked.

"No, I'm staying a few blocks around the corner at the Marriott."

"Please, come in and let's catch up. We can talk inside." Carly motioned for him to follow her inside.

They found an area with a couch and chairs out of the way. "I'm so surprised to see you. I've so much to tell you."

Drake took off his coat and sat beside Carly. She inhaled his cologne, a scent she remembered when he hugged him goodbye in Edinburgh.

"You look wonderful! How did your meeting with Dr. Curry go?"

Drake asked, getting lost in Carly's eyes. A strand of dark hair fell across her face, and he reached out to help her, touching her hand.

The heat radiating from the fire made the area cozy. The flames flickered inside the stone fireplace, casting a warm glow and creating a romantic atmosphere.

Carly explained the theory of epigenetics and how Caroline's memories were imprinted in her DNA, which revealed her relationship to Carly. "I'm still reeling from the connections that Dr. Curry confirmed."

"What's this?" Drake asked, touching the picture frames.

"These are family trees Dr. Curry made for me. This one is mine; the other is Cadence Davis's."

"Refresh my memory." Drake looked at the family tree as Carly explained.

"Cadence Davis appeared to me after her mother came to the television station. She was the first girl I encountered on Johns Island."

Drake remembered and put his arm around Carly.

"So, Caroline Richards is your fifth great-grandmother?"

"It seems that way, according to my family tree. It's mind-boggling how the discovery of her remains at Bethesda led to all these memories and encounters."

"I don't fully understand it all, even though I've had experiences during the paranormal investigations I've conducted over the years." Drake adjusted his position and ran a hand over the stubble on his face.

"I can't explain how you saw Caroline or why you knew to seek me out at the conference," Carly said, feeling Drake's knee brush against hers.

"I'm just going to say it. You captivated me from the beginning. From the moment I saw your picture in the brochure."

She found herself at a loss for words, unsure of what to say. Finally, she found her voice. "I didn't want to admit it, but when you wanted to meet me downstairs that night, at Coombe Abbey, I had no idea who had sent the note." She looked down at her knee, moving against his. "I loved Austin, but I felt a connection to you. I know it was wrong, and I denied it."

"Since we're confessing, I'll burn in hell for this. I wanted to kiss you right there, so much so that it overwhelmed me." Drake's fingers brushed hers.

"So, what's stopping you now?" Carly asked, her voice husky.

Drake's expression changed. He leaned into Carly, putting his hand on the side of her small back. He put his lips on hers, softly, saying, "Helpa fi!". The Welsh term they understood between them was "Help me."

Carly felt his warm breath against her neck as his kisses trailed away from her lips. She felt lightheaded, her heartbeat thumping wildly in her chest.

Drake pulled back, heady from the long-awaited kiss. "I need to confess something else, since I'm already a condemned man."

Carly laughed, "More confessions? It sounds serious."

"I found out something from my Mum. Family history is her thing." Drake sat up, putting space between himself and Carly.

"Go on," Carly said.

"When you told me about seeing Gethen Bowen at the trial, I started doing research for you. I asked my Mum where she grew up in Wales."

Carly interrupted. "Wait, you told me your mother lived in Wales with you. When your parents divorced, she brought you to England."

"Yes, I didn't know the rest when I told you." Drake's difficulty swallowing didn't escape Carly.

Carly didn't comment; instead, she let Drake finish.

"My father's family and I lived in Monmouth. When my parents divorced, we left Wales. But she told me my paternal great-grandparents' last name was Madoc."

Carly rubbed her eyes. The dots started to connect. "You couldn't descend from Stefan, he died. I saw him fall, and I saw his stone."

"It gets dodgier by the moment, I'm afraid. I descended from Brychan Matauc. The spellings, Madoc and Maddoc, are other versions."

"I can't wrap my head around all the coincidences." Carly shook her head, "I guess nothing should surprise me."

"One more thing I discovered but didn't tell you when we spoke about Stefan. Brychan and Stefan were the sons of Dewydd Matauc, of Llancaiach."

"Wait, you mean as in Llancaiach Fawr?" Carly pulled her knee underneath her.

"Yes, I wanted to tell you, but thought you'd find it unbelievable. I'm sorry." Drake took Carly's hand. "It seems we are connected in more ways than we imagined."

She felt a surge of electricity course through her veins as their hands touched. Carly heard the ornate Grandfather clock in the lobby chime four forty-five. "I'm supposed to meet Dr. Curry for supper at a pub around the corner. You should join us."

"I don't want to intrude," Drake said.

"Nonsense, you're coming. Besides, wait until Alston hears about your connection to Stefan Madoc."

After a lovely dinner with Alston, Drake and Carly reached her Bed and Breakfast at the same time that her phone alerted her to a text. "It's Delaney," Carly said. "I'll text her back in a bit."

Drake walked upstairs with Carly to her suite. She used the key card to open the door, and they went inside. Carly placed her purse and key on the dresser and hung her coat in the wardrobe.

They settled on the settee, with Carly tucking her knees beneath her and turning to face Drake. "I thought Alston found your information just as interesting as mine. I really enjoyed our discussion about epigenetics and its paranormal connections."

"Yes, I found it all quite intriguing. But now what?" Drake replied.

"There's so much to explore with what he told me."

"I don't mean that. I mean *us*." Drake looked into Carly's eyes, feeling exposed and vulnerable.

Carly moved closer to him and took his hand in hers. "Our story is just beginning. I'm not going to let you walk out of my life unless you want to."

She welcomed his embrace, which was more passionate than their initial kiss, confirming his feelings.

"Carly, maybe I should go." Drake raked his hand through his hair.

She searched his eyes for a reason to tell him he should leave. "No, don't go."

Carly woke up after midnight, thinking about Drake and his feelings for her. She never thought she would experience this way of feeling after Austin's death.

She remembered kissing Drake and the night they spent together; neither of them questioned the urgency of being with each other in that moment. She caught a glimpse of her reflection in the mirror and noticed that Drake's stubble had left tiny abrasions on her neck. A smile spread across her face as she recalled the memory.

She grabbed her phone and checked the time at home. She decided to FaceTime with Frederick and Vivi. She could sleep on the plane.

Hearing their voices made her miss them more. They told her how much they missed her and how Ms. Dottie made them do their homework.

"Good for Ms. Dottie. I'll be home by tomorrow night."

"We miss you," Frederick said in a low voice, not wanting Dottie or Vivi to hear.

Carly smiled. "I miss you, too. I'll be home tomorrow night." Looking at Frederick, she saw how much he favored Austin.

"I miss you, too, Vivi," Carly said.

After she finished talking to the kids, she spoke to Dottie, telling her about her flight and that she'd have Delaney pick her up at the airport.

Carly called Delaney instead of texting her. "Hey, girl. Do you have time to talk? You're not going to believe what I'm about to tell you."

The two spent the next hour discussing the information Dr. Alston had shared, as well as the surprising revelation that she and Cadence Davis had a common ancestry. Delaney found the information fascinating.

"That explains a lot about why I couldn't see the same things as you at Llachaich Fawr and Ffos y Gerddinen," Delaney said.

"Yes, it explains everything. Caroline's experiences, mostly tragic, were imprinted in my DNA."

"Do you think your Granny experienced the same things? And what about Vivi?"

"Yes, I believe our experiences are connected, especially when someone can communicate with spirits."

Just then, Carly's alarm went off, reminding her it was time to wake up, even though she had slept less than two hours before she called. "Hey, I need to get ready and meet the Uber downstairs. I have a flight to catch."

"Yes, go ahead. I'll see you at the airport tonight. Safe travels!"

Carly placed her phone in her purse, choosing to share the news about Drake in person. For now, she kept the secret to herself.

~

The flight home gave Carly time to sort out the information Alston Curry shared, not to mention the fantastic ability to experience the imprinted memories of her ancestors.

She wanted to tell her parents as soon as she returned home. Paula might come to terms with Carly's ability more so, and perhaps she would come to accept her *gift*.

Carly kept her secret about her night with Drake for only two days. Delaney knew she was holding back on sharing everything, so she made reservations at Rita's on Folly Beach to drag it out of Carly.

She met Delaney for lunch after sleeping off the jet lag. She felt like a new person, no longer feeling apprehension about Caroline Madoc and her daughter, Eira.

"So, give me the low-down on everything. I'm dying here." Delaney grabbed Carly's hands from across the table.

"I thought I told you everything that Dr. Curry said." Carly reveled in letting Delaney squirm for a minute. "I might have left out a detail or two."

"You dirty dog, I knew it!" Delaney exclaimed, her voice rising.

Carly noticed that the attention of other patrons turned toward their booth. "Okay, okay. I haven't told you everything. Drake showed up in Glasgow."

Delaney nodded. "Well, well. This means I'll need a Jack and Coke before you spill the tea." She caught the server's attention and ordered a drink.

Carly continued where she left off. "Drake was waiting for me outside the Alamo Guest House when I came back from meeting Alston."

The server brought Carly another tea and Delaney's drink. They thanked her and resumed their conversation.

"Drake told me he did extensive research on his father's family in Wales while he searched for information on Caroline Madoc's appeal for her land. His ancestor is the twin brother of Stefan Madoc."

Delaney took a drink. "I'm stunned. Why didn't he tell you when you talked earlier?"

"He didn't think I'd believe him, but it explains our connection to Caroline. She would've known his twin brother. It all seems like something out of a movie."

"I have a feeling this is about to get really interesting." Delaney rubbed her hands together.

Carly smiled and sighed. "Oh, it does. Drake told me he felt something the first time we met, at Coombe Abbey." She felt her cheeks flush and lowered her voice. "He said I captivated him."

Delaney put her hand to her mouth to stifle a shout of celebration. "I knew it! I told you he was into you."

"I think he felt a pull towards me, just as I did towards him." Carly twisted her wedding band around her finger. "I've forgiven Austin, and my conscience is clear. I don't feel guilty."

"Oh, sweetie, just enjoy the journey, wherever it takes you. It's an amazing story about how Caroline and Stefan brought you to Drake."

"We'll take things slow, Delaney, especially because of Frederick and Vivi. Our story is only beginning."

Epilogue

After Carly returned home, she and Delaney continued their research on the Foundling Home and Bethesda Orphanage. Drake lent a hand from London, locating information regarding Nathaniel Duncan and Louisa Albertson's involvement in arranging for orphans to come to Savannah.

The newspaper reported that Miss Louisa Albertson, of London, with the help of Nathaniel Duncan, of Savannah, Georgia, arranged for young girls who were about to turn eighteen to be 'adopted' or indentured to wealthy merchants and businessmen in the United States. Many of the teenage girls became prostitutes in various brothels throughout the New England states. At the same time, Albertson and Duncan sold children who were too young for such arrangements to wealthy families for adoption.

Their arrangements came to light when money paid to Louisa Alberton for two teenage girls did not produce the expected cargo, and upon returning to England, she was arrested for criminal behavior involving children. She identified Nathaniel Duncan as the person responsible for arranging the transactions. Both Louisa Albertson and

Nathaniel Duncan went to jail for selling children, thus severing the connection between the London Foundling Hospital and Bethesda.

Carly discovered that Eira Richards had gone to Boston under a similar agreement with the Clarke family. Louisa Albertson employed the alias Susannah Richards to conceal her true identity. As a result, Eira Clarke's parentage remained unknown until Carly persistently pursued the truth, aided in part by her paranormal abilities.

Jeff Sullivan called Carly after she'd returned from Scotland, wanting to start something more than a platonic relationship. After she followed through with her promise to go out, Carly knew where her heart belonged, with a certain someone from England. She and Drake belonged together.

Jeff took Carly's rejection harder than she expected. He stopped emailing her to check on how things were going and started a serious relationship with his co-anchor, Erin, on Channel 5. No surprise to Carly. They acted as if they had a mutual attraction from the beginning.

Later, Carly discovered that Liz Greene had overheard Bauer and Jeff discussing the possibility of replacing Carly with someone younger and more responsible. Liz told Carly that although Jeff acted like he wanted her to stay, he was secretly trying to replace her.

The politics at Channel 5 caused Carly to leave television news for good.

Curt and Paula delivered the two Scottish Terrier puppies as promised. Frederick and Vivi agreed on Isla and Ian for their names. Everyone instantly fell in love with their new pets. Dottie didn't let on, but she, too, loved them.

Elise Ravenel discovered an enthusiastic buyer for Carly's home on King Street. The new CEO at Roper Hospital viewed the house and made a full-price offer immediately. Now, Carly needed to decide where she, her children, and Dottie would go after the sale closed. Her parents hoped she would agree to move back to her grandparents' house in Abilene.

Carly found the perfect house for herself, Dottie, and the children on a quiet street in Mt. Pleasant. It was just two minutes from Delaney's house, and Elise Ravenel lived nearby as well. The area seemed ideal.

Carly and the kids were doing well. Austin's memory remained alive in little things and traditions. Carly determined that Austin would stay at the forefront of the children's lives.

Since his burial, Austin hadn't appeared to Carly again. He found his resting place beside the Tabor family in the small country cemetery. Carly made a promise to return each year to bring the children to pay their respects and visit with family.

Her paranormal experiences persisted, but now she recognized which events were part of her inherited memories and which were truly paranormal. Instead of avoiding her inherited gift, she embraced it and found her place using her ability.

Drake and Carly continued their long-distance relationship after she returned from her visit to Glasgow. They reconnected in Boston for Spirit Seekers 2026. Carly introduced Drake to Boyd Hawley, and they became fast friends. Delaney and Carly spoke at the event, and Dr. Curry enlisted Carly's assistance during his presentation on epigenetics. This led to more conferences and increased her podcast's followers.

Carly realized that she didn't want Drake to return to London after the conference. Their long-distance relationship had become both costly and challenging for them. Drake confessed that he wanted to spend more time with Carly. They had fallen in love, and neither had wanted to be apart from the other.

Drake secured a position at the Charleston Museum as director, earning an impressive salary. He took a leave from his position at the London Foundling Museum to try out his new appointment. He found an apartment in a home on Pitt Street, close to the museum.

Drake purchased an engagement ring sometime after Carly visited Glasgow. Call it a hunch or a spirit's nudge, but something told him that he and Carly would spend the rest of their lives together.

Delaney joined Carly at conferences as often as possible, enjoying the time they shared. She and Boyd Hawley decided it was finally time to tie the knot, planning to get married the following Christmas.

A publisher in Glasgow contacted Carly about writing a book about her paranormal experiences, including her recent discovery of the theory of epigenetics and her connection to the past.

Carly gradually introduced Drake to Frederick and Vivi. Frederick and Vivi slowly accepted another man in their mother's life, warming to his concern for both their mother and them.

Carly was determined not to rush her relationship with Drake. She wanted things to progress naturally. She knew she loved him and wanted to live the rest of her life with him.

Vivi seldom talked about her visits with Granny Eddleman. Carly understood that Vivi shared the same gift, a legacy handed down through their ancestors. Instead of trying to deny it, she embraced her connection to the women who came before her.

Carly watched Ian and Isla sleep peacefully at her feet. During the last year, she experienced a sense of tranquility she hadn't felt since before she lost Austin. The move from Denver to Charleston, the haunting spirits in her house on King Street, and the mystery of the missing girls on Johns Island—all of it had brought her to this moment.

By confronting her haunting dreams and past experiences, Carly discovered love and happiness not only with Drake, but with Frederick and Vivi, too.

Carly put an arm around her children and kissed Drake. "I can't wait to see what our future holds."

~The End~

Author Lori Roberts

Ways to Connect with Lori Roberts:

author_loriroberts@yahoo.com
www.loriroberts.com
https://www.amazon.com/author/loriroberts
https://www.youtube.com/@AuthorLoriRoberts
https://www.facebook.com/Stonewallswife

Other Books by Lori Roberts

Lost Letters ~ A Civil War Love Story

Willow

Sing a Song of Murder

The Lowcountry Ghost Trilogy:

Book 1 -Cries in the Night ~ A Lowcountry Ghost Story

Book 2- Where the Sweetgrass Grows

Tales of Frontier America:

Book 1- This Dark and Bloody Ground ~ Maggie's Story

Coming in 2026 ~ The Ties That Bind

If you are interested in reaching out to Lori Roberts to speak to your school, historical organization, book club, or museum, please contact Lori at her website, www.loriroberts.com or via email, author_loriroberts@yahoo.com